PRAISE FOR *M*

"*Mirth* is that rare thing: a truly absorbing novel that portrays, in all its complexity, a life lived over time. In beautiful, fluent prose Kathleen George follows Harrison Mirth through three marriages and the many vicissitudes of a writer's life. The result is a dazzling portrait of a man who lives up to his name, and of those who love him. A wonderful novel."

—Margot Livesey, author of *The Boy in the Field*

"A beautifully written book. After a childhood of neglect and loneliness, Mirth becomes wildly embracing of all things life-giving: a celebrator of art, and literature, great food, and travel, music and most of all, love. Kathleen George beautifully captures a vulnerable, memorable character and the significant women who have shaped him. This writer has her wise and subtle eye on the contradictions of the heart and extends a spirit of forgiveness to all. She offers up *Mirth* like a talisman to remind readers of the role love and death-defying pleasure play in an all too-brief life."

—Jane McCafferty, Drue Heinz Prize winner; author of *First You Try Everything*

"*Mirth* is a gorgeous and deeply moving novel about the tensions between the life and art of a writer."

—Hilma Wolitzer, author of *Today a Woman Went Mad in the Supermarket*

"Kathleen George's character Liz is a third wife who cobbles together her husband's story via other women—beginning to end; he enchants (sooner or later) and is enchanted by women he loves, who love him. George's treatments of relationships and marriages, the rising and the falling, have the glorious and sad ring of truth to them, how it starts, how it goes at a leisurely pace along its way, and how it closes, the strain. Liz's part of the story has a kind, good heart, so sweet at the outset, just how falling in love is, both tentative and sudden, inevitable. Any man would be honored to be remembered in this way."

—Paul Kameen, poet, author of *Writing/Teaching*

"A life story, a love story, a rich roman a clef—*Mirth* is all these and more. Imagine if John Williams' *Stoner* was about the joys of a life well-lived. Kathleen George has fashioned a tender, knowing portrait of a true American romantic."

—Stewart O'Nan, author of *Emily, Alone* and *Henry, Himself*

"You cannot fail to fall in love with Harrison Mirth. Go ahead. I dare you. In *Mirth*, George has created a character who follows his passions, for better and worse, whose stark and unyielding appreciation for beauty and zest for life permeates every page. A true meditation on how to live and how to love. *Mirth* is a wise and wonderful novel, both an exploration of the undulating freedoms and constraints of love and marriage, and a reminiscence of a life well-lived. *Mirth* will delight you as you read and stay with you long after."

—Meredith Mileti, author of *Aftertaste*

"In *Mirth*, Kathleen George gives us an intimate portrait of a man who lived fully, risked much, and found his truest love in his later years. This is a tender, moving, beautifully written novel."

—Jane Bernstein, author of *The Face Tells the Secret*

Other titles by Kathleen George

MIRTH

Kathleen George

Regal House Publishing

Published by
Regal House Publishing, LLC
Raleigh, NC 27587
All rights reserved

ISBN -13 (paperback): 9781646032716
ISBN -13 (epub): 9781646032723
Library of Congress Control Number: 2021949150

Interior by Lafayette & Greene
Cover images © by C. B. Royal

Regal House Publishing, LLC
https://regalhousepublishing.com

Parts of this novel appeared in different form as the short story, "The
Tractor Accident," in *North American Review* and subsequently in George's
story collection, *The Man in The Buick*.

Printed in the United States of America

For my sisters, Vivian and Janet, and my brother Richard

MIRTH

1

He sits at breakfast, marmalade today on a buttered English muffin with his egg, with his juice—overall a yellow-orange meal. Each day is slightly different to keep breakfast interesting, the sameness and the difference in the right balance. Rhythm, Liz calls it. Sameness: the newspapers, Liz crossing through for coffee, her wiping off the jam he spilled on the newspapers, everything just routinely familiar.

She stops. "Are you all right? You look sad."

He is a little sad, he admits. A dream has been coming toward him, but he's pushed it away and let it get blurred by his satisfaction with the marmalade, and now with her question, there it is, taking form like a building in a lifting fog.

Or a ship.

"I had a dream. Let me think. I was…somewhere. In the ocean, on a raft, maybe a raft, safe but not safe? Just floating. And I saw the most amazing huge ship in the distance. A big black ship. I wondered if it would pass me by or come for me. For some reason I didn't want it to. I tried to make myself invisible. I didn't wave or anything, but it seemed to be coming toward me. I just watched it."

"Did it come very close?"

"I woke up."

"It sounds scary," she says, rubbing his back. "Gotta shake it off, don't you think?"

"I guess so."

"Be super-careful today."

The dream, now in his conscious mind, keeps nagging at him.

Nags at her too.

This is the beginning of the end.

≈

This is the beginning of the beginning of the end:

Harrison is off teaching when Lizzie (his third wife) is removing her school papers from the dining table, thinking to prepare rosemary garlic chicken for supper—and what? Rice? Polenta?—when the doorbell rings. Two elderly women stand there. The small one asks in a strong but crackly voice, "Is this the residence of Harrison Mirth?"

"It is."

"My name is…was Mary Jo Martin. I knew Harrison in grade school. And this is my friend, Carol Ann. We were at a 60th class reunion in St. Louis and, well, he wasn't there because he did *his* high school up in Vermont," she says breathlessly, "but then we were driving across the country on our way to New Jersey and we *thought* we might just manage to *see* him."

"Come in. Come in. He's still at work." Mary Jo Martin. Ha! Isn't this the story of the twenty-eight valentines?

"You mean he still works?"

"Teaches."

"Oh, that's so *interesting*. Good for him."

Guests at dinnertime, then. Harrison will turn somersaults to invite them to stay for dinner, but there are only two chicken breasts, so…he will want to go out to dinner; he'll make the evening festive—he loves that sort of thing.

Mary Jo Martin. He'll be excited.

The other woman, Carol Ann, says, "She hitched a ride with me. She's going to see her daughter in New York. She hates planes. I'm just the chauffeur."

The two women follow Liz into the kitchen where she digs out a good bottle of red. She finds three passable cheeses and puts them on a board. She digs around in the cupboard and manages a whole basketful of assorted crackers. Mary Jo Martin. Yes, she is the little girl who got twenty-eight valentines from Harrison.

Liz loves that story.

He is still like that, a believer in love. He thrives on domestic life—marketing, cooking, table settings, positioning a sculpture just so, gazing at his beloved over dinner, touching hands as they watch a TV program.

Liz pours wine and shows the women Harrison's latest novel, just out, hardcover, to entertain them until he arrives.

"Have you lived here long?" Mary Jo asks as a way of asking if Liz is a permanent fixture.

"Almost twenty years." Pretty permanent.

Harrison gets home from the university about forty minutes later and takes in the guests with a series of expressions ranging from puzzlement to joy. Mary Jo is a squat, chubby, perky, well-groomed older woman. Her friend is a lean, tall, ragged type.

"Tell me about *your* life," Harrison urges Mary Jo. "Catch me up."

"Well," the old flame says, "I now live in Puerto Rico. Long story. But I have a gorgeous villa with a swimming pool and you are welcome to come. Any time." As an afterthought she nods in Lizzie's direction to include her in the invitation. "Really. Any time you want. It's very relaxing. I'm heading back next week after I see my daughter."

Harrison says, "We're in the middle of a school term. But thank you for the thought. So, a long way as they say from St. Louis."

"Oh yes." She sparkles, flirting. "I lived in Germany for a while too."

"Well traveled then."

"*Very well traveled.*"

"And the rest of it? Your daughter? Lives in New York?"

"Quick summary of my life: Married three times. Divorced twice. My daughter looked you up, by the way; that's how we found you. Anyway, widowed once, the third, but now even the other two jokers are dead. (Sorry. That's how I buoy myself up, by calling them names.) One daughter and she's in New York, right. My only child. To my first. She's a mathematician. I have no idea what that means. But she's in a university, too, like you!"

"And like Liz."

"Oh. You too?"

"Yes!" says Harrison, sounding bizarrely proud and urging Liz forward into the kitchen limelight. Liz figures third wives are sort of invisible. She is enjoying thinking about Harrison when he was young. The boy is still there, inside. Liz is fifteen years his junior but today she feels like, oh, the amused and admiring grandmother who gave him paper to make twenty-eight valentines.

"Liz is a writer and professor," he's saying.

Mary Jo turns to Lizzie, whose existence can no longer be ignored, and tells the story of her amazing valentine year. "It was so unusual. Of course I was thrilled. And a couple of years later, I had a piano recital and he sent me a huge bouquet of flowers. He was amazing. I've never been treated so well since. He set a standard. Nobody else met it. Ah well."

Lizzie has asked him at other junctures how he knew to make such gestures as a mere boy in a poor neighborhood in St. Louis.

"Movies. I learned my whole personality from movies." He bought a copy of *Swing Time* to show her his inspiration, and he took her hand as they watched it. He sang along with Astaire doing "The Way You Look Tonight."

There he sits now, a personality formed a long time ago by Fred Astaire, Spencer Tracy, Cary Grant, to name a few—a combination of dash, intelligent wry wit, and looks. Interesting, charming men, doing whatever they had to do to win the girl.

Lizzie offers dinner to the visiting duo, having come up with two more pieces of chicken she could defrost, given a little time.

"Ah no, we really have to get going," says Carol Ann. She seems uncomfortable, restless. It isn't clear whether Mary Jo agrees or not that it's time to go, but after an hour of cheese and wine and some blown kisses, they are gone.

"She got so short," Harrison says of his old flame. "She used to be tall. And she got old."

Lizzie gives him a quick peck on the cheek. *You're old, we're old, you still don't see it.*

"What do you think prompted her to come and observe the wreck?"

"Now don't be coy. You look fantastic."

"'For your age' is the end of that sentence."

Lizzie has always loved looking at him, touching him. He is an incredibly beautiful man. "Still," she says, "still fantastic."

His arms go around her, and his hug, learned from her, is deep, tight.

"She was coming to see if you're available."

"Nah."

"Oh yes. That's how it goes."

"Oh dear. But she met you. She got the message."

"Hope so. I'll start dinner."

"I'm bushed. Don't know why."

"Visions of the inevitable. Eat some cheese. Get your strength up."

He smiles. *Get your strength up* is his line, said every time he presents some temptation in the way of food.

"Did you know the other one?" Liz asks.

"Couldn't place her. She was somehow *familiar* but she didn't seem to want to talk about herself or come forward."

Liz says, "No. She more or less skulked. I'd guess she was a redhead in her youth. That coloring."

Minutes later Harrison says, "Oh. Oh dear. She might have been one of the O'Neal girls. Not very nice, any of them."

Liz doesn't know that story.

She can see him—how he was—at various stages: the little boy who wanted to be like Fred Astaire, the callow, horny, but wholly innocent youth, the angry stoic middle-aged man.

"Lover boy," she says. "Twenty-eight valentines!"

He smiles.

There are times she sees in Harrison everybody she ever loved, the bad ones and the good ones and likely he sees everyone in her. Time travelers all of us, incarnations, all of us.

"Who were the O'Neal girls?"

"Ugh."

"Tell me. I want all your stories. I dunno. I've never wanted to know anything as much as I want to know you."

"Good God."

"You're vivid."

"Not boring anyway."

"Not to me. Never."

"Neighborhood family. The O'Neals."

He tells her the story over dinner.

2

The first woman he married was Amanda, a small, almost square-ish woman who was an accumulation of characteristics that mimicked Mary Jo Martin as well as Maria Aboud, his girlfriend when he was sixteen, and roughly four others, women who'd had a particularly strong impact through his college years. Physically, they would all grow old to look like little chess pieces or Asian sculptures. Amanda was the culmination of something, a wish, an impulse in him, or maybe just a habit. At the time of the marriage, she was fit, five foot two, pressed into business suits and nylons and heels, with an impish face (bright green eyes) and a haircut that wasn't exactly in style but that seemed just right on her. Her hair was one of the things that gave her that square-ish look—almost a medieval pageboy. She bustled with energy; she looked like someone going places; she came into a room and everyone expected her to take over.

She was a would-be journalist, aiming to be an editor, at the moment working for *Time* magazine in the low-down editorial position of assistant copy editor. She hated the work, but she knew she could and would do better.

One day she "walked into a bar" as they say. Several men noticed her, not because she was beautiful, but because of the bristling energy she gave off and also because she'd come in alone and ordered a bourbon. They liked that. Harrison certainly did. He was about to approach her when he was cut off by another man, a tall, good-looking fellow in a suit much superior to the one Harrison wore. Nevertheless, Harrison flashed her a smile that said, *I'm waiting. Patiently.*

He watched the other man talk and talk and listen and listen. Even though he thought it was hopeless and he only had three dollars left, he sent her a drink. "Whatever she's having," he told the bartender. "Say it's from her old friend from college." And in this way he was fitting her into the skin and face of a woman named Didi with whom he'd had many laughs and also a sad and troubled visit to a doctor to terminate what would have bound them together in a hasty marriage. Didi was a little crazy—always in a fierce mood. She was a woman without friends, snobbish and isolated, and yet he liked her and tried to stick with her through everything, including the doctor she insisted she see. Suddenly she tired of him and ran off to China or somewhere in the East—she wouldn't say.

When the bartender presented the drink, Amanda (whose name he didn't yet know and whom he knew not at all) looked up at him. Only a momentary puzzlement crossed her face and then she gave a little wave. Oh, how that wave sustained him! They were in this fiction together. Another half hour went by. He hadn't enough money to stay and drink and have dinner as well. He chose staying.

New York in those days was post-war, the place to be for people of an artistic bent, with a tolerance for poverty and a lust for everything else. It was still a lot like the world of *My Sister Eileen* (the play and the films) in which the Ohio sisters subsisted on sample packets of cereal. The artistic people, many of them, were eating cereal or its analogues daily; in Harrison's case it was whatever leftover deli scraps he was awarded after his morning job making sandwiches. He ate a lot of pastrami in those years. But he didn't want to be anywhere else, not back in Missouri where he had been raised or New Hampshire or Vermont where certain months of his life had been spent, not even in Boston where he'd gone to college before and after his stint in the navy. No. Right smack dab in the middle of Manhattan was the best choice he'd ever made, and deli scraps were not the only inducement. There was promise everywhere. New York was the center of the universe. When Harrison read what J. B. Priestly wrote, he felt his heart sing: "The New York of forty years ago was an American city, but today's glittering cosmopolis belongs to the world, if the world does not belong to it."

The war had given the city an injection of adrenalin. There were jobs everywhere, goods in every window, ships in port, tons of freight going this way and that, huge businesses headquartering right in the city, money passing from one hand to another and from one bank to another.

Romance was not only possible in New York but expected. Harrison had been a sailor. He could have been the one (wasn't!) in the famous photo of a sailor kissing a woman bent backward into an embrace right on the street in celebration of the end of the war. Celebration was still in the air.

He had a cold water flat, which he happily displayed to Amanda—who, counting off steps, said proudly that hers had twelve more square feet than his. There was a refrigerator out in the hall of his place; it made funny noises, but he was used to it. "I like it," he told her, stepping outside his room and patting the refrigerator in an attempt not to go straight to bed. "I think of it as a sort of friendly monster, groaning." He smiled at her and at the refrigerator, his appliance pet.

She said, "Seems more like an old guy huffing and groaning. You know, an old lech." Unfortunately, that remark reminded him of a time he'd walked in on his father grunting and groaning over a woman who was not his mother. He didn't say this to Amanda, but he lost a beat or two on the unwelcome memory.

He showed her the hall where the bathroom was, to be shared, as was the refrigerator, by three tenants. "Most of the time I label my deli bag of scraps and most of the time nobody takes them."

"You're kidding."

"Well, once, twice, they disappeared."

She shook her head at the way he made bookcases—and he was a champion reader—by piling books face up until he got something like two even stacks and then using a board over them and then starting on the next shelf. The rest of the books got shelved upright in between. "What do you do," Amada asked him, "when you want to read something that's being a brick?"

"All hell breaks loose."

"I would think so."

She began to take her clothes off. He made a quick trip to the hall bathroom. When he got back, she was in bed, the covers only loosely over her. She was wonderful! So game! He got his clothes off as quickly as he could and got to work. He ripped the covers off her the whole way. "Aren't we beautiful," he said as he looked at their body parts connecting.

When it was over, she touched his face, two fingers down the side until she came to his chin. "Have you had sex before me?"

He frowned. "Of course." His frown deepened. "Are you criticizing me?"

"No, no, it's just that you seem so grateful."

"I am grateful. I've always been grateful." He dropped to one knee beside the single bed, a mere cot. She adjusted to take up all the available room as he said, "Grateful for you."

"We should get to know each other," she said.

"I thought we were doing that."

"Oh, there's more, much more. I'm not as nice as you think. I'm *interesting* but not nice. You. I'm worried. I don't want to hurt you."

"How?"

"By letting you race ahead into anything. I guess I'm ambitious."

His bedside clock ticked away. A shout from the hallway interrupted them for a second. It was the divorced guy calling down the steps about borrowing a beer from someone else on Harrison's floor. Harrison hesitated, trying to figure out why ambition was bad. "I'm ambitious," he said.

"For what?"

"Being a writer."

"Oh, God help me. I should have guessed. You have the hair. You have writer hair. And enough books around. I just want to be a big-time editor someday."

"That could be a handy match," he teased.

"Ha."

"I'm going to see if there is any corned beef left. Aren't you hungry?"

"Always."

He went into the hallway with his shirt tied around his bottom for decency and tried to remember if he'd eaten what was left of his stack of corned beef around two o'clock when he had to rush out to interview seven dancers for a press release. He'd have to make sure Amanda knew that press articles weren't what he was ambitious to write—whirling in his head was a poetic novel. He didn't know who the characters were or even the plot, but he had…the feeling.

There was no corned beef. Alas. He was out of money. He went back inside.

It was hot. Amanda was fanning herself by riffling the pages of *The Fountainhead*, which she'd taken from the wooden crate that was the nightstand.

"I can offer a spoonful of peanut butter," he said, trying to ignore his rebounding lust under the shirt. Should he be this easy? He was so available. All a woman had to do was remove a sheet. A shoe. A hat.

"Walk me to my place? I have a fan and I have four slices of cheese and a half loaf of bread." She looked at the small clock near the cot. "We're going to need some sleep."

"What time do you get up?"

"Seven-thirty."

He had to be at the deli at eight. "Let's go."

Amanda was insanely drawn to one of the editors at her job at *Time*. Samuel. He tended to get the political articles and was known to be good at his job. He was not very tall, not even handsome, and he was probably married, but he was the drollest man she had ever met. She imagined if she ever got to roll around with him, they would spend 80 percent of the time laughing. After two weeks of seeing Harrison, she found she still thought about Samuel all the time. She couldn't seem to help it.

When she passed him one day at work, he was telling a story about some idiots sitting behind him at a ball game. The man he was talking to smiled broadly, as if waiting to laugh. She made an excuse to gather a fresh tablet and passed them again before going down to the bowels of the building to get to work. This time he was saying, "And all the while they talked about stocks while Robinson was at bat. They never changed the conversation even when he hit a triple." As she got out of earshot, she heard, "My wife turned around and told them to spend their money on something other than baseball."

Yes, okay, he was married.

She hadn't been to a game though everywhere she went baseball seemed to be the subject of conversation. She wanted to get to Ebbets Field soon, partly so she would not be like the idiots who sat behind Samuel, in their own worlds, laughable. She was pretty sure Harrison, so eager to please, would take her if she mentioned it. He liked to go places—he'd be out every night if he could afford it. He'd gone to Fifty-Second Street to hear Charlie Parker and Miles Davis. He did whatever he could to take in Broadway shows—angled to get press work that awarded him comps. His specialty was dance troupes so tickets for dance always came his way. To think she might hear Billie Holiday live, in a club, if she stuck with him. She could not afford to pine after Samuel when with a little effort she could screw her head on right and work with this guy, Harrison.

She got to the basement and started her copyediting. Unbelievable. A *there* instead of a their. Grrr.

She could diagram any sentence you gave her, no matter how complex. She could blast out dangling modifiers. Her blood spiked at pronoun misuse. But she was also aware of content and had what was called good taste. She hoped Harrison was meticulous about these things in case he showed her something he had written, but she was pretty sure, based on the state of his apartment and his wildly tousled hair, that he was not going to turn out to be a grammarian.

What Harrison had felt, throwing on his clothes and running out of Amanda's apartment after that first night was regret that he could not sit and eat and enjoy a lovely, normal morning, lingering over the Grape Nuts or the Corn Flakes she had put on the table. All he could do was pour a handful of cereal into his palm and run. He was five minutes late.

"You're late," said his boss, Eddie Schwartz.

"It was for a good reason."

Schwartz frowned and handed him a bag. "Leftover chips of ham."

"Bless you."

"You're not God. Neither am I. I have to fire you if you're late."

"I'll work extra."

"Pay attention to what the customers are saying. I don't want any waste."

"Right."

Mostly that day, he alternated between thinking about Amanda and about the work he had lined up—some big ones. That day after work at the deli, he was interviewing June Taylor, and he was supposed to ask her about her friendship with Jackie Gleason and make a press release out of it. He tamped down his hair, ran to meet her in a rehearsal hall and asked her in his most quiet voice about aches and pains and lofty goals, and, yes, the big guy, Jackie Gleason. She smiled and said they were very good friends and respected each other *professionally*. Good God, he loved the way she looked aside when she answered. He would try to capture that. He needed a new ribbon for the typewriter in his room and had no time to get it and get his work in so he had to write and type up his interview at the agency.

The next day he had another big one, José Limon. He'd cadged tickets to both dance concerts, Taylor's and Limon's. He called Amanda and she said yes, so he got to take her to both of them. Then, on the next Monday, he had an interview with a theater company that had little chance of making it. Smart Stage it was called. They were doing every play that had been done ten or fifteen years ago. *Idiot's Delight, St. Joan, Murder in the Cathedral.* They specialized in a cheaper version of what had once been big lavish productions. He had tickets for Tuesday. Amanda said she couldn't go to that one, so he went solo.

Two weeks flew by with him seeing Amanda several times but not nearly enough as far as he was concerned.

Friday would be payday, thank God. It was Wednesday.

On his break, he called Amanda at work.

"I shouldn't take this call," she said.

"Well, I can get into the Cotton Club tomorrow night. Interested?"

"Sorry. Busy."

"Um." He hesitated. "Dodgers Friday is a possibility."

"I can do that! I'll come to your place. We can take the subway."

"Great," he said.

Two good things. Harlem tomorrow night and baseball Friday. Three good things, actually—Schwartz had shown him another take-home bag with his name on it. This one with what must be a half-pound of ham. Schwartz put it in the cooler until the end of Harrison's shift.

But all good things aside, Harrison worried as he served customers. Was Amanda being unavailable on principal or was she actually scheduled with someone or something? He couldn't afford to be distracted. He had a lot of regulars and many went so far as to manipulate the line to get him. *How's your day?* they might ask if he didn't ask first. *What's good?*

Schwartz, who often smoked a cigar while working, came up to him. "Hungry now?"

"Always. You already gave me some ham to take home."

"That's for home. Make yourself a nice big something. Next break."

"Thank you."

"Do you ever get to eat vegetables, fruits?"

"I like them. Not much lately."

"Your bowels are okay?"

Harrison was a bit shocked. After a laugh escaped him, he said, "I'm Mr. Steady." He was. His body just kept working no matter what he did to it. He wasn't a He-Man but he was strong enough. Could swim straight for thirty minutes, could lift a pretty big package, move a bureau without scratching the floor. His skin was clear. He could walk fast. He could run.

"Take a banana and an apple. Fruit anyway."

"Thank you." Vegetables. He wondered how he would find and cook the vegetables that were now on his mind, like an assignment. He loved squash, okra, peas, beans, all of that. Thinking about vegetables brought his father to mind. His father had been a famous intellectual, a political pundit and essayist, much in demand, always writing articles. During most of his successful years, he lived in New York and Harrison almost never saw him except for a month or six weeks in summer. His father's idea of summer was to rent a farmhouse in Vermont and get in a garden as soon as the weather allowed, and then to spend lunchtime and evenings sitting on the porch swatting flies. And thinking. And reading. And even during these summer vacation months writing in a crabbed hand in small notebooks.

It was a relief that his mother was off acting in small companies. He and his father felt freer without her.

When he took his lunch break, Harrison made a roast beef and cheese sandwich and then grabbed an apple and a banana. As he ate, sitting on a crate out back, he jotted notes in his own small notebook, describing his father. Big, careless, good at patting a boy on the head, affectionate, stupid about married love, about fidelity at least, but sweet tempered. Hard-working. Idealistic about democracy.

Harrison wrote about being eight and ten, running around, hoping for a playmate from an adjoining farm property, sometimes finding one, often not, so he'd spent hours learning about the garden and running in circles until, finally exhausted with the heat, he spent the rest of the day reading. He'd read all kinds of things and realized he was not lonely when he had a book or a pen and paper.

And then the garden would yield. And there would be vegetables, so beautiful and tender and new, he and his father would eat them raw, laughing at the bounty, before they could find the inclination to cook them.

Harrison smiled to think of his father's joy. He thought maybe he'd caught it in what he'd written today. And then he went back inside and began making sandwiches.

He looked up from his work to see a disapproving face. Theodore, one of the other deli clerks, distinctly disliked him. One day he was going to ask Theodore straight out what the problem was.

But he was shocked moments later when he overheard Theodore telling the manager, "Harrison is stealing. I saw it. He made himself a huge sandwich while he was waiting on customers and he took fruit too."

"Uh-huh. Get back to work."

Harrison thought he'd better straighten this out right now. "Ted. Theodore. Hey. I heard you. I wasn't stealing. I was supposed to. Schwartz told me to."

That didn't much help. Theodore seethed the rest of the day. It was even more galling that Harrison was innocent. And preferred.

She came up to his place on Friday right after work in her navy-blue dress and the lighter blue hat he'd seen before. They allowed a good ten minutes for kissing and flirting with the idea of doing more, but they straightened their clothes and started for the subway to go to the Dodgers game. They dinged in their nickels and passed through the gate just as two boys to their right sprinted over the stiles and ran before an officer could get the gate open for himself. "Youth!" Harrison said, though he was only twenty-three himself. Amanda was a whopping twenty-four, six months older than he. He felt very adult having this woman in his life, a woman who wore suits and hats and had come to New York three years ago and had seen *Brigadoon* and decided she wanted to stay in a city that could so easily combine dirt and whimsy. At first she bunked with other hopefuls in search of work; once she got work, she moved on to her solo flat. Dorm life was not for her.

"No matter what I do, this Theodore is gunning for me," Harrison told her when she asked about his day at the deli. "Instant dislike from the first day," he exclaimed. They bounced and vibrated as the train sped toward baseball. Harrison was nose up to a smelly armpit on a big man.

"He thinks you're rich," Amanda said into his ear.

"That's crazy. Why would he think that? He has way more than I do."

"Well, you look rich. Why don't you pretend it's true, crow about the estate where you grew up, tell him about your gourmet meals in other settings, say you went to Europe every year as a kid. Invent servants!"

"Why would I do that?"

"To test my theory! Also, to torture him," she growled.

Harrison frowned. "You think that's it?"

"Ach," she said. "I don't know how you're going to be a writer if you don't know people. And their foibles."

He brightened. "I love foibles," he said, "the word and the fact of them. *Foibles.* What a great word." He felt in his pocket for his notebook. He had it but couldn't write on the train.

The big smelly man looked down at them, cross-eyed. "You Dodgers fans?"

"Yes. Damn right," Harrison answered. "You?"

"Yep."

"Okay then."

After a while, Harrison asked her, "What makes me look rich?"

The netting on her hat quivered. It was a beautiful shade of light blue. She fidgeted, trying to check the seams of her nylons. These were the days when women wore their suits and hats and nylons and heels to a game and men sweltered in their suits and fedoras. Harrison was thinking that hats didn't suit Amanda. But she was such a trouper of a gal, doing what she figured she should do, dressing as well as she could on her salary. It touched him.

She appeared to be thinking hard. "It's something about your face. And the way you're careless with your clothes. And the hair that won't stay put."

"That makes me look rich?" But he was observant enough to know she was right.

"That and the fact that you don't seem to care, you don't seem desperate."

"Desperate for you," he said, proud of the little transition he'd made.

She shook her head and rolled her eyes.

"Spare a dime?" the big man said. "I get off next stop."

Amanda thought Harrison should not have spared a dime, but he did. They got off the train and she found herself craning her neck to watch a mother and father (she guessed) carrying a weak, clearly ill, child of about six into the stadium. She couldn't stop looking.

"Hot dog?" Harrison asked.

She shook her head. But Harrison had seen her looking at the ill child, and while they watched the warmups, he asked her about her childhood in Ohio. "Did you hate being an only child?" he asked.

"That wasn't exactly it."

He studied her. "One time you said something else about being the neglected one."

"I had a sister. Two years older."

For a while they watched the ball tosses, left field to home, second to first. Finally, he said, "What happened?"

"She was sick. She died."

"How terrible for you." He took her hand, which was sticky from caramel corn and driving her crazy. He didn't seem to notice. "What was she like?"

Amanda shrugged. "I never got to know her really. She was just quiet. More or less invisible."

"Did she go to school?"

"Yeah. Until she couldn't. She loved school."

The game began. During the third inning, Amanda went off to wash her hands and powder her face. She brought back two napkins from the hot dog stand that she had put soap and water on. "For your hand," she said. "The one I held."

He looked puzzled.

"It's sticky from mine."

"Is it?"

"Yes. Ugh. I hate stickiness." He was so odd. Or earthy, maybe.

The Dodgers lost that night, but Harrison took it in stride. "Baseball is life!" he said. He put his arm around her as they left the stadium.

She was glad she'd finally seen a game and felt she had checked an item off her list of things that proved she was aware, awake, in the right city, and healthy.

Back on the train, he asked about her sister again. "What did she like to do? Didn't she have friends?"

"Why?"

"I don't know. I just like to know."

"To write about her?"

"Oh." After his initial surprise, he seemed to entertain the idea. "Maybe one day I will. What were her days like?"

For a while she didn't answer; the train bounced and vibrated them along. Finally, she said, "She had one good friend, a boy, who visited her regularly for maybe five years. I guess he loved her. There is not a lot to say about her. She hated doctors. Loved books."

"Like you."

"Yes, there's that. Loved radio. Could sit and listen forever."

"Maybe couldn't move like you could," he said, thinking it over, sad looking, imagining it. "You'd be out playing dodge ball. She'd have Jack Benny."

"Something like that." She felt herself begin to cry and that made her furious. Why had he dug up her guilt about running out to live instead of spending her time sitting bedside? How she ran. She made friends, went swimming, started dancing, got precocious and called a boy her boyfriend and kissed him, came home late, avoiding the room her sister was in. When she couldn't find playmates, she went to the attic or out to the hammock to read, making a world for herself. And after her sister died, she did the same thing, more so.

"Oh." His arm was around her. He tightened it a little. "Darling," he said, trying out the word. "I'm sure she was happy for you, watching you enjoy life."

And that did it. Because her sister *had* been generous of spirit. Had called out to her one night and said she admired her. After she died, Amanda pushed herself forward, discovered boys for real, and sometimes longed for one who would be like the boy who visited her sister.

Her sister had loved her in spite of how horrible she was.

She had to dab at her eyes, thinking she didn't much like Harrison for digging at that part of her life, for wanting to turn everything into something he could write.

During this first couple of weeks of knowing Amanda, Harrison had other offers. His boss Schwartz suggested he should play the field. He didn't feel like playing the field. One of the clerks at the deli, Franny, with a last name that sounded like *genteel* (but that wasn't it), had pressed for weeks to find something they 'could do together,' so he had taken her with him to the Cotton Club on that Thursday night when Amanda couldn't go. She was wowed and kept snuggling up against him while he kept patting her shoulder in what he hoped was a brotherly manner. She got bolder when he saw her to her door. She'd teased and tugged at his hand to get him inside. And he was tempted too. She was a pale, studious biology student whose teasing and flirting seemed forced, performed maybe. It had probably been a mistake to take her to the Cotton Club, but he'd hated to waste the second ticket. He studied the railings on the ten steps leading up to her door and the lower windows of the building, trying to think how to avoid going inside.

He kissed her a few times, aware of the minty breath she offered him. "Sorry I'm so beat tonight. I still have to write my press release on the changes in the Cotton Club."

"I'll bet you write fast."

"Not always."

He wondered what Amanda was doing. Schwartz would tell him he was foolish, throwing a good fish *out* of the pond. But, no, he inclined toward Amanda with her challenges and her independence. "See you at work."

"I'll save the ends of bread for you."

"Wonderful."

Other people might not put peanut butter on rye, but it was very handy having bread around.

In fact, he had some of that peanut butter on rye when he got home. He made a few notes in his notebook about a cat that watched the street from a lower window as a young woman clung to a railing made of spiral legs on the way to her apartment after a long day. After that, he typed up what he would hand in the next day at noon on his lunch break. He walked around in his skivvies being a movie character trying to win the girl—what Fred Astaire did so well. The Saturday after the ballgame, Amanda was once more unavailable. However, she'd agreed that on Sunday they could go for a walk in Central Park after a subway ride uptown.

He bought a bouquet on the way. When he arrived at her place and handed her the flowers, she looked surprised and a little worried.

She searched for something to put them in, rattling cupboards. "Don't have a vase."

"The pitcher, the pitcher," he said brightly. "That's the right size."

She poured iced tea into three glasses and rinsed out the pitcher handing it over to Harrison for her bouquet of white snapdragons and pink carnations. The ceramic pitcher was a classic blue and white piece, nicer than anything else at her place. "Did you buy that pitcher?" he asked.

"No, it came with the place."

"Amazing," he said. "It's a find."

"Really? I kind of never thought about it."

"Maybe you could offer to buy it when you leave."

"Or just take it," she said. "Old fat man wouldn't know the difference."

He was disturbed that she didn't notice beauty when it was in front of her, but his hat was in the ring and he wasn't going to pluck it back. When he thought about Amanda braving her way through her sister's death, he forgave her.

She got back at him on that Sunday walk for making her sad. Tit for tat, she asked about his father and mother. He'd already told her his father was gone, deceased, and his mother was…somewhere, playing a small role in something.

"That's fantastic. Where?"

The postcard of a couple of weeks ago was his most recent news.

He said, "I think the last I heard was a small role in *The Male Animal* in Rochester Hills, Michigan."

"Will you go see her perform?"

"If she were playing Hamlet, even Gertrude…" He smiled. "By the way, that's her name. Gertrude. No, I can't get off work long enough. She comes to New York fairly often. She comes to see a bunch of shows at a time when she's between roles." *I'll…introduce you* was too presumptuous, *have her get us three tickets* was too hopeful, so he finished with, "I'll let you know when she's in and how much time she has for socializing."

"Good," said Amanda.

Then she hit him with "Tell me about your father. How he died."

Harrison was good at remembering those summers at whatever farm his father found to rent. He could remember the smell of his father—sweat and pipe tobacco. He could, if he wanted, even recall the breath—alcohol, onion, vegetables, newly taken foods, and he recalled a sense of enjoyment over meals and when he was really young, after dinner sitting on the porch, wishing it could be like this forever, and then falling asleep in his father's embrace.

But he wasn't so good at remembering the death because he had, as most people had, guilt about living when someone they loved was dying. "There's time," he told himself twice when he was supposed to visit and cancelled because of school commitments and, to be honest, exciting dates and the possibility of sex.

The truth was, he couldn't stand to see his robust father pale, thin, shuffling, so clearly not his former self. He wanted to say the right thing, but he didn't know what that was. *It's been grand.* Implicit past tense. When he'd managed earlier visits, he asked about his father's essays and criticisms, but he was aware that the work was changing and wasn't as sharp and he never wanted to have to say so.

It was a mess at the end, with his father in a seedy hotel in New York, so downscale that it made Harrison's Boston student apartment look good.

Amanda nudged him. "How did he die?"

"Of old age and neglect. My mother left him for longer and longer periods. She was tired of trying to pretend not to see his younger women friends but then they left him too. He wasn't much fun for them at that point. He apparently forgot to eat. He just existed for a while and then he didn't."

"Letting himself die."

"I guess so." But Harrison kept picturing an earlier visit, a longing look in his father's eyes as he reached to touch his son's face, as if he could absorb youth and get back to his better self.

Harrison had moved out of the way of that touch. Now his reaction haunted him.

At the park, women sweated in their finery and held on to children who tried to pull away. The trees, gorgeously green, not an orange or yellow leaf to be seen, provided some cover but it was hot. The benches were occupied by men smoking and talking as if they hadn't had enough smoke and talk during the week.

Two well-dressed but uncorralled children came toward Harrison and Amanda, dangerously waving huge cotton candies. To avoid them Harrison and Amanda had to dodge out of the way, breaking the hand-holding. Amanda fussed to be sure the little girl hadn't bumped her. "Ugh. I wouldn't want that sugar on my dress."

But Harrison hardly heard. He had abandoned his father. The old man had been declining, sad, lonely, not able to think clearly, and Harrison had wanted to be in Lit classes and in bed with one of his girlfriends. His father had died alone. Not found for two days. Lousy.

Death was lousy. Guilt. Everybody had it. Didn't make it any nicer.

Without Amanda one evening, he went to a movie. He couldn't seem to settle down without something to distract him. His breath got short, his attention scattered, he needed people, needed to be moving, living. Thank God for stories, thank God, thank God, for stories. As a boy he'd learned to depend on books and movies—two movies every Saturday, Tarzan and Jane his favorites, back when he lived at his grandparents' house—and books alone during summers with his father.

Something about June Allyson reminded him of Amanda or vice versa. In her nurse's hat, June Allyson was quite pretty, sparkly eyes and all, but she usually played characters who were too nice for his tastes. Amanda was saltier, which he liked. She could swear, man, could she swear. But Van Johnson, the male lead, was noble and tired with war-doctoring and June Allyson was glamorous and tired with war-nursing—and the best part was how they couldn't stop thinking about each other and wanting each other and waiting for each other. They were Tarzan and Jane in another setting.

Calmer, after the movie, he dropped into a bar and had a whiskey. He talked briefly to a man sitting on the stool next to his. The man had just lost his job as stage manager for a small company. Harrison listened, sympathetic, suspecting drink was the problem. He tucked the man and his story away in his mental notebook, and later made a note about him in his real one.

Pah. He didn't know if anything he was writing down was any good. But he did it anyway, sending demons into hiding.

Calmer, he went back to his place and dropped into sleep.

3

What Harrison couldn't imagine when he was young is what he becomes when he is old. Slow. Waiting and watching for the exit sign. Things are getting grimmer day by day.

Mary Jo died no more than two years after her visit. Several friends are gone too. He is not able to walk very well. He hears a solicitation in the voices of others, which is probably what he sounded like once upon a time. Stupid youth.

"What will you read?" he'd asked his father in the later days, before he abandoned the old man. "Anything, oh, anything," his father said, and this is how Harrison feels about television. He puts any old thing on and gives himself to it, whatever it is, while he waits for Lizzie to arrive home from teaching. She left out a lunch for him today right near the sofa, so he doesn't have to go to the kitchen to fetch it. She always figures things out. Yesterday she was upset to see he hadn't eaten the chicken and rice she left in the icebox (he still calls it an icebox), but he knew in advance that reheating would challenge him—he always ended up burning things and spraying the microwave with bits of food. Because he didn't want the mess, he simply never went to the kitchen to find his lunch. Today there is a sandwich on the end table. Easier. He eats a bit—soft, chicken salad on soft white. A glob falls on his shirt; he picks it off. He does not bother to clean the spot on his shirt, he's just...tired.

Pudding would have been easier still.

Today even TV is good. Today it's *Tarzan*, and Harrison is young again seeing it but, oh, it's terrible to see what young *was*. In the movies, everywhere, a reminder of the whole country's youth—cruelty to Blacks, cruelty to animals. Give to the Wildlife Fund, he reminds himself.

But young was wonderful too. He'd loved his life. *Tarzan, Jane, Tarzan, Jane.* Learning about each other, men and women, women and men. He'd certainly identified with Tarzan as a boy, wanted to sweep up a woman who needed to be swept away from her father, torn from mindless cruelty and stupidity, and he'd wanted to brave every sort of thing to save her, to feed her.

He hears the front door. Lizzie is back! Hooray.

"With you in a second," she says.

He hears her steps go toward the bathroom.

He waits for her to pee.

"I'm coming!" she calls. But he hears her steps go to the kitchen. Water. Water out and then water in. But then it gratifies him to hear her seconds later rushing toward him, and she arrives bearing two glasses of water. "Hey there. So sorry. I was almost dizzy from dehydration. Here. Try." She hands him one of the glasses.

He sips, reaching out an arm toward her at the same time.

"What are you watching?"

"*Tarzan.*"

"Corny, huh?"

After a long time, trying another sip of water, he says, "No, actually wonderful."

She settles beside him to watch. "I saw a part of one of the Tarzan pictures once. What I remember most is that Tarzan went through all kinds of brambles and tree limbs and you know what? Not a scratch, not a mark on his body. I guess they didn't care about credibility."

"He's perfect, that's the whole point, but—" He points to the TV. "See? In this one, he's hurt now. You missed it. Jane's father's party just shot him and then he had to fight a lion and a tiger. So, he's seriously hurt. But, of course, he'll live." He goes silent, watching reverently.

Lizzie, at first about to scoff at the movie, becomes as interested as he. People and animals saving each other, or trying to—what could be more basic?

An elephant is lifting Tarzan and carrying him to safety, then showering him with pond water from its trunk.

"It's very romantic," she says.

"Yes," he says, smiling.

Harrison never had a jungle to manage but he knew to be heroic meant punishing the body. During his long middle age, the long marriage to wife number two, he cleared acres of land and planted thousands of trees to make a better land for his family. That was his heroic deed, small perhaps in the large scheme, but he tries to keep it up even now, with Lizzie, though the scale is laughably even smaller. He is the man who only recently labored in the back yard, pushing and kneeling and digging, denying body aches, and came into the kitchen, proud to present Liz with flowers, not noticing that his legs were bleeding.

"Oh no," she said, "you're hurt."

"I am?" He didn't feel the pain, which even if he had, he would have waved off. She told him his nerve endings were muted—perhaps some sort of balance for the parts of him that had super-sensitivity.

"I'm fine," he told her.

Now he can hardly do anything at all in the yard. His body won't obey him.

"I'll make dinner," she murmurs after a while.

"Sit. Rest." He takes her hand. He keeps holding on. She doesn't move.

He wants her to see it. Without saying it, he wants her to get it.

Tarzan and Jane, Tarzan and Jane, Tarzan and Jane. They can't be without each other. They could almost die from longing when they are without each other. They are *impelled* toward each other. He and Liz, Tarzan and Jane. It's always been like that for them, the eagerness at suppertime to see each other after a day apart.

Even when he was young. Even in his stupid first marriage.

She kisses him. He keeps her hand and squeezes. "Jane," he teases.

"I'm going to make some steaks," Liz says.

"Wonderful." He always liked making steaks—shallots on the stovetop, and with a high temperature, he could get a good salty crust on the grilled meat. *Salty Crust.* There was a title. What would the story be?

4

One Thursday Harrison's co-worker at the press agency gave him tickets to a dance band. "I can't go," the guy said. "The band is okay, but their singer is not very good. They crave word of mouth."

"Harrison to the rescue."

He called Amanda and told her to get decked out—they were going dancing.

That day, he kept thinking of the phrase "word of mouth." He *knew* what it meant. It was just sort of an interesting phrase, Biblical, a bit smutty. He was in high spirits. He had started a novel about a press agent who did everything possible to help a dance troupe fill the seats. He considered *Word of Mouth* as a possible title. A couple kissing, murmuring promises. And then...what next?

As he climbed the steps to Amanda's apartment, Harrison caught up with a woman also climbing. She lived a floor below Amanda. They happened into a conversation about how she wouldn't be doing stairs in the future. She was a pleasant woman; he'd seen her around, neat and clean in her Peter Pan collars, and always with a warm smile.

She said, "I love my apartment. I hate to leave but I'm going to have to. It's just life, making decisions for me."

"Aw. I'm sorry," he said.

"You don't live here?"

"My girlfriend does. We both have tiny places. Maybe we'll look at yours when the time comes."

The woman said, "Come in! I'll let you see it now."

She was some great housekeeper. One floor below Amanda he found an apartment that looked like a real home, with a living room and a bedroom. A rocker, a sofa, canisters, things on the walls, all that stuff. "Oh, this is just exactly, exactly, what we want!"

"I'm moving to my hometown next year. I'll need to stick close to my parents. They need me."

"Whereabouts?"

"Scranton. I haven't told the landlord yet. I don't want him showing it till I'm ready."

"You aren't selling the furniture, are you?"

"I am. I'll let it go cheap. Look, don't say anything. Landlords get stingy when they know you're leaving."

"I'll be ready—I hope—to snap it all up when you give the word. Mum."

"Mum," she answered.

Ha. Luck was coming his way. Now he just had to persuade Amanda a step at a time that they needed to live together.

He reached her floor and tapped on her door.

Amanda wore a red cocktail dress that she had borrowed from a tenant in the building. "Ta da," she said when she let him into the apartment. "Is this what you meant by 'get decked out'?"

"Oh, you look wonderful," he said. The truth was, she didn't look great in red, it paled her, and she also seemed uncomfortable for some reason. He would take the dress off her later and release the devils—perhaps a girdle was tormenting her.

It was a sweet fantasy, to think of living well, one floor down. He twirled her around, all the while almost bursting to tell her that with his salary and hers together, they could make it in the bigger, better place.

But, no, no, first step would be to persuade her that they needed to live together in her place, save money, get used to each other. Then his grand surprise!

He tilted his head waggishly and took her arm as they started down the stairs. Going dancing with my girl, he thought. Going to dance in my white socks and my dress shoes, like Fred Astaire.

There were signs that Samuel might leave his wife. Amanda overheard something amid the dings and clacks of typewriters about a night on a cousin's sofa and a need to wait two days before he could get back into his own apartment. She clocked two sins: the joy she felt at the news that Sam's marriage was in trouble and the guilt that she constantly thought about Sam while Harrison kept treating her with kindness.

And then, to make matters worse, her colleagues—the young women at work—met Harrison for drinks one night when she invited him along to their blowing off steam party; now they swooned in the coffee room every time they talked to her about him. Louise was her best friend of the group, a tall thin woman with a cap of short black hair. Louise, who was almost always in a good mood, who was also quite smart about everything, said, "I watched him. He's polite, he's generous, he's a dreamboat, and he adores you."

They were right about his benevolence. And he *was* lovely to look at with thick wavy honey-colored hair and a face, though conventional, that was perfect in its arrangement. Add blue eyes. Add dimples. Yes, all right it was a face that could look pugnacious, but that expression never lasted long and soon it was back to boyish hope. Carol, another one of her work pals, pretended to pummel her. "Damn. How did you get so lucky?"

And yet she thought of breaking it off. She told herself she should simply make an open play for Samuel and…find out. Take her main chance, whatever it was.

On a Monday night she told Harrison she was unavailable and since it was Monday, he had no tickets to anything to lure her. She followed Samuel as he left the office. "Hey," she said.

"Oh, hi, Amanda."

"Which way are you walking?"

"I hadn't decided."

"If you head downtown, I'll walk with you. We can gripe together."

"A bar is better for that," he said. "I know a good one."

An hour with him was just what she had willed to happen. For that hope, she had worn her most flattering dress, a navy blue with an elongated profile and a kick pleat below the knee. It made her look taller. An hour would allow two drinks, three. She had to get him to talk.

He swung expertly through the streets, sidestepping stray bags of garbage. The air was humid and pressed at them as they ducked between sun and shade, and the car horns made a kind of music with their different notes and rhythms. Samuel looked miserable in his tie and she understood that about him, even before he loosened that tie and then took off his coat, again fluidly, and hung it over one shoulder as they walked, both fast walkers, impatient with those who ambled or looked into windows at watches or sandals or magazines. They could keep pace with the city. They came into a band of sunshine that had them both blinking and then into shadow and a series of smells—roast beef, *some* kind of beef, Chinese spices, tomato sauces, hot dogs. It was hard to ignore hunger.

But Samuel slid expertly past all establishments offering food. The funny thing was, her colleague had more of a Fred Astaire look than

Harrison did. She liked his gritty panache, his lean body—some memory of her first love at thirteen maybe, in the way that successive lovers are amalgams of previous lovers.

He looked at his watch. "Probably should get to where I'm going at seven or so." He felt in his pocket. "I'm okay either way. Got a key."

"At least you have a cousin in New York," she blurted.

He looked at her, surprised, and almost halted his walk, but after the first small hitch, he continued. "Oh. So you know what the key is for."

"Sorry. I overheard you. You were telling people you were like a kid on vacation, sleeping on your cousin's couch."

"I talk too loud. Loudly." He'd corrected himself over a chord of car horns. He was already pushing into a bar that she knew a little. Louie's was at the corner of Broadway and Nineteenth and was usually packed with people after work, most of whom spoke *loudly*, making another music, sometimes discordant.

"If ever you need to have my place—for a night, not permanently, I have a friend I could go to," she said close to his ear in order to be heard. "If your cousin kicks you out."

He looked at her hard. "Are you flirting?"

"Only if you want me to."

The din was almost headache producing but she held on to his voice. Underneath the noise she heard him order two scotches without asking her what she wanted. Then he answered her question. "I might want you to at some point in the future but not now. I have my hands full."

She held on to the phrase about the future. Her smile wouldn't quite come on full force, but she went ahead, "And you love your wife."

"I do."

"She must be amazing."

"She's not amazing. I just love her."

Two very large men with stentorian voices came in behind them and called to the bartender while trying to push themselves through other bodies to the bar. One man shoved Amanda against Samuel, which brought a lot of blood to her face. "I didn't do that," she said, so quietly that it sounded possibly arch. She hoped the noise had erased her dumb comment. But obviously Samuel heard her because he blinked an acknowledgement.

And then he threaded the conversation backwards, telling her, "It's vice versa that's the problem." A little cryptic but she figured he meant his wife no longer loved him.

Before she could censor herself, she said, "I dreamt about you. You were on a stage, being a comedian. And somebody was taping it for radio."

"Ah. Huh. Very interesting. I used to want to do that for a living, actually. But not too many people make a living at it. Jack Benny makes it look easy. I think I'm not dry enough. Sentiment gets in the way. Though almost nobody knows I have any of that. Including Ann." He looked forlorn and took a good slug of his drink.

"Oh, out, out, damned sentiment," she said, trying to lighten things. "It gets in the way, I agree."

Samuel waved to someone down the bar. Amanda didn't want to turn to find out if it was a woman or a man, old or young.

"You don't have that problem," he said. "Sentiment."

"I don't?"

"No, I admire you. You're tough."

"I am?" She didn't think he'd paid enough attention to know, tough or not.

"You appear to think I'm wrong." He drank off his glass and ordered them seconds.

She felt she might cry. He had said nothing about the fact that she dreamt about him. He'd slid right by the importance of what she revealed. He was the tough one, the cynical one.

"Am I to understand you're not dating anybody," he said, presenting her with a second drink.

"I am." She tried to concentrate on the mahogany bar, one of the best she'd seen, and the tin ceiling, the fineness of this place he'd chosen.

"Oh, good. Look, don't think about me. Get married, have children, be happy. Or don't get married but be happy. Seriously, you're a good kid. Ah, why do people get crazy about each other?"

"I think about that all the time."

"And what have you come up with?" He smiled, almost a wink.

"Childhood images. Um. Filling the gap in the personality. Frugality meets spendthrift."

"You got that right. More?"

"Smells, apparently, according to scientists."

"How do I smell?"

"I'm not sure," she answered seriously. "I've never had a whiff."

Amanda had had a boyfriend at sixteen, a lounging tall lanky fellow.

She liked his looks and his personality. He was scrubbed up, clean, but his skin had a smell that was neither cologne nor soap. Just skin, an almost chemical smell to it. She realized at one point that her nose stuffed up and she got a terrible headache every time she got near him. "Maybe I'd be allergic to you," she said.

"Lucky you."

With Samuel, no matter what he said or did, she felt alive around him. Louche, he was louche. Or she wanted him to be.

After the second drink, he asked, "You okay to go home?"

"Sure."

"You walk it?"

"Almost always."

"I'm going to my cousin's, figuring out what obeisance to do next. What a life. All our scrapping. What's it worth?"

She didn't have an answer.

When she got to her building, in spite of the traffic noise, she dropped a dime into the slot in a phone booth and called Harrison's building. Somebody downstairs answered. "Would you put a message under his door?"

"Okay. Shoot."

"*Not busy after all. Have enough pasta for two. Let me know if you are coming.*"

"I could come over if he can't," the guy said.

"Just put the note under his door."

Soon she settled into the evening. She laundered a white cotton blouse, leaning over the kitchen sink and giving it two good scrubs and two rinses before she hung it on the curtain rod to dry. She put her bed pillow on one of the kitchen chairs to read the last fifty pages of *Tales of the South Pacific*, and without missing a beat, began *I, The Jury*, then listened to the comedy hour on the radio. After all that, she finally climbed the seven steep steps on the eighteenth floor that put her out on the roof where she could look at the city she'd chosen. No, she wouldn't want to be anywhere else, no matter how lonely she got. The thrum of the city filled her with love, more love than she felt for any person, even her parents. She knew there were millions of people, Harrison one of them, having an evening just like hers, smarting with rejection, and she felt one with them.

Harrison had gone to a bar because he thought perhaps with people buzzing around him, he could catch a rhythm and make notes that might fit his current novel attempt. When he asked himself who the antagonists of his book about the press agent would be, a pretty basic question, he couldn't decide. Surely that was a bad sign. Did it mean he should drop that idea and start something else? His father had once told him you needed to get to a hundred pages before you knew whether to go forward or to drop something. All he had so far was an emotion he hoped to capture. A story that was bright with a feeling of elation, joy... And it was to be joy *in spite of* evidence to the contrary.

He ordered an American whiskey and made his best attempt to nurse it so that he could stay seated at the bar for a long time. If he was going to be a writer he had to watch people. He studied the people down the bar, trying to guess what they were there for, drink or company. His father used to say, "Just write one good sentence. That is a day's work." And his father worked for hours over a sentence. So Harrison took out his notebook, almost full, a ragged thing about four by six (maybe the fifth of what would be hundreds of similar notebooks in his life).

The men, two of them, focus on the spot behind the bartender, longing for the whole bottle, longing for the blur of a long pour.

Eh.

One woman is looking at one of the men. She wants to talk, she wants to sidle up, to slide into the smallness of an embrace. But she's afraid. She holds back.

Eh.

According to his father, he could revise and polish these sentences for three days and that counted as work. The thought of that kind of patience was both refreshing and daunting.

Behind him a sound went up—women's voices, raucous, and giggling about something. Their squeals mounted in volume and intensity. He turned to see five young women, bright-eyed, all of them. Perhaps they were new to the city. They had the expressions of daring on their faces. Each one was nice looking, carefully dressed, and sexually appealing. He didn't want to stare, so he angled himself away a bit. My God, but they were having a good time.

"And then he said—" one girl began, but they were already in hysterics again and he couldn't hear the rest.

He found himself laughing even though they were no doubt making jokes about men, but women having a good time counted among his favorite things. Even in high school, when he saw women laughing, he felt good. He wasn't feminine himself, didn't want to wear their clothes, didn't want to kiss a guy, but, well, he supposed he had a girlish heart.

When he got back to his place, he learned that he had missed Amanda's phone call, but the fact of her calling made him happy.

The next night he took Amanda to see *It Happened on Fifth Avenue* because he needed a laugh and the reviews had said it was a very funny movie and she, too, clearly needed some cheering up. She was glum, well, actually growling with anger lately. The film was about a charming ne'er-do-well who moves into a rich man's house when the man goes on vacation and then invites all his bum friends in too. For some reason, the movie made Amanda even more furious. As they walked out, he tried to put an arm around her, but she shrugged him off. "I am so sick of seeing these fantasies about rich people suddenly having souls. And we're supposed to believe that the wealthy people let a bunch of bums live in their house and eat their food and wear their clothes because… why? You know people like that are just self-satisfied. They don't want to know about the poor!"

"I think it was just meant to be silly." But he understood what she was saying. There was no credibility to the story; it was all just an arrangement for sentiment to win out. He had always determined that his own stories would not be sentimental in that way—he *hoped* they wouldn't be. "I just don't know why you take it so hard," he said. He bumped her playfully.

She grumbled, head down, "Because I want to be one of them. Rich."

At first, he thought she was joking. But her face was frighteningly angry. "You do?" he asked, puzzled.

"Doesn't everyone? Except priests and nuns and maybe even they do."

He stretched to avoid a puddle. He supposed he wasn't normal. He simply did not want to be wealthy. It wasn't interesting. He had never wanted it. Poverty, making do, was interesting.

"You know when I first saw you, I thought you *were* rich?" She pummeled his upper arm in her irritation. "And you don't have a god-damned thing."

"True, I don't." If that's what she'd wanted from him, and still wanted, they were doomed. "Let's get something to eat." They were passing a row of shops and restaurants, sandwiches, pizza, soups, Chinese.

"I ate. Let's just drink."

"Someplace where they have peanuts or pretzels at least. I need something," he insisted. "I haven't had dinner. Think of me for once."

"I know a bar where they can make you a sandwich. I'll pay. I owe you. I want to treat you."

He said all right. He was down to almost nothing. Did she seriously want to hobnob with the rich? "You're just in a state for some reason."

She paused. "All I know right now is I really need a drink."

He pulled up a Fred Astaire. "Mandy. Darling. Let's be rich then if that's what you want."

"How?"

"I don't know. I'd have to write something great."

"Oh, hell, the truth is, I don't know what I want. This and that." She swung into a bar he hadn't even seen they were approaching. She ordered a Seagram's for each of them and a club sandwich without asking Harrison if that would do it for him. "I'll eat a quarter of the sandwich," she announced.

He touched her hair, then her face near her ear, a gesture learned from the movies. He'd seen some movie star do that just recently. Was it Van Johnson? It meant *I see you are having a hard day. I am strong and I comfort you.*

"Ugh. Don't touch my face. Feels scary."

What the hell? Dozens of actresses in great movies *put up* with a touch to the face, in fact appeared to be *seduced* by it.

She said, "We should stop seeing each other."

He said, "Okay" so fast he couldn't identify any thought that had gone into it.

She said, "Well then."

He said, "I'll walk you home. I do need to eat first though."

"We can wait that long."

The sandwich came and he swallowed hard, each bite going down scratchily. He ordered a beer. She put money down for it. She seemed determined to pay, perhaps to prove to him that he would never be able to support her. When she went to the ladies' room, two women approached him, one on each side.

"Are you in movies?" one asked. "We've been trying to identify you."

"Good God, no. Sorry I can't offer a drink. I'm broke." And he felt bitter about it suddenly, the lack of cash, the non-rich life he was destined to lead which was *perhaps* what had made Amanda crazy to get rid of him. But he really didn't want much money. Just enough.

"I'd stand you to a drink," said the one. He looked up at her. She wasn't attractive, too much dark hair crowding her face, a long nose, but it was also a surprisingly jolly face.

"I would, too," said the other one. He turned. The second woman was quite attractive, a dark-haired girl who didn't try to fit into the current fashions. She looked almost gypsy-like with a peasant blouse and skirt. It was odd clothing, like a costume, but pretty.

"I saw you looking at my outfit. I admit they're my own clothes but I was auditioning for a role, honest. I'm not quite as weird as I look."

"An actress!"

"Maybe. If they take me. What are you?"

"A writer."

"Oh, how wonderful. What have you written?"

"Lots of pages. Nothing published yet."

He was morose but he had the slightly happy thought that Amanda would see he was sought after. He waited a long time, but she did not come back. After a while he took the change the bartender had brought for her and bought the other two each a beer.

Two weeks later, Amanda said, well, she was thinking about it and if she still felt good about it in a month or two, he could move in.

Once, early on, Harrison took Liz to New York and insisted on several long walks. "I used to live there," he said. "Cold water flat. I hope they improved it." After a few blocks, he pointed again, "There too. Long ago."

Liz tried to imagine it.

"Too hot or too cold," he said. He shook his head.

What Liz was pretty sure of was that he loved it.

5

Amanda had the fan going, and she was drinking what looked like iced tea. It was sweltering and on the stovetop was a pot of rice with chicken in it, wrong for the weather. Amanda wasn't much of a cook.

She looked beat. She was plugging in an iron.

"I got an invitation I think you'll like!" Harrison announced.

"What?" she asked grumpily, moving some dirty clothes into a single pile.

"Reserve the date: September 12. A party with the upper crust." He showed her an invitation that had come through his press agent's office. He handed it over with a stack of pastrami chips and said, "I think your great little rice dish is done," as he turned off the fire under it.

"Fifth Avenue. Wow. Good address. How…"

"I hear the food is going to be fabulous."

"How did you…?"

"I don't know. Someone apparently asked for me."

"Huh. It says formal. Dear God, I don't have formal." She wiped an arm across her forehead, looking like a washerwoman in a film, someone who had to be Cinderella-ed to go to the ball.

"Well. We need to borrow from friends or go to a secondhand shop. I think I know a guy who has a tux that might work for me. I'll look into it. Do you know someone? The woman who lent the red dress?"

"That was a crappy dress."

"Yes."

"No. That's just it. I don't know people who have things like I'm supposed to wear to this do. That's the whole point."

Two days later he arrived back at her place, beaming. "Try this." He unwrapped from paper a silvery gown. She hesitated and then went into the bathroom to try it on, modest about her lack of confidence that she could pull it off.

When she emerged, she said, "How did you figure the size? It's not even too long."

"I have an eye. I, ahem, know your measure."

"Golly. The cost."

"We could try to sell it back to the secondhand shop. They had jewelry but the dress broke our little bank. You'll have to go unadorned. Or I could ask around at work in case someone has little sparkly earrings. Don't you have women friends?"

"Nope. I'm not that kind of girl."

"Well, you're my kind of girl."

The way Cary Grant might have said it.

The house that held the party was a huge brownstone; a doorman made it look like a hotel to an unknowing observer. Another liveried man on the street parked cars for those who owned them. Harrison and Amanda were cab people that night—they had considered the bus, but they were too fancily dressed to manage that comfortably. Harrison had adorned Amanda with rhinestones borrowed from his work pal, Franny, who still liked him enough to help him out with another date; she lent them with a grumble and a whole lot of undisguised curiosity.

The first floor of the house was decked with flowers, but Harrison could see beyond the entranceway to what looked like the largest kitchen he had ever seen outside of a restaurant. There were some dozen people rushing back and forth in that space, all of them dressed in white.

"Upstairs, please," said a man in a plain black suit and white shirt, pointing them to a grand staircase that was wide enough to accommodate a trio or quartet of people walking in tandem.

At the top, another man in a black suit and white shirt ushered them forward into a salon that appeared to take up the whole floor or most of it. The windows were framed in red velvet draperies swagged aside. Several of the tables were glass and gilt. Harrison quickly counted five sofas in the room. There were people of a certain look—wizened women with flat chests and hair harshly combed back. Balding men with paunches they tried to be proud of. Everyone held a drink. Why had he been invited? "Five minutes," he said, "and we'll go unless I start to feel this wasn't some crazy error."

But what his eye caught next and made him want to stay were the walls full of paintings. It was amazing to see so much art in one place that was not a gallery. In a way it *was* a gallery. Understanding this—that someone named Jones had opted to hold, to own, what others had painted—intrigued him.

Amanda had drifted to a wall that featured several framed paintings that could have appeared in a drawing room centuries earlier because they showed men in a hunt, horses eager, skies a perfect blue. These weren't the paintings Harrison admired; to him they were copies of an old idea, but they were well done, he granted that. He crossed the room to join her.

"You like these?" he asked.

"They're so…English."

"Yeah. My family would have been working the stables. Writing poetry on the side. Yours?"

"Angling to get into the hunt."

"*That* close to the powers that be?"

"Way back, I mean. My parents' generation has fallen much, much lower. Did you see on the wall behind the bar service—"

Several guests passed balancing gold-rimmed martini glasses. "Speaking of—" he said. "Let's get a couple of those."

"Oh yes, I'll have a martini tonight."

They were three-deep at the bar, waiting for their drinks, but they got a good look at the paintings of one figure after another behind the bar. They were of women dressed for a gala ball in 1870 and later up to 1920, and the men, no matter the period, sat stiffly in suited wear. "Looks like family portraits," she murmured.

"I feel like one of those guys," he said because his borrowed tux, one size too small, forced him into that same posed stiffness. He laughed, imagining himself older and paunchy, and partly playing that role, he said in plummy voice, "You can sit, my dear. I'll get your drink."

As he stayed in line, he was cataloguing the fact that she had liked something about the portraits. He turned and watched as she crossed the room and sat on a beautiful chair with gold-painted legs and gold-upholstery fabric, and he had the horrible feeling she was imagining doing so every day.

Carrying both martinis several minutes later, Harrison saw Amanda leaning forward and flirting with an old man. Her conversation allowed him to stall at a third wall of paintings. He sipped his drink, then some of hers to avoid a spill. *Now, these works*, he thought, *bring the hosts up several notches*. He absorbed the dizzying colors of Norman W. Lewis, the filmy, tired farmer couple by a fellow named Curry, and then he stood dazzled by a collage—never thought he would love a collage, but he did—paint, ink, papers, paste, a work of art done by Robert Motherwell. Oh God, to live with these things right on your wall. If he ever had money it would go to painters.

"Gorgeous, right?" said a woman behind him. He turned to see a girdled, décollotaged blonde of about forty with majestically swept-back hair, carrying what looked like an almost finished Manhattan, cherry on the bottom.

"Can't stop looking at it."

"That's a sign."

"Of what?"

"An eye maybe? I helped hang these."

"You did? Wow. This one—"

"Motherwell. What got you?"

"That line. The saturated red."

"Well, when you have money, come see me. The gallery is called Stephen. My stuff is very expensive."

"I'll never be able to afford anything like these."

"Start small. Trust your eye. I already do." She saw a waiter with a pickup tray and moved off. He watched her deposit her glass and hail a waiter for another.

He went to Amanda and handed over her drink, but since she was still in deep conversation with the old fellow, he moved to the fourth wall of paintings. They were among the ones he liked, totally different from those on other walls. All abstract, pointillist. He loved one by someone named Leonardi. He drowned for a moment in the colors before turning back to the main room and the food that was now being circulated by a bevy of waiters. At least a hundred servers had been hired for the evening.

The first throng of waiters missed him completely. He saw Amanda now standing and talking to a well-put-together middle-aged man who halted a waiter to get her some lobster in a puff of pastry.

He watched her, and she seemed, even at a distance, fake. When he caught up to her, he said, "Aha, so avoiding the fellow in the cheap borrowed tux."

She blanched. "This is secondhand after all. I'm sure everyone knows. I'm just doing my best to fit."

Poverty embarrassed her. Right. He was more sanguine about being the stable boy writing poetry, not aspiring to the house that owned the stable, that is, until he saw artworks. Then he had second thoughts.

Finally, they left and decided to walk a long way before hailing a cab. A delicious cool breeze picked up just enough to dry the sweat on the backs of their necks. The street was quieter than usual and the moon was full.

"I noticed you really like paintings," she grumbled.

He did. He did.

If they could borrow a car and drive to Provincetown, he could show her works of art in a calmer setting. He could show her how to live beautifully without riches. Like in the French paintings—a tumble of flowers, fruit, an antique table, a worn chair. There could be joy in poverty when it came with beauty and sensuality and always cheese, bread, fruit, red wine.

"Paintings and vases and pitchers," she murmured.

Traffic for some reason quieted down even more as they walked and there was a hum of it, moving steadily.

"Why paintings?"

He had the horrible thought that Amanda was not right for him. "Just...I guess I have an eye. I got hooked in Provincetown. I think we should go soon. You'll see what I mean."

She shook her head and tilted it, trying to know him. His face took on some years in the moonlight.

6

Amanda gave in and agreed, took Monday off work, packed a small suitcase, and they headed out the very next weekend to Provincetown (Harrison had borrowed an ancient truck from a guy at the agency, and it was uncomfortable). They got there and immediately started walking up and down the streets. She'd thought the first thing she was going to do was dip her toes in the bay.

There were what seemed like a hundred galleries along Commercial Street, dizzying to Amanda. They strolled slowly, being bumped by people in more of a hurry. She kept an eye on Harrison's face as he stretched toward the galleries' windows, hungry, looking.

"What kind of prices are they?"

"Two hundred, four hundred, seven hundred, a thousand."

"Yikes. Har, you really can't afford to buy anything."

He said, "We're going to have to give up that drink at the Colony. Also, maybe dinner."

Before she could ask if he was serious, he was taking her hand and leading her into a gallery.

He studied a seascape for a long time.

"You love that?" she asked.

"No, there's something wrong with it."

"What?"

"Sort of playing to the crowd too much. Wanting to be on the wall in a middle-class home."

"Is that bad?"

"It isn't good."

She was embarrassed that she'd liked the painting. High class was her aim after all, back with her great great ancestors. In her imagination as she hosted a party backgrounded by paintings while she, wearing a spectacular gown better than anything she had ever yet seen, descended a staircase with her husband. But in the vision her husband was Sam. Dumb, dumb, dumb. The heart was dumb. She shook the image away and slipped an arm through Harrison's and squeezed, wanting to give herself to him, touched by his longing. "Okay, sweet man," she said. "I am your student in these matters."

His face brightened. "Well, okay. I like the rough edges of these figures," he said at one painting. At another, he said, "I get something from that."

"What?"

"Fury. Angry paint."

"Really?"

He nodded. And just when they were about to go to dinner, there was another gallery and a shout of laughter escaped him as they stood looking in the window. "Oh, we have to stop here!"

Inside he asked the owner, "Could we see the one in the window close up?"

The man took his time fetching it and propped it on the countertop, holding it delicately.

Amanda saw that it was abstract but after a while she saw, too, that the subject was an old-fashioned hunt.

"It's a sendup, sort of handed to us. Magic."

"What do you mean?"

"It's for you. The gods intended it. Of course, we might have to do dishes for dinner. For real."

He bought the painting over her protests, the owner nodding and saying, "Witty, isn't it?"

It was about eighteen by thirty inches, now wrapped in brown paper. Harrison said, "I'll carry it for you."

"I won't know what to do with it."

"I'll help. I wanted to find just the right thing for you. And now some dinner. Whatever you want. I'll eat bread."

She felt both irritable and affectionate, and for some reason, perhaps simply hormonal, she couldn't stop touching him. If she couldn't have Samuel, well, Harrison was second best.

They got back to their room at midnight. It was comically small and could have existed in Manhattan except that the walls were decorated with fishnets. A couple of oars welded together made a coat rack—well, *dress rack*—since it was still warm out. There was no closet or wardrobe in the place. They made love and crashed into sleep and woke to make love in the morning. For breakfast they had fried dough at the Portuguese Bakery and lots of coffee until they couldn't sit there any longer without ordering again. "I think I should move into your place," he said. She had admitted a few days ago that they could afford more pleasure if they paid less rent.

"Yes," she said. "But how will we fit?"

"Snugly."

"You need a table for your typewriter. If you're going to be a writer."

"What if I set up my typewriter in the hall outside your door?"

"Someone would steal it."

"That's no good then."

"I can't think where to put it. And your clothes."

"I'll roll most of them up. I could keep them in a suitcase under the bed."

She nodded, feeling glad he did not want her closet space.

"And I think the table with the typewriter could double as a bed stand. I could type there."

She had been thinking the kitchen might be better—strawberry jam on the pages, that sort of thing. But she didn't say. They were sealing something, and it seemed delicate and precious.

"All right," she said.

He sublet his place the next week, sent his boxes of books, then packed the rest of his belongings in one suitcase and three paper bags and moved. They would have a little cash now as a result of the merger, he reminded her when she looked alarmed at the additions to her place. Things were looking up.

Thank God they were in New York, where cohabitation went by the excuse of anonymity. Thank God Amanda's parents lived in Akron and didn't ever leave home. And that she had neighbors who knew to look aside.

Once Amanda let him move into her place, she determined to make it work. They now had money to eat and drink in the way they liked and besides he was a good guy—kind, if innocent. She won points everywhere she went with him. People thought, however (and she'd called this shot at the beginning), that she'd snagged a rich guy who was only playing at living simply. If only they knew.

7

Forty-five days after Provincetown, Amanda said, "We have to do something. I mean...I'm late."

It took Harrison a moment to register and then he said, "Damn. Oh, damn."

"We can't—"

"We'd better get you to a doctor to be sure."

She nodded. "I made an appointment. Next Thursday. But that guy won't do it. I have to find someone else who will."

Harrison took another moment to answer. "I'm thinking. I mean I'm thinking all kinds of things." He stood up, sat back down. He said, "We could just go to a justice of the peace."

"Wow. What a proposal."

"I'm sorry. It's not how I would do it."

"You've never met my family. They would just die. What are you thinking? I've never even met your mother."

"She'll disapprove of anything I do, that's flat."

But Amanda didn't want a child. That would really change everything about her plans for herself. If they'd had more room, another bed, or if he still had his own place, she would have booted him out of her place that night. But they had only the double bed and no floor space, so they climbed in together and he held her until she fell asleep.

All week Harrison mentioned the justice of the peace, and all week Amanda nodded and dabbed at her eyes.

He called his mother. "I think I'm going to get married soon. Something simple. No honeymoon as yet."

"That woman you told me about? A month, two months ago?"

"Yes, Amanda."

"Well. You must like her?"

Like didn't seem the right word, but he said, "Yes."

He did not get a blessing, but then he never got a blessing from his mother about anything. Other women liked him, coddled him and beamed in his presence, but his mother was always frowning, picking at his clothes, scrutinizing his haircuts. Around her he felt awkward in a way he never had with his father who was perhaps equally sloppy and charming and also, like Harrison, intense underneath while easygoing on the surface. He thought it couldn't be helped, that he was a bit like his father. He promised himself again that he would, however, never be unfaithful.

Why the hell he still wished to please his mother, he didn't know.

Amanda looked at him kindly these days, perhaps coming to like and accept the idea that he had fathered her child. Sometimes she touched his hair and he felt…such a rush of warmth. Oh, maybe she was just smoothing it into place, but he felt…lovingly touched, nicely touched. Not the rough way his mother had laid hands on him.

Still, things weren't as happy as he wished. He couldn't type late into the night because Amanda needed to sleep. He snuck home between press-agentry assignments and began a short story about a man who learned he was going to be a father. In the story the man imagined a son and what he would say to him, only to realize suddenly that the child might be a daughter. Harrison was to learn years later that this emotion made a very good song in *Carousel*. How to love and care for a daughter was, at any rate, the thrust of the story he began and managed to finish in a week. It wasn't bad. It had feeling and the feeling was that women were wonderful, to be loved and loved. Amanda cried when she read it.

Then Thursday came and Amanda woke and took his hand while he lay there, awake, thinking. She was scared, he knew. She got up after five minutes and went to the bathroom. She came out seconds later, looking happy. "We're free," she said. "I got my period."

He couldn't think. "You didn't do something?"

"I took no coat hanger in there with me."

He didn't ask if she had ingested something the night before. He had heard of such things among friends in college. She was so happy that he couldn't bear to ask the question. She climbed back in. He held her and they were both late for work, not caring at all. He didn't, anyway. He felt close to her and that was worth it all.

Harrison slapped sandwiches together, finding himself sad that marriage wasn't imminent. He wanted to do right by Amanda. If even a few people in her building thought less of her for living with him, wasn't he responsible? They *should* get married. But it was true, he hadn't met her family and she hadn't met his mother. Wasn't that how it should be done?

Then as if thinking about it made it so, two weeks later his mother announced she was coming to town. Harrison gave her his new address.

A day later she arrived, dumping her suitcases at their front door, assuming she would stay with them, so they fluttered about, trying to fit a borrowed cot in the kitchen/living room while she watched and smoked and dug into her luggage for a change of clothes. "I can change in the bathroom, right?"

They looked at each other when she was gone. The cot didn't fit anywhere, she'd seen that. She came back in a beige dress and low heels, saying, "You know Mary Sue has been begging me to stay with her. I really ought to try. I'll call in a bit." She wandered to the counter in the kitchen, checking the liquor bottles, saying, "Now don't overdo the booze." Before she made moves to leave, she scanned the books on the shelves, the contents of the refrigerator, and Amanda—her clothes, her legs, her hair—with a smile of approval and an equal whiff of disapproval. She was in the theater, after all. She had practice switching facial expressions for a knowing audience.

Harrison saw Amanda could hardly breathe. Finally, his mother left for the afternoon.

"She usually stayed with friends," he said weakly, "so I thought…"

"Oh God," Amanda said. "Did you see? She wanted to sleep right here while we passed back and forth to the bathroom."

Harrison was starting to laugh. He couldn't stand to wear anything at all to bed. He tried to remember to wrap a towel around him for decency when he went to the hallway, but late at night he was fairly careless about the towel, more or less carried it in front of him for show. His mother disapproved of everything about him so he had to hope her friend Mary Sue would come through.

"She didn't like me."

"She doesn't much like me either. Maybe she'll warm up tomorrow when her other friends get bored with her."

And Gertrude Mirth *was* a tad nicer the next day. She asked her son and Amanda all kinds of questions about their work, and she listened judiciously, but if Amanda turned away, her lips would purse, or she would blow a stream of smoke to the side, skewing her mouth, trying for her best Lady Bracknell. Though he laughed it off, his mother made him terribly nervous.

And she was so dramatic. Well, yes, he'd got a bit of that from her, but it sat better on luggish men, didn't it? There his mother was, with her hat cocked to the side—rakishly, he thought, though she was not a feminine version of rakish at all—pontificating about the state of the arts.

"I'm taking us all out to dinner," Harrison announced.

"Lovely," his mother said.

People looked when they walked into his favorite little Greek dive in the Village. Soon she was holding forth about the current state of the theater in a way that made people at neighboring tables drop their own conversations to listen to her, often looking puzzled at why they suddenly cared about the health of that art form.

Amanda tried to join the conversation. "You said yesterday you lost your director?"

"We surely did. And he was good too. *But* we learned he had his own way with accounting, and we were not getting a quarter of what the house took in! A petty criminal, yes, a dirty thief, but with a great sense of how to *block a play, alas.* We were *very* frustrated when we figured it out. *I* figured it out first, actually. I always had a *math* sort of brain."

Harrison was definitely going to be paying for all her dinners. Mama was on the skids.

Three days, three meals together and then his mother left, waving a queen's goodbye.

The aftermath of her visit was even worse than the visit itself. As usual, he'd made it through, but he was shaking. She'd never thought much of him and yet he loved her and kept trying to change her mind. How dumb was that?

Very dumb. He admired her pluck though, crazy as that might be.

While Amanda was out late at work, Harrison roamed the apartment, restless, wanting to write, trying to write but he couldn't calm himself until she came home, and routine was established.

One night when Amanda was out, Harrison did manage to get down a few paragraphs of description about a small-town man going about his workday, only to see that he was fashioning the beginning of a story about a cuckolded man. Was that what he feared? Every man did. And of course, it made a good story, and he wanted a good story.

Amanda got home at eight-thirty. He threw his arms around her and got her supper out of the oven. "I made a kind of a pasta concoction," he said.

She ate it greedily while he read her his pages about an unfaithful woman.

"Well, there has to be trouble in a story, right? Choose money, illness, infidelity," she said with a sort of authority. "This one has more trouble than your earlier ones, so I think it's on the right track. Actually, I think it's pretty good."

He waited for her to say more but she didn't.

It was cold outside and in their place. She grabbed the coat she'd tossed on a chair and slung it around her while she finished the pasta dish and had a cup of tea.

She said, "I have to go to Ohio. My pops is not happy about having me far away, so I have to go in for Thanksgiving."

November was upon them, with all the promise (and threat) of holiday parties and family get-togethers. They hadn't sorted all that out.

"Do you…um, want me to come?"

"Sure. If…yes. I thought your mother might be lighting down again or vice versa."

"More like swooping. No, unless there's a postcard I missed?"

"Well, all right. If you want to come to Akron, okay, but you'll have to stay at a hotel. I mean we can't…and besides the house is small."

He wanted to meet his future in-laws. It seemed they could find a sofa for him, which is what his mother had done when she was forced to host him over a school holiday break—when his grandparents sent him to wherever she was. He'd slept on plenty of sofas over the years. Plenty. But of course, Amanda was nervous about showing him and he was nervous, too, to present himself to hardworking conservative Ohioans. He agreed to stay in a hotel, assuming there was a cheap one.

They took a bus, which got them in late on the Wednesday before the holiday. Amanda instructed him to walk two blocks to the hotel before her father came to pick her up. "Keep an eye out. It doesn't look like anything. It's a dinky little thing."

It was already after midnight. "What if the hotel doesn't let me in?" he asked.

"They will. It's a hotel."

He wanted to ask, "Can't your father give me a ride?" but he saw she was terribly tense. He kissed her goodbye and found his way to the Akronia.

Good God, small towns were dead things, weren't they, nobody much around in those two blocks, the desk clerk asleep in his cubby hole of an office. Suddenly he wished he'd stayed back in New York. But finally, he was in a room, with nothing much to recommend it, a crooked painting on the wall, if you could call it a painting—somebody's literal image of a house. The sheets smelled clean, though. He stood at the window, smoking and looking down over nothing and hoping all would be well. He felt like someone else, a character in a film, smoking and looking out a window.

On Thanksgiving Day, Amanda called the hotel and gave Harrison the address and there he was, after a long walk from the hotel, sitting in her parents' living room, looking stiff and strange. Amanda's mother pulled her toward the kitchen, saying, "Please slice the cranberry. Nobody does it as well as you."

Amanda flushed at the lame excuse, but she followed her mother, a stolid Ohio Republican in a navy-blue dress with a gold belt, the dress that had graced every Thanksgiving and Christmas dinner for as long as Amanda could remember. How could parents and their offspring be so mismatched? Her mother often told people, "My daughter likes to write little articles. I just don't know why she can't do them here in Akron." Case in point.

"He's very handsome," her mother said.

"I know."

"Well, do you trust him?"

"With what?"

"To be true to you."

The problem—she didn't say—was her own wobbly fidelity. She sliced the cranberry too thin as the stupidest act of revenge. When her mother hugged her, she started to cry. Marriage was a practical thing, right? Two by two. She would marry him and get it over with.

At dinner, Amanda's father, a quiet, somewhat bloated man, a plumber, asked, once they sat down to dinner, "You do something with entertainment groups? Is that right?"

"Yes, sir. Press agentry."

"What is that, exactly?"

"Groups pay, say, dance companies, theater troupes, to have publicity done. Anything I can come up with to get their names in newspapers and even on the radio. I help promote them."

"So, you like what they do?"

"Usually. Not necessarily. I'm like a lawyer, paid to defend, not to believe."

Amanda, assuming this thought went a little ahead of her father, interrupted with, "Harrison's father was famous. He was a political essayist. In all the big publications."

"That sounds interesting," said Amanda's mother. "And what does he do now?"

"Not much," Harrison said. "Pushes up daisies these days."

A horrible spell fell over the table for a moment.

Amanda's mother said, "That's right. You told me. I'm so sorry. Sometimes I don't know where my mind is."

The turkey was dry, the stuffing was dull, and only the mashed potatoes were very good. The cranberry sauce required a spoon, cut as it was, so thin.

To everything he was served, Harrison said, "Thank you. Very nice." Or when he could manage it, "Marvelous."

Amanda mouthed, *Sorry*.

Amanda's mum served store-bought pie and weak coffee after the meal. While they ate dessert, Amanda's father asked, "This is what your job will be? This publicizing? Or is it temporary?"

"Oh, temporary. For sure. So is the deli I work at. I'm going to be a writer. In my case novels."

"Books," Amanda said impatiently. She made a large wide space with her hands. "Fiction. Long stories."

He told Amanda when she drove him back to the hotel, "We're even. Yours don't like me either."

"It's hard to say."

"My parents were full of…problems of all kinds but I have things in common with them at least. Experiences, I mean. Reading, writing, attending theater, looking at artworks. Yours don't have any idea who you are. That has to be hard."

"Well, yes, it is, if I let myself think about it."

"Even so, bottom line, they don't like me."

"And dittoing you here, they don't even like me."

"I see that. They love you but they don't like you."

She began sniffling. He hugged her and persuaded her to come up to his room for a while. They got the fisheye from the hotel clerk—to quote a musical that hadn't yet been written. They sat on the edge of the bed and held hands. "I'll win them over," he said.

"Thanks. Do you ever think we're not supposed to be together?"

"Never. Never," he lied.

A smudged round clock ticked on the nightstand.

"I should go. I hate to leave you here."

"I hate it pretty much too. I'll be okay. I have this." He took up the book he had been reading on the bus while she slept. *The Stories of Anton Chekhov.* "He makes my brain work. He's how I want to write."

On that evening after Amanda left, and while he fretted, he had an image of happy families sitting around talking, listening to music, having leftovers. His heart ached to think he had never had this thing, this very ordinary thing that for some reason he wanted badly. The years he lived with his grandparents, his grandmother made a turkey, and they ate it early and she went to bed. His grandfather read, trying to better himself, as he said, and never, skinny and intense, craved leftovers. Harrison somehow, even as a boy, thought there should be more celebration, more indulging.

He paced his room and stood at the window and smoked. For a while he listened for sounds in the hallway, thinking he might drum up a conversation with another lonely human, but when he did hear sounds and popped his head out, he found an old drunk standing in the hallway, cursing, trying to open his own door.

"Did you get yourself a nice dinner?" Harrison asked.

"I don't care about dinner. Goddamn door. There."

The door opened and the man disappeared.

Something Amanda accused him of never feeling came over him. Anger. She'd told him he was lacking in natural anger. Oh, it was there. Lots of times he wished he could break something. He paced and smoked and finally settled down and read his Chekhov. While he read, he got an image of a character he might write, a man who married, who persuaded himself to happiness in spite of evidence promising the opposite.

Amanda insisted on a solo bus trip to Akron for a few days during the Christmas holidays, and she timed it in such a way that Harrison could put up his mother who was making another quick visit to town. He suspected she wasn't wanted by the people from her theater company—not at the holidays, at any rate. When she arrived, she dropped her bags and plopped onto a chair and defended herself before he had a chance to intimate that she'd put herself through a lot of travel within a month.

"Oh, I could have gone to the Chipmans or had Christmas dinner with our leading man. He's, you know, not a date, he's that way, likes men. But I thought, no, New York is where I want to be. Just a New York break."

"Everybody else is leaving, getting away from the city," he said, laughing. He'd prepared the bed for her, absolutely clean sheets of course.

She got up, looked around, her eyes avoiding the chair she'd just vacated. "Where will you sleep?"

He teased her. "Well, I could go to the almost in-laws in Ohio, but I thought, no, New York is where I want to be." He pointed to the chair and dragged two crates in front of it to extend it. "I'll manage on that."

"Oh, maybe I should…"

She looked old and frail suddenly. Why, she was fifty—so she *was* old. He wondered when she would die and how he would feel about it. He imagined himself mourning, feeling philosophical about death. He saw himself sitting for a long time, facing his typewriter or having a beer in a bar, taking in her demise.

She poked at the crates, performing the self-sacrificing mother who would gladly sleep on a chair to be near her son.

He showed her how he could curl up and when he needed a change of position, stretch out by getting his legs over yet another addition, a stiff kitchen chair.

"You must have done that before!" she exclaimed. "Perhaps when you're in the doghouse."

"That hasn't happened yet."

She studied him for a moment. "Oh, let's go out to dinner. Let me treat you."

"I can't refuse."

They went to a small Armenian place. She liked ethnicity in her food though not in her friends.

He watched the expressions that crossed her face—all of them usable in the little parts she got to play in Michigan, he assumed. But some of them were real. The tight-jawed determination was one of his favorites. She'd put her acting career on hold several times to sit with his father, to tend to him, to make sure he didn't drink excessively. She had always made do and didn't know how not to. Struggle was her middle name, even when there was no need for it. If a kind, affluent elderly man got interested in her, she would refuse because…where was the struggle in that?

"Do you think about Dad? "

"I ache for him." Dramatically said of course. Did she?

"I thought you were pretty angry with him in the last days."

"But that doesn't mean I don't ache."

"Okay."

"In my little room I have four—count them—suitcases, old things I picked up at secondhand shops, with his papers in them. You know, drafts of articles and things like that. I have to go through them before I send them somewhere. There are things in there I don't want anyone to see."

He was surprised. What kinds of things? Bad notes about her? Badly written drafts?

"Because he did love me. He *did*. He just needed someone to do that other stuff for him."

Women. Other women in his notebooks.

Harrison as a boy had blocked out the womanizing, known it and not known it because it seemed that was what his father asked of him, to know and understand and also to banish knowledge. What remained was a memory of being nine years old and alone in a cottage at night listening to the sounds of nature outside his window and reading reading reading, waiting for his father to come home from Mrs. This or Mary That.

"Let's get more of their bread and dessert too!"

When she played expansive, the performance wobbled a bit.

"Good idea!"

"Yes! Filling up!"

"What will you do with those suitcases full of papers?"

"Libraries have shown an interest. I have to decide which. Your father hated Harvard, thought they were all snobs, so…I don't know yet. I'll get advice. I'll let you know."

To think someone wanted the bits and scraps his father had jotted down. Harrison felt a prickling envy. He just threw his bits and scraps in the trash, never thinking anyone would want them. And, well, certainly no one did at the moment.

Amanda didn't know what kinds of messages her body was sending her. Upon her return from Ohio, she had terrible cramping and once more she was late. She loped out of the shower and confronted Harrison who was typing, the clackety-clack of his thinking and pausing and thinking about the next word driving her crazy. "I have bad news," she said. She was way steadier than the first time. "We're going to need money, we're going to have to find the right doctor, you know. I'm really, really sorry."

Outside it was snowing. Ten at night and she could just tell the sidewalks were going to be slippery. She got a welcome vision of falling and causing a miscarriage.

Harrison clambered up from the crate on which he sat and held her. "Listen," he said. "Why are we waiting? We could get our blood tests tomorrow; we could get married in a week. The little kid won't ever know it was shotgun. I can't wait to meet the little bugger."

But she didn't want the little bugger.

Harrison swayed her back and forth, back and forth. "Oh, I know just how it should be. I don't mean a picket fence. I haven't lost my identity. I mean a building here in the city, you know. But kids running around and saying kid things. I think it's the best of life. I wish I'd been one of those."

"Those what?"

"A kid with siblings and a yard to run in or a hallway and a mother and father in residence."

"Why are you always so happy then? You had shit." She knew he often shrugged off the solo childhood and the parents too busy to raise him, so a wash of feeling came over her and she managed to return the embrace.

"I don't know. I like *our life* I guess."

But multiple kids? He was nuts.

It was the next day, of all things, when she got her period. She felt as if she had slipped on the ice, which she hadn't, but there it was, done, over.

Harrison said, "It doesn't mean we drop the marriage idea. Right?"

"I guess."

He gathered his coins up and bought two inexpensive wedding rings.

And then the day after that, a Friday, Amanda was leaving work when she heard footsteps hurrying after her. She turned to see Samuel.

"Drink?" he asked.

"Oh, sure, yeah, okay."

He dove into the first bar they passed. He ordered two martinis. She didn't care that he'd ordered for her again. She drank everything and anything. Martinis were fine.

They drank and talked about work. He was angry about an article, which purported to be about the financial benefits of war, and he thought he had sensed an anti-Semitic undertone in the piece.

She had copyedited that piece and saw what he meant.

She was wondering if they would have a second drink and she was rehearsing what she would tell Harrison about it when her thoughts were interrupted by Sam who said, "I'm still bunking at my cousin's place. Seems forever."

"Terrible. So, you haven't been forgiven."

He shook his head. "My cousin is away. You want to come up?"

She shrugged as if it meant nothing, like visiting his cubicle at work. More talk about undertones and overtones. "Why not?"

"I have more gin there."

When his hand went up her skirt, an hour later, after an elevator ride to an ordinary apartment, though bigger than hers, one bedroom and a separate kitchen, she managed to say, "I just...I'm getting married. I... we set a date. Three weeks from tomorrow."

She thought he was going to say, "Don't. Put it off."

But he said, "Perfect. Wonderful."

And the way he was groaning, wanting her, she didn't have the will to stop him.

8

Everything about the transaction at City Hall was as unromantic as it could be. Harrison had invited everyone at the deli to come to the apartment for a wedding celebration. Things would finally feel joyful if they could make it through the wait, the lines, the paperwork, the certifications—without giving up.

Harrison's spirits lifted with every hurdle overcome. Amanda had a book in hand that she kept trying to read. He practiced his skills of observation, watching couples. Some looked happy and others he deemed would not make it past a year. There were short-haired soldier types pawing their intendeds. One tough-looking duo might very well be a thug and his moll. Several other pairs, two of them elderly, looked simply weary. Some of the couples were so young he could pretty much guess that the women sloping along—girls, really—were pregnant.

"At least we're not shotgun," Amanda said, looking up from her book and seeing him watching others.

He'd found the prospect of a shotgun wedding a little bit exciting, dramatic. He'd worked over in his mind a day when his own imaginary shotgun kid would notice the dates and get angry, having worked it all out. He imagined himself saying, "We love all of you. Your little brother, your sister, and you."

"I don't understand," his puritanical fictional son would retort, "how you could be such a bastard, getting her pregnant."

"We loved each other. You'll come to understand some day very soon."

His imaginary kid quizzed him about the woman next door who had been pregnant and now wasn't—and there was no baby. "What did they do with it?"

"It was a stillbirth," he explained. "They call it a stillbirth when the baby in the mother's belly isn't strong enough to survive and the body makes the birth happen even though the baby is, um, already gone."

Yes, he'd be a good father, explaining all things calmly.

"What are you thinking?" Amanda asked. They were almost at the front of the line.

"Nothing."

"Didn't look like nothing."

"Just imagining our future, our family. What are you thinking?"

"I'm wondering how we're going to feed forty people who are going to be squeezed into our apartment—I'm working on that more immediate future, three hours from now."

"People will sit on the bed. Some will spill out into the hall. We'll manage."

Thank God his mother was in a show, unable to come in. Otherwise, he'd have to suffer Gertrude tugging at his jacket, picking lint off him, adjusting his hair, and making sure he knew that everything about him frustrated her civilizing attempts. He hadn't actually announced the marriage or invited her, only asked her performance schedule and determined she couldn't be there. She often said, "The only excuse for missing a rehearsal or a performance is death. Your own." She had gone on stage with a hundred and four fever and claimed it was down to a hundred by the end of the night, work being the cure.

He thought of his father a little. His father, if he were alive and mobile and younger than he was when he died—if you could put this marriage back twenty years in a defeat of logic—his father would nod and offer a cigar and clap him on the back and jot a few notes for his next article on the back of an envelope while he waited for the ceremony to begin. Yep. And he'd make a marvelous speech and a gorgeously literate toast. That was Pop. In his mind, Harrison let him attend.

He had three siblings from his father's first marriage, a dreadful affair with a bitter ending. But those three were like distant cousins four times removed and it would have made no sense to invite them. They didn't like him because they saw his mother as the interloper who had stolen their father's affections. It wasn't up to him to explain their father had had plenty of affections, stolen and not, before he met the young flapper who was to become Harrison's mother. Harrison had only met those half siblings once when the three had driven across country to a funeral of a cousin and stopped for tea one day at the New York apartment in the Chelsea Hotel. It was some holiday or other, so Harrison happened to be there, instead of with his grandparents in St. Louis, which was rare. His brother and sisters were adult creatures who frowned mightily in his direction.

"How old are you?" the half-brother asked.

"Ten."

That was about the extent of their conversation.

The line inched forward, and he allowed in the thought that almost all the couples in front of and behind him had someone who cared about them. But soon he would be a husband and that would be his connection. He kept trying out the word *wife*. "This is my wife, Amanda," he murmured to himself.

The ceremony was quick. A few words, a putting on of rings, and it was done.

At the party afterward, most of the food was from the deli, most of the breads a day old. The guests came from Harrison's two endeavors, the deli staff and the press business. He included among his invitees two dancers who had given him extensive interviews and who had then bought him a really nice dinner that included appetizers and desserts and wine, the whole gloss of a sophisticated meal. Amanda had only invited three women from work, Louise, Nan, and Carol.

She, like Harrison, had not yet told her parents about the marriage. Neither had relatives there. In that way, at any rate, they were a match.

9

Amanda told Samuel no the next time he offered a bounce on the sofa at his cousin's place. But she carried his disappointed look around with her, seeing it at lunch when she sat alone and even while she showered and came back drying her hair and waited for Harrison to finish typing. She began to ask herself what she would do if Samuel left his wife. She imagined asking for a separation, breaking it as gently as possible. Sam had no place to live, so she would have to ask Harrison to be the one to leave—but that wasn't exactly fair. It was too much for her to figure out. She had to trust to fate. And a certain amount of mental oblivion, helped by drink. Time would solve it.

Sam didn't ask her again to spend an evening with him, to go for a drink after work. His hellos were a little shy, his exits to doorways or elevators somewhat abrupt. They behaved to each other like lovers who had had a breakup, but really, she had only been with him three times altogether, all before the marriage. It seemed his cousin regularly ate out on Thursday nights—she'd worked out that pattern. The second and third times they didn't even bounce on the sofa, only threw the sofa sheet over the bed and used that bigger more comfortable surface.

Oh, what was sex anyway? Just a bodily function. She liked it, but what she wanted more from Samuel was the worldliness, the cynicism, and the time after they made love when the cynicism disappeared, and he held her and told her he had been thinking about her and that she was terrific.

Sex was a trap. Sometimes she just hated the idea of it, but that never lasted too long.

The women from work who had come to her wedding always asked about Harrison and they told her at regular intervals how lucky she was.

One day in February in a snowstorm, she got into the office five minutes late, having been buffeted by the windy blizzard, and asked breathlessly, "Is there coffee?"

Louise, the only one in the kitchen, cheerful as always, said, "You! You've got your love to keep you warm."

"Didn't help on the way here," Amanda muttered. She didn't even take off her coat and gloves before she poured herself a coffee.

Louise said, "You don't want him, send him my way."

"No, I want him."

Just then Samuel came into the coffee room. "Is there coffee?" he asked.

"I made it," Louise said.

"Hey, take your coat off, stay!" he said to Amanda.

"Maybe I will."

After he poured and left, Louise whispered, "Guess what I heard? Yesterday he told the guys he was getting divorced and that he was happy about it."

Amanda almost dropped her coffee cup.

"I have my eye on him, actually. He's not gorgeous like yours, but he's funny. There's something...I don't know. You know?" Louise's face sought some sort of approval from Amanda.

"Yeah. No words for it. But we're word people. So, we shouldn't say there are no words for it. There must be."

Louise said, "Okay. He exudes some kind of power, doesn't he? Or is it danger?"

"Raffish." Amanda slipped her coat off.

"Charming."

"Louche."

"Wow. Okay. You sort of dislike him."

"Not at all. Don't really have the mind to figure it out right now. I just get attached to certain words." Her eyes were practically crossing with fury. He was getting divorced and he hadn't told her and Louise was interested in him. Who else was? Probably half the other women at *Time*. So, he didn't want her. It stung. Badly. She did her work in a fog, slowly, claiming to everyone that she was getting sick with a cold or the flu, which accounted for the errors she was making.

The women friends drifted toward Louise's desk at lunchtime. On the way Nan was saying, "I love a hot tea or cocoa and a book and peace, just being alone in my place."

"And the radio," Louise said, catching up to the conversation.

"No radio," Nan said. "Just me and my thoughts. I love being alone."

They sat and opened sandwiches just as Carol joined them with two boiled eggs.

"Stinky," Nan said.

Amanda was trying to figure when she had last been alone. Did she need a vacation from Harrison? To experience her thoughts while reading and having tea and allowing herself to feel as alone as she truly was? She thought maybe that was it.

That night Harrison greeted her at the door with a bottle of wine and a letter.

"Something got accepted?"

"Rejected. But read it. I mean, *read it.*"

This story shows promise. The language is engaging. But the story feels hurried. I did not always believe the characters. Do try us again with something new.

It was from *The Atlantic*, so a celebration ensued. They polished off the bottle of wine that night, promising to meet at the library to figure out where else he might send the story. Hope, promise, was an amazing thing.

The next day the streets were treacherous with hardened snow that had become iced over during the afternoon. Amanda was huddled in her coat just outside the building, trying to decide, bus or subway or walk, when she heard a voice, Samuel's, in her ear. "Drink? Please say yes."

Louise came out of the building just then and said, "Nasty weather. Will it ever end?"

"Not till it's beaten us," Samuel said.

"Maybe we should treat it with Manhattans." Louise had come around to face them and her face was flushed.

"I need to get home," Samuel said.

"Oh. Some other time then."

"Definitely," he said.

"I, damn, I forgot something in my desk," Amanda said. "I'm running back in."

"What was it?" Louise called.

"A letter. Well, a package with a piece of jewelry in it. From my mother."

Amanda went back inside. There was actually an envelope with a small gold bangle that had belonged to her grandmother and that her mother had sent her after Amanda admitted to the marriage. The clasp was broken so she'd brought it to work thinking she would stop at a jeweler someday. She felt a deep gratitude to her mother that there was an envelope and a bracelet she could show Louise.

Her breath came raspily and irregularly as she rushed into the elevator and back into her cubicle to fetch the thing that proved her innocence. She rehearsed the sentence, "We were just talking about the commas in the Pierce piece when I remembered—"

Then she got back downstairs and through the front door, where she found Louise was gone but Samuel was still there, smoking.

"Drink?" he said. "Bar or my place?"

Harrison went to a number of dance performances and theater events alone through March and April. He thought it was such a treat that he got two tickets to most things and a shame that he couldn't always persuade his wife to go along. And at times he minded being away from his typewriter at night. But the way he thought about it—and loved to describe it—was that there were two terribly ambitious people snug in the little apartment. She was going to be a major editor one day, he was sure. He was going to be a published writer. End of report. They both had passion and intelligence. They worked at one thing or another way more than eight hours a day. Twelve, fifteen, was more like it. Amanda often read for three hours. He wrote for two most nights. And when he went out it was fodder, right, stimulation? One day they would move to a bigger place, *the bigger place downstairs*, and if things went well, they would buy a brownstone and make a living room upstairs and hang paintings on all the walls.

"Do you ever have extra tickets to anything?" asked Franny, the pale young woman who had lent him jewelry for Amanda. He wondered where in her life she had had time to wear fancy jewelry. Lately she talked about going to grad school when she had enough money.

"Deli work is *not* going to be my future," she complained when she joined him out back and bummed a cigarette. He lit it for her. She appeared to be new to smoking, coughing once, eyes going wide with the adjustment to smoke getting in them. "I hope people know that. I never get to do anything interesting after work. In the arts, especially."

He felt bad wasting a ticket, so he said, "I have one for the Southern Dance Company for tonight."

"Your wife not going?"

"She can't."

"Well, I'd be thrilled to go."

He worried that she still looked at him with a little too much interest. Not wanting to give her the wrong idea, he asked her to meet him over on Second Avenue where the troupe had rented and refurbished an old movie theater. He'd written about how they'd had to make the floor right for dancers—wood, no splinters, no uneven boards. Their preparation made for a good little feature. "Five minutes to eight," he said.

He ate out near the theater, dinner on his own. The restaurant was the tiniest little railroad car of a place. It featured mousaka and an accented cook and waitress—and owners who were too busy to chat with him. He listened to their banter with each other, considering it his sad little bit of social life, but he reasoned that since Amanda was eating alone at her office, he would do her the favor of aching and suffering instead of enjoying himself. He took a small notebook from his pocket and made notes about the owners who he thought would make good characters, working and striving as they did to succeed. Every time he looked up, he feared he would see Franny entering, having chosen this place too, thus making him feel shabby about not inviting her.

While he ate an eggplant beef thing, he made notes, which after he read them over, surprised him with their sadness. There was too much "lonely" and "alone" in his jottings. The solitariness of his childhood was still with him.

The Southern Dance Company was not stellar. One of the women dancers stamped around while looking lovingly at a male dancer whose face showed something like grim determination. The rest of the company—those who played farm workers were pretty to look at while they worshiped the earth and the crops and the sky. They weren't tortured by love, so that helped. "Um," Harrison said at intermission. "Well." And then he said, "Would you like something to drink?"

"Sure."

In what wasn't a lobby exactly there were glasses of cheap whiskey poured, a small sign asking seventy-five cents a tumbler. "Warm us up," he said, because the theater was low on heat as well as talent. He would do his best for them, but he doubted publicity was going to save them.

"You looked like Joel McCrea just a minute ago—whatever you were thinking, some...angle."

"Um," he said again. He was lost for words tonight, just lost. His heart hurt. He felt nervous. Amanda was very distant these days. He tried to turn his thoughts to happy memories.

He had to walk Franny to her place, the whole way over on Cannon—he was not enough of a lout to just go off and leave her to the streets. When they got to her building, she said, "I owe you a coffee or a drink."

"Oh, couldn't. Just too knocked out."

"From processing the great dance show," she teased.

"Kind of. It didn't energize me, I can say that. Oh, man. All the hopefuls. It's sad."

"You're very kind."

"Oh, I don't think so. Just as ambitious and nuts as the next guy." He was almost tempted to take her up on a drink.

She rose up on tiptoe and kissed him on the cheek. "I think you must be a good writer."

He walked home, almost slouchily slow, hoping to kill enough time that he would walk in on Amanda, nicely tucked in bed, reading a novel, asking how the dance program was. And he let himself imagine her in the future reading a novel with his name on the cover, looking up at him, cheering his success.

She was sitting in a kitchen chair, having a cup of tea, but also reading a novel. "Good?" she asked.

He wasn't sure if she meant him or the dance program. "They have some work to do," he said. "And they need an injection of genius. But you never know for sure."

"Should I make you tea?"

"I'll get it." He wanted to tell her he'd taken the woman from the deli and made sure Franny didn't think of it as a date, but Amanda was engrossed in her reading. "You like that book?" he asked. It was Josephine Tey's *The Franchise Affair.*

She turned it over as if to see what it was called. "Yes, excellent writer."

He got the water boiling. "Save it for me. I'll read it next." They were known at the library, grabbing up the new books as soon as they came in. Amanda carried hers to work. She snuck in pages between assignments and even when she went to the loo and she made great headway at lunch. He admired that in her. "Going to bed?"

"In a bit."

He took his tea to bedside where *The Heart of the Matter* sat. He envied Graham Greene's agonies. They helped propel him into his novel's world. Guilt, pressure, all of that Catholic suffering made good copy.

He patted the bed.

She looked up. "In a minute."

When she came to bed, he smelled rye or something close. "What did you get for dinner?"

"A ham sandwich."

"And a drink."

"Needed that drink. I should go brush my teeth again."

"No, no. Stay."

She did, arms around him, patting him on the back until he slept.

A few weeks later, Amanda, tromping to the office, coat flying open because it was a warm May day, saw herself in the glass of a jewelry store. Her head tilted forward, her attempt at a mild pompadour was already coming unpinned, and her clothes were, if anything, undistinguished. All around her strutting the street were women who had prepared their looks. Ditto on the subway when she took it if the weather was bad. If she *remade* herself, she couldn't help wondering, would there be a change in her relationship with Samuel? He didn't talk about the divorce, only to mention that it was in the works and that, no, his wife was not changing her mind.

At work they avoided each other, so much so that she was sure most people had figured out why. She badly needed a confidante, but she didn't know whom to choose. It couldn't be Louise for obvious reasons. She'd been thinking maybe Carol, her other friend. Carol was not fantastic at her job, always missing mistakes that Amanda then caught, so in a way Carol owed her. If accepting a confidence could be banked. That morning it happened that they went to the coffee room at the same time, and each poured a cup and with a little orchestrating from Amanda, they meandered toward an agreement to meet at noon for a walk.

Samuel happened into the coffee room seconds after Carol left. "Ho, hi, you did something with your hair," he said in full voice, apparently in case Carol could still hear.

"Undid something." She was beyond, beneath, and above style.

A chunk of hair fell over her left eye, making no statement at all, except perhaps washerwoman up out of bed and facing her workday.

He said, "You always get *fewer* and *less* correct. Why don't the others?"

She considered. "One: bad grammar-school teachers. Two: *Fewer* seems like a snotty word. Not enough regular people say it."

"Fascinating. Would you be willing to discuss changing language over lunch today?"

"I have an appointment. I'll have to see about canceling it."

Louise entered the coffee room at that point, ears pricked. She said, "Oh, hell, the last drop. I'll have to brew again."

"You do it well," Samuel said.

"Oh, I don't need false praise. I know I make a good pot. Anything exciting today?"

"We're lamenting changing grammar. *Fewer* and *less.*"

"I think I always get that right."

"You do. You are not among the bad ones."

"I love your dress," Amanda said, heading out of the room.

When she got to her desk, she wrote a note to Carol. *Can't walk today after all. Have to work through lunch. Maybe soon, maybe tomorrow.*

A little later she was called to the phone. "Meet me over at the Empire Bar. We shouldn't go out together."

"Right," she said. "A flabby paragraph for sure."

Less and fewer. Less and fewer.

"I ordered you a grilled cheese," he said when she arrived. He displayed a sheaf of papers and a pen. "Hold these, in case someone sees us."

"Right." She was sure this was the big blow off. She was ready but worried she might begin crying and it might show at work. A cold, stomach cramps, she'd have to complain—how lame she will seem.

"Do you want a drink?"

"Why not? Sure. How about just a bourbon?"

He ordered a martini for himself and a bourbon for her. "You are pretty tough," he said.

"Pretty tough."

"I've been worried about us. I've been worried I'm ruining your marriage." He paused and drank a little water and shifted the papers. "The thing is, I'm not ready for a major commitment. Not for a long time."

"I thought you weren't going to try to get her back."

"I couldn't even if I wanted to. She's apparently moved on."

"Is that new?"

"Only new to me. She pretended to be unattached to anyone else. It hasn't been going on for a long time, just something recent, but it seems to have sealed things for her."

"But you long for her?"

"No, I don't long. I feel empty, puzzled."

Empty and puzzled were two words that could describe Amanda too. Their drinks arrived. She could feel breadcrumbs on the banquette and found herself worrying them with her left hand while she took up her drink with her right. She got a quarter of it down on the first sip. So, say it, she thought.

"It's just that I know I'm not capable of anything permanent for a long time and I know you have a great guy. And I've been feeling I should give you fair warning."

"You can say it. I should stop coming over."

He looked sad and uncomfortable and unhealthily thin. "That's not what I want. But it's what I feel I should do, for your sake."

Because he didn't love her and assumed he couldn't. But she wasn't so sure of that. She had a sort of staying power with people.

"You're my good friend. I want to see you have a happy life."

"I forgot how much I love bourbon." She took another drink of it. "Is your martini good?"

He looked at it and speared the olive. "I haven't tasted it yet. I worry when you change the subject."

"It's so I won't cry. I hate to cry. Let's talk about grammar or something else."

He considered. "All right. Tell me three things you know you will never do."

So not grammar. She scratched her head under the unintended bang. "One: go back to Ohio to live. Two: do manual labor. I'd die first. I can't even cleanser the sink without wanting to shoot myself."

"Cleanser is not a verb."

"It's my word for the act. Like Shakespeare, I can make language when I want. Three: ever stop reading. I live through others. In books. Are you going to do three?"

"No. It was a one-way game."

She knew his three. He didn't have to say: One: leave New York. Two: marry her. Three: ever give her the serious bum's rush.

"I love grilled cheese," she said. "So glad you knew what to order."

He smiled. He did like the fact that she could always bounce back, especially with the help of food and booze. She knew that, so she hauled out all her positivity. "I'd better read these pages. If somebody comes in, I'll have to know what I'm supposed to be talking about."

"True." And he smiled again. Each smile she got from him was a great triumph. In a week, he would probably want her in his bed again, good friend that she was.

On a break at the back door of the deli, Harrison smoked and wondered who lived in all the apartments across the way—big brick buildings; he counted eighteen floors in one, twenty-one in another—and he wondered, too, if the rat he saw crossing the alley had many mates and if he gave equal opportunity to all the stores or if this particular guy was partial to the deli. There were, after all, good crumbs to be had here. He hauled out his notebook and wrote about the rat.

The owner, Schwartz, came out and lit up. He brushed sawdust from his shoes and then sat. He smelled of mustard and garlic. "I need a break too. What a weekend. My wife dragged me all over creation wanting to buy furniture. She says ours is crap. It's perfectly nice stuff."

"If I can fit some nice crap, I might buy it."

"You want it? No, seriously, I'd give it to you, happily. Otherwise, we'll be putting it on the street."

"I'd better ask my wife."

"Ask your wife. They always have opinions."

"Wisdom on marriages? I could use some. It was lots more fun before."

"Oh, that's normal. You wonder why anybody takes the step. Well, you don't wonder. The women insist on it."

But Harrison had been the one to insist. He wished he felt happier. He wished Amanda would pay some attention to him. He said, "I don't think she notices me. I'm like a chair or something."

"That's normal," his boss said. "Just one crazy thing we all have to go through."

The boss went in before Harrison finished his cigarette. He felt a little better, being normal, being a chair or whatever other image there was for an unremarkable lummox. He accepted joining the parade of men who didn't know how they happened to be marching or where they were going.

That night, before a theater program he had taken only a single ticket to—not wanting to be greedy—only to find that Amanda would have gone had he asked in time, he stopped for a drink before the show. He had a new client to see the next day and that was good. He'd met her earlier today but not interviewed her yet. Maggie Clifton. Margaret. She was spirited and stringy (lean and full of pronouncements). He told her about the deli work and his evening schedule of seeing shows, one after another. She was very curious about that part of his work.

A gaggle of women had gathered at the bar and were murmuring, then laughing joyously about something—and that "girlish laughter," as always, cheered him. A man at the next bar seat had a little wooden machine he kept showing people. It was about six inches square with a toy figure of a man standing on a box with a noose around his neck. If you put a penny in the box, the man got jerked upward. If you put in a nickel, the man jumped off the box and raised his hands in jubilation.

"That's fantastic!" Harrison said. "Where did you get it?"

"Made it."

"Could you make me one?"

"Yes, yes, I could. But you'd have to pay for my time. A week's work."

"Hm. Could I have a phone number? If I find the funds?"

The man wrote a phone number on a bar napkin. Others gathered to look at the toy.

That night he went to the theater on Houston where he was seeing *The Skin of Our Teeth* on a comp ticket. To his surprise, standing in the lobby was Maggie Clifton, the woman he'd met earlier that day and who ran the theater company he had to interview her about tomorrow.

"You!" he said. "What a coincidence."

She didn't say, "My goodness, yes." Nor did she say, "Oh, I need to see everything." She made no excuses. "Got my eye on you," she said in an accent with just a tinge of the South. He wasn't sure she'd sounded like that earlier in the day. "Truth is, I asked your boss what you were covering."

"You didn't sound Southern this morning," he said, confused. "Now you do, I think."

"I am. I was. Trying not to be."

"Oh, I see."

"I hope you don't hate Southerners."

He shook his head, laughing a little. He drifted toward a board of publicity photos a few feet away. Maggie followed. "I liked this play when I saw it a couple of years ago," he said.

"Won't you get bored?"

"I don't know. Since I'm writing for the company, I feel a sort of obligation."

"It's going to be rough. I can tell by the photos. Very amateurish. We can always slip out for a drink."

Which they did after one act. He thought, Well, I'm sort of doing the interview tonight. Maggie was a sometime actress turned theater entrepreneur, with classic actress red hair and a lean, eager look.

She entertained him over their scotches, telling about her bad stint as a hoofer before she had her moderately successful few roles. "You can't imagine how that sat with a family of real estate developers. They practically disowned me."

It occurred to him that Maggie was a red-haired cheerful version of his mother, but she had seen reality and decided to *run* a company rather than spend a lifetime seeking stardom. "I hope you like my troupe better than the one we saw tonight."

He hoped so too. He'd always rather be impressed than not. "Your family approves?"

"They haven't seen anything. They don't want to come into New York to witness it, but it sounds better to them—entrepreneurial being more respectable than being *on* the stage."

She was spikey and memorable—though her constant sarcasm, her main form of discourse, jangled him a little.

Amanda had folded into herself all through spring. Samuel was holding firm. His resolve to spare her—or rather reject her, which she allowed herself the luxury of understanding—made her critical of everything. She hated the articles she worked on. She hated people.

She decided she hated her hair. It had gotten long so she began pinning it back, but that style didn't look good on her. She even tried going to bed in rollers. "Afraid to get near you," Harrison said.

Right after the night with the painful rollers she went to a beauty shop and got it cut and rinsed red, which she was sorry for as soon as she saw it.

When she entered their apartment, Harrison stopped, then just said, "Oh. It's very different. You don't look like yourself. I mean…I'll get used to it."

She hated their apartment, which was hot, and she decided, without consulting Harrison, to move to a bigger place in their building. Later that week, she signed a new lease before he got home. When she told him, he dropped the bag of groceries he'd just bought. "What are you saying? Is it—the one I was keeping a secret—the place on six? Six C. Is it on six?"

"No. A place came up across the hall. I signed a lease for Seven B."

"No, wait, *B*? Why would you do that?"

"Because we need more room." She lifted up the bag of groceries at his feet. "I hope there aren't eggs in here."

"I don't like the view from B."

"Well, I don't know about *view* but it's lots bigger than this. Two actual bedrooms."

"That means it's more expensive than the one I had my eye on."

"But look, this way you can type in some other room, so I won't go crazy."

"So that's the problem? And we'll be buried in B, no light; you know how dark those rooms are, so what do we end up with—no light, no money for things."

"What things?"

"Art maybe, a thing, a gadget, a little man getting hanged, like that thing I told you about, or a painting."

"You have no concept of how to live."

"You're saying *I* don't!" He was apoplectic. "*You* don't. You don't have a glimmer." He slammed out of the house, angry.

She thought, Good, good, he'll leave me, that will be that.

The things he wanted to buy! Artworks! Some stupid toy! Food and drink, she could understand. She had something to tell her mother now when things fell apart: He was unreasonable, a dreamer. Her speech was ready.

But as she sat trying to read, later attempting to eat a sandwich, she wondered where he was, and she felt worried about him and awful about herself. She began crying when she pictured his shocked face as she'd told him what she'd done and once she started crying, she couldn't stop. The new place was going to be dark, that was true. She hadn't thought about it, but the views from B were awful, nose-to-nose with other buildings. She would have to try to reverse the decision. That meant charming the landlord, which she wasn't sure she could do. Maybe that could be Harrison's job.

Harrison came back at eleven at night. She told him she would try to undo her mistake.

He shook his head. "I didn't know you hated the typing."

"It's hard."

"Okay."

"Go ahead. You can be angry again."

"Why?"

"All the best people are angry. There is so much in life to be angry about."

"I have anger. I tamp it down."

"You shouldn't."

He shook his head. He was tired, wanting bed, she could see. "I'll make it work," he said before tossing unbearably all night long.

There was a chance to make more money by going in to work on Saturdays. She decided to make it up to Harrison by doing that—and it was innocent because Samuel didn't go in on Saturdays. Instead, she sat in an almost empty office—sweltering because by now it was July—feeling virtuous and horrible. When she passed a mirror, she thought she saw a woman hiding under a bad red wig—because that's how she looked these days. She wished she could take the red helmet off and be herself.

Harrison had looked at her the day she came back from the beauty shop, and she knew he was not only surprised but also uneasy. Later that night, he managed to ask her, "Red? Why?"

"Why not?"

"I don't know how to read it."

"You could say I look nice."

"Sorry. Yes. I was just surprised. Like you were trying to be somebody else."

"Myself. Whatever that is."

He pulled her toward him. "Come on. You're strong."

She was. She wasn't. The usual story.

August 1 was the date they set to move to the bigger place. Some friends came over to help. Most of them marveled at the number of mirrors Harrison had bought to bring in light. They began helping him mount them. "Only problem," his boss joked, "is you get a gander at yourself everywhere you turn."

There wasn't much furniture of their own to move, but there was the influx of his boss's furniture. His boss had arranged for some of the deli people to gather and help get it there. They kept tromping up the steps, panting and cursing cheerfully.

Harrison was making a spaghetti sauce and boiling up some pasta for the party. He had thick breads he needed to cut, and a few appetizers he was ready to put out, mostly deli items, pastrami, beef, cheese, salami, and some pickles. It was only right to order from Schwartz because the guy was being so generous with him.

"Didn't know you were a cook," Schwartz declared.

Harrison wore an oversized white shirt that got spattered with red sauce, but the stains pleased him. For the moment he was a cook and a painter. He had never been afraid of mess, but it was another step to glory in it, which he did. He'd wanted this big party, fun, people laughing and joking and wishing them well. He invited Franny from work because he hoped she would see he was in a marriage. She arrived bringing cookies and asked Amanda if she could help unpack dishes. Amanda shrugged and said okay. So, there, the marriage was established.

He had considered inviting Maggie Clifton for the same reason, but Amanda had never met her and besides he felt there was already some sort of infraction in the way Maggie had showed up at the theater. However, stirring the sauce, he found himself wishing she were around to quip about the food or his clothing or the many things she was ready to pronounce about. She was tough. She had opinions about everything. She had pronounced *The Skin Of Our Teeth* "a high school workbook of a production."

He stirred the sauce and looked over at all the activity and he loved it—it was like having a huge family buzzing around. Amanda was live-ly today, too, which gave him hope for the future as he watched her giving people orders about where to put the seven boxes and the bed and the newly acquired used sofa from Harrison's boss. Plus, also from Schwartz, three little tables and a chair and two bureaus. They were going to be like regular people any day now, coming up in the world for sure. As he cooked, Amanda tapped him on the backside each time she passed him. Thank heavens something was making her happy. This move was making her happy.

"I'll get some music going," she said. "Almost everything's in."

"Come have dinner!" he called out to the group.

Later, as people danced, they caused the needle of the record player to jump, but they kept dancing, so Amanda tried a radio station people could dance to. Drink loosened their bodies. Schwarz stayed on, but he slumped in a corner, saying, "I'm older."

"Good signs," he said to Amanda when the last person left and they agreed to clean up tomorrow. "We're good. We did the right thing. I felt the blessings."

She hugged him tight.

A week later he was at a movie alone. And he was only seeing the film because Amanda kept telling him he should go out to Hollywood and write thrillers, and make some money as a writer, but he couldn't get his mind around the kinds of stories she wanted him to tell—"the kind ev-eryone *likes*," she told him. It was true, it was exciting to watch murder and suspense, even when there was little credibility, like this one with Humphrey Bogart not on camera for half the movie because the idea was he was supposed to look completely different before undergoing plastic surgery, which when accomplished (off camera of course) made him look like Humphrey Bogart!

One thing he was learning was that things changed week by week in his home life. They just did. Affection one week, nothing the next. So that was life as an adult, huh? Schwartz would tell him sure, yes, that was what women were all about.

Dark Passage. He tried to study the script writing, but he laughed at the movie's scheme—the camera somewhere behind Bogart's shoulder and no view of him until halfway through the movie. Only his voice. Very bold. Oh, wasn't cinema wonderful, always up to something even if it didn't work, which Harrison thought was the case with this one. It did make him laugh, though, sometimes out loud.

The two couples in his row shushed him, as Amanda would have done if she'd been with him.

The character Bogart was playing got excessive kindness from men, women, strangers. Oh, they really extended themselves—gave him money, gave him a place to stay. It didn't seem like human nature at all. Harrison laughed again. No one else in the theater was reacting. Bogart meanwhile made one mistake after another until just about every nice character except Bacall's ended up dead, making Bogart a suspect. Man, nobody could have luck that bad.

This was what Amanda wanted him to write. Something surprising, sensational.

Harrison almost left, restless. And yet. Bacall beckoned. She was the "someone to watch over me," the lover/protector he craved. If the song was right, everyone wanted that giant embrace. When the movie ended, he stayed in his seat and watched the whole all over again, not laughing the second time, but drifting into a fantasy of learning his way around Hollywood, toughening himself, being lonely but productive, giving in to writing the fantasies that united people, the simple dumb truths. Amanda hadn't said she would go *out there* with him. "People fly back and forth," is what she'd said.

He stopped at a bar after. He didn't want to get home just yet. As his thoughts tumbled, he hoped to get a little drunk and get a good sleep going.

Amanda had told Harrison to treat himself to a movie that night. She hoped he did.

Because Samuel had said at lunchtime where she sat in the break room reading, "Okay, you win. Just keep drinking your coffee and reading your novel, Bob is watching." The door was open and Bob and who knows who else was watching from the floor.

She pretended to read. "How do you figure I win?"

"You're fetching. You've fetched me. Will you come over again?"

"Perhaps I lose," she said, turning a page and doing her best to understand what she was reading—which was hopeless. Her heart was beating rapidly, her throat was full. "That's it? Come to bed?"

"Um, yes." His eyes sparkled, he got a one-sided smile, and his body went on alert as if to jump out of the way of danger.

He loved it when she resisted him, didn't he? "How's your wife?"

"She's lovely. We had a civilized lunch the other day. She told me I was wonderful but that she just happened to love someone else."

Lot of that going around, she thought.

He poured a coffee and made a to-do about finding the cream and sugar. "I can't stay in here long. People talk."

"I know they do. So?"

"A. No conjoining among workers. B. You're still married. It casts both of us in an unflattering light."

"Give me today to think."

He left the room abruptly, though whether he was performing for the watchers or angry, she couldn't tell. She'd meant what she said. She needed to think. Or rather feel. What would it be like to say no? How would she feel?

Steinbeck blurred as she realized what she wanted to do. She wanted to ask him to take her to dinner and a movie, not go back to his cousin's place. He would probably call her at her desk. She would say something like, "Getting dinner with a friend from work and then seeing a movie." He would have to figure out he was the friend. Maybe he wouldn't figure it out and that would be that.

He called at three. She threw all pretense out the window. "Dinner and a movie," she said.

There was a slight pause. "Fine, fine. I'm trying to figure out where. You might be seen."

"I don't care." Louise, two desks away, stared at her when she repeated, "I don't care." Right. It certainly didn't sound as if they were talking about comma errors.

Samuel had brown hair, straight, not thick at all. A straight nose. Slightly lopsided features—well, everybody had inequality of the two sides of the face, mostly not noticeable, but his was a bit more see-able. He was waggish and seemed to be winking most of the time. He ate—everybody saw him eating, but he burned up whatever he put in. Lucky, people said. He was thin—bony, concave—but there was some-thing elegant about it. Blue eyes, some days very blue, some days not.

The novel Harrison had recently begun and worked on that night was about an old man who regretted sorely that he had not married. The old guy was in the early stages of Harrison's exploration, a fine furniture craftsman, who could do curved legs, dentils, anything. But that night, Harrison went out and got a burger and suddenly realized, no, no, his character was a sculptor in Provincetown! Aha, he needed to get there again to do research. When Amanda got home, late, saying she'd had to have dinner with someone from work, he was spirited about his writing. He told her he wanted them to go for another long weekend in Prov-incetown.

"I don't have time!" she screamed at him.

"Okay, okay, I understand. All right. I can go on my own."

"There you are, not being angry!" she yelled. She threw a blue saucer across the room. It hit the wall and broke. "*Why* don't you ever blow up?"

His heart hammered. The agony on her face—was it hatred?

He stood at the door for a moment, then began to pick up the pieces of broken saucer. Now they were down to three blue saucers. He was starting to say, "Of course I get angry, but—" when he saw she was crying uncontrollably. He put the pieces back down on the floor and brushed off shards from his fingertips. He went over to where she had collapsed on a kitchen chair, and he lifted her and held her. "I know something is awful. But I don't know what it is."

"I neglect you."

"You do. Honestly, I get very discouraged."

"You should hate me."

"How could I? There are times I don't like you, but I could never hate you."

"Oh, hell," she said. "Go for walk. I'll clean up."

"I'd rather stay in. I want to be with you. Let's have a calm night. I won't bother you. I'll write a couple of pages—"

"Then I'll go." She stomped out the door.

Fear, hurt, and anger vied for dominance. There was so much of all that in the large cavern of his body that he didn't know how to parcel it out normally. It felt so much better to walk the high road, skimming above it, making peace.

When she came back, she said, "We should separate, a trial separation, but that means two places. Two cheaper places."

He couldn't look at his pages once it was actually spoken. Everything slid downhill, all hopes, all at once. After a pause, he asked a simple question. "You don't love me?" She didn't answer.   "Where did it go?"

She took off a sweater and hung it on the back of the chair. She looked beaten, very sad. It took her a long time to make her way around the chair and sit. "I don't know. I'm not sure I ever did and it's not your fault. I don't think I'm meant for marriage. I should never have said yes. I tried not to say yes."

What he had loved, her sassiness, was gone these days. There were circles under her eyes and her hair was often unkempt. How could she have fallen apart so completely? "Is everything okay at work? You're not fired?" he asked.

"No. They can't do without me." She shoved what was on the table away from her—sugar bowl, napkins, saltshaker—as if that could help solve something. "Can you look for a place? For yourself?"

He wanted to scream, but he answered levelly. "We need our money for this place."

"What about all those women who are after you? Huh? Couldn't you use a couch someplace?"

A couch. When all his stuff was here. When he'd worked for this. "Who's after me? What are you talking about? Is this why you're asking to separate?

"I don't know all the contestants. But that Franny from the deli for sure. And that woman who blew into town and runs some theater company."

She'd been aware. "Maybe they think they're interested. I don't know that they are, and I don't care."

"Give it a test run. I give it two seconds to become clear."

"Man, you really want to be rid of me."

"I only know I'm not good for you. Earlier tonight, I read your pages by the way. I copyedited. Lots of punctuation errors. You need to re-type." She staggered toward their bedroom and once there fetched a set of pages, returned, and dropped them on the table. "I wish I could die."

Good God, she was dramatic.

He tried to read her copyedits for a while, too distracted to digest most of them. Finally, he decided he deserved to sleep in a bed. That's all there was—Amanda had gotten rid of the hand-me-down sofa with a criticism about the color of it, which she hated, and how stiff it was, but she hadn't replaced it yet. He rolled up a blanket and used it as a barrier in the bed, furious about the twelve inches that remained on which to lay his body down. *It's called bundling*, he said to no one. *We're Pennsylvania Dutch. Intimacy without sex.*

"Women," Schwartz said. "They are trouble for sure. Best to get it in your head they don't matter."

"How does a person do that?" he asked. He felt so miserable that nothing, not the novel which was coming along surprisingly well, not the cigarette in his hand as he stood out the back of the deli with his boss who liked him, not the great bag of leftovers he was taking home, nothing, nothing cheered him.

"I think she's going to ask for a divorce."

"They do that. A lot of times the marriage goes pouf in a year. If it lasts a year, it might go thirty years. And then they want a divorce anyway."

"How do you know all this?" Harrison asked, even though he doubt-ed the supposed knowledge. He would learn years later how right old Schwartz was.

"I been watching people. Observation." He pointed vaguely toward his ear rather than his eye. Probably accurate. He was a listener.

"I always thought I would get married. I never thought I would get divorced. I wanted to be the guy asking his kids how school was, play-ing Santa Claus, you know, the whole bit, bringing roses home, saying 'Happy birthday, sweetheart,' all that."

"Man, you're nuts. None of that is the fun you think it is. You been watching too many movies."

Birds flew into the yard, desperate for crumbs—and there were some. Harrison and Schwartz watched them.

"Some people actually have that," Harrison said.

Schwartz said, "Yeah. Some do."

Harrison went back in to resume his work of making thick sandwiches. Schwartz followed and was soon making clean signs with crayon on butcher paper, which he'd torn into squares. *Roast beef special. Cheese sandwich special.* Schwartz was a generous owner and manager in that he didn't cheat the customer with piles of lettuce. He prided himself on a great sandwich.

Harrison asked, "Rye, brown, white?" and kept piling things onto the sandwiches he was making. He liked to give a little fold to the beef and pastrami at just the right moment to make the guts of the sandwich line up with the bread. He looked up at his line—several regulars and then behind them a surprise: his own wife, Amanda, standing there, waiting like any other customer. He got rattled when he noticed her, which was stupid. Why would he feel nervous around his own wife? He made five sandwiches before facing her. "What can I do for you?" he asked, trying to make a joke of it.

Her eyes were glittering, bright. "I missed you," she said. "I wanted to see you."

"Oh."

She was grinning broadly. She said, "It's like seeing a stranger for a moment when the setting changes."

"Wow. Yeah, I think I know that feeling. I should make something, though. People are waiting. Don't worry, I'll pay."

"Make me a roast beef with the works." She took out a five-dollar bill.

He got two slices of the best bread, a thick marbled rye, smeared mayonnaise on one slice, mustard on the other, lettuce, tomato, pickle, and two slices of roast beef, folded just so. "Why aren't you at work?"

"I called off sick. I wanted to spend some time with you. I'll hang out until you take a break."

"That's an hour from now."

She kept smiling. Even then he knew it was the healing before the death, the sunshine before the storm. He observed things too. He knew plenty more than he was ready to acknowledge.

"I'll walk for an hour," she said. "I can shop."

He took her five; she took her change.

Watching her walk out of the store, he understood, even though she walked fast, that there was uncertainty in her step, something about the way she leaned forward, a little like an old person who wished she could take her shoes off and collapse on a sofa, wrong color or not, and stare at the wall.

10

When Harrison was fourteen, he fell for a gorgeous redheaded Irish girl in his class. All the boys (older than he) said every one of the O'Neal sisters was gorgeous. Harrison ran after Sarah O'Neal as they exited the school one day and in a trembling voice asked her if she would go to a movie with him.

She said, "Um, I guess."

He said, "Friday night, okay?"

She said, "Okay."

The night before the date he bought a box of candy and the Friday of the date he went to a flower shop and bought a bouquet.

"Wrap it?" asked the male clerk. "Or vase?"

"Wrap," he said.

He scrubbed his face and his neck and behind his ears and dressed himself in his church suit.

His grandmother said, "There's nothing for dinner. I just can't. You can make yourself an egg."

Which he proceeded to do.

"What's so important? Why do you have your suit on?"

"I have a date."

"Oh, sweetie! Why would you want a date at your age?"

"I just do." He scrambled the egg, which looked small in the pan. He was hungry, but also his stomach was jumpy. He took out a slice of bread to eat with the egg. Carefully, he ate his tiny dinner. He tended to get food on his clothes.

"It tires me to think of cooking," his grandmother said. She shambled into the living room and lay on the sofa. His grandfather was napping on the glider on the front porch, so both grandparents were lying down, but he was aware that they did anything they could to not get into that position together on the same surface. Their unhappiness saddened him. After all, he'd seen some old folks totter down the street together, holding hands.

After he finished eating, he took the candy and flowers from where he'd put them in the living room.

"My, my, you are doing it up right," his grandmother said. With a puff of effort, she added, "Good boy. You are a lovely lad."

With that compliment, he felt correct as he trotted down the street to Sarah's house, knocked on the door, and waited.

Sarah did not answer the door. Instead, four beautiful redheads did. They ranged in age, he estimated, from seventeen to seven. All of them had curly hair, masses of it, and blue eyes and pure complexions. He actually liked dark haired women best, but sometimes he made exceptions.

The girls were laughing.

"So, who are you?"

"Harrison," he said. "From school."

"And are we supposed to let you in?"

"I can wait out here. I'm taking Sarah to the movies."

"Oh, you are, are you?" said the eldest. "Why didn't she tell us?"

He felt alarmed. "She didn't? Is she home?"

"Upstairs."

"Oh, could you ask her to come down?"

"Why don't you come in?" said the eldest. "Let's get to the bottom of this."

She opened the door then and he entered, relieved.

Again, the sisters laughed, high screechy giggles, but he wasn't sure why.

"Tell you what," said the eldest. "You hide in the coat closet and we'll quiz her."

"She didn't say anything about our date?"

The littlest girl took the candy from him. He clutched the flowers and pulled them toward his chest. The eldest had opened the closet door and two others more or less pushed him toward it. There were too many coats in the closet as it was, so he was a hard fit. Coats rubbed against his neck, his head, his arms, pushing his hair up, and all the while he tried to protect the flowers. The door shut and he was in the dark.

There was more laughter and now whispering. He couldn't make out what they were saying but finally he heard a call, "Sarah! Oh, Sarah! Are you home?"

And then footsteps and then the voice that certainly sounded like Sarah's voice. "Where is he?"

"Oh, you're *not* going to a movie with *him*, are you?"

"I suppose I have to."

"But he's wearing a suit. The pants are short. Is he dumb in school?"

"Pretty dumb."

His heart dropped. It wasn't true! He was one of the smartest.

They were laughing again.

"And he thinks it's a date?"

"I guess he does. Let me have one of the chocolates. Don't eat them all, you little pest."

"At least we get chocolate." That came from a little piping voice.

"Well, where is he?"

"Scared. Scared of you. And well he might be. He doesn't look at all courageous. Can all the boys thrash him?"

"I suppose so. I never noticed."

It wasn't true! He fought his battles. It simply wasn't true. He opened the door.

"Good heavens, what are you doing in *there?*" said the eldest.

And of course, they laughed.

"Look at his hair. It's all over the place," said another.

He presented the bouquet. He understood the candies were a lost cause. "I brought you these."

"Oh." Sarah held them for a minute. He used his hands to try to tamp down his hair.

They weren't laughing but there was on each face something of a smirk and their eyes examined him.

"We should get going," he said.

"Oh. Okay." Sarah walked toward the door. On the way she put the flowers on an end table.

He couldn't think of much to say as they walked. Old women, young women, teachers—all described him as handsome and smart. But the O'Neal sisters found him ridiculous for reasons he didn't understand and yet it was familiar from the tone his mother often took with him. He felt sick, almost dizzy. He was hungry too. The egg hadn't been enough at all. And now there was no candy. He wished he could use his pocket money for a meal somewhere. But when they got to the theater, he bought two tickets and a box of popcorn and guided Sarah O'Neal to her seat. He wanted to leave her there but couldn't bring himself to do so.

He knew she would tell this story and he felt a shame so deep that his face flushed all the while he watched the movie.

11

They lay in bed, with the glow of Christmas around them. Amanda had strung lights across the bedroom window, almost as an answer to the lights in apartments across the street. Tonight, they went out to dinner, a more expensive dinner than usual, Amanda's treat since her bonus money had come in. They both had appetizers of shrimp and then steaks and baked potatoes and a side dish of green beans amandine, a side dish Harrison said he wanted to make soon, now that he knew almonds and butter turned good old green beans into something special.

Amanda's hair had settled on a more sober red color this last week. It looked good. She did too. She was dieting these days. The icebox always held carrots and boiled eggs for her.

"I guess it's the carrots," he said, tracing her hip as they lay there. "Your shape is beautiful."

"Better, anyway."

"We should have another party."

"Why?"

"Get dressed up, have friends over, make...something nice to eat. A ham. Lots of good bread."

"Green beans," she added teasingly, "with almonds!"

"Why not? That would go with ham. I could make a potato salad."

"Is that in your rep?"

"No, but I see them make it at the deli. It's not hard."

"You could just bring some home."

"I'd like to make it. I want it in my repertoire! So, who will we have? Theresa, Evelyn, Monty, Bill from the agency. Tom, Franny, George from the deli. And their wives or dates. And you?"

"I don't know."

"Louise is nice."

"She is. But I don't know. Why do I want work people here?"

"For fun. To be festive and happy. Ask people. Maybe six people from work. Okay?"

She nodded.

Slowly they found each other. They touched hands, arms, and when they felt enough go-ahead signals, they got to the other parts of them. Harrison thought that finally this was a good day, that things were turning around.

But after they held each other and then grumbled about being hungry again, and ate toast with peanut butter, and repositioned themselves, Amanda said, "We're not right for each other."

Harrison went still. After a while he said, "It sort of seemed we were. Are. I was feeling hopeful."

"We should both move on. I never thought I would get divorced but it's what we should do. I don't think I'm a person who should be married."

The lights twinkled here and across the street. It was all beautiful and peaceful.

"How does a person get divorced?" he asked. "And…and not let it get awful?"

"They pick a guy like you," she said. She began to cry.

Oh, the truth was, he knew how it was done. He'd read about it when working on a story. But now he said, "We should take our time. We should be sure. If we're sure, we'd have to go to Las Vegas or Reno and we'd have to stay for a period of time to establish residency. Like three weeks. In case there is some red tape."

"Gambling and meals included," she sniffled. "That's the way, then."

He looked out the window at the brick wall he'd become used to.

Suddenly, she sat up in bed. "If we go on a weekend, I could fly back and go to work and then fly out there again. If we need longer, I could take a vacation week… So maybe if you would be willing—"

"To lose both of my jobs? Is that what you're asking? I get to hold the fort in Nevada?"

"I'm sorry." She began to cry again.

Selfish! He caught his face in the mirror and it terrified him, so he just said, "I'll make some calls Monday."

He didn't tell her he had jumped the gun about a party and already told people to come over on New Year's Eve. Everybody he told was clearly happy to have a *plan* for that night. He couldn't undo it. Besides he needed people and cheer and strong drink to swallow what was happening. So, he didn't nix the party invitation over the next week, casual as it had been. He and Amanda would blow a lot of money they couldn't spare.

Then New Year's Eve arrived, and people came bearing good cheer.

It was a good party; nobody guessed a thing was wrong. Calendars now said 1949.

There was a good month to go before they made the trip to Reno. He kept getting tickets to shows, and Amanda said each time she didn't want to go with him.

Maggie Clifton, the other redhead in his life, kept seeking him out, calling him, and asking if they could see the things he had to see together. "Perfect," she kept saying. "I love going to the theater with you. Plus, you're willing to leave when it's bad and all the while I get to sample the competition."

They had a couple of dinners together. As always, he walked her home. When they stood before her apartment one night, she said, "Are you *ever ever* going to kiss me?"

He said, "Not now. Maybe eventually."

"Hm. Are you being noble?"

"I think so."

"Don't. It's so out of fashion." She kissed him. "Was that so bad?"

"It wasn't bad at all." He laughed. She could be funny for sure.

But he didn't go up to her place.

"Play the field," Schwartz always said.

For a while he thought about eventually starting something up with a cellist who had four young children. An instant family. Children for whom he could scare away the monsters.

Would he ever figure out how to have that life? Family life with all its chaos.

Eight years later he would have that life—it was sort of handed to him as if he'd ordered it up, like a sandwich—and it was great and it was not.

In the middle of January, before the trip to Reno, Harrison and Amanda sat at the kitchen table. He said, "I hope we will do this in such a way that we will always be friends."

She said, "Of course."

It was a confusing time, with Maggie making it clear she was waiting in the wings. She was a pal, a friend, a good person, but he could hardly experience his own feelings of despair when she kept joking and telling him his life was just fine.

The plan (he agreed to it) was for Amanda to establish residence and then sneak back to New York if possible and work for two weeks and then return to Reno. He understood work was important to her and he couldn't deny she had a better job than he did. She was banking on a combination of vacation time and, well, lies to get her through the divorce.

"I'll say my mother is sick," she said. "Or I could say you are. Then we have to tell some lawyer in Reno we have irreconcilable differences and it's done."

Harrison went to the library and did some research the next day. He brought what he'd learned to the kitchen table. Nevada had nine possibilities for divorce; irreconcilable differences was not one of them.

It was bizarre to research details for something he didn't want to do. What he'd learned was that they would have to choose from among the following: Impotency, adultery, desertion, conviction of a felony, habitual drunkenness, neglect to provide the common necessities of life, insanity, living apart for three years, and extreme cruelty entirely mental in nature.

Amanda made them each a pastrami sandwich as they sat, talking it over, choosing among the possibilities. He wasn't impotent, he had not committed adultery, and he had not deserted her, or she him for that matter, he was not felonious, and though he liked a drink, he was not a habitual drunkard. And what *were* the necessities of life, anyway?

"I really don't care what we say," Amanda told him. "Say I've committed adultery. I don't care."

He didn't want to ask her if it was true.

"I care," he said simply. "Words, after all, do hurt."

"We should just choose the most popular one. Extreme mental cruelty."

He choked on a bite of sandwich. "What have I done to you?"

"Typing when I need to sleep."

"Is that all you can come up with?"

"Inviting people to the house without consulting me."

"I don't know that those things are going to do it."

"Calling me names."

"I never."

"But we can *say* so."

"Aarrggh."

He bought her a little box of candy before they made the train trip. He saw the little foil box with the gold ribbon in Macy's and tried not to buy it, but it called to him.

He and Amanda took the train together. They had to get sleeping compartments, bunks, which solved one problem at any rate—he slept above. It was strange. He read for a while, being jostled so that it was hard to focus his eyes. He sensed she was awake below. "Good night," he said.

After a while she said, "Good night."

When they arrived in Reno, he found a cab and asked to be taken to a reasonably priced ranch. "Is this a divorce?" the driver asked, but there was no question in the question.

"Yes."

"I know where to take you. Just leave it to me."

What an ugly city, Harrison thought. I can't bear to stay here.

At the ranch that the taxi driver had chosen for them, they were welcomed by a woman who was costumed to fit the setting, dressed in a skirt, boots, and a Western-style shirt, but otherwise fairly staid. As soon as she spoke, they saw she was bent on respectability.

"I don't lie in court," she said. "You have to stay six weeks."

"Six! I can't," Amanda declared.

"She'll lose her job," Harrison cried.

"Listen. My people get nice clean divorces. This place is affordable. What you do is you call in sick and say you have a problem pregnancy and have to have bed rest. If you're any good at your job, they'll take you back."

"Oh, God," Amanda said. She and Harrison went out to the yard to talk it over. They *could* go to another ranch. But what if they ran into the same rules?

"Who is on your side at work?" he asked. "Who would go to bat for you?"

After a long pause, she said, "Let me try a phone call." He followed her inside but thought better of it and dawdled near the door reading the brochure. He'd never had a real vacation. The brochure advertised *Horseback riding in the morning after breakfast, then lunch, then a ride to a shopping area or a lawyer, then dinner with everybody staying at the ranch, then a trip to a casino for gambling and dancing and drinking.*

Harrison had packed a lined tablet, a stack of newsprint paper, and a portable typewriter to put a positive print on the time he would have to spend uncoupling. He decided he would skip the horseback riding to write in the morning, then perhaps allow himself to partake of the other vacation offerings later in the day.

He could hear Amanda on the phone. "Yes. No, it's my choice. I'm not asking anything, only that you support me when I say I took a vacation and got sick and am under medical care and will come back as soon as possible. Six weeks. If you have to say that, say that. No, no, I'll call, or I'll get Harrison to call but I need your support. I can't lose the job. I can't." She was crying.

Six weeks. He was in trouble, too, at work. The agency had replaced him and even Schwartz was going to have to reduce his hours. Well, a divorce was supposed to shake things up, right? It was *a divorce* after all. It was big. And sad. But it sure was hard to reconcile that with the joy he witnessed all around him—people raising their voices to call out plans to each other, wearing Western gear, yeehawing their way to the stables.

After Amanda's phone call, they nodded to the manager that they would stay.

"Two rooms, of course. That's my policy," she said.

"I'm going to learn to ride," Amanda announced as they walked to their rooms that first day. "That will take care of mornings and distract me from worrying about losing my job. I'm also going to shop and gamble when they offer those trips. That will distract me the rest of the day from…thinking about losing my job."

Nothing about losing her marriage. "Why did you marry me to begin with?" he asked. "I really don't know."

She sniffled but didn't answer.

Everywhere Harrison looked, he saw couples. He got an explanation from the bartender on the second night. Many trios and quadruples came here to the ranch, he learned—the divorcing two plus their new partners waiting to get married as soon as the divorce was final. Groups of four were very common—and certain rooms went empty most nights. But there was love in the air in Reno. People being people, several residents who were bunking alone and avoiding the one they were divorcing found other residents they liked lots better and new love flowered. For many, the whole thing was a lark.

Maggie Clifton had begged him to write her a postcard, so he did.

Harrison wrote two short stories in the first week. The first came right out of what he saw around him and was about a quartet at a Reno divorce ranch. In his story, the rejecteds got together; everybody went through the motions of establishing new arrangements, but all four were riddled with doubts about their decisions.

The second story was about a kind deli owner with a fatherly demeanor and an illogical hurt over things that happened to his employees.

He got a long chatty letter from Maggie. He didn't write back. It felt wrong.

Instead, he worked many hours a day but couldn't get his latest attempt at a novel going. When he needed to quit typing, he read whatever he found in the paltry library of the ranch. *The Green Years.* Even though he'd seen the movie. *A Lion in the Streets.*

A few days later another letter from Maggie arrived, telling him about her current rehearsals and referring to things they might do when he returned.

He firmly believed letters should be a back and forth. With some reluctance, he wrote a short note to Maggie.

"Hey, handsome," said a woman at lunch one day. She was new. She slid in across from him at the trestle table. Amanda was nowhere in sight. "I'm going dancing tonight with the group. You?"

"I'm not a good dancer."

"He really isn't," said Amanda, suddenly coming up behind him.

"Oh, I don't care. It's just something to do. Healthy."

Harrison said, "This is my almost ex. Amanda. I'm Harrison."

"Lucy." She shook hands with each of them. "Apparently everybody goes to this club in town. It kills the time."

Amanda said, "Probably a good idea. Cheaper than gambling, anyway. We're all in danger of losing our shirts here."

Lucy said, "Have you noticed? Some of these people sort of own the shirt factory, so to speak."

Rich people. Harrison had of course noticed. Other divorce seekers bought Western wear, the high-priced stuff for themselves and versions of it in small sizes for children. They gambled long into the night, sometimes losing in an hour as much as the whole trip cost him and Amanda.

Lucy said, "Look. I just want to dance. It's the only thing I like to do."

He would dance with her though she might regret it. "How can you not *hear the music?*" Amanda had scolded him once.

He loved music. All sorts. He could sing the whole of Mozart's piano concerto in C. He listened to jazz and knew what the musical jokes were. He not only heard music; he absorbed it *and* loved it. He knew when it was a clarinet giving way to a trumpet. When there was a key change, he felt it in his whole body and applauded that thrill. That he couldn't get his legs to keep time was a distress to him, but even so, there were times he felt immense joy at moving to music, badly as he apparently did it.

Amanda danced with Harrison once. A few others asked her to dance, and she accepted.

At the end of the second week, they had an appointment with a lawyer who sported a string tie and greasy hair; he suggested they choose mental cruelty. The fellow listened to Amanda for the next five minutes and then wrote it all up. "Man, I'd never be able to stand the sound of typing," he said. "Sleep deprivation makes a person go nuts."

They thought at one point they might take a day trip to the Grand Canyon, but it was too far. Amanda had found a pond off the ranch where she went to swim most afternoons and she declared she was content with that. Harrison read and wrote, read and wrote.

He asked the owner if there was a bookstore in the vicinity and she directed him to an old guy in a small shop selling used books. He stayed for an afternoon and left with Chekhov's collected stories, *War and Peace*, which he'd already read twice, and a paperback edition of *The Franchise Affair*, a book he'd once promised Amanda he would read.

The remaining weeks stretched out. Altogether he got fifteen letters from Maggie. Amanda couldn't help noticing. She said, "That one really, really wants you."

"I haven't encouraged her."

"The more fool you."

He replayed that comment as he took long walks. One night at dinner he watched a newly formed couple as they leaned toward each other, holding hands. How he envied them even if soon it turned out to be a brief self-deception.

"You made me up," Amanda said, sitting across from him at breakfast. "I'm not so nice."

Eventually, they signed papers and were told they could finally go home.

A couple of people had apparently put in a really good plug for Amanda because she got her job back. And she kept their place. Harrison moved to a smaller place two blocks away.

And in the midst of a lot of nothing, Harrison getting only a few hours from Schwartz, *The Atlantic* took the second story he'd sent them—the one about the divorce farm. He was astounded. It felt like years before he saw it in print, but then there it was, real, his name, his words. He told Maggie, whom he was seeing pretty often by then, that he was going to sit around at the Algonquin and feel the feeling of being a published writer. She said, "I'm for that. You deserve to feel that way."

His intention was to sit there alone, letting his thoughts drift, enjoying his new confidence. He ordered a bourbon. Just sat.

Then he looked up and saw Maggie coming through the front door. A strange combination of elation and disappointment overtook him.

She announced that she had a pocketful of money and three copies of *The Atlantic* that she quickly spread on the table. "Someone will ask!" she said. They sat back on the cushioned sofa and had several drinks each. Maggie blushed and told the waiter, "He's in here. A story! Talented guy!"

He'd have liked to be deep inside himself, even anonymous, but it was too late to do anything other than thank her.

She was a marvelous woman, he knew that, even though he felt himself disappearing under her generosity.

He told Liz he was deeply unhappy through all his middle years, but she didn't believe it. Or she thought it was both true and untrue.

12

1958

They were in a VW, Maggie in the passenger seat holding the baby and trying to read at the same time, while their daughters tumbled around in the backseat, arguing and slapping each other. They were on an excursion to see a corner china cupboard like one they had seen at a neighbor's house. The day was damp, bracing though, with wafts of wet air coming through the windows.

"She tore up my letter," Emma screamed, referring to her younger sister. "Now I have to write it again." She could get a good huff going, Emma could. "Anna is just stupid, stupid, stupid."

"Don't use that word," Maggie told them. "That is not a word we use."

"Anna is, though," Emma said. "What else do you call it?"

Harrison jettisoned his thoughts to the little shop with scones that was two doors away from the antique shop and he also thought about the long cool martinis he would make that night when they had friends over.

Anna reached forward over the seat to pull at her little brother's leg, Thomas screamed, the magazine fell, and her mother leaned forward to retrieve it and bumped her head.

"Damn. Why did you have to upset Thomas?" Maggie asked her younger daughter in a dangerously level tone. "Why can't you sit still?"

"Because she's telling lies."

"Because she's stupid," said the more knowledgeable older sister.

Harrison leaned over and took Maggie's hand. "Are you okay?"

"Just my noggin." She held Thomas up to her shoulder and kept patting him to quiet him down. Today Harrison wasn't so happy about the chaos he had so craved. He'd been working out how to make a character like his father in a story. The idea had come in a flash, but he didn't get it down right away and now it was gone. Or going.

"Emma, stop calling your sister names," he commanded.

He knew before looking into the rearview mirror that there was a trembling lip to be seen. Emma was a talker so when she paused it was because she simply couldn't go on. "What exactly is the problem?"

"She tore up my letter to the Easter Bunny. I wrote out all the candies I like, and she tore it up. In tiny pieces."

"Would you like to write it again?"

"I don't have any paper! We're in a car. Easter is tomorrow."

"Indeed, it is." He wished he hadn't trained them to be formal letter writers—stamps, mailbox, the whole thing. "We'll have to leave your note on the table. Hopefully he'll be well stocked."

He felt the children staring at him and then he heard them luxuriating in a good cry. Through hiccups Emma was saying, "How will the Easter Bunny know to stock what I want? The red licorice, not the black."

"He'll know."

"But *how?*"

"Oh, shut up," Maggie said, throwing up her arms. "There is no disaster happening here. You'll get your candy."

"How?"

"Just because. You will."

"How!"

"Because there is no damned Easter Bunny. Your father is the damned Easter Bunny."

There was a stunned silence in the car. Emma was busy adding ten more years to her life, figuring it all out, and that job of maturing on the spot cost her a bit of time. "Is he Santa Claus too?" she asked quietly.

"Yes. Yes! He is! So there! Now sit still until we can get you some ice cream."

The car went silent at any rate as the children put aside childish illusions.

Harrison had to work hard to stifle a laugh in spite of himself. Maggie was at times a pushover for sentiment and at other times, like today, just dismissive of everything, including her own children and the happy illusions of childhood. And as a disciplinarian she was full of contradictions. He'd heard her say, "No *Gunsmoke*, no *I Love Lucy*, no *Wagon Train*, for a week," only to see the girls watching one of those things that very night. He had mixed feelings about Maggie's attempts at discipline, sometimes admiring, other times condemning. Mixed feelings down the line, that was life, right, and what he wrote about. Paradox! Ambiguity! If only someone wanted to publish it.

All the work on the land—digging is what it mostly amounted to, holes for trees, trenches, space for the new shed because the builder would get started earlier if Harrison prepped the land—all that was both fulfilling and boring as hell. And more to the point, time-consuming. His body acted out the tasks of somebody else's life, the guy who wanted nothing more than a beer after a long day of bringing up earth but meanwhile the other guy in his head was spinning glorious phrases he planned to write and was sure he would remember…and many times lost.

He'd had two more short stories published in the intervening years, but none in as high profile a publication as *The Atlantic*. One was the deli owner story and the new one was about a father of a newborn girl wanting to tell her all she needed to know, committing it to a letter, ultimately destroying it. Those stories did not pay. He had not had a paycheck in eight years. Man, it hurt.

Well, he had kids, great kids, and he loved them and wanted to save them from everything bad. But they didn't much want their parents' wisdom. They were born with their futures already etched in them. He wondered what Thomas would be. So far quiet, except for the occasional ear-splitting scream. He was not yet living up to his literary forebear Tom Jones.

Emma was a golden-haired beauty, upturned nose, tilted upward face, clear blue eyes. Smart, too. He loved the name because he loved the character Emma Bovary with her fire and her wishing and her belief in love. Anyway, his Emma was going to have it easy in life, he thought, if anybody ever did.

Anna (Maggie's choice of a name, secretly Karenina to him, so the name pleased him) seemed to understand there were pitfalls everywhere and she was often just in a bad mood. *I get it*, he thought. *I get it, honey. It's shitty to be the younger one.* Also, come to think of it, the older one. Also, as in his case, the only one.

When Anna enjoyed something, it was wonderful to see the sunshine cracking through, erasing her frown. Tolsoy's Anna Karenina was a great character and she, too, believed in love.

Maggie was good at giving the girls lessons, teaching them numbers and clocks and whatnot. He was the family scholar, Maggie insisted, but the little ones didn't come to him for learning. They ran to him to be lifted up or they sidled up against him, wanting to feel a shoulder, a thigh muscle, a nose. He remembered being young, running, wanting the touch and sound of his father too. Sometimes Thomas went still with concentration at the sound of his father's voice. Harrison almost captured in writing the longing for the human baritone and bass notes the other day and then he lost it halfway through the sentence which now, driving along, he thought he could retrieve possibly...and lost again.

"I'm worried about getting the roasts on," Maggie said.

"If it's late, they'll forgive us."

"But then we'll need more appetizers."

"Buy something in town?" He was very much looking forward to the adult conversation—talking books, trading jokes.

"I guess so."

"I hate everything and everybody," Anna pronounced.

He put on the radio, which soon played "Tom Dooley" and he sang the lyrics along with the radio to entertain the family.

Whenever Maggie looked at Harrison, she felt she'd gone fishing and ended up with the prize fish. Today he was in his wooly blue shirt and a pair of pants that wasn't too terribly stained. In her girlhood she had had numerous crushes on well-dressed, neat boys, and even for a while thought she was madly in love (as her mother and brother wanted her to be) with a man like her father who believed a stray hair was an abomination. She was supposed to marry this clean man, but one day she just ran away to New York, flummoxing them all.

When she finally phoned home, she told them she didn't know why she had to be so upstanding while she was young, that it was normal to break rules at her age, and she wanted to be around people who did.

And then she'd clapped her eyes on Harrison with his tousled hair and his exuberances. A steak fallen to the floor was still a good steak, he said. Dirt was normal, natural, even desirable. He had no money and seemed almost to like poverty. He was devoted to the arts—dance, film, the stage, books—and he was ruddy and four square and about as straight a shooter in bed as she'd come across. The fact that he was married provided her a thrilling chance to break rules.

She told him she had enough money for the both of them. Her father was immensely successful. She said something human and good ought to come of office buildings and shopping plazas and fancy dinners with influential politicos.

She said her family's money would make it possible for him to be able to sit in a quiet place and read and write all day, a dream come true.

He told her reality was tough. "Children make noise. It's who they are. The land needs tending. It's what land requires. So much for dreams."

But for some reason other things inspired him or had in the past, he explained. He wrote when he got squashed on a subway car or got jangled by someone spouting nonsense. What did that mean?

She didn't know.

She watched him filling up notebook after notebook. Would he ever *be* a writer?

Once when he was out hoeing, she grabbed a few of his notebooks and snuck off to the bathroom to read them. She was astounded that every entry was filled with despair. It made no sense. This was the part of his life that was the happy family life, with children crawling all over him, exactly what he'd always wanted. And he seemed cheerful, so how could he be as sad as the journals suggested?

People always remarked about his good spirits.

She fretted over the dark musings in his journals.

He wrote a lot about wishing they were still in the city, but he was turning into a good farmer. The journals, she decided, were a way of exercising (and exorcising) a part of him, a ten percent, not the whole of him.

Today he was singing along to the radio while he drove to Poughkeepsie and to Keepers, the antique shop they had been headed to. She looked at him. He did not seem despairing. Her irritability with the girls lifted. She felt, as she often did, that they were blessed, *celebrities* though the audience was only small and rural. Golden, some people said. A pretty couple with pretty children, a grand house, smarts to spare between them, a sense of style, wit.

Robert MacAfee, owner of Keepers, shook their hands and said, "You aren't from about here—I mean not born and raised here, I take it."

"No, we bought up here," Harrison said.

"Lots of stage people," Robert said. "Even some movie people up here these days."

"And us" was Harrison's way of straightening out that situation. "We're residents, not weekenders."

"He's a writer," Maggie said, and she slid her hand up her husband's back in an affectionate ownership. She handed over Thomas to give herself a break.

MacAfee said, "He's been in before, looking at this piece. Brought the troops along this time, I see."

They all stared at the corner cupboard. "Will it fit?" she asked. "I mean if it sticks out too much, look out for the china when these two are running after each other." She nodded toward the girls who were examining the table full of antique toys. "Speaking of, they want a treat." She'd already bought Easter gifts and done the baskets of candies and eggs.

Harrison said, "I measured eight times. It's a beautiful piece."

She, holder of the purse strings, nodded sagely. He was never careless, didn't ask for much, hardly spent anything, but still, she had more than a right to veto a purchase. "I like it," she pronounced.

She liked to give things. As a child she took extra sandwiches for kids at school. She paid the whole bill for a hotel room when she and friends went on vacation. Maybe it was guilt money because she was fortunate to be the child of people who dealt in land and buildings. She was smart enough to know it wasn't something she had earned by wit or labor, so she spread it when she could.

"We had a piece like this at home," she told MacAfee. She turned to her husband and nodded, then back to the owner. "I guess we should get down to business. How much?"

"Two hundred," he said.

"I have one fifty with me. Would you take the rest when you deliver?"

"Yes, might even make it just twenty-five at the time."

"Well, thank you, sir!" she said. She was excellent at receiving as well as giving, and she'd discovered that generosity usually bought her second favors.

Harrison wandered over to the toy table. She heard him say, "If you promise not to fight, you can choose one to share."

"He's being the Easter Bunny," Emma reminded her sister.

"Do you have money?" Maggie called to her husband.

"Some."

Maggie's brother and his wife had wanted to come up for Easter, but their kids were sick. She heard their voices anyway. "What kind of a writer *is* he?" "Does he have an income yet?" "Can you talk him into something sensible?" "And now he wants antiques."

Maggie loved the fact that he had an eye for fine things.

If only he could write something fast, popular, a moneymaker, oh, that would finally shut up her family. They thought he was lazy, which he wasn't—quite the opposite, always working at something. At least they couldn't accuse him of not being smart. He was plenty smart.

"Move down here," Maggie's father had told her at the wedding. "We'll find something he can do. I'll put the big dope to work writing up land deeds." Her father died a year after the wedding, leaving Maggie's brother to take up the complaints about her choice of a mate.

But she didn't want to go home again, hadn't then and didn't now. She wanted her own life and she had found it, a fairy tale life. An estate, living with land around her, neighbors a mile and half off, all of them accomplished, fascinating people. And her guy. The prince. Why would she want to go back to a Southern town where everybody would ask her what happened to her stage career? And how could she say that it had been merely a rebellious escape, a way of running away from a straight and narrow life?

Harrison was staring at a poster in the inner door of the antique shop. It showed a man named Buster Corrigan running for state assembly. "I'm going to get myself into politics one day," Harrison told Maggie who came toward him, counting out cash. "Do some good around our neck of the woods. I need to be useful."

Where had this come from? "But your writing?"

"I'll fit it in. Somehow."

He got up at four and wrote until daylight. Then he worked the grounds and the house, which always needed something. He'd started writing again from three to five in the afternoon but there were often interruptions, today for example, shopping and then entertaining tonight.

She hoped not to have to tell her family, if he became political, that she had to hire men to dig this or that. How did her husband even imagine he could do it all? But she didn't nag. He had a determined look, happy right now, yes, happy, looking at the poster.

Huh. Politics. Of all things.

He took the children outside the shop.

Anna said, "Daddy, can we have ice cream sodas?" Her face was collapsed in on itself. There was some guilt in her wanting a treat, he didn't know for sure why.

"Absolutely," he said.

He was staring back at the poster of Corrigan when his wife came out of the shop and said, "Delivery next weekend."

He gave up the idea of the scone he'd wanted and began to move toward the pharmacy that sold ice cream—better to get his kids what they wanted.

"Are you serious? About running?"

"I want to."

"You have to be Irish and dogged and cynical."

"You don't think I am?"

"You've got the first two."

"I'm cynical!" he declared.

Laughing, she said, "I'd have to disagree. Let's get these kids what you promised them."

The party they gave that night was small, about a dozen people. Harrison was especially keen to see their friends Oscar and Betty and just plain glad they had been able to make it. They had places both up in the country and in the city. Oscar, gregarious and constantly having lunches and dinners with famous people, was an attorney specializing in entertainment law and Betty, very quiet, was a teacher. They had three kids as Harrison and Maggie did and the kids had met and gotten along. They didn't bring their kids with them to this party though they knew they could have.

Harrison clapped his friend into a big hug. Oscar was just lovable. Everybody wanted to hug him and be hugged by him.

"What I have up my sleeve (hopefully not too literally)," Harrison said when a group gathered around him, "is either Manhattans or martinis. You're on your own if you want something else. I have achieved perfection in the making of these two elegant drinks." He tossed ingredients into a shaker in his signature slapdash manner and people cheered.

"How are those proportions?" their neighbor John called out.

"Perfect, I hope. I do it by feel."

"To the best party givers!" Sophie, also a neighbor, called out. She was a petite, thin, muscular blond who looked as if she should be wearing tennis whites even when she wore a light blue wool dress, as she did on this evening.

Sophie had a degree from the Rhode Island School of Design and had begun making unique earthy jewelry. Maggie had ordered gifts for everyone she knew to get Sophie started. Sophie had told Maggie that her husband, an attorney who was seldom around, was probably going to leave her. He *had* shown up tonight though. He was Douglas.

Tonight, Maggie was her old self—theatrical. Harrison still wished she hadn't given up the theater business that had brought them together.

Sophie's husband, Douglas, raised his Manhattan glass at that moment to say, "To all of us. To us. To this lifestyle we landed. People aren't going to be able to live like this ever again. We had...the luck of perfect timing."

True. They had all lucked into amazing houses, two hundred years old or more, and for astounding prices. Now people were beginning to pay sixfold and more for historic buildings from Great Falls up to Sharon, Connecticut.

Douglas and Sophie had brought their three daughters tonight, one older than Emma, one her age, and one younger than Anna. Emma was in charge of all of them. She'd slapped stuffed toys into the hands of the younger kids and started the rest on some word game that would feature how smart she was. She hadn't yet figured out that praise for smashing her opponents came from her elders, but not necessarily from her peers. Oh, Emma might need some soothing tomorrow.

The other people at the party were Bill and Louise, both writers and illustrators; John and Susan, an elderly couple who had just retired from the *New Yorker*; Sandy and Dave, she a nurse, he an anesthesiologist (good to know such people who might have connections when you needed them); and Harrison's error (according to Maggie), their handyman Nick and his wife Bibi, both awkward and out of place. They tilted their heads toward conversations, trying to figure out how to leap in. Russia, India, Gandhi? their faces said, *Oh, oh, oh, wasn't that that skinny guy in the news?*

Harrison *liked* Nick and Bibi, too bad.

"Hey, sweetheart," Maggie, said, coming up to him. "Make me a martini?"

"Coming up."

She shivered a little. "Cold tonight," she said. This was one of those Easters that felt all wrong. There would be at least two more weeks of winter. While he poured her drink, she went out to the porch and ordered the kids to play in Emma's room.

Soon, fresh drink in hand, she was telling theater stories to entertain the guests—crazy things people had said, the time a whole cast had to cover for a guy who went up in his lines.

"We made no sense," she was saying, "but we all kept talking. Somebody said, 'I know your leg hurts,' and so the guy started limping and one of us cracked up. Supposedly the audience never saw a thing. That was the report, anyway. Oh, did you ever hear that story about John Gielgud coming on stage with his zipper or rather his codpiece undone and then when the next night, he said, 'Will this thing appear again tonight,' the company fell apart. And that was *Hamlet*. In *England*. So, I guess I don't feel so bad." She told the story of hiring a somewhat normal weight young woman only to find her months later having gained sixty pounds or so. Harrison had heard this story several times.

"The young man playing her boyfriend was supposed to carry her over a threshold. One day he came to me and said, 'I can't lift her. What do I do?'

"So, I said, 'Tell her we'll have to solve it somehow.' I couldn't bear to fire her. I was stuck. I suffered. Couldn't sleep. I was surprised at the next rehearsal when the two appeared at the door and the boy said his lines and this actress kissed him and put him over her shoulder and carried him."

"And that was all right?" Bibi asked.

"It was funny, but it wasn't really anything we could keep. The girl knew it. She quit the next day. A year later I ran into her. She was thin."

Nick said, "Aw, that's good."

Bibi asked shyly, "Who did you get for the part?"

"Oh God. The big girl broke our budget. I had to play the part. It took a lot of acting. I never was a teenager, you know, even when I was."

"I can imagine," said Sophie's husband, Douglas.

Harrison was swimming in martinis; he could almost float. He wondered for the tenth time if the big girl in Maggie's story had been pregnant. He went out the back door to the grounds he sometimes walked, wondering how he had become a landowner, talking alfalfa and trout and streams. He lit up a cigarette. This one was a Lucky Strike. Last year he'd played with Gaullois in their slim packs. They made him feel European and he loved it. One day when he was working with Nick, they rolled their own and those were good too. Tonight, he took a long slow drag and made his way, wobbly for sure, to the gazebo. He put his head back against the laced wood and was almost asleep when he was aroused by a throaty, "Hey, there."

"Oh, hi."

"What's happening?"

"Getting sober."

"Too early for that," Sophie said. "It's cold out here. I came out to shock myself."

"I know. It feels good though."

She took the seat beside him and ran her hands over her arms. Then she extended her right leg and tapped her foot against Harrison's left foot. "You want to mess around?"

"Well, that would be lovely, but I don't think Maggie or Douglas would be too happy with us."

She sighed. "Douglas wouldn't care. He's having an affair."

"For sure?"

"I know what I know." She kept rubbing her foot against his. She looked at him sadly. "Shitty, huh?"

"Yeah. Are you two…breaking up?"

"Not until he leaves me. I've no money. At the rate my necklaces sell, the kids and I'll be living in one room in Queens and eating deli scraps."

Oh, it sounded wonderful to him. Deli scraps! "I'm sorry," he said. "I'm so sorry you have that to figure out."

"It's no big deal. Everybody's having affairs. Everybody."

He sensed that was true. At least writers were writing about people who were having affairs. In the current literature, my God, it was an epidemic. He'd just read three, or was it four, novels that turned on infidelity.

"Is Maggie having an affair?" he asked as casually as he could.

Her eyes lit with hope that she could make some headway here, then she shook her head. "If I'm honest, I don't know. I really don't. Douglas would take a spin with her if she agreed. He likes her."

He stood abruptly, saying, "I need a drink" and pointed his body toward the house. Then he turned back to the gazebo and planted a kiss on Sophie's forehead. "You're pretty," he said, though she wasn't his type. "And you're going to be okay."

Back at the house, he had another martini, thinking, What the hell. Everything is wrong. He told each person who sat beside him that he was going to run for political office, maybe in the next year or two. "If I can improve the school system, the roads, if I can get better people to take positions of importance, I will feel I've earned this glorious life we're all living." One room and deli scraps and love in the afternoon, galleries and concerts and shows of all sorts for the picking in the evening—secretly more glorious to his mind.

The next day he was sick. It was part hangover, part flu. Maggie was buzzing around hiding eggs and doing the final cleanups from the party. "Go, lie down," she said.

He didn't want to, but he had to. She plopped Thomas on the bed beside him and the boy slept contentedly.

Lying there, he tried to imagine himself an assemblyman. He'd feel better about living up here, being of use. But could he do whatever he had to do to fix the bridges, upgrade the schools?

He sat up carefully so as not to wake his son. From his jacket pocket, thrown over a chair at the side of the bed, he took a notebook, perhaps the fifteenth of its like, that held all kinds of things from ideas for stories to observations on people he met or those he knew. And he wrote out his feelings. *All these people recognize what a good sport Maggie is, and I know it too; she's strong, she's marvelous in many ways, but there are times I think if I died today, her life would go on as she wants it with or without me. I'm the decoration.*

For him—and he felt as if he were one of the heroines in a Chekhov play—life was about work, that was all there was, work, work, work. It gave dignity to an otherwise crazy existence. He had inherited that belief from his father who always studied and wrote, ill or well, happy or sad, city or country, and to be fair from his mother who plugged away at getting roles in plays. Who could guess how much grit it took to get those roles, let alone play them? Actresses were, as they say, a dime a dozen. Probably even in Michigan. Even in Minnesota. He wrote and, looking over what he wrote, shook his head at the Chekhovian sentiments and erased them as well as he could.

As Harrison leafed back through his journal, Thomas let out a cry. He lifted the boy and held him on his chest, heartbeat to heartbeat. "There you go. Better, right?"

Thomas was so undemanding. Would he always be this way? "You want to cry, cry," he said. "Live hard, Tom Jones, Tom Jones."

But the boy decided to simply study his father's flannel shirt.

Harrison lay there unable to write in his journal because of Thomas; he let his mind wander. The current novel attempt was stalled. He had been writing about a small-town mayor who was being used and abused by those around him.

"What's the damn story?" Maggie had asked him. "Just that people *use* him?"

"Sort of. Probably. He's nice, my character."

"Nice isn't very interesting," she said smugly, in that voice she used to criticize theater productions when he first met her. "I think something more has to happen."

Lying there, Harrison toyed with the idea of having the mayor pack his bags and disappear, strike out for new territory. Hm. He sat up and put Thomas on his lap and took up his notebook. He jotted, *He gets out.* He considered that for a while. What if he had the mayor adopt a difficult child? He made some notes about an angry six-year-old. He tried to imagine the kid's physical appearance—my God, the way Willa Cather could describe a character. She was damned good. He gave the boy a curl to the lips, a wide forehead, squinty eyes. And yet, he was still without the one telling detail that Cather would find. All right, an ungenerous mouth. He would try this new wrinkle with the mayor and the kid tomorrow when he did his morning writing hours.

"What do you think?" he asked Thomas who studied his face. "Will it work?"

The girls were squealing and running. Clomp clomp went their steps, so heavy, how could they run and also land that hard? How could skinny little bodies make that much noise? For peace he put on the radio, tuning and tuning until he found a Guy Lombardo recording. Nice, so smooth.

Maggie came in and kissed him on the lips. "You feel better?"

"Starting to. I'm getting up. I think he's probably hungry."

"I'll feed him. The ham's in. Three more hours."

Easter ham. As soon as she said it, the smell clicked in, making him wonder why he hadn't noticed. "Aren't you tired?" he asked his wife. "The party and now today?"

"A little. But I'm happy," she said.

13

Maggie's family almost always called her on Saturday afternoons. She almost always had to tell lies.

"I thought for once Harrison might answer the phone," her sister-in-law said in a call later that spring.

"Oh, he's busy outside." Actually, he was holed up, writing, but he had spent days on the garden so he deserved credit.

"That's good," her sister-in-law said.

"He's talking about going into politics." Was this a way of defending him? Or would it cause more grief?

"Politics?"

"Yes, isn't that great? He got the idea about a month ago and he's been looking into it." As she talked, she unwrapped purchases she'd made that afternoon.

"A whole new Harrison. Something completely different," her brother, on the second line, declared.

Her mother and her brother and sister-in-law knew nothing of the artist's life. "Not completely. It doesn't mean he's giving *up* the writing."

"How can he be a politician of any worth? Does he know anything about it?"

"Well, he's smart. He'll figure it out." She lowered her voice, aware she wasn't hearing the tac tac tac of his typewriter keys where he worked in the mudroom just off the kitchen.

"How's Thomas?"

"The sweetest baby."

She had him in a bassinet in the kitchen. She stretched the phone cord to look into the living room where Emma was curled into a pretzel and deep into a book. Since Anna was waiting for a promised game of cards, she beckoned Anna toward the kitchen and pointed to the bottle on the stove and to the baby.

Maggie continued unwrapping packages—meat, a pork roast for tomorrow. Potatoes. Milk, cereal, eggs. What a lot of food they went through. She was a favorite at the local store because she bought a lot and never haggled, understanding the grocers had to make a living too.

"Do you think his stuff is any good?"

"Well, yes, I do think so. I wish he'd do something flashy with a disastrous accident or a big event and tougher characters, but I tell him that when I can, and he listens." The last package was a book for Harrison, a novel by John Cheever, which she was pretty sure he'd been wanting to read. A little gift. A gift on a Saturday afternoon. Just for the heck of it.

Harrison had stopped typing because he couldn't help hearing some of the conversation Maggie was having. He knew she spoke just quietly enough to pretend he couldn't hear her, just loudly enough to make it possible for him to pick up the gist of it. He'd been writing a scene in which a young couple walked through wildflowers, feeling the redness of the flowers was part of their passion, mirroring it. Bee balm it was this time, but they'd also identified with red columbine and cardinal flowers at other points in the story. Harrison found the flowers sensuous, bordering on obscene and he wanted to capture that. He'd enjoyed writing the scene though he wasn't sure where it belonged in his current work or even if it belonged. Lord, there was so much to know about writing. Why couldn't he have put off the marriage for a couple of years and cloistered himself to work, building on that lucky hit at *The Atlantic*? The answer came as soon as he'd asked himself the question. His energy doesn't come from cloistering. It comes from the opposite—people buzzing and being.

When Maggie came in, he looked up. "Want me to read?" she asked, nodding toward his pages. She was acting very girlish, holding something behind her back.

"Not yet. Thanks."

"Got something for you."

"Cookies!"

"No, not cookies, though I could scare one or two up if you have a need."

He waved that aside. It was almost cocktail time. Peanuts, cheeses, Manhattans.

"Well, here it is." She presented the Cheever novel. He'd rather she'd brought cookies. It felt like an assignment, like a *Here's a model. Do one like this.* "I hear it's witty," she said brightly.

"Witty is always good." Wit was one form of smartness. His father had that satirical edge in all the political writings. The heir apparent to that sort of fame was Gore Vidal. While his father had impressed with a kind of ponderous solidity (and wit, yes, wit too), Vidal had brilliance and dash. He was movie-star-ish. Would nothing short of that satisfy Maggie's family? Or his own mother who kept asking in phone calls, "What are you doing *these* days?" her phrasing a suggestion he needed to transition to something other than what he was doing these days.

"Maybe when you get into politics, you'll write about politics some more," Maggie said. "Your mayor—"

"Could be. Could be."

"Come out when you're ready. I'll make you a drink. Oh, we should put in those trees tomorrow. Some of them."

"I know."

When Maggie left, he went back to his pages. What he wanted to capture was the difference between the lovers and the old lady watching them. When he saw old people he studied the way they wore their shoulders so close to their ears. There was some physical or psychological reason for that constant shrug. He sat there trying it out. It was…a humbling of some sort. *I don't mean to be a bother, I'm just…*

Physically maybe the head was too heavy to support without the extra push of the raised shoulders. He kept trying it, figuring. His mother didn't stand like that. She was still preparing to come into a room (on stage or in real life) like a purposeful much younger woman. She kept her shoulders down and her head back. He wrote for a while, creating two women—deciding to make it the middle-aged one who disapproved of the lovers and the older one who did not, because the older one could remember love and longing. He felt good; he felt he had found some truth in their attitudes. He wrote the older one kneeling down to pinch a wildflower, knowing it would wilt in her hand before she got it home.

"Drinks are made!" Maggie sang outside the door.

He took up his journal, paused, wrote: *I am two people. I am the cheerful dope who is going to run for office having been told he has personality and has a good chance at charming the electorate, but a small chance of getting enough votes to actually win. I am Caliban, trapped and angry and inarticulate. I have everything I need except myself. I have drink and I have drunken companions to keep me entertained, but when I'm sober I resent being a dog.*

No, not a dog. Dogs are loving. Give them food and love, they ask for nothing else; they return it tenfold. He is some other beast.

Her family thinks he's nothing. That wedding. How he'd kept up a good front. They bought his clothes, finding the ones he brought inadequate. They smirked. Maggie's brother said to her, "So you are marrying a pretty face!" Maggie had retorted at the time—he'll give her that—"He's more than a pretty face. You'll see. Just you wait."

She opened the door. "Ready? Manhattan awaits."

Manhattan awaits. The phrase kept going through his head.

He got himself up and out of the mudroom where he'd been spinning his wheels. They were due for the real Manhattan, the place of his youth and confidence. They only got there once a year before Thomas and now that they had an infant, Maggie hadn't even mentioned it.

One day—oh this was five years ago now—Maggie was opening the mail and she said, "Oh, well, I'll be. John Randolph."

Yes. An actor. Harrison remembered Maggie had worked with Randolph once though he had not seen the show, had only heard about it. What was the role? He couldn't come up with it.

That day, five years ago, Maggie said, "He's on Broadway. *Seagulls Over Sorrento.* Isn't that great? We've got to go see him. Weekend after next?"

"I'll consult my calendar," Harrison had said drily because he was digging soil then (as he was digging now) and any day was a good day to stop digging and go into the city.

That trip to see *Sorrento,* Maggie had been thrilled, too, saying, "And we've got to see *Wonderful Town.* Everybody's seen it already but us."

She certainly didn't have as much oomph about getting away from the farm these days.

Harrison went into the living room now and sat on the sofa with the girls on his lap, one leg for each, while he held Thomas against his chest, and he found himself humming snatches from *Wonderful Town.*

"What's that?" Anna asked.

"It was a play first and then it was a musical. Your mum and I saw it five years ago."

"You liked it?" Anna asked.

"I think he did," Emma said.

He gave them each a squeeze. "Two young girls discovering New York. Starving. Loving their life. We did that. Me and your mum."

"Starving isn't wise," Emma said.

"I was doing that artistic exaggeration. You eat deli scraps and peanut butter or cereal. The girls eat *a lot of* cereal in the musical. 'Starve' means wanting a four-course meal you can't afford and eating peanut butter."

"And Mom liked it?"

"Loved it."

Now she ordered things for the house and read a lot, pretty much indiscriminately.

He'd watched her, theorized. He'd concluded: A. She was actually shy. There was an awkwardness about her that she had disguised with a lot of bravado when he first met her. And he'd been impressed by what she did. After all, she was a producer, she made big decisions, she paid salaries, she made witty if devastating pronouncements about people. He thought now—he was not sure—but he thought she was actually a little afraid of people. B. She had money. She didn't *have* to work and so she decided to live well on family money—what nicer way to bring up a family, she said (she insisted the right size was three kids), giving them what they needed—nothing excessive, but also no strain, no panicking about money. Sweetness and goodness all around. In fact, he could hear her in the kitchen now, humming. He had bought it—the calm civilized life. Emma had been such a good baby. It seemed the right way to live—making young people for the next generation, guiding their learning.

"My calendar is free weekend after next," he called into the kitchen.

"For what? Oh, right. I'll see what's playing and I'll get Janet to babysit."

"For a whole weekend?"

"Right. Janet can use the money."

Maggie made a lot of financial decisions, like the theater producer she had been, always parceling out payments to someone, him included, and enjoying that role. She had told him, "You work the land. You repair things in the house. You've earned it."

He *had* earned it. The money wasn't excessive, but he could buy a breakfast out if he wanted.

"Don't order tickets until I've seen the listings," he called.

Anna slipped off his lap. Emma stayed, smoothing his hair, watching him.

In the kitchen Maggie was laughing about the onions making her cry.

"Want any help?" He took Thomas to the kitchen and she put him in the bassinet. "Here. Let me do the onions."

"No. Go do something fun."

He went back to the mudroom and opened his mail, which he had allowed to sit, knowing it was going to depress him. Not exactly fun, facing a rejection which was surely what was in the thick envelope. It was his novel, an earlier draft of the one about a young couple— He opened the letter enclosed and read the rejection, which said nothing specific, only that the novel was not ready yet, not mature.

Everything about his ambitions felt foolish. He went back out into the kitchen. "Maybe call that John Randolph again. If he's there, we can have drinks with him and his wife. They were interesting."

The next weekend they were on the train to Manhattan.

As soon as his feet hit the pavement of the train station, Harrison felt himself buoyed up. And the din—he welcomed it. The crowds pushing past him—fine with him. Maggie looked plenty happy too.

She'd booked rooms at the Algonquin; she revealed that surprise with a wink to Harrison when she told the cab driver where to go.

"Are you kidding?" They'd stayed at less expensive hotels on past trips.

"Where else!" she said. "You're a writer! Maybe you'll meet an editor in the lobby."

After they put their bags in the room, she and Harrison went back down and sat in the lobby, the two of them on a sofa together, the same sofa they'd sat on when he had his celebration of *The Atlantic* story. He reached for a menu card on the table.

"I think I want scotch this time. A little smoke in the booze," she said. She smiled disarmingly and took his hand.

He called over a waiter and asked for two scotches. And peanuts. The day's newspapers were on a rack near the elevator. By now each section must be wearing a splash of egg or coffee, but when he saw a wheezing rotund man put the *Times* back on the rack, he went to fetch it. His fantasy played—here he was in his future, a novel published, him living around the corner, coming into the hotel for meetings with friends or just for the buzz of human intellectual life, a bourbon or a scotch or in summer a gin and tonic. A show every night. Or, well, many nights anyway. The kids in a great school with brilliant teachers.

They were seeing a show tonight and having dinner after with John Randolph. This was the life, Harrison thought as he opened the newspaper. Maggie put a hand on his thigh, proprietary, suggestive.

Oh, he wanted…everything, everything, everything.

He watched Maggie get up and weave to the desk to ask something. Today she was wearing a tailored navy-blue suit. Nobody would accuse her of not being proper in all situations—which was a surprise from the person who'd first presented herself to him as unconventional, almost reckless.

That first full novel of his, the one he'd finished and sent, had been about a young marriage that didn't work. It sat in an envelope on the floor of the mudroom now. He wasn't sure if he would revise it or work on one of his other starts. Another editor who had recently rejected it said, and now the few words were fixed in his brain, "Not enough of a story here, but good writing. The only cure is to write another."

Ha. Easy to say. You had to be pressed by an idea before you could just "write another." Right? He could hear his father in his mind, outraged by such a command. Even though his father didn't write fiction, he would have made a speech about heartbreak and the need for strong feeling in the gut before a writer knew what to attack next.

The rotund wheezing man who had returned the *Times* sat in an adjoining chair, this time with a whiskey. "Hallo," he said.

"Hello to you."

"Mind my asking, are you somebody famous?"

Harrison laughed. Not yet, he wanted to say, but he just said, "No. Afraid not." He gave his name as an afterthought. "Harrison Mirth."

"Mirth, did you say? With a *u* or like laughter, cheer?"

"The latter."

"Interesting. No relations to the political—"

"Afraid so."

"I'll be. James McConnell, writer." He extended a hand.

Harrison wasn't sure he knew the name. "Excellent," he said. "Happy to meet you."

"Travel writing mostly."

"That sounds wonderful. Benefits there!"

"Tiring sometimes. You?"

"Just a farmer. In town for a couple of shows."

McConnell nodded skeptically. "Auditioning?"

"No, no, just watching. My wife knows a number of actors. She was in the business a couple of years ago."

"Always hooked, I hear, once you start. The theater bug."

"Well, she's a sensible gal and we have a family, so…"

"So, farming. Aha. I see she is chatting up the desk. Very wise. You get good service if they know you. She's probably figured that out."

"She has."

"Well, enjoy your shows." McConnell heaved himself up. "I have to get back to work, alas."

"Who was that?" Maggie asked.

"A travel writer."

"Plenty of small fry around," she said.

"Of which we can be counted."

"I guess so," she said, frowning.

When the bill came, and was presented to Harrison, he knew he could put the drinks and nuts on the room ticket, but it felt good to pull out what cash he had and tell the waiter to keep the change.

As Maggie applauded the curtain call for *Epitaph for George Dillon,* her brain ticked off the things that would have made the play stronger—a more likeable protagonist, a stronger through line. But Robert Stephens was fantastic, a mean and intelligent cynic. Her brain still worked. She could feel Harrison's wanting and wondered if he perhaps should try writing plays. She had read and reread his novel about a failed marriage and given him as much feedback as he could take. Privately, she thought it needed more humor. She told him, "Make it funny. That's my advice."

Sometimes he *was* funny. Sometimes, oh, so whimsical and truly Mr. Mirth. The stories he told the kids! Wonderful! But there was a bigger and bigger cloud lately. She was trying to figure out how to lift it. Surely the four hours every morning (it was four now) and the two every late afternoon was enough time to write. Why she could pen eight novels in a year with that much time. They wouldn't necessarily be good, but they would *exist*.

They saw a small alley between people ahead and pushed forward. She would talk to Harrison about trying a play.

They whisked themselves to Frankie and Johnnie's to meet John Randolph and his wife.

They got to the restaurant in good time and as they got seated, Randolph and Sarah came rushing in, all moving in a very Manhattan rhythm.

The first time Harrison met them they assumed he was an actor. Maggie admitted that when she was desperate in their early days, he'd done a couple of small roles for her. But he'd been kind of awful. Too dramatic, over-eager. They had all laughed about it, Harrison included. It hadn't been a goal of his. He admired those who could.

Randolph continued to act, and he had good news. "I think I've got a film role. Fingers crossed. They're looking at Sarah too."

"How do you do it, with children and all?" Harrison asked now.

"I don't know. Every day is a challenge. But we do. Along with all the Communist activity we engage in," Randolph said drily. "Be warned. The Red Scare ain't completely over. You may be investigated for drinking with us."

"Proudly," Maggie said. "Proudly. Anything I can do to stand against the idiots…"

"Well, the truth is, Sarah and I have both been blacklisted," Randolph continued. "All kinds of film work we could have had went down the drain for a while, so that's why this new movie thing is such good news. Bah. Let's drink."

"Absolutely. This is on us," Maggie said. "Dinner and drinks."

"No, no," Randolph protested. "A whole dinner?"

"Oh yes." They ordered drinks and then Maggie raised a glass. "A toast to your continued success."

"Thank you, thank you," Sarah said. "As long as I can act, all is well."

Maggie examined Sarah's clothes—stylish, a full skirt and bold jewelry. And short hair swept back. Sarah had the panache of an actress.

"What roles have you loved?" Harrison asked her.

"Me? I love the ones I haven't landed yet. The ones with wit. Ruth in *Blithe Spirit*. All of Coward. God, *Design for Living*. Oh, *Present Laughter*. That's playing now but I'm not in it, alas."

Maggie said, "We're seeing *Shadow of a Gunman* tomorrow. I wonder if we could fit in a matinee of *Present Laughter*."

"It's good," Sarah said.

Maggie turned to Harrison.

"Sure," he said, completely game.

"Why did you drop it all?" Randolph asked Maggie. "You clearly still have the bug."

She had dreaded that question. Bad enough that her own husband asked it from time to time. It was because her extroversion left her one day; it was like watching a bird flying off. She felt herself reverting to the thirteen-year-old who was a little afraid of the world. Just because. It had just happened. "Well…"

Randolph rescued her. "Finances. I know. Stupid of me to ask."

She told Randolph, "Seriously, I'm lucky." Without voicing it, she tried to communicate *husband, children, home, peace.*

Sarah said, "I *know*. Sometimes I wonder at our capacity for stress and rejection."

Over dinner, the Randolphs told stories of those stresses. Travel from coast to coast. Betrayals. Harrison listened with rapt attention.

A year passed.

Emma and Anna loved playing with Thomas. They taught him to walk. They taught him to say Mama, Dada. They dangled toys in front of him as if he were a cat. The boy seemed smart—he took things in quickly, remembered what he'd seen, but he kept his own counsel. He rarely asked for anything, rarely cried.

"What will he be?" Maggie asked. "A doctor? A writer?"

Were his silences a kind of unhappiness? Did children, like spies, steal their parents' secrets?

But birds sang, holidays came, there were more parties.

Harrison got three more rejections on his first novel. After three, he wrote an alternate version about a failed marriage in which the protagonist, a woman, was more sympathetic than the man who was a high school teacher who had to battle school politics. The people in this version were sweet. He wrote fast, noting his progress with the skill of fixing scenes and sentences. By mid-winter he'd sent that novel out to seven editors.

He got seven rejections.

He thought he would now just write for his own pleasure, perhaps only a few hours a day. He would go into politics as he'd been promising to do and make the community he lived in a better place.

14

The snow was high, maybe four feet, and nobody wanted to go out of the house, not even the kids. In coat and boots, Harrison pushed out of the mudroom with a shovel. It would do no good to spread breadcrumbs, of which his pockets were full, in the snow. They would sink and the birds would starve. Heaving snow up and over, he made a person-sized pile to his right and cleared a patch of about six feet long by two wide. He'd have to do more when he fueled up with coffee and something sugary, perhaps one of the muffins Maggie stocked. When he thought the patch of ground was safe from drifts, he turned out his pockets—sprinkling crumbs like something out of Hansel and Gretel. "Follow this and find me," he said aloud. But when he looked up, there were no birds around. All this for nothing? He stood there pondering, having deep thoughts about the seasons. To think that in three months he would be planting a garden or at least preparing the ground for one.

And then what seemed like a piece of white fluff in his eye turned and revealed yellow feathers. The goldfinch hesitated and then flew to his feet. It had perhaps made a sound he didn't hear with his earmuffs on. Four other finches flew in to partake of the winter treat.

When he went back inside, Maggie said, "You didn't take the bowl. I mean, it's here, but the crumbs are gone."

"I dumped them in my pockets."

"Oh, dear."

"What?"

"You'll get moths. They'll get stale in your pockets."

"Huh." He went back outside and emptied his pockets better, frightening the goldfinches for a moment, but they got used to him.

His coat was wet, but he was too chilled to take it off. Back inside he lay down on the living room floor and wrestled his daughters to the ground.

"Ugh. You're wet!"

"I know. Isn't it fun?"

Anna seized him and held him tight, but Emma got up and brushed herself off and went to the kitchen to help her mother.

Winter. Just Maggie and the kids. Right. Right. Everybody got depressed.

Maggie called out, "The temperature is supposed to rise by twenty degrees tomorrow and the next day. We ought to melt pretty well."

"Good."

Oh, it wasn't going to be spring yet, far from. He went to the mudroom and unearthed the seed catalogue. His father had written glowingly about the agrarian life, saying we would not be sane, not ever, until we got back to the earth and learned to grow what we ate. This was sort of funny since his father had also liked the Manhattan restaurants where most of the staff had never seen a plot of land in their lives.

Still his father was romantic about land, about the country and the promise of America. And Harrison couldn't help wanting to please his father's ghost. He told his father silently that he had planted trees, that he'd nearly killed his aching body planting pine trees, six hundred forty of them. Before the huge blizzard he had walked out to see them and almost cried to see how well they were doing. He'd done right. The oaks were there, too, they'd come with the place, and a few maples and birches, gorgeous birches they could see through the dining room window. But the pine trees were all his and they bordered the property.

When the snows melted days later, there was slush everywhere and then it got cold and the path to the car was more treacherous, not to mention the somewhat longer path to the barn. Sometimes he considered an oil heater for the barn with the idea that he would write there. But it was dangerous, everything there ready to go up in flames, including the storage of their baby clothes and papers and bits of furniture they had replaced. No, he was safer in the mudroom. The barn held no cattle, no horses. Just stuff. Not to mention his marvelous tractor.

"Why do I have all my theater accounts in those damned boxes in the bedroom?" Maggie asked aloud just as he went to the mudroom to work.

He answered silently that it was because she constantly promised to review them to find out if she'd been cheated nine years ago. She couldn't face those records or the idea that maybe a guy she'd once trusted to keep the books before Harrison came along had skimmed profits she never saw. After all, she'd heard more than once about Harrison's mother's criminal boss.

"Just take the boxes to the barn. I can't stand how crowded our room is. And I can't face looking inside them."

"To the barn? Now? And then what?"

"I don't know. Just take them."

He fetched them, one box on top of another, and walked out without his coat, goose-stepping over the ice that had formed when the temperature dropped again, coating a wet ground with dangerous almost unseeable slickness. Three times he almost fell. Why did this have to happen today, he thought, during his writing time? Why did he not drop the damned boxes of papers in the wet and cold and see if, like certain animals, they survived the winter.

But he didn't. He tripped, skated, and cursed his way to the barn. He knew he was going mad. He could feel the madness right there, in his throat, in his heart. He yelled at his daughters who had gotten so bored they were dressed to go outdoors. "It's too slippery! Get back. Play something inside. Use your damned brains. If you have any."

They cried.

He held on to his fury. He said, "Come on, don't be babies." He slammed into the mudroom. Oh God, he thought, I'll tell them a story tonight. Something long and complicated and… He banged his fist against his head to get rid of the anger. One day he would not be able to get rid of it.

When the weather broke, that is, when the ice melted, there were two visits that pleased Maggie. The first was from a neighbor, Old Wilson, who came to the door with a small box from which emanated a yippy noise.

"You always said you was going to get a dog," said Old Wilson who had a son they called Young Wilson. "This here was birthed a couple weeks ago. He's a good one. My son says it's yours now."

Maggie had not asked for it, but she hated to say no to anyone. And she did think the comfort of a dog, a creature that looked longingly at her, would be nice. And…always, truly, she thought a dog was a good thing for the children, to teach them responsibility and the love of all living things. "Can I look?"

Old Wilson put the box on the ground and lifted a wriggling black and white mutt that personified curiosity. The dog couldn't look at everything fast enough. "Brought an extra leash here in the box. He's a good one. Best of the litter."

"Did you name him?"

"Oh no, that's for you. We just said, 'Here, dog' and 'Boy Dog.' He came. He's a good one."

The mutt was handsome, and Maggie fell in love. She lifted and held the dog and kissed it somewhere between the eye and the top of the head. "How much do you want for him?"

"Oh, nothing."

"You must take something."

"Well, he's not bred or anything."

She rooted around in the bowl in the kitchen where she kept cash. Handing over a twenty, which certainly pleased Old Wilson, she said, "Thank you for remembering us."

When he left, the dog barked a goodbye and the children, hearing that sound, ran in, jumping and squealing with delight. Outside the door, up about fifty yards Harrison was splitting and stacking wood. He wore the old blue wool shirt that had bits of crumbs in the pockets but had not yet attracted moths. The bowl of crumbs he carried out these days were useful for the other birds that came around now, but the goldfinches preferred seeds and they had them, too, because things were popping up everywhere. Daffodils waved all along the pathway to the barn.

Old Wilson was talking with Harrison who looked surprised. The two men shook hands and Harrison watched him go off. The way he scratched at his face, he was thinking of something, forgetting the logs for a moment. Then he started in again, swinging the ax.

That night after supper he said, "Old Wilson is a tricky bugger. I want you to watch out for him. He'll always be hitting us up for a few bucks."

"But he needs it."

"I'd rather it was direct."

"Oh, I don't think a person like him can be direct."

"Maybe not. Notice he didn't come to me with the dog."

"Noted."

But the dog went to Harrison anytime Harrison was within reach. In fact, the dog was in love. He followed his new master everywhere, panting, looking longingly at him, rubbing himself against Harrison's leg.

"Tell him to play with *us*!" Emma cried.

"Go!" said Harrison.

But the dog was in love.

They had to name him. "Spots," Anna suggested. Emma told her that was too common. "We should try names, see what he responds to." The dog looked as nervous as a kid on a quiz show. His legs buckled and he peed on the living room rug.

"Oh dear," Maggie said. "I'll get rags."

"And a rolled-up newspaper," Harrison told her. His father had had dogs and he knew how to train one.

"Pepper," tried Emma. The dog looked down, embarrassed.

"Junior," tried Anna. "Youngest Wilson."

"That's good!" Emma granted.

Thomas said something that sounded possibly like "Junior," but probably wasn't.

"Jonah!" Maggie said, returning with the rags and rolled-up newspaper.

"Casey!" Harrison growled. The dog went to him. He spanked the dog and put his nose in the urine. "No. Not in here. No." He hit him again. The dog looked up at him, apologizing it seemed, adoring, and wrapped itself around his leg.

"Casey, it is," Maggie pronounced. And the kids did a chorus of 'Caseys' until they were all used to the name.

On the Tuesday of the next week of the long winter, another visitor came by. This one was a salesman for the *Encyclopedia Britannica*. He was tall and lanky and wore a cheap suit.

Maggie invited him in for coffee.

"Thank you, ma'am." He plunked down three brochures in a line on the chest they used for a coffee table. "What a beautiful house."

"Well, we're working on it. These old houses need a lot of love."

"I'm sure." He saw Thomas sitting on the living room floor, playing with Casey. Do you have other children? School age?"

"The two eldest are in school, yes."

"And how are they at learning?"

"Brilliant. My kids are very, very smart it turns out."

"Then you're going to want to give them every advantage. I came here primarily with the intention of getting you a full set of the Compton's from *Encyclopedia Britannica*, but I've changed my mind. You should have the better set. And more. I have something else, too, you might like. I'll tell you about that in a minute. I can see you care about your children."

Of course, she did. Who didn't? "So, you're selling something."

Harrison was out back, turning the soil, adding manure he'd bought from Old Wilson. He had the seedlings in their various containers lined up and ready to go in. Tonight, he would realize he had a backache, and she would prepare him a hot water bottle and he would thank her as if he had never had such a gift before. How she knew him. She could predict him. Which was scary because she knew he would leave one day.

"You already value encyclopedias, I'll bet. Do you have a set?"

"Not here. When I was a child, my parents had them in the house. Could I get you a coffee?"

"Well, all right."

She brought the coffee saying, "At times when I'm doing a cross-word, I'll admit, I want to check something. Oh, I know that's cheating!" she said cheerfully.

"Sure, a clue like Ptolemy, and you think, how do I spell that. Sure."

"We have a library down the road in Pine Plains of course. And they have the whole—"

"Yes, of course. Libraries are the life of a community. But long nights doing homework or the instant answer when you think of something you want to know, well, these wonderful Britannica editions can't be beat. And you don't have to go out for an answer!"

She turned over the brochure looking at the price tag. Her mother would approve. They had had a set of Britannica at home, feeling anything that had a British name would bring them up in the social set.

And it would help Harrison when he needed to look something up. He was always running off to the library.

"Yes," she said. "I think this is a good idea."

"Yes," the salesman pressed, seeing his advantage—she didn't mind, he had to make a living—"what I'm going to propose next is the combined deal for people who have readers in the family. For those people there is nothing like a collection we call The Great Books." He handed her another brochure.

She read the list. It felt like college all over again. Homer, Aeschylus, Sophocles, Euripides, Aristophanes, Aristotle, Virgil, Plutarch, Machiavelli, and more. She read mostly contemporary authors lately. These were challenging titles, all right. She thought she might dabble, but her kids should and could tackle them, if not today then soon. And Harrison liked his classical references. He'd used them as epigraphs in two manuscripts. So, she said, "Yes." She had been planning to ask for another two thousand from her mother for a few things and now she was sure she would go ahead with that request, specifying something her mother would be in favor of and hopefully heading off the usual questions about how noncommercial Harrison's writing was.

How many times would she have to explain that his father's career was the unusual one, a person who could be paid for writing his opinions about things? It took much longer for a novelist to make money if he or she ever did. And she was here in this marvelous place, just what she wanted. They weren't lacking anything. They were now a family of six, counting the dog. They were all smart and healthy and full of life, also counting the dog.

When the spring reverted to winter temporarily, there was another sheet of ice over everything. The daffodils bent over and gave up. Harrison surveyed the damage, thinking all he had planted would die. He slid and skated to the car and drove to the public library. The encyclopedias were going to be a reason to stay home, but he wasn't going to give into it. He could still talk to a librarian when he needed to look something up or find the next read. He felt his voice rise up in cheer as he greeted the old woman behind the checkout desk. "I need a novel to distract me," he said.

"Have you read *Wapshot?*"

"Yes, I have. I own it."

"Oh, how impressive. Your wife always tells me you're a writer."

"Working away at it."

"She used to bring the kids here a lot. Winter, of course, people stay home."

"I'm sure she'll be back soon."

"I hope so. Lovely woman."

Kind to everyone. Right, right, right. He browsed the newly acquired fiction holdings and chose *Exodus*.

The winter had done him in. He felt as if he'd just broken out of prison. He sat at the library for a while just watching people think and make decisions. Then, heaving a big breath of courage, he drove to a diner where he'd heard the politicos hung out. For some reason (perhaps a lack of other customers?) the staff let them sit there most of the day.

He went in. They were there, three of them, leaning toward each other, speaking softly, one of them using a forefinger to make a point of some sort on the table as if something written there needed to be flicked away. They stopped talking when Harrison approached.

He took in the grumpy-looking men. All were smoking, one a pipe, the others, cigars. He was reminded of his father who was old and crusty, too, and a pipe smoker. "Gentlemen," he said, "excuse the interruption. I've been wanting to meet someone who could connect me to the party. I want to be put to work."

They shifted.

"Sit down," the pipe smoker said. His face was lined with the effects of smoke and outdoor work. He was strongly built, about sixty. He thrust out a hand. "I'm Jack Emory. This here is Paul Martin," he said, pointing to a grinning man with rutted skin.

"Hello!" said Paul. "You want to work? We got work. Couple of questions first though." He, like Emory, wore a suit and tie, like something right out of Ireland where the only clothes any man had were out-of-fashion suits and ties.

The third man said, "I'm Paul's cousin, just here for the eggs today. James Martin." Tighter grin, flat gray hair, a judgmental type, a flannel shirt rather than the rumpled suit and tie uniform of the others.

Harrison hadn't thought to put on a jacket and tie though he wasn't as casual as the Martin cousin. "How do I start?"

"Sit," said Emory. "Are you a Communist?"

"Not so I've noticed."

Paul moved over another few inches and Harrison sat.

"Democrat?"

"Nothing else will do."

"Experience?"

"None."

"What is it you want?'

"To be useful. To make things better."

"What things?"

"Schools, roads, county taxes."

"What have you been doing with your life?"

He explained.

"What will you give up?"

He didn't know the answer to that. "I always fit everything in. If I run for office—"

"We start you on other things. Organizer. That kind of thing. You're a writer, you say?"

"Novels."

"You could correct our grammar if we write up some speech?"

"Oh, sure." It became clear in that first half hour there was no money involved in the early stages of political life. That was something he had to swallow.

"Get this guy a cup of coffee," Jack Emory said to the waitress. "We got us here a possibility." He looked at Harrison. "We groom you, you run for office, right?"

"Yes."

The waitress hurried over with a cup of coffee Harrison didn't particularly want. But he sipped at it. First lesson—he already knew it. You get invited to a chicken dinner you'd better eat the chicken. It's coming back up on you, doesn't matter, you push it back down your gullet. It's a contract.

"You know who he puts me in mind of?" Jack asked his compatriots.

"Kinda looks like a Kennedy," answered Paul Martin. "Kinda."

"That's gonna help," said Jack. To Harrison, he said, "You know this is Republican territory. We haven't gotten somebody elected for a while. You up for a fight?"

"Yes. Show me where."

"In time, my son, in time."

Harrison got himself a new father and a brother and a cousin all in a little trip to a diner. He didn't think that at first, that it was a substitute family, but after a while he realized that's what he'd bought.

When the ice melted, green things began to sprout again. It became apparent that the massive amounts of snow had done no serious harm to the roots. Vegetables grew shyly at first, then boldly, breaking earth, needing stakes, announcing, *Pow. I'm here. Don't stop me now.*

15

Harrison and Maggie went into Manhattan more often the next year and usually managed three shows in a weekend plus dinners with friends, like Oscar and Betty.

Harrison, in spite of his promise to himself that he would write only for his own pleasure, had finished another version of the marriage novel and was shopping it around on his own. He couldn't seem to give up. Then one day an editor named Collins from Simon and Schuster called him to come in for an appointment and he and Maggie rushed into the city early on a Friday so he could meet the editor on Friday afternoon.

He thought this was it. His heart hammered when he was shown into an office piled high with manuscripts and saw his own on the desk of a tall, slim, bespectacled man.

"I'm dying to get out of town," Collins said, looking at his watch. "I have friends who have a house up North. I go for the weekend, but I stayed a little late this time. Wanted to meet you."

Harrison did not tell him he had just come in from the north.

"You have talent."

"Thank you." There was a pause. What was the man saying? What was he *saying*?

"I can't take this novel. It isn't ready, not ripe yet. And don't ask me what you should do to it, you just need to write another one."

Harrison shook his head to clear it. He knew he would forever dream those words. *Just write another one.*

Collins said, "But you need an agent next time. I almost never look at an author submission. You need someone to fight for you."

That sounded right. He was not a fighter. Not in that way. Fighting embarrassed him. "So how do I—"

Collins handed over a note card. "I'm giving you three names. Do not send anything until it's ready. Understand? Your next one will hit."

He'd worked on this one in its various versions for five years, but he knew not to say it. Five years was nothing. Collins led him to the door. They were like ships passing, him rushing in from the North, Collins heading out to someplace perhaps not far from Harrison's house.

Maggie was waiting in the hotel room with a bottle of champagne and open arms. He shook his head. "Not yet," he said. "Apparently I have talent. But no publication yet."

"We can still drink the champagne," she said.

What Maggie had imagined the result of this trip would be was a husband so happy and full of himself that he would toss down a glass of champagne and then toss her onto the bed and then, full of ego, would ravish her. She had always wanted to be ravished. It didn't much look like she was going to get her wish tonight.

She kissed him on the forehead and said, "Well, it's good news overall, isn't it? He'll remember your name."

"I can hope."

She looked over his shoulder to where there was a mirror. The new dress was very stylish, and she loved the wide belt. The saleslady had said it was amazing that she'd had three kids, so good was her figure. That and the fresh haircut—well, she hadn't felt or looked this good in a while.

A few moments later, she sat beside him on the bed, holding the champagne. "Should I open? It will cheer us?"

"I don't know about cheer. Give it here. I'll open it."

She hadn't wanted him to unleash the cork. He could be slapdash, ruin clothes, but this was not a good night to criticize him. She watched him and then, unable to help herself, hurried to fetch a towel from the bathroom.

Their sex lives had fallen into a pattern, not one she loved. Saturdays. They would announce to the kids that they were having a nap. And they did—nap. But then in the drowsy way of Saturday afternoons, he would reach for her and after a few caresses, they would remove their clothes, or in summer had already done so.

There were times she'd tried to role-play. Once she danced around with only an apron on. Oh dear, he didn't much like that. "Who are you being?" he said irritably.

"I thought you might like this persona better." And then her voice caught, and she thought, Please God, don't let me cry.

"Oh no," he said. "Come here. I'm sorry." And he held her tenderly. She got it, that he liked her best that way, plain, no apron or other costume, and to be honest, perhaps a little thoughtful and sad, a side of her that she hated.

He liked examining her body. In bed, he was a boy, forever playing doctor, fascinated anew by the tender, meaty, private parts. "Beautiful," he would say.

She did not find genitals beautiful. They were there. You clothed them. They did their work. Amen.

She tried to maneuver him to lovemaking other times, other days of the week. She turned toward him only last week early in the morning. He was hardly awake. He kissed her nicely for a while, but it was clear he wanted to be up and typing something or other.

Twice she asked, "Why Saturday afternoons?"

He didn't know at first. When he worked it out, it was a bit of celebration at the end of the week and before they had people over or went someplace; it was what they did between work and socializing.

It was better than some, but she wished they could be more flexible. Didn't a lot of people make love before sleep? Instead, she read in bed long into the night and he either read some history tome in the big chair in the living room or put aside a book for some television. It was easy to get addicted to Johnny Carson. Lots of people watched every night, but she wasn't sure they were people who got up at four or five to write.

When he got the champagne open that day in New York, the day on which he was told he had talent but had to keep working, he said politely, almost as if they were strangers, "Thank you for this. Thank you for your faith in me."

"Endless faith. *Ab*solutely endless."

She saw by his face that he found her phrase too facile. His look said there was surely an end to her support and in fact he hoped there was.

He poured the champagne sloppily—she had expected that. He paced, drinking, thinking.

"How about a murder mystery?" she said.

"That isn't...something I know about or get interested in."

"Something about a child. Like Dickens. A child in trouble?"

He appeared to consider this. "A child. Maybe you could tell me about *your* childhood again," he said bitterly. "Some Dickensian details."

"Mine? But I had it good. Why aren't you writing about yours?"

He shook his head and looked as if he might answer but didn't right away. Finally, he sat down again. "Maybe someday I'll want to write about my grandmother—all her life, stymied. She had so much talent. Singing, sewing, speaking—and God, she was smart. And my grandfather...kept her down."

"That's a good story. There's your villain, then."

"No, no, no, he wasn't a villain. They were immigrants, without connections, without money. He was proud that he made a living. That was his understanding of what he was supposed to do. And he did it."

"So, write it!" she said. "*I'm* interested."

"Really, Maggie, stop. Don't tell me what to write. I can't just do assignments."

She forced herself to shut up, remembering that he had said several times when he got an idea that seemed right, it was something that just wouldn't let go, and that was the sign that he should write it.

"I need a walk," he said, grabbing up the room key and leaving abruptly.

She wished he would write something easy, accessible, clearly sad or funny, not that strange middle ground. She finished off the bottle of champagne. Well, at least tonight they would go to Frankie and Johnny's for a steak and then to their show, *A Raisin in the Sun,* something serious, and tomorrow to *Gypsy,* something fun.

It was 1960. They'd been married for ten years.

The next morning Harrison went for a walk again.

All he ever wanted to write about was love. And as he walked—and he didn't have time for it today—he wanted to get downtown to look at the place he'd once lived in and at Amanda's address. He was no longer in love with Amanda—but he was in love with the memory of those days when everything was at his fingertips. He had tomorrow afternoon to make that walk and he determined to do it. Maggie would be happy shopping and it would do them good to spend some time apart.

Somebody he didn't even see brushed past him. He had to feel for his wallet since that was a pickpocket's trick. Maggie would tell him, "Use it. Write about a pickpocket."

He walked fast, got jostled a few times, but that was something he was used to, part of the memory.

No, what he wanted to write about was love. People in relationships, hurting each other, forgiving each other. He felt his latest manuscript was good and he decided he would go against Collins' advice and try for an agent with that manuscript.

Walking past all the unlit neon, he toted up his life so far.

He wanted to be making a living. He worked all the time, but he badly needed somebody other than Maggie to be his paymaster. He wanted money to be handed over to him in a check, weekly or monthly, as it had been at the agency job. If he ran for state rep and got elected, that would happen.

He checked his watch and headed back to the hotel. But when he got there, he checked his watch again and sat in the lobby instead of going straight to the room.

A woman handed him a brochure for a gallery opening that night. The thrill he felt looking at the brochure made him know he had to get back to Provincetown and its artists. He would persuade Maggie to make the Cape their vacation trip—instead of going to Virginia to see her mother and brother.

And so began a pattern of expansion over the years, first a week, then two weeks, then a month in Provincetown where Maggie and the kids got suntans and Harrison got a couple of burns. They drove to the ocean side of the Cape most days of the week and frolicked in the bayside the other days. They made a lot of friends and were told that they were lucky, perfect.

Liz, later, thought it *was* true, that they had been a wonderful family, golden, fifty percent of the time at least. Those middle years with all the sameness of daily life made people try to budge this or that to explore (or mourn) paths not taken.

Or maybe it was forty-nine percent happy because something tipped the balance, and it blew up.

16

Midway through summer a few years after Provincetown had been established as the vacation destination, Maggie got a call from her brother. Her mother had come down with some sort of bronchial infection and was taking a long time recovering. Maggie drove south with the kids—a long trip but she kept the car windows open and the radio on.

When they got there, her mother looked at the kids who crowded behind Maggie. "Kids. Go to the kitchen. Cassie has a surprise for you."

Cassie! Maggie started to go too. She had essentially been raised by Cassie.

"Wait." Her mother put out a hand. "In a minute. Sit."

Maggie sat.

"He's not with you."

"He's busy. I didn't need him to drive."

Her mother was tiny and fully gray and pale, all the more so since she'd been sick. She heaved a sigh and said, "He's no good. Just keep being sweet to him; he'll stick with you. That's what I did."

Maggie said, "That's not it. He's busy."

Her mother was still wearing a robe. She looked down at herself and said, "I'm going to put some real clothes on."

Maggie, released, couldn't wait to see Cassie. When she got to the kitchen, her children were eating Whoopie pies and each of them had a mustache of white icing. Cassie was unwrapping the wax paper on another and handing it over shyly to Maggie.

"You get over here," Maggie said, "and hug me first. I never was so glad to see someone." She knew she was going to cry. Her children looked at her curiously, but she didn't care. She hugged Cassie long and hard.

The kids watched as she took a chair and wiped at her eyes. "Yum," she said, diving into the Whoopee pie. "I've had dreams about these things."

Cassie said, "You look good, Miss Maggie."

"Do I? Well, my life is busy. I guess that's the recipe."

"I'll bet. No more acting? I know you were good."

"I didn't love doing it anymore."

"Is that right?"

"It's as if, once I loved a *person*, I didn't love all that theater anymore. I liked it, but I didn't…need it."

"I understand."

"Do you? You were always wonderfully smart about things."

"There's nothing like loving a person. It's what we live for."

Maggie nodded. Perhaps she had come to see Cassie and her mother was simply the excuse.

17

Well done. Your tan conjures John Kennedy," Jack Emory said, post-Provincetown. "We're considering pushing you earlier than we thought. We're going to need you to attend some community gatherings—church suppers and such. See where we are."

The church suppers began. He wanted to eat Maggie's good meals, but he was always stuffed when he got home.

At one church basement while Jack spoke, a very old woman shuffled toward him with two small plates. One held a Jell-O salad and the other a macaroni salad. "These are two of my specialties," she said, beaming. "My kids and my grandkids are crazy for them."

She had a sweet hopeful face and he liked her, and he ate her offerings, saying, "Don't run off. Tell me about your grandkids."

"Oh, they're all grown up now. One sells insurance. One is a mother. The other one, I don't know, various jobs. A guy. He was always a dreamer."

The Jell-O salad was almost good. Banana in lime.

He liked the people who made up the congregation, but many of them looked tired, or was it resigned? He understood the demographic. Most of the wives worked at home all day and the husbands went out to make a living. Some were laborers, others modest white-collar workers. These were not the weekend people Maggie invited to parties.

Jack, about to introduce him, was at the ancient microphone which was screechy.

Though Jack had always lived in upstate New York, he had an almost southern folksy quality when he spoke. He was saying, "We need new blood in the state house, you know. We need some good red Democratic *blood*. I ask you to think hard about what the Republicans have done for you. Nothing. Right? A big nothing. Those roads they were promising to fix? It did not happen. Those additions to the school building? Where are they? And the library is living on donated funds. Yes, thank heaven for our wealthy weekend visitors, and hey, I'm not disparaging them, but we also have a community with a history here and they should feel the library is theirs. Every time you have a frustration in the next year, I want you to say to yourself, 'We need new blood. We need a Democrat.' If we're lucky, we are going to have a Democrat who can do what we need. So, pay attention now and applaud a most wonderful and brilliant man—he's a writer—who is running for office. Wouldn't you like to see Harrison Mirth representing you? He knows you. He likes you. He understands your lives. Stand up, Harrison. I call him Har, even Harry, sometimes for short but it's Harrison. Stand up. Let them see you. Give him your encouragement, if you will."

The applause was loud and genuine.

Yes, it was heady, even this, even church basement fame. He walked up to the mike.

"Yes," he told the audience. "Yes, I do care about making lives better and I want to be your next assemblyman."

They applauded heartily and he told himself this was good, this was what he was supposed to do.

Even though he thought he wouldn't be able to manage it, he began writing furiously every morning, re-imagining the mayor character as instead a political candidate, an old guy in a long-term marriage falling hard for a young woman who was a waitress at the diner he frequented. She was a sweet sad character and he loved writing her scenes.

That summer, one day when Harrison got home from meetings, Maggie sat him down. "You want an iced tea?"

"Why not a seventh glass of tea?" he joked. He felt jazzed up from all the caffeine.

"Seems we got an interesting phone call from your mother."

"Interesting?" He found himself sipping at the tea in spite of himself.

"Well, it seems the theater troupe she's acting in is disbanding for the summer and she has to be somewhere."

"Oh no."

"Oh yes. Now I think she didn't want to say but my guess is the troupe is falling apart. I didn't press your mother on that. By the way I kept calling her *Mother* and she kept asking me to call her Gertrude, so I'd better get used to it."

"Oh God. Just say it."

"Anyway, Gertrude Mirth is coming to stay for the summer. Now we'll be a family of seven, counting Casey."

"We don't have room," he said. "We have to talk her into a sensible plan."

"The kids will have to sleep together in Emma's room."

Funny, Maggie had not offered that solution for him when he needed a room to use as a study. On the other hand, the mudroom had appeal. He liked the smell of it, the fact that it was right off the kitchen, but damn it was cold in winter.

"Just for the summer," she added, aware of the alarm on his face.

He said tersely, "We have to build. It's silly to keep putting it off. We need two more rooms."

She sighed. "I actually wish for three, but I'd take two. I did talk to that guy Greg Johnson a while back. He did the renovation for Sophie and Doug, you know—I liked what he did, didn't you? He made it look like the new parts were there originally. He's expensive. But he's good."

"I could do some of the labor."

"If he lets you."

"Let's just do it, build."

He needed to grow some tough skin too. His mother would blow in and make him feel awful. If there was a phrase that he was likely to hear seven times a day, it was "Oh, Harrison!" He'd either said something naïve or spilled something or married Amanda in his stupid youth or tripped over a rug or…it could be anything. With his kids, too, by the second week, her manner would be corrective.

"I know this is hard," Maggie said. She slid his glass of tea over toward her and sipped. "Jeez, I can't imagine saying no to her. She's your mother! She needs someplace to stay. Right?"

"That's what she said?"

"Um, yes. She made it all very jolly about being with us finally."

"And you already told her yes."

"Well, sort of. I said I'd talk to you. I mean, let's face it. I was cowardly. I know perfectly well you needed a place to stay a thousand times in your childhood and she never did it for you. So, you could conceivably say no."

His mother, to pursue acting, had left him with his grandparents during the school year, or shipped him to his father in summers. But there were times she put him on friends' couches and finally sent him to a badly run boarding school just so she could play some dowager in a play nobody would ever hear of again.

He didn't like the rage that was building in him as he imagined a whole summer with her. He didn't want to boot his mother out. He wanted to *change* her. He wanted to *extract apologies* from her.

"The thing is you're a good person. And so am I. We can't say no."

Maggie was wearing a pinafore apron. She looked pretty and nice and somewhat cowardly.

"Maybe we're just dumb."

She laughed a little. "Dumb and good."

In spite of himself, his thoughts turned to celebratory events, parties and picnics. It was the way his mind worked. His mother could be so charming, so literate, so much the belle of the ball, holding forth wittily about all kinds of things. People up here would love her and she'd be happy with an audience. He was willing to let his kids see her *ambition*, her *energy*, her insistence on making a mark, small as it was. They'd see her determination to do something, to be someone—it would be instructive.

She arrived in May. He and Maggie went to the train station holding on to each other as if a terrible wind were blowing them off balance. And yet when his mother appeared, there was a grin on his face, and he held his arms out wide—his signature gesture. He couldn't help it. He did it with Maggie all the time—in the swimming pool, when she came out of the hairdresser's shop. *Come to me, come to me. I take you in my embrace.* Did he think he was Jesus? Maggie asked him once.

"Hi, Mum, you must be weary."

"I'm not so bad."

"Fighting the good fight."

"Which fight is that?" she asked, untangling from his embrace.

"Against the great unread."

"Ha, that's good. I was sure you were going to say 'unwashed.'"

"That was the intention."

If anything, she looked a little confused. He took her arm. "Car is right over there."

She said, "Maggie, you are a sight for sore eyes. A flowered dress! That is perfect for the season. I think I want one just like that."

"I can show you the shop."

"That would be fantastic."

Maggie said, "I should warn you. We have some banging and sawing going on. It gets kind of noisy."

"Oh dear, headache noisy?"

"Sometimes."

"We can run you over to the library if you like. It might be more peaceful."

"I might very well take you up on that. What are you building?"

"Two more rooms," Harrison said. "I'll show you the plans. I actually designed them. I could have been an architect."

She looked at him skeptically. "That's very mathematical work."

"Harrison is the idea man," Maggie said. "And he's pretty brilliant at it. The other guy does the math. Anyway, are you hungry? It's just omelets and salad and crusty bread for supper. We're very French these days."

"I love a French supper. You married a darling," she told her son. "She does everything right."

Maggie raised her eyebrows for Harrison to see. She knew when she was being flattered by a pro. But she said brightly, "We're having a party for you on Saturday. Our most accomplished neighbors. They'll want to know all about your theater company."

From the series of expressions that passed quickly over his mother's face, Harrison knew Maggie had been right and that the company was either kaput or they had fired her. Exactly how many interesting old women were there to play in a season? He understood that having a forty-year-old who was a whiz with age makeup and could play sixty or thirty was more financially viable than having a sixty-year-old trying to pass as forty. They probably needed someone who could play mothers of teenagers, leading ladies.

"The children are excited to see you," Maggie told Gertrude. "They say everyone else has dull grandmothers who just bake cookies. They have one who bakes *stories*, so to speak—that was Emma, of course."

"I will keep them entertained. Are they still good in school?"

"Sure. Oh yes. They're fantastic."

"Now, are you sending your work out?" Harrison's mother asked him just as they put her in the front passenger seat of the car.

"I did. For a bit. Not now. I met an editor—I think I told you—"

"Yes, you told me he said some nice things."

When Harrison got into the driver's seat, he told his mother, "Well, one of the things this guy Collins wrote in his notes to me is that it generally takes ten to fifteen years to get published. And that most writers have five in the drawer before one gets out."

"Okay, you're thirty-four, no, thirty-six…"

In the rearview mirror, he saw Maggie wince. He said, "Give me two more years before you give up on me."

Later that night Harrison said, "I guess we'll have to take her to Provincetown with us."

"We can't leave her alone with the saws and hammers. Which I am dying to get away from, by the way."

He had begun carrying a table and chair and typewriter out to the pond to write out there. Sometimes the morning dew chilled him. And he was easily distracted by animal life out there. One morning when he was mesmerized by the ducks gliding along in the pond, he went back to the house for his camera. He had black-and-white film and thought the camera might very well catch the way the ripples in the water imitated the visual rhythm of the ducks' feathers. He had tried to describe it, but he also wanted to capture it visually. When he went into town to get the printed photos, the man in the shop told him. "These are good. You do this for a living?"

He laughed, saying, "Why, no!"

"Guess not. You'd have your own darkroom if you did."

Seeds got planted like that. He began to take more photos—of the trees, then of the neighbor's cows, then of people. He *was* good. He caught the people in their most characteristic expressions; his pictures made windows right into their souls.

"The kids need new bathing suits, but I guess we can buy up there. You need a new one too," Maggie said.

"Do I? I'm not particular."

"Your old one has a tear down the back, shows your butt. Anyway, I'll start packing this week. Should I pack you some film? Pack your camera?"

"You can pack film. I'll be using the camera this week."

He had been thinking about installing a darkroom, but he didn't want to say just yet. It would have to go in the basement, with a wall partitioning off a section. It *could* be done. More building! It would cost. The thought stayed up on a shelf until it might be time to take it down.

He reached for Maggie, began to take off her nightgown by pulling a section down over her shoulder. He kissed her shoulder, then moved to her breast."

"On a Sunday!" she said.

"Never say we have no flexibility."

"Stop. I need to get my diaphragm. I love our kids, but I don't want another now. And you—Mr. Fertility."

The unhappy interruption made Harrison lose the moment, the naturalness of their talking about their combined lives, the sweet mood she was in, the look of her almost exposed shoulder. Now she came back to bed, trying too hard, making a joke of pulling her nightgown off one shoulder. He had to figure out how to get his desire back, but a part of him wanted to remember this delicate situation, how, whether bad or good or neither, desire came to him, a normal male, when the prey was innocent and unsuspecting. He knew a lot of men were like him, needing discovery, exploration, predation, shitty as that was, maybe, to feel sexy.

He worked on inching her gown up from the bottom. Desire hiccoughed to a return and he managed a pretty good session in spite of the early interruption, and when they finished, they lay still for a while.

Half their friends were getting divorced. It was the high season for partings, it seemed. Even some old folks were getting divorced. Maggie had told him their neighbor John was going to have to pay Susan $300 per month in alimony, but the amount was supposed to go up as he figured out some long-term investments. Harrison couldn't help imagining (as he supposed Maggie did also) what a judge would order him to do, were they to divorce. If he had $300 a month (neither he nor Maggie kept track of the transfers of money), it was for the work he did on the house and grounds. If a judge threw up his hands and said she must not give him money, she would have to hire someone to do the things that needed to be done, certainly at a much greater cost. The judge might order Harrison to become a trucker or a mailman to provide alimony. Or would it work that way? That's what he thought about as they lay side by side in the summer heat.

As he imagined this alternate future, the idea of being a trucker or mailman, meeting people, having adventures, writing at rest stops, excited him. He couldn't get himself to sleep from thinking himself into that life.

Maggie was awake too. She said, "We'll have fun in Provincetown. We'll be relaxed. You can take pictures."

"Sure can."

If things went right, he was going to be an assemblyman. Every day he did some work on the house. He was writing. He was 'taking pictures,' as Maggie had phrased it. A literary agent he had written to had agreed to represent him. Fred Lewis. The road signs were all good.

Harrison wasn't a praying man, but he sent up a wish that something, something to do with his writing, would break soon.

Maggie said in a sleepy voice, "I really like our builders. Especially Marshall. Such a nice guy. I'm glad I baked. They absolutely loved the cookies."

He'd tasted the really chunky tollhouse cookies as they came out of the oven. Maggie had to keep a fan on her as she stood waiting for them to brown. The fan turned, stopped, thought about it, and turned back the other way. It was his old one, tentative, the secondhand one he'd bought in the city when he was with Amanda. He supposed they needed a new one for the kitchen.

He imagined Maggie running off with Marshall. Or rather Marshall moving in, pushing him out. Marshall would work at other jobs during the day and take care of their property at night and cheerfully adopt the kids. Maggie would persuade Marshall he didn't need to work elsewhere. She could cover it all, she could pay him. Harrison would be allowed to visit his kids, but mostly he'd live in the city again. Maggie would always be nice to him and he to her.

Escape fantasies—everybody had them, right?

This was still long before the tractor accident.

18

July was hot and by then Gertrude had worn out Harrison and Maggie. They snuck off midweek to go into the city.

They had dinner with Oscar and Betty and heard about Oscar's adventures with celebrities—mixed briefcases, cancelled fights, always something of a comic struggle.

On the second day there, after breakfast, Maggie snuggled back in to read.

"Mind if I take a walk then?" Harrison asked.

"Not at all."

He made his way downtown, stopping at the Chelsea Hotel where his mother and father had lived for five years and where he had spent some days in summers as a boy. He stood in the lobby and looked at the familiar walls, floors, ceiling light fixtures, elevators. The desk clerks were busy, and they probably wouldn't remember him. He soaked it in and, after a while, he just left.

Next, he made it to City Hall Park to wander and sit, after that to the Woolworth building, then to Vesey Street and had a cup of coffee over which he lingered as long as he felt able, and finally down to his old apartment. How could a person be nostalgic for the hallway bathroom, the shared refrigerator, the tiny space he had once called home? Foolishness. Of course, it was foolishness. He now had a luxurious bed, several sofas to choose from, a brilliantly stocked kitchen, and acres, acres of land—which he quickly reminded himself he was responsible for.

When he approached the newsstand at the corner of Houston and Varick, he was thrilled to see the same ancient owner of the stand, a bald man who wore an apron, whose fingernails were dirty, but who had a most cheerful disposition, rain, shine, or snow.

"Hi! It's me. Visiting."

He saw immediately that he was not remembered. Before he could feel embarassed, the man said, "Remind me. Tell me when and where."

Harrison pointed. "Used to live up there, fourth floor. Worked as a press agent and a deli clerk. I brought you some pastrami once."

"Of course," said the cheerful man. "I never forget a feed! How are things?"

"Wonderful. Terrific. Three kids. Moved up north two hours away."

"They do. They do."

"Some of us do, yes." Harrison bought a paper even though he'd already read it in the Algonquin lobby. He moved onto the corner across the street and just stood there for a while, taking it in. The vacuum cleaner shop had become an Asian takeout place and the hardware store had become a stationery store. In place of a million dusty bolts and nuts in bins were now polished counters featuring embossed linen papers.

He wasn't a churchgoer though his grandparents were Catholic. Because he had never, when he lived there, out of some odd fear of being pulled back to religiosity, entered Our Lady of Pompeii, he had always walked around it, passing the old men and babushkaed women streaming into it. This time, he went in.

He caught his breath. There was statuary and painting *every-where*—right, left, above him. He thought, "Man, those Italians. They just keep making art." He sat in a pew and looked at the painted images on the ceilings, but for some reason, fan of painting though he was, he was more captivated today by the sculpted figures—life-like, blue-robed figures some artists had carved. He could see how those figures helped belief that the dead, the unmoving, could somehow live forever.

It made him miss his father.

Amanda's street was the last place he visited. He didn't think about her much anymore, but he wished her well. He supposed she lived somewhere else now. He had made her up, he understood that.

On impulse he went to a phone booth to check on her current address. The phone books, hanging by chains were tattered. There was always the chance that the page you needed was the one someone had put gum on or torn out. But he had luck. He found her name. Yes, she had moved. To an apartment in the Chelsea area. He put in a dime and made the call. Her phone rang twenty times, no answer. Of course, she was at work.

She'd probably had three promotions by now. He retrieved his dime and called *Time*. A grouchy operator put him through to some desk or other where the person who answered said, "Everybody is at lunch. Call back."

He considered the subway back to the hotel but decided to walk. He was a very fast walker. Unfortunately, he saw a diner on the way with a chalkboard advertising a hot beef sandwich special. Of course, Maggie would need lunch, but he couldn't beat down the craving for a good old grandmother-style hot roast beef sandwich with gravy. He took a stool at the counter and indulged.

While he ate, he watched a gorgeous young woman with long black hair torture a horny guy who didn't seem up to the challenge. The young man's eyes almost closed several times with the exhaustion of fending off desire in a public location. Oh, she swung her hair, nudged him, smiled, scolded, in such a profusion of expressions that Harrison dug into his pocket for the notebook he was committed to carrying and he wrote about these two, thinking that perhaps he could use this impossibly flirtatious young woman to shape out his waitress character.

With a loaded belly, he walked back uptown, arriving at 1:30 at the hotel. "Sorry I'm late. I'll take you to lunch."

"No need. I ordered a sandwich from downstairs."

She was still reading, propped up in bed, reading John Updike.

She was in the middle of the bed so he couldn't slide in beside her. "Tell me something."

"This book is pretty damned good."

He stood at the window looking down at traffic. "Tell me something else."

"We're going to have to pull weeds when we go back."

"I know." He did know. That was real life.

19

D oor to door," Jack Emory instructed him. "Personal contact." It meant Harrison had to leave the weeding to a hired boy, but at least the garden had yielded some beautiful produce and Maggie was still harvesting.

It suited him, talking to people.

One day he tapped on the door of a frame house that had a fence needing a coat of paint. A woman wearing a loose dress and a sweater came to the door, carrying a broom. "What is it?" she said irritably—and called back toward the kitchen to say, "Stay out of there. You hear? Let me see you on the stairs. Don't go near the kitchen." To Harrison, she said, "My kid broke a glass. I have to sweep it up. What is it?"

"The vote is coming up in a month. I'm running for office." He handed her two brochures and a card with his photo. "I can't— Look, let me get the broken glass for you."

"No. Why would you?"

"I do it with my kids all the time."

She let him in, and he went straight to the kitchen with her broom and began cleaning up, not only the glass, but the spilled milk. Twin boys stood at the door watching him soberly.

"Oh, don't, that's my good dishtowel— Never mind." She took the kids to the stairs and gave them each a lollypop.

"Who's that man?" Harrison heard.

"Just some politician."

Just was a word he hated. A speech formed in his mind, a speech he planned to use. He rinsed the good dishtowel out in the sink, watching the water run white. "Can you talk for a minute?"

"A minute, yes."

"You told your kids I was 'just some politician.' That's the last thing I want to be. I'm a family man, I'm a writer, I'm a photographer, and I happen to be running for Assembly because I think I can do some good. I hate to say squeaky wheel on top of everything else, but I might have to be that."

She stared at him.

"Do you vote?"

"Usually. Not always for Assembly though."

"I'm hoping you will."

"Do you…want a cup of coffee?"

"A wee one. I have lots of houses to go to."

"What happens when you go to the other houses?"

"People generally stop what they're doing and give me a listen."
She poured him a half-cup. "And you have kids?"

"Three. Two girls, one boy."

"It's a lot of work, isn't it?"

"Yes."

"What kind of writer are you?"

"Novels."

"Really?"

"Yes. Call me an apprentice, but very serious."

"Do you write about other times? Kings?"

He laughed to think of what he would write if he had that sort
of imagination. "Afraid not. Just regular people. Like people living up
here, mostly." He forced himself to finish the coffee. "I should go. Do
vote—I hope for me."

She nodded. "Mirth. I'll remember that name. Doesn't it mean—?"

"Laughter, sort of, yes. Kind of high spirits."

He bid her goodbye. He felt so bad for women stuck at home. He
tried to canvass in the evenings, too, so he could meet the men. What
he thought he saw was consistent determination among the people up
here to be responsible and grown up and a decent citizen, and most
terrifying of all, he saw boredom.

He tried to do fifty contacts every afternoon and church dinners and
any other large gatherings in the evenings or another fifty contacts. He
gained ten pounds, which he realized when his pants didn't button easily
and in one case not at all. He also suffered from indigestion—which
was odd since he had a steel drum of a stomach.

Jack Emory told him, "We have a chance. I don't know percentages
yet, but, informally, people are telling me it looks close."

He had always thought he had endless energy but at four in the
morning when he woke to write, he always wished for two more hours
of sleep.

His mother had found a small apartment in Pine Plains and got some
work as a substitute teacher at the school, and *that* thrilled his daughters.
They kept hoping one day they would have a teacher out with a sore

throat and there'd be Grandma in the classroom! She had applications out for full-time jobs at other places away from Pine Plains. She was definitely a worker.

He met his mother for lunch on a Thursday in Pine Plains when there were no sore throats or other ills to give her employment.

Their waitress wore a starched pink uniform that strained at the waist. She offered them a grim expression as she rattled through her speech: "We have an egg salad, tuna salad combo on special today. All the usuals, too, BLT, club, burger."

His mother looked good, cheerful, in her fall dress and sweater. Her hair was getting quite gray now and she pinned it back into a low knot at her neck, accepting this latest role, rural schoolteacher.

They ordered a BLT and a club, Cokes, water (Harrison had had fourteen cups of coffee this morning already). He really could not finish all of them—and had to beg entrance to six or so bathrooms. Desperation of any sort didn't look good on a candidate.

"I see your picture everywhere," his mother said. "I've been getting the local paper of course, keeping up, and you are always in it. Every day."

"Well, I write the press releases!"

"Ha. Good trick. I never thought you could do all this. Do you like it?"

"Pretty well."

"What happens if you lose?"

"Well, I would still do work for the party."

"Sounds positively Communist!" she declared.

"Don't!" he shushed her. "You don't know how seriously people take that threat."

"I do know. The whole theater and movie industry is still reeling."

The tough waitress in her starched pink delivered their drinks, which his mother downed in seconds. "Ah, I was thirsty. Look at that waitress. Sour puss. Letting herself go."

"Do you ever think you'll perhaps date someone again?" Harrison asked his mother.

"Good heavens, no. Why do you ask?"

"I wondered if you get lonely. I mean Pop has been gone."

"But I loved him."

"Did you?"

"His mind. A fascinating man. He found me fascinating too."

Harrison wasn't sure he believed her. He'd hardly known her, growing up. And his parents were rarely together. Now, there she was a few
miles from him, and she still revealed little about herself.

"Are you gaining weight?" she asked.

"A bit. But I'm not a sour puss."

"You have to watch that."

He laughed.

"What are you laughing about?"

"Nothing. I don't know. I really don't." *Her.* His mother. She was
consistent at any rate.

"You aren't going to go crazy, are you?"

He shrugged. "Probably. Someday I'm going to explode. I can feel
it building."

"Good heavens."

A different waitress, same uniform, approached him. "Excuse me.
I know you're in politics. I heard you speak at my church and I just
wanted to say I'm going to vote for you."

"Thank you. Just a couple weeks to go! Thank you!"

"I know. My sister has a crush on you."

"Aw, thank her. That's sweet."

"You are married though, aren't you?"

"Oh yes."

"She told me to check."

"Well, yes, I really am."

"Oh, well. Okay, then." She smiled and went off.

"Temptation, temptation," his mother sang.

"Two votes. I sometimes feel I'm counting them."

"Oh, the Republicans have this county sewed up. But it's good to see
a Don Quixote every once in a while."

He paid the check. Oh, he knew his mama. She'd suggested the lunch,
but she was probably figuring it in as a free meal. She was negative and a
skinflint and probably afraid of just about everything and everyone, but
he felt a need to protect her from herself.

"What's this afternoon?" she asked.

"Door to door."

"Sometimes I think how your father reached thousands of people
with a single article. Maybe you might take up political writing."

She stood at the doorway to the diner without realizing she was blocking people trying to exit. He moved her aside a little. She carried a huge handbag. What did she need to keep with her all the time?

"I think I'm going to relocate," she said when she realized he wasn't about to defend his wish to write fiction. "Possible job in Philly."

"Doing what?"

"Teaching acting. I know how to teach it."

"Do you know anyone in Philly?"

She shook her head. "A person has to be brave."

Maggie got his mother to babysit on election night and went with him to the smoke-filled back room of the bar Emory had said was the place to be. Jack Emory was already there with several cronies. They kept ordering beers and toasting Harrison as the rumors swelled: *He got it. He didn't get it. He got it.* Somebody Harrison had never met said he personally knew ten folks who had always voted Republican and were going for Mirth this time.

Maggie knew Harrison's mother told him he was going to lose. Maggie insisted he was going to win, but in her heart, she felt the tug of premonition. Still she had a gift for him, a big surprise.

When the votes were finally in, it turned out that Harrison had lost by 900 votes. It was the closest a Democrat had ever come to winning the seat.

In her cups, she stood up somewhat unsteadily and gave a toast. "It's hard being part of a party that always loses up here but has conviction and will and spirit. And is *in the right.* I continue to be proud."

People applauded. Jack toasted her for her generosity.

Then Harrison took the microphone. "Thank you for believing in me," he said to the whole room. "I hope our standing, our 'almost' win will make a difference. You've all been wonderful, and I thank you."

Cheers and applause. God, he did love that part of it. Maggie came to him and he put an arm around her.

"How do you feel?" she whispered when the hubbub died down.

"Lousy. And sad."

"Should we go?"

"Not yet. I can't leave." People kept coming up to him and touching him—hand, shoulder, head. "Oh, oh, well," he would say to John or Martin or Peggy, to all of them, "let's keep fighting." Between handshakes and hugs, he told Maggie, "I'm trying to hold on to names and faces. I don't want to come up empty if I run into someone who worked on the campaign." He added wistfully, "They liked me."

"Well, you're very likeable."

Things finally quieted down. "Let's get some air," she said.

They drifted outside. Maggie unearthed a pack of cigarettes and the red leather lighter he'd bought her. She'd quit but was back on it lately. He took the lighter and fired her up, then unearthed a cigar from his pocket—saying, "Celebratory, you know, and I don't even like the damned things." He lit it anyway.

Maggie could hardly breathe. She'd been holding in her secret, what she now hoped would cheer him. She said, "I have a surprise for you. I bought us something. For you. Well, rented, I guess is the correct word."

He frowned mightily. "Someplace for the summer on the Cape?"

"No, but we'll have that too."

"Good golly, Mollie, what?"

But she could see his eyes were moving fast, taking in the truth. After digging into her handbag and producing a key, she said, "A *pied a terre*. For us. West Village. Weekends. I rented for a year and a half. I'm committed to getting you there just about every weekend."

He collapsed against the building, neon yellow light now splashing on his face.

"We gotta move back there," he said.

Maggie panicked. She knew her face showed horror, but she couldn't live in the city. She had the gorgeous house and grounds, a life she could control. "It's not a place for kids," she said.

"Oh, sure it is. I know plenty of people who bring up kids there. Randolph and Sarah do. Oscar and Betty."

"Well, we'll need another time to talk about this, then. Tonight is not the night. But we do have a place, an apartment for two to enjoy. Please say you're happy."

"I've just lost an election and I can't quite take it in, any of it, tonight or the future." He kissed her. "I can't believe it. What's it like?"

"Bedroom, living room, kitchen. I snuck in one day and looked at it. The previous tenant was a successful academic at NYU, but she got another job, in Texas, I think, and she wanted to be rid of all her furniture. I took it. It's not bad. I mean we can replace, but she was a nice old gal and pretty clean. Greens. Sofa and armchair, kind of muted sage greens. Bookcases. That's a plus. Double bed. Fairly well-equipped kitchen—not that I ever feel like cooking in the city."

"I am so…"

"You'll miss the Algonquin, I know, but no reason you can't take a book and hang out there."

"When do we go?"

"This weekend."

He smiled slowly. "I know you thought of it as a victory prize…"

"You're still a hero."

"A Don Quixote anyway. Right now, I have to spend some time with Jack before we go home. He gave me his all. He's the real thing."

He went inside while she went to sit in the car. She was shaking from having given her little performance. And she was wobbly, a bit drunk. She knew he needed the city, so she gave it to him.

One day Harrison dug a box out of a drawer in his desk and came up with three lapel buttons. There he was, younger, his face as it had been when he ran for office. "What do I do with these?" he asked Liz.

She took them and examined them. "Would you have been good?"

"I think so. Tireless anyway."

She put two buttons in her pocket and pinned one on her sweater. How differently their lives would have turned out had he been elected. She would probably never have met him. She figured the election might have been the halfway point, the crisis point, when Maggie, to keep him, had sent him into Manhattan for a taste of independence and youth. It was a peripety—a reversal of intention, according to Aristotle, the point at which direction changes.

20

The next weekend Maggie showed him the *pied a terre*. They got in on Friday at one. She encouraged him to use his key so he would feel ownership of the place.

When he opened the door, there weren't any lights on and it was not the brightest apartment, close as it was to another building. Plus, it was a gray day outside. But he went around eagerly turning on lamps. "I'll put a mirror here and here," he said, pointing to two walls. "We'll catch what light there is." Oddly most of the light was in the bedroom. "Maybe shutters. Or blinds. I'll figure it out."

He bounced on the bed once, pronounced it good, and hurried back out to the living area, taking a long look at the kitchen table. "Maybe I'll keep the smaller typewriter here and some paper. There's still room to eat."

"But we love breakfast out. There's a good greasy spoon next door, did you notice? That's one of the reasons I took this."

"I did notice. Oh, this is grand. I wish I'd brought the typewriter this trip. I have my journal though."

"I take it you like it?" she teased.

"My God, Maggie, it's…thank you for this. It's the best thing you could have done. Ever." Well, no, he didn't quite mean it because she read the expression crossing his face. In her mind, she heard him say what he didn't say, *The best thing would be to buy a brownstone and move the kids here and set them up in a good school. The best thing would be to hobnob with other artists and go to the theater three times a week and to lectures and jazz two times a week.*

He had told her once that he wished she were more flirtatious. He said, well, it…did something to him. It was chemical and primitive and that was just how things were.

She refused to bat her eyes—that was going too far. But she ran her hands over his body—it was a very nice body—and then she stopped suddenly, so he would want more. She wasn't great at sexy, girlish behavior, but she gave it a go.

Her timing was off. He was thinking about work. He kissed her on the forehead. "Thank you," he said. "I feel overwhelmed. I don't know how to tell you. I feel so…"

Far away from the election, she hoped. Far away from despair, she hoped.

She went out for some groceries and was quick about it. When she got back, she caught him writing something and saw that as he wrote he was close to crying.

Liz was sure she would like Maggie. She was also sure she would be afraid of her. The time to test that was when Thomas was graduating from vet school and everybody gathered for the ceremony. Liz found herself saying dumb things, like, "Great to be in the city for a weekend," and Maggie said things like, "I have to shop for a Pooh bear, just the right one," and Liz said, "I'm sure you'll find something nice," and Maggie said in her most withering voice, "I'm not looking for *nice.*"

She liked her and was afraid of her. A correct prediction.

21

Between November 1961 and 1963 he spent most weekends in the city, always taking his work, always working. He managed each spring to get seedlings going in the house, to dig up the earth so the robins could find the worms, and generally to make a presence, so the neighbors knew he was still in charge. When the manure of the guy in the next property (not Wilson, the other side, Fentek) leached down to the stream and poisoned the trout, he called in the experts and got verification of the problem. "Don't take him to court," Maggie said. "He's a neighbor!"

He didn't. But he got the man to quit poisoning the stream the next year. He still split and stacked the firewood.

Casey was a good dog, nuts with joy when Harrison was there, sad and slowed down when he was not, spending much of his time sitting at the window, waiting.

Maggie went with Harrison to the city each weekend for a while, but the girls needed her, so then it was every other weekend, and then they took the kids with them a couple of times but that was too crowded and soon it was more like once a month that she got there. They talked by phone every day.

It was okay; she had him home during the week. She would embrace him from behind when she brought him a tea or coffee in the new study where he was set up to work at the house upstate. The weekend absences made their hearts grow fonder.

He listed the shows he saw and showed her the pages he had written there.

In the city, he often had lunch with Oscar Brandt. God, the people Oscar knew—Uta Hagen, Spencer Tracy. Oscar had to attend events multiple times a week because famous people apparently adored him and asked him to everything. All the big show biz names needed lawyers at some point. Not only did Oscar have a great reputation, but he was a man who liked to please everyone, therefore was always running to take care of someone or something. Though he was heavyset, he was always beautifully dressed and as graceful in his movements as if he'd been trained for the stage or for dancing. His face was a jowly version of kind. He was definitely the savior in a Dickens novel—the solid guy who rescues the orphan.

Harrison had just arrived in Manhattan on Friday November 22, looking forward to a cocktail or two with Oscar, when he discovered the city had gone crazy. All plans were off. All lives were altered.

On the street, friends were collapsing against each other. Strangers were trading information of which there was little. Harrison asked a stranger what was going on.

Jack Kennedy had been shot.

He had to find a television store to watch the news. He borrowed their phone to leave a message for Oscar that he was cancelling their plan and getting the train for home.

On the train, there was no information, only talk, conjecture, misinformation. When he was almost home, the conductor made an announcement. "The president is dead. The doctors in Dallas confirmed it. They could not save him." Silence first. Then expressions of disbelief and some sounds of weeping.

When he walked into the house, he discovered the children had been sent home from school. He searched for what calm he could find—children needed that. "They couldn't save him," he said quietly. "I think it was a good hospital. I think they did everything right."

"Now what will happen?"

"Now we'll have another president. Johnson. That's how it works."

They could hardly get a moment of silence before the phone calls started. Maggie's mother. Friends. Oscar called to say he'd gotten Harrison's message and that he was as shaken as he'd ever been over anything. Maggie called her brother and Harrison called his mother, then Jack Emory.

Jack was crying, trying to get the words out. "He was…oh, you know what I mean. People loved him."

"I know. He wasn't all we…never mind. I know."

"A symbol," Jack said, "of a certain kind of person who knew the world and who had a good mind."

"I know."

"Like you."

"No, please, I don't stack up."

"You do. You could…"

"I'll keep working for you but I'm a writer. That's what I'm meant to do."

"I never do understand all that."

"I have an agent now."

"Is that good?"

"Very good. It's…hope. Keys to the doors."

"This Kennedy business…I don't think Johnson can do it, do you?"

"We have to hope he can."

"Come have dinner," Maggie said. They all went to the dining room.

By seven that evening Maggie was telling friends, "I'll cook tomorrow. I have plenty. Come over." They kept the television on all evening and even when they lowered it to talk on the phone, it was there, a constant murmur. "Why did we invite people over tomorrow?" she muttered, moving in a daze. "I guess I needed to do something." She made a long list of foods and liquors they had to buy for the next day.

And that was her comfort, being a hostess.

The television continued news coverage late into the night. Any place there was a television, people were watching. Was this the 'world soul' he'd read about?

The next night, there were twenty people at their house.

Harrison kept making and serving drinks, mostly whiskey and water, whiskey and soda. Maggie had made three meatloaves and a vat of mashed potatoes and there was also bread and gravy for those who wanted the hot sandwich experience. The guests mostly attended to the TV.

Sophie came to him. "Bourbon?"

"Yeah. Could we go out to the gazebo again?" she asked.

He didn't want to, but she was crying a little and it didn't seem right to say no.

When they sat, she took his hand and held it tight. "We're finally getting a divorce," she said. "I knew it was coming eons ago and it finally arrived."

"Oh, I'm sorry to hear that."

"He wants to marry the skinny co-worker, not the gorgeous one I thought was the problem. It's like an epidemic. We know four couples getting divorced. We trade recommendations for lawyers."

"The kids?"

"That's the thing. We want to share them so that means I get them during the week, and he gets them weekends. And summers to make up for the number of days. He wants me to move to New York and just make it easier on all of us."

"Will you do that? Move?" he asked. Two apartments in New York, he thought. That's how it was done.

"I might. Are you staying married?"

"Yes," he said. "Seems so."

"How do you do it?"

"I don't know."

"Maggie is such a good sport. I guess that's it. I'm not. I'm a complainer."

He laughed, nodding.

"What do you do in the city when you're there?"

"Write and walk and go to shows."

"Girlfriends?"

"No."

"You've had offers?"

"A few."

"I don't get it."

"Actually, I don't either."

She punched him lightly on the arm. "You're sort of a true-blue stalwart or something."

"The city is good for me," he said to shift the subject. "I get a lot of work done. I now have an agent and he's shopping my novel around. It used to be an old mayor and a waitress and now it's a young mayor and a waitress. Otherwise, a pretty total remake. I've actually started another—well, it's a new version of an old idea. It's all about revision, scavenging."

"What happens in your mayor book?"

"The usual. Love. And people doing bad things to other people. Listen, I should get back inside. I have to find more bourbon somewhere. We went through all I bought yesterday."

"You're very generous, both of you. I'll bring two bottles next time I come over."

"Not necessary."

"I want to. Maggie is really such a good sport. She's been serving us all evening. Those little mushroom puffs…"

"She likes doing it." He chewed his lip, thinking how nervous Maggie was. Underneath her cheer was the worry that people might not love her if she didn't entertain and treat on a constant basis.

He had ideas, things he didn't dare say to an outsider, about his need to make a salary and to live on just what he made. He and Maggie had

had huge arguments before—*You only want a field hand, you don't love me so don't pretend you do.* And her saying, *You have some allergy to money, something perverse in you, like you don't think you should be treated well. You're plain nuts. Why don't you want to live well?* And he would counter, *I'm a servant. It's an awful feeling.* Only to hear, *You think that's different in corporate America, and you think that's different in politics? How can you write anything very good if you remain naïve?*

He only knew that in the city, his heart soared. Ideas came faster. When, last month, he sold four photographs through a company that accepted him as one of their stock photographers, he took the money with such joy, and everything he bought with it, including a scarf for Maggie glowed with significance. It was a Friday, and he took himself out to dinner, just a simple roast beef dinner but it tasted special the night he got paid.

It would be stupid to tell Sophie, who was in a needy state, that he knew one day all his springs would pop and, well, he would go crazy, he knew he would.

The next week, with the world focused on the loss of Kennedy, Harrison spent some time with Jack Emory, doing his best to say the right things. "I'll keep working. I'll write what you need me to write."

"Run again."

He shook his head.

They were in Jack's basement where the cigar smoke was almost unbearable. Harrison was just about to make an excuse to go outside when Jack's phone rang and after answering, he covered the receiver and whispered, "Wife tracked you down." It was like the routine at bars, wives calling to demand their husbands get home to dinner or to some task or other, but Maggie never did things like that.

Harrison took the phone and listened. He was supposed to call his agent, Fred Lewis, she said.

"Now?"

"Yes. What does it mean?" Maggie asked.

"I don't know." He took a big breath.

"Do you have his number?"

"Yeah. Back of my journal." He tapped the notebook in his pocket though he was pretty sure he remembered the number.

"Call me back."

"I will."

"Bad? Good?" Jack asked.

"Not sure."

Jack hobbled across the room to the basement refrigerator, which held mostly beer, to give Harrison some privacy as he dialed the number.

When Fred answered, he said, "Well, about time. I'm feeling pretty excited here. Got you an offer. Simon and Schuster. They want this novel and another one in a year."

Harrison shouted. It was an odd sound, almost a roar. It froze Jack to his spot.

Fred continued. "Yeah. Let it out. We can get some time on that deadline if we need it, but we're in business. They plan to give you the treatment—photographers and features, the works. You know, 'best new writer to come along in ten years' and all that."

Harrison was stupefied, having been full of grief because of the assassination and now it seemed almost wrong to get good news. "I need a minute," he said. His voice sounded odd to him as if he had a cold. "I can't believe it. I mean I do, but…"

"Believe me, I know. You work for fifteen years or so and you pretty much wonder if you're deceiving yourself. But you're not. You're good, really good, and people are going to know it."

"When do you want me to come in?" It was Thursday.

"Let's target a week from now, next Thursday. Signing and planning. Meetings basically, people meeting you. Ad campaign guy. Photographer, all that."

"Next Thursday. Okay."

"Go have a drink. We'll have a few ourselves when we meet. Celebrate, my good man. This is it."

Jack grabbed Harrison and hugged him and kept patting at his back. "I'm happy for you, son," he said.

With a furious energy in the next days, Harrison did everything around the house and grounds that he could think to do. He made sure there was enough firewood to get them through the winter. He went into the city earlier than he had to, on Tuesday, to get himself in the right frame of mind to meet whomever he had to meet to get his career going. The first piece of mail he got in the city was that four more photographs had sold.

He stared at the notice, terrified of good fortune. Were the gods tricking him?

Too scattered to work on his current manuscript, he grabbed his camera and went looking for pictures—which were, in a way, a second journal. He didn't know it, but he was on his way to a series of people he got enchanted by—a scrubbed-up Jewish deli owner surveying his cases (not Schwartz but a different owner whose expression drew Harrison into his shop), the newspaper seller he knew and loved with hands grimed by newsprint, a woman with stout legs who handed out doughnuts as if they were prizes.

The photography was a terrific boon to his spirits, but it got second place. It was an "instead of" when he wasn't writing. "I'm a writer," he said to himself as he walked and focused and snapped. "Honest to God, I'm a writer."

The photographer who came to Fred Lewis's office was a woman. She gave Harrison a once-over and said, "I don't think you should have a city photo. What's this farm I hear about?"

He described the house, the grounds, the trees he'd planted, wondering what she would choose.

"Sounds glorious."

"Stark sometimes in winter," he explained. "Gorgeous in spring."

She had an interesting job, which is what he wanted for his daughters. This woman was out in the world, being a part of it. She was maybe thirty, maybe forty. She wore no makeup that he could see, but she was attractive, partly because of her energy and the confidence she gave off.

She had her own notebook out and she was writing, then tapped her pen and squinted. "They won't need the photos till spring. You'll have editing and copyediting and all that to keep you busy anyway. Let's get you under the trees. Or at the woodpile. Right? Man of the soil and yet he can write." She turned to Lewis who gave her a nod to continue. "Sell him as the man who lives the dream—a peaceful place in nature in which to let his poetic imagination soar."

Fred said, "I think that's great. That's why I always ask for you."

It wasn't quite like that, poetry and trees, Harrison thought, but he didn't say.

She said, "I'll come up to your farm. What a treat for me. We'll choose a shirt or sweater. Show me what you have when I get there. Now just be aware I'm going to take a lot of pictures. Your job is to be calm and let me. I'm going to want to catch the…for lack of a better word, a *natural* look."

"I understand. I'm a photographer."

"Truly?"

"I sell through Cantor and Jenkins."

"Oh, terrific. Terrific. You'll completely get it, then."

Fred took him to dinner on the house, as he put it, and they had several martinis each, Fred's favorite drink. "Man, you write sexy stuff," he said. "I love it, all that attention to a woman's thighs, backside, breasts. That's some maddening, appealing woman you created. Readers are going to love it."

"I hope so."

Harrison felt those three martinis and the headiness of his new success so when he dropped his token in the subway slot, eager to get back to the little apartment, he lost his balance in a vertiginous turn from the stile as the train came whizzing in.

But somehow, bouncing along, holding the strap above him, he began budgeting. If he found a cheaper apartment and paid the rent for it himself, it would be the mark of what he did with his new income, the advance, plus some each month from the photographs. He couldn't know if it could hold him until the next advance or the royalties came in, so that part was hopeful guessing. But it was like the old days, poor but independent. Working out the figures, he thought he ought to eat out less. And clothes—he never cared about them anyway—his old ones were plenty good.

He went out searching the very next day. The place he found was on Second Avenue and Eighth Street, just in from the corner, second floor. There was plenty of room for Maggie when she came in and the sofa and some cushions or sleeping bags would do for the kids on the occasions they got to the city. He would sleep in the larger bedroom; the small one would be his workspace; and he had a good kitchen and living room. There was a cheap hamburger place next door that had other sorts of specials. The owners were Mexican, but the menu was totally American, a shame though the offerings were well-done, plentiful and cheap. The apartment was also right next to a movie theater—what could be better?

Maggie might like the old apartment better—it had a more respectable address, but this cheaper location had life. He could feel a vibration coming up off the pavement. Poverty, he laughed. It was true. He loved it.

He went to his old deli to visit Schwartz to tell him the good news about the publishing contract and to ask about getting some hands to move the furniture from one apartment to another.

As they talked, Harrison was seeing change was inevitable. Everywhere. There was still sawdust on the floor, but the workers now wore white shirts and green aprons; the butcher paper signs were gone, replaced by lacquered white boards with looped letters in red and black.

Eventually Harrison and Schwartz stood outside in the back, smoking as they had fifteen years ago.

"What, you've left the wife?"

"No, I just work in the city. Like a lot of folks."

Schwartz raised his eyebrows. "I remember when she came in the store, looking for you one day. I could see there was trouble."

"Oh, that wife. Yeah, there was. No, I have a second wife, Maggie. You met her."

"Where is she?"

"Up north. Beautiful house. Lots of land."

Schwartz nodded for a long time. "You're a city boy."

"I guess I am. I can appreciate the other when it doesn't exhaust me."

"Of course. Let's get you some cheap labor. You aren't a rich writer yet."

"Not yet."

Two clerks liked to make extra money and they had two friends with a truck, so it was settled, all in an afternoon. He was moving.

He told Maggie after he did it when there was no point in arguing.

He had his radio for company. When he wasn't writing or sprinting out to photograph a bridge or a person, he listened to his favorite stations, writing down lists of the music he loved and determined to own when he could. DeKoven drove him nuts. Just when Harrison was immersed in the rhythm and melody of a passage, the disk jockey would stop the music to pontificate. But Harrison kept tuning in. Either that or the jazz station, a substitute for going out to hear live jazz.

Maggie came to look at the new place. "It's okay," she said, "I mean, it's fine. But if I paid for the old one—"

"I sublet the other one. The checks will go to you."

"I mean, don't be silly, why don't I just pay for this one?"

"I want to pay for it. I want to."

She went out shopping and filled the refrigerator with groceries.

22

He started to spend more of his week in New York. One day, before the novel was out but after the publicity machine had started, Harrison decided to call Amanda. He called after supper and she answered right away. "I've seen the press releases," she said. "I saw them at work when I was running through a bunch of stuff. I think we're going to review you. Which is a big deal, I hope you know."

"I know."

"They say no to 99 percent. I was going to find a way to write to you to say congratulations. So, anyway, congratulations."

"Thank you. And you? How are you?"

"Fine. Not remarried if that's what you're asking. I do have someone though. He stays at his place and I stay at mine and I like it that way."

That was close to his arrangement these days, but he couldn't agree that it was ideal. The luckiest people were close soul mates who couldn't do without each other. A few years ago, when he read "The Bird and the Machine," he gasped at the point where the hawks find each other again and reunite in the open sky. People in train stations and airports running toward each other—the scene captivates him every time. To want someone that much...

"And work?" he asks Amanda.

"Good. I'm editing now. It's good."

"Same friends on the staff?"

"Pretty much. You okay—beyond the total high of getting your novel out?"

"Yep. Three kids. Big house. Lots of acres. I'm spending more time in the city these days because I work better here."

"You married that theater director?"

"Yes. Maggie."

She said, "Look, this is a totally innocent invitation, but if you want to have a drink to catch up or close the case or whatever, I'm willing."

"Yes. I always felt we needed a punctuation mark after Reno."

"So, okay. Tomorrow night, six o'clock, maybe White Horse. You okay with that?"

"*Saloon Society*," he said.

And she said, "Yeah, I read it too."

The bar would be a little noisy, busier than he liked, but she might be more comfortable with chaos around them.

He almost didn't recognize her. She looked more or less the same, but his eye didn't put her image together right away. His confusion reminded him of the way in a dream a person is both the same and different. He leaned over to give her a quick embrace. She gave his forearms a solid hold.

"You seem fit," she said. "You cut a good figure. I'm guessing Maggie is good to you."

He was wearing a jacket and shirt Maggie had picked out for him. Is that what Amanda meant?

He wanted to answer fairly. "Maggie does more for me than I ask for or deserve. She's pretty terrific."

"That's the deal everyone wants."

He didn't argue the complications—how he didn't *want* to have things bought for him, how Maggie's manner got in the way of romance. Most people would tell him he was nuts.

"Will you tell Maggie we met?"

"Yes."

"Good."

She wanted a martini. He went to order two at the bar, saying, "One olive, one lemon twist, both very dry."

When he brought them back to the table, she said, "Tell me about the book."

"I started it years ago. It's gone through many changes. Complete changes. It's a novel about a couple, of course, what isn't? But in the political world. I dabbled a bit in that. I mean personally."

"Someone told me."

"Who?"

"I can't remember, honestly. Am I in anything? Please warn me if I am."

"Not exactly. It's not like that. My characters are composites. You are maybe a fourth of the woman in the current novel that's coming out soon, and a few other people, including my wife make the other three quarters of the character. She's a waitress."

"Good heavens, that doesn't sound like me."

"You see. That's what I mean. The problem with the first one, the one you saw part of, was the editor who liked my writing didn't much like the story in its original version, which was all about the relationship. I'm resetting that one in a family fishing business—"

"What do you know about that?"

"Research. Reading. Plus, the chance to set something in Provincetown. And I think now that you ask maybe you are a little part of a babysitter in that novel but mostly she's based on a friend who is getting a divorce and the rest of her—I don't know who she is, maybe some ideal woman in my mind."

"Huh. Do you still write a lot of sex?"

"Can't seem to help it."

"Horny bastard."

"I guess so."

"Harrison," she said. "I owe you an explanation. I know I do. You wanted to know why I wanted out and I couldn't talk about it, but now I'm okay and I will. It was Samuel at work. I knew he was getting divorced, and I probably sent out plenty of signals to him even when I didn't want to. I was crazy about him. He finally picked up on the messages and then he wanted me too and then he changed his mind. You were the good guy. You wanted to love me, and I let you try."

He didn't want to be stunned, but he was. "Is this who you're with now?"

"Oh no, not at all. He's married to Louise. She was crazy about him too. And so were a few others."

"I hardly remember him."

"Really thin? Intellectual and sort of odd?"

He'd suspected someone but not *that* guy who seemed awfully dull. "Are you over him?"

"Completely. And you're the better guy. But that's where I was."

"Emotionally."

"And…literally. I'm sorry. You sensed something, I know."

He felt the blood rush up to his face, making it hard to stay calm. "I guess I didn't want to believe it."

"I'm so sorry. Ask anything."

He tried to make a joke. "Did you two rush into each other's arms?"

"No, he just poured some drinks and took his clothes off. It wasn't particularly fulfilling. I've wanted to admit how stupid I was."

"I wouldn't use that word." He was stupid, too, old fashioned, probably responsible for thwarting her honesty. They drank, listening to conversations swirling around them, seductions in progress mostly, and they laughed when they recognized what they were hearing. He got up to get two more drinks. That took a bit of time and he saw Amanda fend off an admirer, which it appeared she still did really well. She was still almost plain and yet she drew men in.

"How's your mother," she asked when he got back to her. "Still acting?"

"Teaching acting these days."

"Is she still a terror?"

"Afraid so."

He had some perspective, a little, but did not feel like talking about it in the bar with an ex-wife. He remembered seeing *Auntie Mame* five or six years ago and laughing heartily at everything the Rosalind Russell character said. Her nephew, her ward, asked, after a party, "Who was that English lady?" or something like that and Mame said, "Oh, she's not English. She's from Pittsburgh."

"Why does she sound English?" the kid asked.

"When you're from Pittsburgh, you have to do something!" Mame pronounced.

Maggie thought that line was particularly funny. Neither of them could have guessed that Pittsburgh was one day going to be Harrison's home, a city to which he would become very attached.

"That kid was *good*," Harrison said of the boy who'd played an utter devotion to his aunt, no matter that she was a terrible parent.

And Maggie had said, "That's you, of course. You and your mother."

At first, he'd scoffed, and then within the hour he saw that Maggie was right. His mother, also a terrible mother, was entertaining and theatrical and he had been her page. He hadn't quite thrown off that role, even now, even though his mother was nowhere as sweet as Rosalind Russell.

He didn't want to have dinner with Amanda, but his breeding made him ask if he could get her something to eat.

"No, sorry, I have plans with my guy."

Relieved, he said, "I hope he's good to you."

"Medium good. Doing his best. His name is Mike, just an ordinary guy—like 'just my Bill' in the song." She described him as a smart, preoccupied (often with sports), slightly overweight, sturdy printer, expecting very little of life. Bill left her alone when she needed to be alone. That she liked.

Harrison watched other bar customers while searching for an exit line.

After a moment, she said, "You're funny. Still the same." She described how he'd come into the bar, seen her, and opened his arms wide in greeting as he'd used to do with her, with everyone.

23

In 1967 the springs popped. He was spending much more time in the city—going as if to work like the other men did but not taking a train back North most evenings. Like Oscar and others, he thought of his work as belonging to the city.

He tried to work at home on the weekends as well, but the kids would *clomp*—the only word for it—up and down stairs. His daughters would play rock and roll loudly enough that he knew the words to "It's My Party" and "My Boyfriend's Back." They were normal kids, passionate about the music of their generation, but the lyrics they needed to hear fought with the lines he was composing.

He was growly and the kids started avoiding him, especially Thomas who could spend his days communing with an ant or leafing through one of the encyclopedias.

Emma had a boyfriend. She was too young for any of that. As a father he was the direct opposite of what he'd been as a horny boy. "I don't want her alone, do you hear, with that boy or any boy," he said to Maggie and she tried not to laugh.

"The problem is the kids her age are dating," she tried to tell him. "It's considered *normal.*"

"I don't care. Knock some sense into her. You know about hormones. We had them."

"Once upon a time."

One weekend he came home early and found her in the kitchen *tete a tete* with a neighbor. Not Douglas, but a new guy who had bought in the vicinity of Great Falls and who lived alone. They blushed and pulled apart.

"Just learning the secrets of the area shops," the man said. He stood and shook hands. "Everett," he said. "We've met at a party."

"Right," Harrison said. He hated the way his voice sounded. Hollow as if he'd been hit in the stomach.

"What was that about?" he asked Maggie when Everett drove away.

"He's learning the secrets of the area shops," Maggie said, shrugging.

He didn't pursue it. Was she an unlikely Bovary or Karenina? She hardly seemed the type. Trembling, he dropped it that day, but it stayed under the surface, nagging.

Another weekend he went home and after hours of chatting with Maggie realized he had not seen Anna. He found her in her room in bed. She jumped when he came in, a terrified expression on her face.

"What's up? Are you sick?" he asked.

"Kind of. A little bit."

"Let me feel your head." He felt no fever. "Where does it hurt?"

"Nowhere. I'll be okay."

"Come on downstairs. Is it cramps?'

"Um. Kind of. Mom said I could be alone."

"Okay."

"Lots of drama," Emma said cryptically as she passed him on the stairs.

"What's wrong with Anna?" he asked Maggie. "She's going to stay holed up all night. Exercise would do her better."

Maggie looked shaky, almost tearful.

"What is it?"

"Don't bother her. Please leave her alone."

"Wait. I'm her father. Talk to me."

"She's had…a little bit of a shock. Okay? It's over."

Words flew through his mind. Rape, depression, what? "A boy?" he asked.

"I promised her I wouldn't tell you. I promised."

"It was a boy, right? My God. Anna is still a *child*."

"Don't talk to her. You'll devastate her. Leave it to me."

"But why doesn't she want to talk to me?"

"Because you're busy. Because she adores you. Because she's uncomfortable with you."

"This is ridiculous. We're both her parents. She needs to be able to talk to us. Let's go deal with it."

"Do *not* go up there again. I'm telling you she begged me not to let you talk to her."

Maggie's command floored him. He could hear what she wasn't saying. *You're not here enough.* He flew out the door and walked so fast it was almost a run. His fault, his fault, his fault. He'd been gone, he hadn't been watching, and the end result—something bad, something very bad. Now he wasn't needed or wanted at all.

He came back to the house, threw a few things into a satchel and went to get a train back to the city early, aware that only Casey stood at the door looking out at his departing figure.

Why was Maggie encouraging Anna to do without him?

When he got back to the city, he dumped his things and went out. St. Mark's place was a crowded circus of batik and long hair and people selling earrings and smoking pot. He didn't fit here either. Tonight, an old geezer offered him a roach, but he refused it. Their friends up around the farm had given him pot a couple of times and he discovered he didn't do well with it. While his friends were enviably happy and hungry, amused by everything, wildly affectionate, he got jumpy and morose and headachy.

Anyway, he'd failed at hippiedom and really he was too old to be a hippie though his hair was a touch longer than it used to be. Were these people actually as free as they said they were?

He had left the apartment, thinking he would pop into the St. Mark's movie house or walk several blocks to one of the bars where there was conversation to be had. But as he passed the Electric Circus, it beckoned to him. He'd heard about it plenty—the lights and sound were like an LSD trip without the drugs, people claimed. *With* drugs, the place apparently blew a person's mind. Maybe a little mind-bending was what he needed.

He hoped he would not be the only person over forty in the Circus.

The lights and sound grabbed him the moment he entered. There was blue, then red, swirling at his feet and climbing the walls, while a different light, a strobe was going all the time. He could hardly sense the floor beneath him.

"Reefer?" asked a boy with hair to his waist.

"No, thanks. A drink."

"You have to get that yourself."

He squeezed past colorfully costumed kids who either were, or were *performing being*, relaxed, laid back. To his right hundreds were dancing on a thickly crowded floor, but since there wasn't enough room to dance, mostly they ground against each other. Emma and Anna were in danger of all this in the next few years. He got himself a bourbon and found a wall to be a flower on.

A woman came up to him, saying, "Piece of wall for me."

"Certainly."

"I'm so glad to see someone here who isn't twenty-two," she said.

He looked at her then. She was dressed for the scene—a Mexican vest, a flowy cotton top, and a long flower-print skirt. He guessed her to be not quite his age. Maybe thirty, thirty-something. She had a strong nose, bright dancing eyes, and long dark hair.

"Are you a tourist?" she asked.

"No, I live around the corner."

"Aha. Will you take me there later? Sorry, I'm a little drunk."

"No. If things were different, I would."

"I see. Can I lean on you?"

She meant it literally, her head on his shoulder.

Well, he wasn't much of a dancer, so this was how he'd experience the club, swaying and holding up a wasted woman. At first, he just looked, taking the whole place in. Then he thought he wanted to remember and maybe at some point write about it. The dancers, pelvis to pelvis, aroused him. And then the woman who attached herself to him was rubbing her hand along his ribs. It felt very nice. He had what felt like a significant hard on.

He steadied her against the wall and got himself another drink. She'd wanted one but he persuaded her to make it a Coke. As he carried those drinks back to her wall space, he saw that she was quite pretty. And of a personality that was constantly ready to be amused.

"Here you go."

"You're a cheerful guy. What's your name?"

"Mirth."

"Okay. You're a joker."

"No, it's my name."

She blinked rapidly. "Really?"

In the end he walked her home. She had sobered considerably. She kissed him and said, "Please come in. I went there hoping I'd meet someone like you."

"You don't know me. We don't— I'm not available."

"Neither am I. I just want to mess around a wee little bit. Why not, huh? Never see you again. Who's to know?"

Her apartment was fairly well put together. There was an antique dining table and chairs and then the bench made of three chairs—Amish. The draperies were attractive and, he could tell, expensive, a subtle version of the ones Scarlett O'Hara used when she needed to make a dress.

"My father bought me all this," she said.

"What do you do?"

"Disappoint him. Ha. No, I'm in law school. Finally gave in to it. Family business. Trying to keep up the standard."

She had announced that she wanted to mess around some, which they did on the couch. He felt young and awkward and needy as he had when, at fifteen years old, he tried to seduce his fourteen-year-old neighbor, Beth Ann.

"I'm married. This is a first for me."

"It won't be a last, probably. We can just make each other feel good and then go our separate ways. It's innocent. Nice, huh?"

In the end he slept with her and it felt both familiar and unfamiliar, like ice-skating after you'd let ten years elapse, the surprise of walking on blades again. "What's your name?" he asked at three in the morning when he roused himself to get started walking home.

"Beth."

"Huh. My first girlfriend was Beth Ann."

"I'm Beth Cohen."

He'd made a mistake, stepped over the line that kept him faithful. But he couldn't remember the last time Maggie wanted him, needed him for something. And now she was mooning over that Everett guy.

When he got back to his place, he couldn't sleep so he sat down and wrote. Or tried.

Maggie didn't call the next day or the day after.

A week later he tapped on Beth Cohen's door.

"I hoped you'd come by. But you have to agree, no strings and I'm sticking to it." She led him inside. She'd been nibbling at cheese and crackers and she had the television on. Her dining table was piled with books and papers.

"How's school?"

"Second year woes. It's not what I want but I'm not getting any younger and I'm going to see it through."

She looked voluptuous in jeans and a dashiki top.

"Can you take a break? Dinner? My treat."

"Never mind dinner," she said. "We know what we want with each other."

They went to her bedroom and kissed and took off their clothes. But when he touched her, he realized she was shaking. "You're a bit nervous too," he said.

"I seem to be. Without the benefit of drink." She looked at him seriously.

He kissed her. He had thought about doing this all week, but it felt strange to him, too, now that he was sober. He said, "I'm sorry. I can't. I guess I'm uptight."

"Drink helps, doesn't it?"

"It does."

"Want something?"

"No."

He stayed for two hours. Mostly they talked, eventually nibbling at cheese. She offered a peanut butter and jelly sandwich, which reminded him of his early days with Amanda.

She cut the sandwich diagonally and put it on a plate and brought it to him in her living room. "Are you unhappy? Personal life, I mean."

He stared at the sandwich, really wanting a good dinner. "A little. We seem to be going through something."

"I hear marriage is very hard. That's why I'm never going to do it."

"You might change your mind. People do."

"How old are your kids?"

"Fifteen, fourteen, nine."

"Good kids?"

"Wonderful. I need to start spending more time with them."

He stood and looked out the window. "What a wonderful apartment this is." And Beth was quite a complete housekeeper. Everything about her place seemed permanent and purposeful. "I've always wanted to buy a house here—three stories, whatever—and bring the family here. But they like it there, up north, so I'm outvoted."

"I see."

"Are you really doing homework tonight?"

"Until ten. Then some friends are coming by and we're going out as a group. I'd invite you, but…"

He finished her sentence in his mind a couple of different ways. *Too many questions. I wouldn't feel as free. I'm really sort of dating one of the guys who's coming by. You're too old for the group.*

Ha. To be unwanted in yet another setting. He said an awkward, polite goodbye, then walked up the street, past the revelers, wondering where to go next.

And then he was at his apartment. He put his key in the lock of his place. He needed dinner, real food. He would boil up some pasta or go next door for a burger and fries.

His apartment was not empty.

Maggie was sitting on the couch, reading. She said, "We need to talk. I want to make up. I can't stand it when you don't call."

"Me neither."

"You were probably out to dinner. I ate one of your cans of tuna but I'm still hungry. Would you? Could we? Maybe we can even talk there."

"Thank you for coming in." He peed and washed up, thanking his stars he hadn't gotten into bed with Beth Cohen.

"Can we go to that Hungarian place? I've had it on my mind." She sounded spirited, almost happy. She picked up her handbag. She wore pants and a designer version of a hippie blouse, great colors but very finished lines and he felt a pang, seeing how she wanted to fit in.

From a bowl in the kitchen, he took out some cash.

They had to move single file through the throngs. Maggie lit a cigarette and smoked as they walked, in a sense, carving her path with the burning tip.

Sadness filled him. He persuaded himself the incense burning on several tables bathed them both in exotic aromas, erasing his almost mistake, softening Maggie's faux hippie.

"About Anna," she said when they were seated. "I know you don't feel it, but she's afraid of you."

"Good God, why? Wait. You haven't told me what happened. I'm capable of imagining horrible things. You might as well let me know."

Instead of answering that, she said, "She thinks you're amazing and that everything about her disappoints you."

"Ridiculous. It doesn't."

"No matter. It's how she feels."

"But…? I have to talk to her."

"Please, we need you to make things normal."

A waiter was approaching with menus. Harrison waved them away distractedly. "Beef goulash, right, you said?" he asked Maggie. She nodded. "And bread and red wine," he told the waiter.

"If you could know how much she wants to please you," Maggie said when the waiter left.

"She *does* please me. Always. But…"

"Just come home. That's what she needs. But no inquisition. Just be there."

A long silence went by. He was stymied but caught by the idea that he was needed for something. He wanted to comfort his daughter—that he was clear on. "She doesn't know she's wonderful, does she?"

Maggie shook her head. "She doesn't care about that. She thinks about being pretty, about being a desirable girl. She wishes she were unselfconscious."

"She *is* pretty."

"I know that. She doesn't."

"Who? Just tell me who the kid is."

"If you ask that, you'd better not come home."

Knowledge was dangerous. Would he strangle the kid?

He picked at bread and got images of Anna, hesitating in doorways, reluctant to speak up when they had company. He had to give her confidence.

How witty Anna was. How did she not know that? And yet, as he twirled the breadbasket, he wondered what was the trick to giving a child courage? "I want her to know she's wonderful."

"Please just keep everything normal. Quizzing her would kill her."

Finally, he nodded. Maggie gave him a warm smile. As he ate and settled into the evening with his wife, as he determined to make Anna happy and confident, he felt re-glued to the family.

One of the things he struggled with when he was writing was explaining ambivalence. His characters had a lot of to/from feelings. As people do. He wrote in his journal:

> Memory. I am four years old. Grandma says my mother is coming to visit and she will stay two whole weeks. Grandma's voice, the way she looks down at the floor, tells me she feels two ways about it—glad to see her daughter, and completely exhausted before the visit has begun. And I, not necessarily influenced by her, feel the same way. I have a memory of previous visits. My mother bursting in, looking at me, saying something approving about how I have grown. And also, yes, my mother taking all the available air in the room and soon enough, after about five minutes, finding something wrong with me. Another memory: two kids at school asking me on the playground why I didn't have a mother and father. "I do," I said. "They both work." "When do they come home?" "Sometimes. They don't live here. My mother comes on holidays. I go to New York to see them." Puzzlement. They think I'm lying. "Do you like going to New York?" one asks. The fact was, I loved it and told them so and I told them one more thing so they would

envy me. "I get money to go to the corner place and order whatever I want. A hot dog or tuna salad. I always get a milkshake." They are impressed by the milkshake. And by the independence. I can't remember what I felt inside about having a family so different from everybody else's. I think I must have been a little sad. Photos seem to show me looking preoccupied. But I thought I was happy at the time. I told myself I was. How can that be? And I was proud of my parents being interesting people. It's that divided feeling that gets me, to be enchanted by my parents who seemed almost strangers to me, and at the same time to wish to God they were more ordinary.

Glad and sad. He was glad Maggie had come to New York for him. He was sad about it too. But he determined to be a better person, to put his indiscretion aside and to do something to cement his marriage. After all he had been faithful for nearly twenty years. That counted for something.

The first thing he did was sublet his apartment for three months of the summer so he could spend all his time with his family, both at the Cape and at home. The tenant, a graduate student taking two summer classes, would take over tomorrow.

The writing was going well, his second book had been accepted, so why not get some confidence and assure himself he could write anywhere? Why not be all right in the world? A model for Anna.

Why not remind himself that he had found Maggie *interesting* when she kept showing up to rescue him from his first marriage?

Maggie was picking him up in Poughkeepsie this time so they could meet with friends which meant he had to take the train from Grand Central instead of Penn. But, oh, the Oyster Bar! It was just one of the things he would miss desperately.

He loved his apartment in St. Mark's place. He loved the mess of the city. The lights, the shows. Actors everywhere. He would miss other writers he was getting to know. He had seen Malamud at a restaurant eating with Philip Roth and Joseph Heller and they had asked him to join them. They were friendly and treated him as an equal. There was brainy talk, yeah, some of the time, about politics, but also food, also baseball.

He loved everything about the city, but he would recover, adjust. Maggie had pointed out to him that every time his mother announced she was coming, he sank at first and then suddenly his spirits would rise, no matter the history.

It would be all right. He loved the garden at the farm, the pillows he'd chosen for the living room sofa, the gorgeous corner cabinet he had found when the kids were small, how hilarious Anna was, how serene Emma was, how smart and full of feeling Thomas was. He loved hugging them and getting hugged back, being welcomed by Casey.

As he waited for his train, he took out his notebook to capture a woman dressed splendidly, just showing off all her stuff in bright yellow. She was the image of confidence. What would happen to her? Something would. She cared too much about being lovely.

A different woman, this one dressed badly, also caught his attention. He jotted down that her jacket did not match her skirt; her shoes were down at heels. She sighed with every breath. He could see she was sad and wondered if that was why she had let herself go. He made a note, too, about the shoeshine guy with his weary cheer, the energetic way he swished the cloth back and forth, fighting the hard shoes and maybe the men in them, and then smiled and said warmly, "There you go, sir."

Maggie had to admit the house was happier now that her husband was home. It was messier with books, papers, coffee cups, and there was a certain impulsive quality to their lives—*let's go out to lunch, let's go to the library today, let's just take a ride, anybody want to go for an ice cream?*

The kids were brightening, all of them. *Look at this. Read what I wrote. See what I painted. You know what I just read in the encyclopedia?*

Anna showed him a painting she had done which he studied for a long time after which he said, "This is really very good. Your eye is… mature. Do you have more?"

After that, Maggie found Anna sketching things every day. Birds, trees, tables. Her own favorite was an abstract sketch Anna did of her father gardening. She was still shy around him, a little tentative, but also clearly a little in love. She blushed at every compliment.

Today Anna was sketching again, and Harrison was back to working on the vegetable patch. Maggie went out to see both the gardening and the sketch only to find Harrison was kneeling and had once again not changed to work clothes—she knew his new khaki pants would be hard to clean. He didn't distinguish between work clothes and good clothes. He just wore everything hard. She bit her tongue. He was weeding around the eggplant. No gloves of course, just him and soil.

She stood a few feet behind Anna to see that the sketch had some-how caught the way he was immersed in soil.

He looked up. "Hey, Anna," he said, "your hair looks cute that way."

It was just a loose ponytail with some wisps on the sides.

Maggie sashayed toward him and said, "And mine?" Her hair was a mess because she was long overdue for a visit to the beauty shop where they made her a more convincing redhead. Now the roots hinted at her natural color, a mousy brown. She ran her fingers through her already tousled hair. "Very stylish, right?"

He complied. "Very fetching."

"Fetching," Anna said. "I like that word, Pop. I don't know why."

See, she was talking. Good.

A little jealous, but also grateful, Maggie watched him work the kids. He was back. But things weren't perfect. Eventually he couldn't hold on and his temper flared when there was too much to do, and he wanted to get back to his real work. Maggie thought he needed at least six more hours in a day.

His temper also flared when she corralled him. He felt it immediate-ly. She'd gone ahead and booked a place for August in Wellfleet instead of Provincetown without running the place or dates by him. When she told him, he slammed dinner dishes into the sink, saying, "You don't need me much for decisions, do you? You just go your own way."

"I did it to take the pressure off you."

"You did it because you need to have your own way." He stood and faced her. "Why not Provincetown?"

"It's more peaceful in Wellfleet. Good for writing."

"No, don't give me that. You know I work—"

"Provincetown is a zoo."

"I *like* late July up there. The people I want to talk to go in July." That included people he sometimes saw in the city, she knew, Misha Richter, the Bodians. "I like people. I like to be *with* the crowd, not run away from it."

"You can drive into Provincetown every day."

"It's not the same as wandering into galleries on the way to get milk. It isn't the same. And half of our friends won't still be there."

"It will work out."

"For you!"

"All right. Never again. You can make the plans from here on out."

"Who the hell are you afraid of?"

"I don't know what you're talking about."

"Yes, you do. You're avoiding the interesting people up there."

It was true. He was right. It was *true*. In P-town there were women who flirted unmercifully with her husband—right in front of her face. They were lean and suntanned and free-spirited and they talked and talked about everything from travel to Maui to the latest political news.

And when she and Harrison went to a gallery opening, there were men and women talking fast about this and that and who and which gallery and who had read what. It wasn't exactly what she thought of as a vacation.

She chose her words carefully to defend herself. "This year's place is better for the kids. To have more room to roam. And we'll drive to the beach. The girls are boy crazy. We need to have some control over what they do."

He harrumphed a little. She supposed he could at least see the wisdom in that.

She caught her advantage and continued. "At least in August, Oscar and Betty will be up there. You like them. We both do. *They'll* be in Wellfleet. Somewhere. Maybe at a walkable distance. You'll be happy to see them."

But his top began to blow again. "I hate when you tell me how I'll react to what you decide for me. You want to tell me what to write this summer? You want that too?"

"Maybe I do. Why don't you write about us?"

"Ha. You wouldn't like it if I did."

He flew out of the house and walked a zigzag around the property for a good two hours. Then from what she could see, he came back, got into the car and went off driving. Her stomach shook. She picked up the phone and called to see if she could change the reservation to Provincetown, the place they used to stay. "It's booked," she was told. She called the Wellfleet owners and asked if they had rented July. They had it open still for two weeks at the end of July, that was it, and she would have to hurry if she wanted it.

"Let me talk to my husband tonight," she said.

That didn't happen.

She was asleep by the time he came home. She found him splayed out on the wicker couch in the sunroom in the morning.

As she made coffee, she heard him stirring. Emma came downstairs and took it all in. She wanted to know what the fight was about.

"It was nothing. People argue. It's healthy. It's supposed to be lots better than holding things in."

"Pop holds things in," Emma said sagely. "I try to poke him to say stuff."

"Well, writing is hard."

Her daughter buttered a piece of toast. "I guess it must be. But he's a success, right?" Even in the kitchen there was a copy of the second book with a full back cover photo of him, looking peaceful and brilliant and happy under his trees.

"I don't know what success is. I suspect it's only as good as the last time you get a sale or a compliment. Then suddenly nobody remembers you and you have to do it again. I remember that from the theater and the actors I hired. They were always being remade by the latest compliment."

But Emma was bored with definitions of success. "I need two summer dresses," she said. "Mine are old fashioned. I'll show you the magazines if you want."

"No need to prove it. We'll get you dresses."

"Great." Emma put a second piece of bread in the toaster.

"Don't overdo the toast. I'm making pancakes and sausages. Eggs, too, if you want."

"Everything," Emma said. The child ate like a truck driver and never gained a pound.

"Morning," they heard, and looked up to see Harrison, still dressed in his clothing of last night, standing at the kitchen door.

"Pancakes? Sausage?"

"Sounds good," he said. He turned on the radio for some news. The station came in staticky, but Maggie didn't say anything.

Emma went to the radio and adjusted it. "Why did you sleep downstairs?" she asked.

Her pop looked at her. "Try it sometime. The air is good. It's cooler."

She nodded, unfooled.

"I made some calls," Maggie said. "One place in Provincetown out of the center of town might have two weeks in July but they don't know for sure yet. Would you prefer two weeks in July to four in August?"

"Only two weeks?" Emma said.

He appeared to think about it for some time. He nodded, "August then. I'll manage."

"Thanks."

24

He wrote in the mornings in Wellfleet and drove the kids and Maggie to Herring Cove or Race Point, where most days, he lay with them, reading. But on other days, he ducked away from the beach and went into Provincetown, shorts over his wet trunks—he didn't care. Provincetown tolerated messiness. He wandered into galleries one after another. It was a real shame he couldn't paint—God, how he loved it.

One day he took a folder with his photographs to a gallery that had once done an exhibit of such things. "Would you take a look?" he asked, shrugging an apology. "People and buildings. Mostly Manhattan."

The small man with thick wire-rimmed spectacles studied each photograph. He wore a perfectly ironed shirt and a bow tie. When he looked up, he said, "I could give you a week next summer. It's the people's faces I'm interested in. Maybe these and ten more. Then, once I have those, we'd have to figure out how we want to hang them." The gallery owner, whose name he had hardly learned, so sure he was on a fool's mission, was Edward Mann, and he handed Harrison a card. "I'd want to firm it up. I do contracts."

"Absolutely."

"Show me what you have by January?"

Harrison was bursting to share this news with Maggie or the first friend he saw coming down the street. At the grocery store where he stopped to buy a bottle of wine, he picked up an attractive card sitting on the counter. It was done by a painter who was advertising that he sold paintings from his home address. It meant, what, that he didn't have a gallery yet? Harrison liked the small sketch on the card—a sort of quick abstract of a painter working in a garage. And he liked the entrepreneurial push of making these cards.

He looked at the address and decided to walk it, knowing he might very well find a locked garage, nobody around, but the walk itself was worth it. After twenty minutes he was gratified to discover the doors open, a fan blowing, and a paint-spattered man concentrating so fiercely on putting a daub to a canvas that he didn't see he had a guest.

Andrew Rosen was a handsome man, large, with a large nose and glasses dropped low on that nose—old person style, though he was perhaps Harrison's age. When he finally sensed a presence, he turned. "Sorry. Can I help you?"

"May I look at what you have?" He could see there were about a dozen canvases along one wall in two rows, propped on a long table and then in front of the table on a couple of two by fours.

"I don't have a gallery yet."

"I understand." Harrison moved to the paintings, which were mainly abstracted seascapes, boats, humans, water, sky. He got that feeling, that heart-racing feeling that told him he saw genius. "These are wonderful."

"Uh, thank you."

"How much?"

Arthur breathed heavily. "I usually ask four hundred. I would take less. If you can't."

"I'm going to come back tonight. Will you be here?"

"Here or in the kitchen." He pointed to the house.

"I want to bring my daughter."

Impulsively, because he saw that this painter was suffering hard times, Harrison handed him the bottle of wine. "Here's my word. I'll be back."

He trotted back to town, bought another bottle of wine, and hurried to pick up the family at the beach.

"We're burnt to a crisp," Emma complained. "We ran out of suntan lotions."

"Your hat? Your towel?"

"Used them. Not much help in the water."

"She was in the water playing with two guys," Anna said, eyes wide. She was still lying down, completely covered by two towels. "Up to no good."

Good for Anna, he thought, prudishness was preferable at this age.

"Shut *up*," Emma cried.

Maggie looked terribly sunburned.

He said, "Let's get you some lotion and some ice on that. Hungry?"

All four said they were. "Okay. Let's get something quick up at the Seafood Shack and then go into town tonight. I need to go in again." The phrasing made them all aware that Wellfleet was to Provincetown as the farm was to New York—the peace that Maggie needed, the excitement that he needed.

Anna was hardly moving. He told her, "I've seen some wonderful paintings I can't stop thinking about. I want your opinion."

She sat up. "Mine? You want me to look at them?"

"Absolutely," he told her, though he knew which two he was crazy about. "Come on. I have a bottle of wine sort of boiling in the car. Let's move."

And they trudged up the dunes.

"Are the rest of us invited?" Maggie asked with a decided edge to her voice.

"Of course. Don't be silly."

That night they walked Commercial Street in a crowd thick enough to be a parade. Anna marched in front—she had an erect posture, felt her importance to what was happening. The crowd thinned as they got to the East End.

They entered the garage where Andrew Rosen sat looking at his own work, which he had spread out for better viewing. He'd propped some against a second worktable on another wall.

"Spectacular!" Maggie said in a burst.

"This is Maggie. These are my children. Emma, Anna, Thomas (our scholar)." (Thomas was carrying a book.)

Andrew sat with the open bottle of wine Harrison had left him. It was full. "I thought you might want a drink. I brought clean glasses." Behind him a woman, thin and exotic, edged into the garage. "My wife," he said. "Rachel."

Anna was studying the paintings, all of them of Provincetown, shacks and seascapes and bits of ocean light. There was one Harrison wanted badly and now he was afraid Anna would choose different ones—though they were all gorgeous.

He put an arm around his daughter. "Do you like them as much as I do?"

She pointed, saying, "Those two are my favorites."

Ah, one of them was his choice, the shack, the roughness against the glistening bay.

"Me, too!" he said. He turned to Maggie. "I want to hang it in our living room. I'd like to see it every day." He pulled a thin stack of bills from his pocket. What he had made in book royalties was going to another artist, but that was right, wasn't it? He pointed to the one Anna had chosen. "Okay with everyone?" he asked, though he wasn't sure what he would do if any of them said no. He looked briefly at the other one he thought was fabulous.

Rosen was close to tears. "Really?" he asked.

"Absolutely." Harrison handed over four hundred dollars.

Thrills were in the air. Rosen was so happy he didn't know whether to laugh or cry.

"And I'm buying the second one," Maggie said. "You choose," she told Harrison.

He understood she was trying to apologize for Wellfleet. He pointed to the other one he had been longing for. "I think that's superb," he said quietly.

"I have to go get the cash, but you can trust me," Maggie told the artist.

Rosen handed out glasses of wine. "Just bring two hundred more tomorrow. I'm charging three hundred each for you," he told Harrison. "I don't know how to tell you, but you changed my life tonight."

Harrison said, "You don't have to explain. I understand. Completely."

Maggie murmured when they left, "We're giving him the full amount. People don't know when they're good, do they?"

He shook his head. He took her arm and tucked it under his elbow. Partners, he thought. For life, he thought. He would make it so.

After the intensive family summer, Harrison went back to spending his weeks in the city. He began accumulating friends he could count on there. The Rosens lived in the city during the winter months and so they got added to the city contacts.

Then there was Dick Rovere of the *New Yorker* whom Harrison met through the Brandts and there were a dozen new people that Harrison gathered along the way once his second book was out. They looked at him sagely after reading his novels, the horny young mayor, the doomed couple in the other. Now he was working on one about a woman who was uncomfortable around her husband's wealthy relatives, but the husband also had goals that intimidated her. Somewhat a reverse of his life, but he was spurred on by the conflict.

Several of Harrison's newest friends were writers, hopeful as he was, to be validated by publication. He'd met several of them at a gathering at Malamud's place.

Tucked in his wallet was a tear-out of a mini-review from the *New Yorker*. It had the phrase "his graceful and subtle observations," words he sometimes whispered to himself when the going got rough. The third book was taking longer than the first two. He was nervous as hell. But he had wanted to do this thing and he was doing it.

25

One day, carrying his camera, he noticed a woman in the park, just sitting. She had lovely bone structure and bright interested eyes. He thought she was arresting, though he was not physically drawn to blondes. He stopped and asked if he might photograph her.

She said, "Sure." She shrugged and crossed her legs and threw her arms against the back of the bench so readily that he thought perhaps she had been a photographic model or *was* one now.

He adjusted the focus and began clicking.

"Do I get to see them?" she asked.

"They won't be ready for a week. But I could meet you somewhere. I'd get a few copies made for you, maybe three that I think are good if that's okay. I'm gathering photos of people for a show."

"I hang out at a bar on the corner of Broadway and Fourteenth."

"You work near there?"

"I don't work. Well, not much. I'm a kept woman."

He laughed, thinking she meant she was married though he didn't notice a ring. Her name was Mary Kaminski.

He learned more about her when the photos were ready, and he took them to her—they had turned out marvelously. He went to the bar at six and sure enough she was there, at a stool, having a straight bourbon. She wore a black low-cut dress and high heels. When she saw him, she tapped the stool next to her.

"My exhibit is next summer," he explained. "I'd like permission to use one of these." He handed her an envelope. "These prints are for you." Waving the bartender over he pointed to her drink and then to his empty spot.

"Man, you made me look good," Mary said.

"You helped."

"Did I?" She had a throaty voice, almost a learned toughness. He couldn't help wanting to know more about her—how she had the money to dress and drink. As they sat together, hearing bits of other people's conversations, making small talk, he managed to ask how she didn't do much of anything but seemed happy.

"Well, I have a boyfriend in the rackets."

"No! Really?"

"Yes. This dress, for instance, is very expensive. He gets me things that are a little…*warm* shall we say."

Stolen. He felt slow-witted. Catching up to her explanation, he asked, "Are you safe? He's okay to you?"

"Mostly. He gets jealous, I'll admit."

She was either very worldly or very naïve. "It's not for me to say, but is it the best idea, being with someone like him?"

She appeared to think for a long time. "I wasn't always attractive. He makes me feel attractive."

"I don't think you need him for that." Harrison didn't feel any lust toward her, but he was impelled by a deep curiosity. He prompted her by shaking his head in puzzlement.

"I used to be fat. Pretty darned fat."

"Hard to imagine. How did you turn that around?"

"Drinking. Not eating." She lifted her glass and took a sip, blinking her eyes to show it was delicious.

"Probably not recommended, the not eating part."

"But effective," she laughed. "You're sort of square, aren't you?"

His drink arrived and as soon as he had some, he felt it immediately. He had been writing all morning and snapping photos all afternoon and then running around to his photo bank and had eaten only a hot dog at a stand. "If I ordered a sandwich, would you eat half?"

"Okay."

He ordered a club to soak up the next glass of booze. "How did you meet this mobster?"

"At a bar."

"And what does he *do*, exactly?"

"You don't want to know. I mean *I* don't want to know. He carries a gun, he drives around the city, he has a nice place——so it pays, whatever he does."

"Am I in trouble if I take more photos of you? You're a terrific model."

"I don't know. But I want more pictures now that I'm pretty and vain."

As she got boozier, she told him her life story. She'd been an ugly, awkward kid and a fat teenager. "I was what you call a loose girl. Basically, I slept with every guy who asked me. And you know teenage boys;

a lot of them asked me. They made fun of me and I knew they did but I couldn't seem to stop. They apparently called me the town pump."

He winced at her phrasing but tucked it away in his mind's notebook. "Where was this?"

"New Jersey. Where else? I killed the accent, huh? Not a trace."

"And you don't actually work?"

"I play secretary at his cousin's trucking company. I don't do much, just make it look like a business."

"I'm worried for you. Maybe you should give me his name."

"No. Shhh. Don't worry. This is the happiest I've ever been. I got a man, I got goods, and I'm thin." She said it in her tough voice, maybe having studied Lauren Bacall. "I'm going to tell you a story. Ready?" She shifted in her seat and said, "Last summer, I went back to my home-town—Podunck, New Jersey. And I went into a bar. And I was dressed to the nines, hair just done, bleached if you want the truth, and I sat at the bar and ordered a drink. I have to tell you how my town is. Half the men in that bar went to high school there and never got out of the town. It was crowded, they all knew each other, and I was the event of the decade. They were buzzing, they were talking, *who is she,* who *is* she, that kind of thing, and some asked to buy me a drink, and I refused, *modestly,* shaking my head. I recognized maybe six of them. Most of them I'm sure had *heard* of me, but not a *one* of them recognized me. Ha. I loved that. So, I had my drink. I paid. I put a hundred on the bar and told the bartender, "Buy the boys a drink on me. Tell them Fat Mary's back in town."

She pulled herself up a few inches. Her eyes glistened.

Harrison had tears threatening.

She said, "Oh, don't cry. You see, I'm okay now."

"What a story," he managed to say, his voice hoarse with the tears he was fighting.

"Take more pictures of me?" she asked.

"Yes, for sure." He gestured to an empty booth. "Let's move over there."

She slid onto the red leather bench, each move she made pho-tographable. She probably could have been cast in movies. He asked her to hold her hair back with her hands and she did. She could take direction like an actress (or a model), no fuss, no questions.

The photo he got back a week later was a winner—everyone who saw it stopped for a long time, taking it in.

One day, a couple of weeks later, they met for a drink at her request. He'd already given her a copy of the great photo with her hands in her hair. Man, she looked like a woman who'd triumphed.

She said, out of the blue, "I just wanted to explain I'm not going to sleep with you."

He was a little taken aback. He had not intended to try to sleep with her, but it was not the first time his interest in a woman as a person had been mistaken for attempted seduction.

"I mean, I like you and you're the nicest guy I ever met, I think, and the happiest, too, but there's the age difference. It bothers me."

He laughed later to think of how he was perceived by her. Happy. And a lecherous forty-four to her twenty-eight or so. With her, he didn't feel lecherous at all. He got the occasional twinge but that was just normal daily life, nothing like lustful drive. He thought it was important to let her feel he wanted her, so he just nodded.

"Very fair," he said. "Very fair. Plus, I'm married."

"That doesn't seem to stop anyone I know."

Mostly as he drifted away from her and these meetings, he began to realize he identified with her, wanted to be the kid who plunked down a hundred-dollar bill to say, *I'm okay. No longer a nothing. Now a something.* Writer.

Photographer, too, but that didn't count exactly.

Writer.

Five bookstore readings, two parties, seven dinners with editors or agents later, photos of him all over the place (one used for publicity, the other on the covers of his books)—he managed to think briefly, *I'm doing okay.* Most times, he thought, *Really, is that me? Why can't I feel it?*

He answered his own question: Because you're only as good as your next one when the few people who read quiet novels make a fuss over you. Then down in the pit again.

He had to get the third novel in shape.

26

One day, a year later, he arrived early at a restaurant in midtown to meet Dick Rovere for lunch. As he waited, he sat reading and drinking a lunchtime martini. A woman sitting at the next table asked, "What's the book?"

He showed her. Cheever again. Another gift from Maggie…

"Like it?"

"I admire it…"

"I totally understand." She held out a hand. "I work for Harper and Rowe. I'm an editor there. Well, assistant editor. I met him. He's neurotic. Writers! All of them are nuts."

He felt a sudden anger. Writers always said editors secretly despised them, thought them too needy, but hell, it was exhausting work, and editors should, if anyone should, appreciate the work and forgive the neediness. "I'm afraid I'm one of them."

She paused. Bit her lip. "I am incredibly stupid. I was trying to impress you. I'm sorry. I've never…I should move to another table, I think."

"If I were meeting my editor, I'd say yes, probably, but it's just another writer I'm meeting, so if you listen in you can have more fuel for your scorn."

"Oh God. I am really sorry."

He thought she was about to cry. Unfortunately, that made him somewhat sympathetic. And she was quite beautiful. She had streaming shiny black hair and dark flashing eyes. She quickly dabbed at her eyes. "I'll ask the waiter if he can move me."

Just then Harrison's pal Dick Rovere came in. The woman almost fainted. She said, "You're Dick Rovere."

"Certainly am."

"I read you all the time! I'm with Harper and Rowe. Just an assistant editor."

"Thank you." He appeared to take her in and approve of her. He dug in his pockets. "I have a card somewhere, I think. In case you're having a terrific party some night."

"I *do* have terrific parties actually." She handed him a card and shyly offered one to Harrison. Her name was Laura Michelman.

"You met my friend here?" Rovere pointed to Harrison.

"Sort of met. Didn't get a name."

"He's not seeking parties, I guess. This is Harrison Mirth. Two novels out. I hear there's a third. Right?"

"Almost done. Difficult birth, the third." Why had he revealed that? He was altogether too truthful about such things. He shook his head to censure himself.

Rovere was saying, "Aw. I know how that goes. On a happier note—how's Maggie?"

"Fine. And Eleanor?"

"Good, good. We should find a restaurant halfway between our houses," he said, "and get together more often."

"I love that idea. So. What are you assigned to these days?"

"You wouldn't believe—England again."

"Could be worse."

Michelman whispered to her waiter and made a change of table.

"She's a beauty," Rovere said, watching her walk away.

"She hates writers."

"So do I." They laughed.

It was only a week later that Harrison got a note forwarded from his publisher and it was from Laura Michelman. *I would like to make it up to you. I'll tell everyone about your books. I'm going to have a party, too, Halloween. Costumes if you want. Optional. Otherwise, would you let me—actually Harper—buy you lunch? I can write it off as exploratory raiding. I looked up your phone number in the directory. Is it okay to call?*

He thought to say no, but how could he pass up a possible connection. If Simon and Schuster didn't like number three, he had to go somewhere else. He thought about it and wrote back, using the return address. *Yes to lunch. Okay to call.*

He tried not to think about her beauty. What a crazy thing the body was, rebelling as it did against the mind. After the Electric Circus escapade, he'd stayed faithful again and was glad of it. He called Maggie that same night and said, "Let's talk seriously about moving to the city."

He could hear her moving a glass with ice cubes in it. He could hear the puff of breath as she smoked. "Oh, sweetie, we have the best of worlds now. You get your chance to work, I can come in whenever I want and be with you. It's good. Isn't it good?"

"It's not ideal. We're not together very often."

"But we both get what we want. I don't think I could ever leave this place. I don't think I would be okay. Somehow we have to make it work."

How could he argue that a place shouldn't be so important? Because it *was*—to him too. St. Mark's corner meant life to him. He'd witnessed the Summer of Love there. He'd gone to old movies around the corner a couple of times a week. He'd been there for the opening of the Negro Ensemble Company. Right on his corner, the country was *becoming* the country it was going to be. Right there in his neighborhood there was authentic mourning for Martin Luther King and Bobby. He could feel it, right up off the pavement, every day. He didn't want to be soothed by the rolling lands of a historic farm up north, remote from the stress and pain of the times. He wanted to say that to Maggie, but he felt too agitated. "I'm going to write you a letter."

"A letter! I love it."

"Things I'm feeling."

"Okay. I know writing is your way to get it out."

"It is. I'd better get back to work."

"I thought you were ten pages from done."

"It's those ten pages. I can't seem to end the damned thing."

"Right. Okay." She let out a long exhale. Hearing that, he pulled out a stale, crushed cigarette, scowled at it, and then lit it to join her. After they hung up, he began his letter. He began it several times. *There are times I think... I don't know what to say but...* Never mind. It was going to be a self-pitying letter. He turned to his manuscript but soon left it and went out for a drink—expensive, but he needed voices, always had, always would.

Laura lost no time in calling him. By the next Friday he was slated for a lunch. Would she bring bad luck or good? He still tried seven different endings to his novel and none of them seemed right. His agent was bugging him for the completed manuscript, and he knew he had to send it in in the next couple of days.

He tossed on a shirt and tie and his corduroy jacket for the lunch. And a wool cap. There was a bracing coolness in the air. He looked a little rumpled; actually, he simply looked Irish. Which he was, partly. He belonged to a tribe with a history of being lively and disparaged.

Laura had named a different restaurant from the one in which she insulted him. She was sitting in a booth, reading, when he walked in.

The book, he saw, getting closer, was his second novel. She had done her hair pinned up in the back with tendrils coming down around her face. She wore a print blouse that had a lot of pink in it and a jacket that was a more subdued mauve shade. She looked gorgeous.

"I see what you're reading," he said, sitting across from her.

"It's very good. I read *The Twist* too. Both, excellent."

He looked around. Pots hanging, cheeses hanging. "Never been here. I'll have to do this in my apartment. What a great idea. The space over my head is going to waste! How did I not know that?"

She smiled, calmly it seemed, serenely, as if she'd lost the flustered person from the previous meeting. "I ordered you a martini by the way just the way you ordered the one in the other place. That's why he's bringing two over."

"I'm preparing my taste buds."

"You're down on Second Avenue?"

"Right."

"You probably have more space than most people."

"You?"

"I'm the exception. I actually have plenty of space. I've been living in my parents' apartment ever since they moved to Florida. I hate to admit it, but it's rent controlled. I'm very lucky in almost all things. Except love." She toyed with the collar of her blouse, letting her hand stray to her chin, in a gesture that was kind to herself, a small caress.

"Those things change," he said, tapping his glass against hers. "To better times."

They ordered—pork roast for him, fish for her. Thick bread arrived first. Harrison was hungry.

"Tell me what you're writing. Can you?"

"Should I? You're at a rival house."

She thought about it. "Okay. No expense account. This is a private meeting, just us. I wouldn't talk about your book to anyone at Harper unless we were trying to get you over to us, but you have no way of believing that, so if you're willing, I just want to know."

"It's supposed to be done. It's almost done. The ending doesn't feel right."

"Endings fail sixty percent of the time."

He told her the story. A Bobby Kennedy supporter and friend, a man who was all work and no play being crushed by Bobby's death.

He explained that he had started the novel when he had full faith in Kennedy's being alive, but he'd had to trash the whole thing or deal with the death because he, too, was crushed by it. "Bobby *became* someone. He changed."

"I know. People loved him and believed he could—" She stopped short of finishing. He thought "fix us" was the end of her sentence. "Then your character is in mourning?"

"Yes. It's affecting his marriage."

"Why? Are you willing to say why?"

"Well, she's already intimidated by him, the wife is. How can I explain? He's lost without a cause to keep him going. She doesn't feel as strongly about things as he does. She comes from poverty and she never was taught to notice the outside world. Her mind doesn't tune in to the national stuff—I don't mean on TV, of course, she watches TV. He comes from privilege, but he's cursed with a sensitivity and he's a loner of sorts."

"They're mismatched."

"Perhaps."

"And now it ends how?"

"He's on a trip to Ireland, solo, considering staying on."

"You're saying the ending doesn't work…"

"It doesn't have punch. A lot of it is about her. She's crazy about him. She won't go along with him on this trip, but he goes and he's sad, destroyed by the American election. And alone in Ireland. It ends with him alone."

"What if he comes back, then? Loving arms. Succor, but not. He's compromised."

"Huh. I'll think about it." But, damn, he was already thinking about it. A scene of homecoming was forming full-blown in his mind. "Sorry, I got a bit distracted."

"That's okay."

"I'm going to work on it."

They talked about the state of publishing, who the greats were. Pritchard, Trevor. (Those were two he hadn't met.) Laura was a woman with literary standards. When the check came, he insisted on paying.

"But I invited—"

He waved away her protest. He always felt good picking up the check. He'd picked it up with Dick Rovere though Dick had more money than he did.

They walked out together. "In what way are you unlucky in love?" he asked.

"Every way you can think of. I'm married by the way. Separated. I should get a divorce. I keep not deciding. It's easier to just let things go."

"You wouldn't be alone in that.."

They had both misspoken that first day. Now they were becoming friends. They liked each other. Which was worrisome in its own way since, as he made his way home, he found himself imagining a real kiss, and then imagining the removal of her fine well-chosen clothes.

It turned out a lot of people were waiting for, even asking about, Laura's annual Halloween party. She had little choice but to start drafting an invitation. *Ghosts and goblins welcome, in costume or not, proffering gifts of drink or not, food provided, dancing encouraged, Friday, October 31.*

She mimeographed fifty copies and spent the evening writing out envelopes to the people who were not colleagues or neighbors in her building where delivery was a simple matter.

That night, she asked neighbors if they would stockpile ice cubes for her—she was probably going to need the bathtub for some of the drinks. She would have to leave work early the Friday of the party but on Thursday she could make deviled eggs and get out the fondue pot and order an emergency platter from the deli—foods that if not consumed would provide her lunches for the next week. On Friday she could do the cheese balls and the shrimp cocktail.

A week and a half flew by and the Friday of the party arrived and she was as ready as she was going to be. She wore a slinky black dress and a witch's hat, both of which suddenly felt foolish. Guests began arriving, one, two, three, four. Harrison was among the first dozen. He came to the party un-costumed but bearing two bottles of wine and one of bourbon and a bowl of potato salad, all of which had been so awkward to carry that he had needed to take a taxi to her place on Fifth.

"You brought so much!"

"I figured you might need some help. Stash the booze if you don't need it."

"I don't know if I will or not. I'd love to stash it and give it back if I don't." People were pressing in at the door, hugging her, joking, and at times handing some sort of booze over. "There's punch on the table," she told them. "If you're in the mood for punchy things."

She kept putting things away and putting other things out, overhearing bits of conversation.

Wow. Look at this table.

What's the music?

Rolling Stones is what we need. I'll go through the records.

No, I will.

She decided to let her guests fight it out. One of her bosses, Ben, about sixty and fat, dressed as a cowboy (and without his wife, she noted), followed her to the kitchen. "Hey, gorgeous witch. I think you look smashing."

"Oh, thanks."

"Are you a little bit evil?" He put an arm around her.

"Um. Not too evil. Plus, married."

He looked at her skeptically. "Where is he, this mysterious person you talk about?"

"Working. In Stamford."

"Why isn't he here? Is he dull? He sounds…awfully dull."

"He's not. Oh, gosh, I keep forgetting things. Would you take this potato salad out to the table?" She poured herself a glass of red and sipped. Alienating a boss was not wise. Perhaps she could get him good and drunk with no memory of having been rejected.

Dick Rovere didn't show up. She peered out to the main room where a few people were dancing, and she was glad to see that three people sat across from Harrison, leaning forward, interested in what he was saying.

When she got closer, a publicist from her office was saying, "And *if* you're on the same train some Friday, we can talk."

"Great," agreed Harrison.

"Or we could just get together sometime for a drink or a dinner."

"Fine with me. Fantastic." Harrison wrote down the man's phone number.

The publicist was a bit of a climber. Harrison was awfully trusting.

And she was a fool, a little crazy.

By eleven o'clock almost everyone was dancing. If literary types looked foolish doing anything, it was the frug or the twist. Harrison didn't ask anyone to dance. A group pulled him up, insisting he join them.

Around midnight, he came to Laura in the kitchen to say good night. "Wonderful party. Thank you."

"I'm glad you could make it."

"I had a good time." He leaned over and kissed her on the cheek just as her cowboy boss came in.

"Ahem. Excuse me," her boss said and left. But his tone was bitter.

"You're fighting him off?" Harrison asked, but mostly it was an observation, not a question.

"Trying to. Tonight, he got a little sure of himself."

"Do you want me to stay a little longer? I have to get the morning train."

"If you can spare a couple of minutes. Lots of people are leaving. Maybe he will."

Harrison stuck by her, making it look as if they exchanged secrets. Finally, her boss left, and then Harrison bid Laura good night.

The first time they made it to bed, it was easy; they sort of flowed right into it, a kiss and then a long embrace against a wall in her apartment, hands tracing the length of each other, and a walk to the bedroom. He was guilty, having thought about it, fought it, known it was going to happen; she was lovely, and he was weak, unable to resist. The thing that surprised him, though, was that she was suddenly different, almost tentative. "Are you all right?" he asked.

"I think so."

"Should I stop?" He stood a few feet behind her on the way to her bedroom.

"No."

To feel lust again—how could anyone do without it? Discovery—lips, breasts, belly, all that was below—it was wonderful, the best exploration in the world.

Two hours later, Laura touched his back as he sat at the edge of the bed stunned. *Now what, now what?* he kept thinking. Would he take a train tomorrow, sit across from Maggie, tell her their life together was over?

"Please don't hate me," Laura said. "I know I flirted, I know I did this."

"I don't hate you. We're complicit."

"If we saw each other once a week, would that be so bad, would we be hurting anyone?"

He wasn't exactly thinking clearly, but the phrase "once a week" made it through to him.

"Should I make us a drink?"

"Yes."

"Will you stay the night?"

"Maybe not. No."

"Don't worry. I won't pressure you." She moved fluidly. The robe she had put on was a gorgeous pattern of pinks, exotic, maybe silk, not fastened in front. It billowed as she walked to her kitchen. After a few minutes he got up and went to the window and watched the flow of traffic on Fifth, then began to dress. Déjà vu. Electric Circus. Laura came back with two drinks, robe fastened.

He tried to sound light. "What is this to you—what we just did?"

"An affair? We both seem to need each other. We both work hard." She pulled her hair over her shoulder, for a moment becoming a woman in a Japanese painting. "I wanted this. I admit it."

The whiskey burned a nice path going down. "You are very beautiful," he said.

"And a little bit smart."

"More than a little."

He went back to his place. It was three in the morning. This is real life, he told himself. People do this all the time. Beth had only wanted one night. Laura wanted a routine, a once-a-week affair that might go on forever. People make arrangements like this, he kept reminding himself. He couldn't think past the moment. He felt the room wanting to spin.

Laura had given him the ending to his novel, which he had written and revised in two days and hurriedly turned in to his agent, who pronounced it fine. His character had gone back to his wife and that was the right ending. Ironic, sad. Everyone was compromised.

Laura's offer had depressed him. But he went home and wrote and came back to the city and wrote. Work was salvation. Chekhov knew that.

He saw Laura three more times.

He hadn't seen or heard of Everett in a while and didn't know if Maggie was still close to him. He didn't want to know.

Mostly he was alone. Lunch, dinner, evenings.

With each paycheck he became more himself. And when he couldn't write anymore, he took his camera out and went out and captured what he could.

27

Ohe day—he was in the city apartment—Maggie called and told him he'd had a phone call from some guy at Vassar and was supposed to call the guy back.

"A question about my work?"

"It sounded that way. I mean, he asked for Harrison Mirth, *the writer.*" A slight scolding in her tone was probably meant to keep him humble.

The third novel was out, respectable reviews, but only respectable. He was tired, but mostly worried about what was next.

He dialed the number she'd given him, reaching to turn the radio down just as someone said, "Jonathan Smith here."

"It's Harrison Mirth. I got a message to call you."

"Oh, wonderful, yes. We had a meeting here at the department yesterday and the thing is we wanted to know if you would like to teach for a year as a guest artist."

Harrison adjusted his chair, which scraped loudly, and he sat. "I've never taught."

"But you do the job of writing. You'd show them what you do, ask them to write things, tell them what you think of what they wrote. That's pretty much the job description."

"I'm being taken by surprise here."

"This is a good school."

"I know it is."

His mind raced. Would he make a decent salary? Would he have time to do his own work? Would he make a fool of himself, talking about what he did?

It would mean living at home again, wouldn't it? It was a sign, a way back to his family life and Maggie.

Smith continued. "It would be Tuesday and Thursday classes. We'd expect several weekends of readings and special seminars, maybe six of them over the year. The Tuesdays and Thursdays would be pretty heavy teaching days. The salary would be sixteen-five for the year.

Sixteen-five in addition to royalties from books and photographs. He'd be self-sufficient.

And thus, he agreed to begin a new pattern of going into the city

only when he could. Some weekends would be possible still. He worked
to get used to the idea.

And as if he hadn't been shaken enough—he had to believe
Shakespeare was onto something with the constant references to the
stars—his friend Oscar came to him, almost teary-eyed, asking, "Old
friend, I hate to ask, but you are often gone from your place and…I'd
like to rent it those times."

"Rent? Ridiculous. Just use when you want." As he said that, he realized the reason. "Are you all right?"

"Not too good."

"Betty?"

"I'm in love with someone else."

"Oh."

"I mean really in love."

"Oh."

"I need a place to see her. She's married too. I'm going to get a place
soon. I'm going to make the move to divorce. I just need to do it right.
Carefully. The least amount of hurt."

Harrison nodded that he understood a need to do it right. *Irreconcilable differences.*

"Betty is good and nice, but we never should have married. I can't go
on. Walk with me?" And without more words, they started out.

Oscar wore a well-made suit—very proper. He was beginning to
bald a little. He still moved with the grace of a dancer or an actor who
had learned how to turn on a dime. Harrison was only wearing jeans
and a sweater.

They walked for twenty blocks up Fifth Avenue and then back down.
Harrison told him he understood, but he didn't. Oscar had declared he
was in love. Harrison couldn't remember what that felt like. He had only
felt the need for romance. And when it came down to it, he could not
really imagine leaving Maggie, carefully or not.

"You've been tempted?" Oscar asked.

"Not like you. Not leading to anything like your certainty."

"Maybe I'm just a bad guy," Oscar said. "But I wish you this pain, my
friend. There's nothing quite like it."

To be so sure. He envied Oscar.

And so, he became a teacher, commuting from farm to class.

"What's it like," Maggie asked, over a Monday night pasta she made
him, "looking at beautiful young women every day?"

"Just Tuesdays and Thursdays. I guess it's bearable."

They laughed companionably.

Smith called him aside as soon as he got to work one Tuesday early on and said, "Come to dinner this Saturday night. Bring your wife. I'll have a few colleagues over to get to know you."

Maggie was skittish about the dinner party, their first in academic circles. She said, "I'd much rather be a host than a guest."

"You'll be terrific," Harrison assured her.

"What do people do, read Proust aloud?" she grumbled.

"Maybe Joyce," he joked. "No, I don't know! Just be yourself."

"What should we take? Should I make a pie?"

"Flowers, wine, for sure, and pie if you want."

When they got to the party, Harrison saw his colleagues through Maggie's eyes, knowing she would eventually make jokes about the bespectacled, bearded, long-haired, bleary-eyed oddballs who lived the intellectual life. He was one of them, he supposed, and he liked them. And he liked the work more than he could have guessed. Maggie was dreaming that he'd get a permanent position at Vassar, close to home, just a short commute away, and then their lives would be settled.

After a while he went into the kitchen where Maggie was helping Penelope Smith who was saying, "So nice of you to bring a pie. I have angel food cake and cut fruits. We can serve everything. Hey, here he is, my husband's favorite new person."

"I heard you might want a gravy maker. I make a pretty good gravy," he offered.

"Please, be my guest."

He sifted some flour into the meat fat and listened to the women talking. "I understand you were a theater producer. Is that right?" Penelope asked.

"A long time ago now."

"I love theater. I used to think I wanted it for a career."

"I…understand. Lots of us go that way when we're first smitten. I think Harrison told me you work with young people?"

"Social work, yes."

"Some very difficult cases, I imagine."

"Um. I would say *all* difficult cases. Lots of sadness out there."

"Maggie gives all her time to the school board. Noble work too," he interjected. He began to stir. He knew her. He knew how she was measuring herself.

When the gravy looked good, Penelope said, "All right. Everything is ready. Let's call them to the table. Would you do that, Maggie?"

Out in the living room, Maggie called out, "Dinner's on!" And everybody trooped to the table.

"So, Harrison," began the most awkward of the professors, a longhaired, sleepy-looking fellow, "how are book sales?"

Harrison frowned and scratched at his neck. "I don't know. I'm not being coy. I try not to ask. It's good to stay in a cloud, maybe, you know, away from all that reality."

"Indeed," Smith said levelly. "Only a few make a living. Who would expect to?"

"That's what I mean," said the awkward one. "Universities become patrons. At least there's that."

"He loves teaching," Maggie said, unabashedly putting in a plug for that permanent position.

Harrison shrugged. But the truth was, the students found him inspiring. They loved his classes and were starting a magazine.

Smith slapped a hand on the table. "I can pick 'em. And now, here's the question! How do you feel about Kentucky, you two?"

Maggie turned to Harrison, puzzled. He was puzzled too. Kentucky?

"Because I hear—and this is just a rumor at this point—that they're going to spring for a guest artist next year. Nice money. I'd definitely recommend you."

"Kentucky," Harrison said. "Never been there."

"We thought we'd have a permanent position, but they cut the line, alas. I wish it could be otherwise. But you are a teacher, for sure."

Kentucky. Harrison was already figuring out what he would have to send ahead and what would fit in the new Volkswagen beetle.

The next time he went into the city, Harrison found an envelope with cash under his typewriter. Oscar. He wrote on it. *Never. It goes back to you.*

And the next time he went in, he found a note with the names of three restaurants on them. *There is a dinner for two at the first two and a dinner for one at the third, already paid for. You only need give your name. Please enjoy. You have saved my life—my heart at least.*

Harrison first thought he would take Maggie to one of the dinners when she came in with him, but he couldn't figure out how to explain the gift from Oscar. The woman Oscar was mad about worked at his law firm. Harrison thought again about the fact that Oscar had let himself feel volcanic emotions which caused an upending of his whole life. Oscar was mad with love.

Harrison called his friend and said, "Let's use one of these dinners to get together. You and me."

"All right, all right," Oscar said. "Friendship I can use. But I'll make it up to you some other way."

They went to a steakhouse off Fifth. "You're changed," Harrison said at dinner. "This new woman has changed you."

"She's a realist. She doesn't pretend to be anything but who she is—lustful, impatient, practical, cynical, generous. She doesn't try to be good. I think I was dying of goodness."

Harrison couldn't help wanting to write that line.

"What?" Oscar said.

"Am I dying of goodness?"

"Look, go to Kentucky. I don't know if you'll love Kentucky, but they'll love you. And they'll pay you for it. Beats being ruled by Maggie's checkbook."

There it was, opening like a flower on the table. Money. Maggie's. Harrison hated money. He thought people should have just enough, not extra, not enough to buy someone's cooperation. But what a fool he was to think anyone avoided that.

"I begged her to go with me for the year. To bring the family. They're giving me a whole house."

"She won't. She's making a stand."

"She agreed to visit twice. I agreed to drive home four times over the year and fly home twice. It's going to be rough."

"That's it, then."

28

Maggie answered the phone one morning in November, early; she was shuffling toward the kitchen in slippers and robe, thinking to make coffee.

Her brother on the other end said, "Honey. I have bad news. It's— Mom died last night."

"Oh. Oh no. How?"

"Heart attack. It was her heart."

"Are you okay?"

"I'm okay. Drink didn't help. She was pretty pickled."

"It got worse, then."

"She blotted out a lot."

Maggie could hear the kids stirring.

"I put off the funeral for three days so you could get here. Do you want to fly?"

"No, I'll drive. I like to drive."

"Think you can get the great writer to come too?"

"Of course, he'll come. I'll call him as soon as we hang up."

"Well, it'll be good to see you."

"I could use a big brother hug."

After they hung up, Maggie sat for a while at the kitchen table, doing nothing. Mama. Always there, now gone. And yet her mother's voice played easily. *Are you keeping hold of that character you married? I tried to read one of his books, but I just couldn't get interested. He's certainly not Southern, is he? So bouncy—where did he get that? See if you can't calm him down some if you're going to bring him around.*

She cried a little, but not for her pickled mother who had had little to live for, more for her mother's constant sadness while alive.

Her eldest daughter, dressed for school, found her in the kitchen, doing nothing about breakfast. "What's wrong, Mom?"

"Grandma died."

"Which one?"

"Virginia. My mother. We have to go. I'll get us packed as soon as I make coffee. You don't have to go to school."

Emma sat down, weighing that news. Her hair was very long, and she wore lipstick and mascara. After she saw her mother moving, she got up and went to tell her sister and brother.

Minutes later, the coffee maker was gurgling.

Maggie dialed Kentucky. Her husband answered brightly.

"You were up!" she said.

"I was up." He had asked not to be called in the morning when he was working, but this was an emergency.

"My mother died."

"Oh, I'm sorry, honey."

"Yeah. She wasn't too good for a while. I guess we expected it."

"Still—"

"Anyway, I'm taking the kids down. We'll start this morning, driving, soon as I get us together and tell Old Wilson to watch the place. Can you get to Virginia in a couple of days for the funeral?"

"Of course. I'll see about how to cancel class. Do you want me to fly up and drive with you?"

"No. The drive will do me good. I think when I drive."

"Me, too. The same. Thinking time."

"Right."

"Maggie. Be careful, okay? I know this is hard."

"She loved me in her way, I guess."

Thomas came into the kitchen, still hardly awake. He rubbed his mother's arm and hugged her.

"I'm okay," she said.

He kept rubbing her arm worriedly.

She drank coffee slowly, then roused herself and packed fast. Her brother was saying in her head what he would no doubt say at the funeral home: *Now you just sit him down and tell him after this residency thing in Kentucky, he should come home.*

On his desk, two months after the funeral, Harrison had four notices about possible jobs. Two had come from Smith and two from his current chair, all four of them telling him about guest teaching positions. It was real, this was what he was doing, this was his life. One position was in Ohio for one term only, another in Arizona for a year, another in Seattle for a year, and one closer to home, in Boston.

Type up a resume and get it out! Smith had written.

He was a terrible typist as his editors had let him know. He got excited, went too fast, hunted and pecked like a manic chicken, partly enchanted by the tap tap tap and ding of work being done. But this was serious, so he tried hard. He typed a resume slowly and finding six errors, used white tape, but it looked bad, so he decided to retype it and got it down to two errors. It would have to do. He wrote four letters to the four universities and got those letters in envelopes with stamps and carried the packet in to work with him, asking for the outgoing mail.

The envelopes had a few mistakes on them, too, with cross outs, the secretary pointed out.

Pam Weid was her name. She was a sweet earnest woman who disliked the hippie contingent at the school and fought it with her own hair skimmed back tight. She wore a rotating selection of sober skirts and blouses. "You didn't have to use your own stamps. If this is business, we mail it for you."

"Oh. I didn't know that."

"Would you like for me to retype the envelopes? I can make them look more… "

He laughed. "Professional." He'd been trying to persuade himself that errors would make him more sympathetic. "I would be grateful."

She opened the first envelope and looked worriedly at the letter and resume she took out. "Would you mind if I retyped everything? I wouldn't get these out until tomorrow. Would that be too late?"

"That would be fine."

In class he talked about voice, the author's voice. *Do you believe in the person telling the story? Do you sympathize with the person telling the story? Is that necessary? Do you think the person telling the story has moral values?*

A boy in the front row squinted. Harrison said, "I'm not talking about sex. A writer can write about sex and have or not have moral values. I'm talking in a bigger sense about recognizing hypocrisy or cruelty or prejudice. Do you see what I mean?"

He was becoming very fond of all of them, the angry, the slovenly, the overly clean and stiff-backed, the ones who wrote about loneliness, the ones who were trying to punish bad parents by capturing them on paper. He took the kids home in his heart. How had he not known he could do this job? It was constantly fascinating. Some kids wrote because they had nothing else to occupy them. Others were hurt and needed to find a way to get it out. He had been one of the latter. Each day he came closer to acknowledging the truth of the ambitious father and mother he hardly ever saw when growing up. Their insistent absences had hurt him and made him feel he was less than his peers. He could even now so easily, because of these kids, call back the offhand compliments of his accomplished father (were they true, real?) the focused criticisms of his diva mother (they felt very real).

The students had brought him closer to himself.

One boy had written a story of an adventurous childhood filled with love—not much conflict but a hell of a lot of joy in the piece. What a lucky, lucky kid.

One book, two late papers, and a letter from Maggie were in his mailbox. He carried them awkwardly, reading over one of the late papers.

The secretary called out, "Mr. Mirth. I started on your letters. One is done. Do you need it now?"

"Tomorrow is fine, Pam. Put your blessing on them." He would stop and get her a vase of flowers tomorrow before coming in.

She said, "You are the most cheerful teacher we've ever had around here. We all talk about how funny it is that you have that name. Aren't names strange? I once knew a guy whose last name was Lively and he was!"

"I wonder sometimes. It *is* possible I had a bunch of merry knights in my background. Maybe my father's ancestors were full of jokes. I should look into that." He got an image of jolly old men laughing as they threw meat over their shoulders to the dogs in the manor house. "I'll check in with you tomorrow. Again, thanks."

"My pleasure."

Walking down the hall, he opened Maggie's letter. She missed him, she wrote. The French drain needed some work. Anna had won a prize for writing poetry. Maggie's brother was in a deeper state of mourning than she was over their mother's death, maybe because he lived closer and saw their mother more often. She wondered where her own feelings were sometimes.

He read and re-read the letter, walking to his car. Other people had abandoned letter writing now that they could make phone calls so easily, but he had joined the campaign to keep letters alive and Maggie was on board with it. In fact, she was a very good writer, but she didn't want to do anything with it.

He sat in the VW reading over the late papers he'd picked up. It was a trifle chilly, so he started the engine but kept sitting there until he located his red pen and began marking. The radio came on, too, scratching out a Mozart piano concerto on the only station that offered such things.

He sat there going through what Maggie had sent—a Robert Lud-
lum. Two days ago, it was *Fear of Flying.* He read a few pages of the Lud-
lam and even though it was well done, he began to doze. A tap on the
window awoke him. A guy from the history department said, "Careful
with the carbon monoxide. We don't want to lose our famous writer."

Famous. It didn't feel like it. His agent had said recently that he didn't
think he could sell a story collection, so Harrison was trying everything.
A play. A satirical novel. Nothing felt right. Maggie had suggested again,
"Write something like a mystery. Something suspenseful."

He couldn't bring himself to tell Maggie about the death knell he'd
heard the last time he was in New York. His agent, Lewis, wasn't the
only one sounding warnings. He and his editor had gone to dinner—a
celebration, Harrison thought at first. But he was very wrong. The mood
was fairly low as he sensed a speech coming from Walter Tomjanovich.
"Things are changing," Walter said. "I love *Friday.* I think it's a great
book, but it's the end of an era. Novels like that won't be published
anymore."

"Like…what?"

"Smart. Quiet. Works of observation."

"Why not?"

"Changing times, changing personnel, the market. They keep asking
for more, well, what's the word, inflammatory novels or more innova-
tive novels. I hope you have something wild in you for the future. Take
your time. I mean, really, take your time, explore, experiment."

Harrison had tried not to feel defeated. Change with the times, he
told himself. Smart, quiet observations—out of fashion. Passé! Okay.

He'd carried that conversation around with him for a year now. He'd
told only Oscar. Meanwhile, as fate would have it, Maggie wanted to
collaborate on something highly commercial and kept firing ideas, but
when he presented this dilemma to Oscar, his friend just shook his
head, saying, "Is collaboration your thing?"

Harrison started for home and his tuna salad sandwich, a nod to
his boyhood. Emma was a freshman already, studying history. Anna
was seventeen but wanted to delay college for a year. She was writing
poetry intensely these days. Maggie had insisted she would pay all their
tuitions and costs out of her inheritance and her investments but Harrison wanted to be involved in this major aspect of the kids' lives, so he
sent Emma money anyway, no doubt a laughable sum compared to the
amount Maggie sent.

A permanent position, should the possibility ever arise, would put his kids through school the rest of the way. How good that would make him feel!

He wrote three novels in the next years, but nobody took them.

Emma graduated with a major in history and Anna began her freshman year, after two years of putting it off, announcing a major in linguistics. Thomas became a teenager. He hated everybody at his school and Maggie told him that was okay because he was smarter than half his teachers. It was true. He corrected the teachers all the time, which Harrison explained in a letter, was not going to make things go more smoothly.

Harrison taught at three more schools in the next three years, making good friends at all of them. Colleagues from the previous schools called and wrote and asked him to visit them when he could. Students from old roll books sent him manuscripts, which he always read—if the kids were serious, someone had to take them seriously, right? His life had a shape if not the one he most wanted.

Then the Seattle position came up again. It was such a long way from home, but this time he took it. "Maggie, come with me," he begged once more.

"I'll visit."

"Let Thomas come to live. A new school."

"He won't want that."

Apparently, when questioned, Thomas, too, said no to Seattle.

There had been three novels, three schools, and a few temptations of the flirtatious sort, which he fought successfully. I'm a traveler, he thought, a bit of a strange old sod with a strange old life. None of the wandering he did pushed Harrison over the precipice to consider divorce until Denise Amott.

Seattle.

As if she'd been on his schedule all along.

29

She wasn't beautiful but he couldn't stop looking at her. In seminar she'd sat to his right, at an angle, looking down. He couldn't even remember which student name went with what face until he got their first extended sketches. Hers was the best, hands down. Then he knew her name. Denise.

She came to his office one day to talk.

"About your work?" he asked.

"About what you're reading," she clarified. "I read a lot. I want the expert's opinion."

In the classroom, he'd wracked his brain, wondering, Did he know her? He felt he knew her. Her eyes were such an intense shade of blue, it hurt to look at them. He'd read something once by Josephine Tey about the color of the eyes of sociopaths, dense blue, unusual blue. This grad student was intense, sharp, possibly a little older than some of the others.

"I tried to write a novel," she said. "Twice. Two novels. I don't know if I ever will be able to do anything good, but I do read everything."

"That's a good start. Most writers read a lot."

"I've read yours."

He wasn't sure he should respond to that. He never assigned his own work and never knew if the students read it.

She had a tiny mouth, a long nose. He watched her speak. She said, "I don't always stick to things. I went to med school, but I dropped it after the first year."

"I'm sure it was beastly hard."

"No, I did well. I just didn't want it anymore. I was flirting with architecture for a while too."

"How does a person flirt with architecture?"

"A year. Grad school. I didn't put that in my application. I wanted to make this stick. The one thing I'm sure of is that I'm always reading and always will be."

He nodded. He identified with that. He was trying to think who she reminded him of. "I hope you'll tell me what you're reading. That way, I could compare notes with you along the way."

He had been about to say, "What I've finished, I will gladly lend you," but that might not work with "along the way."

She held his gaze and there was some kind of challenge in it.

He couldn't think clearly at first. Then he wrote down three titles and handed the sheet of paper over.

"Difficult handwriting," she observed.

"You can't read it?"

"No, I can. I can still make it out." She folded the paper and put it in her breast pocket.

"My daughter always says she can't. My second daughter. She's still in college." Ha, as if talking about his children could put off Denise.

Recklessness invaded him. He bumped into chairs as he left his office. Of course, of course, lots of students wrote about sex, maybe not as explicitly as she had. They were feeling their oats, trying to pin down their longings, but Denise's first assignment had featured dangerous mean sex. In workshop, one guy said, "Whoa. Very disturbing but good, really good," and one young woman called her sketch *tough*. Those were true. The sex was between an angry man, a carpenter, and a woman he was building a cabinet for. His hands were thick, calloused, talented. He was rough with tools. He hated being servant to a privileged woman who could pay him. Domination was his goal.

Back when that workshop critique was in session and Denise's turn came to speak, she said, "Good, yes, I thought he was angry, definitely seducing her, but with anger. You know, like in the play, *Miss Julie*."

Some of them had read *Miss Julie*, some of them hadn't.

Anyway, as a student she was impressive, and she was clearly ambitious which was why Harrison gave her the titles he was reading.

Harrison went to his apartment, a second-floor flat in a blank gray building, where he settled on the sofa to read. Stacked on his coffee table were an Edna O'Brien, another Graham Greene, the Edward Said everyone was talking about, God, another Cheever because he simply couldn't get away from Cheever, the Garp book people were loving, but right now he'd been alternating between *The Cement Garden* by Ian McEwan and *The Book of Laughter and Forgetting* by Milan Kundera.

There was incest in the McEwan. And it was disturbing. He suspected Denise was going to like that book. He began to write in it as he read, pointing out places that the author had chosen sensationalism when you could feel—Harrison could feel—that it wasn't the organic choice. He made notes, writing things like, *Calculating? Sensational only?*

Ha, who was giving assignments to whom?

He switched to the Kundera, very challenging and given a big boost by Updike, who found it brilliant. It was modern—or rather post-modern, in being all broken up and making the reader do the math, so to speak. Yes, Denise was going to like this one; she'd rise to the challenge. And if she wanted sex, there was plenty of it in the novel or whatever you wanted to call Kundera's book. She was going to love part two—the harridan mother-in-law and the ménage a trois she almost discovers. Denise had already shown she liked danger and the unearthing of the dark impulses.

He read late into the afternoon; it was evening when he stopped and realized he was hungry and still had tons of work to do.

But he'd gotten to Part Five where it turned out a woman tried to start a romantic relationship with a young man who was a student. He turned the book over. The jacket copy described the book's theme as "the examination of a glimpse of one's own inferiority and its relationship to troubled lust." Whoa. Thick stuff. Harrison didn't exactly look forward to discussing this section with Denise. He'd ask her to write up some notes.

A question he would ask his workshop: Should there be philosophy, undisguised, in a novel? Another subject for another day.

He check-marked passages that were already being quoted everywhere. There was the one about how a woman's sadness was the key to her genitals. And the one about how the person (man, likely) who has been awkward and unseemly all his life becomes charming once he is loved.

Two martinis on an empty stomach and he was rocking, happy and miserable. Thinking to get a burrito or a burger, something fast, he left the apartment, but suddenly turned around and headed back up the stairs. There was some cheese, some crackers; then he found a sliver of ham, two kinds of bread to clothe it. He stayed in, watching mindless sitcoms to clear out his head.

Denise tried to run into him outside of class for the whole of the next week, but it didn't work. He'd vaporized. The more she tried, the more determined she became that she would be his special one, his favorite, and he would dispense all his wisdom to her.

The next week, on the day of the workshop, she brushed her hair to a gloss and dressed carefully in fitted jeans and a shirt that buttoned low.

But looking at herself in the mirror, she thought, *What a slut I am.* She ripped off the top, put on a sweatshirt, and slammed out of the house. Her next assignment was shit. He was going to hate her anyway.

The usual. He was there in class early. She figured the other profs were trying to say, by being late, *I am awfully busy, but I will attend to you as I can.*

He laughed with one girl about something that had been on TV and listened to an account of the plot of *Death on the Nile*, which two students had seen. "I'll have to see that for sure," he joked. "Maybe I can learn something about plot."

"Do you still have something to learn?" the bright boy, Josh, asked. He was the one Denise usually tried to sit next to. She told the class one day she thought he was going to be published sooner than all of them. (She was right, it turned out, and Josh stayed devoted to Harrison for the next thirty years.)

Harrison said, "I have everything to learn. It never ends."

Two more students came in.

"Welcome, welcome," Mirth said. Most of them called him Harrison. He told them it was okay. Others stuck to Professor Mirth. Denise didn't know what to call him. Nothing felt right.

"Did you write something good this week?" he asked them.

Many groans made them one, comfortable with each other.

"Good sign. If you like what you write, you're probably not in the ballpark. It's only important to do it."

"Interesting!" Josh said. "I get that."

Denise tapped Josh on the shoulder and asked in a whisper if he could have coffee after class. "Oh, sure," he said, blushing.

Class was good, it was useful, she took notes; she tried not to be special, but felt that she was, anyway.

After class she hurried out with Josh. "What are you reading, what are you seeing?" she asked him as they walked.

Flattered, he named the titles of movies and TV shows and books.

They went to the coffee shop around the corner and talked for an hour. He was enchanted, which gave her faith that she still had some charms. "Thanks." She kissed him on the cheek and left.

And found herself minutes later in the office of her professor, still wondering if she should call him Mr. Mirth or Professor or Harrison or just Mirth? She greeted him with, "Hey, sweetheart, read anything good today?"

He thought about her a lot. Her determination touched him. He also refused to be ridiculous, a cliché. Plenty of colleagues along the way boffed their students. Oh no, he told himself, not me. I will not be my father looking for Mrs. Something or Edna Whatever while my mother was away. Yet he caught himself thinking with relief that the fall term would be over in two more months and perhaps Denise wouldn't take another course from him next term and would that by chance make it all right to—? And he thought, Look, in a year, I'll escape; I'll be teaching somewhere else, I'll be safe.

Two months later, secure that she had earned an A+, tired of the many meetings over coffees and glasses of wine to talk about the things he was reading (and, man, he was exhausted by her need to know), Harrison nevertheless agreed to another sit down at a bar and this time he touched her hand. She had told him in one of their previous meetings that he was the best teacher she had ever had and that he blew her away as a writer. She'd quoted his lines, chapter and verse.

He knew what she was doing, but she did it so damned well, getting his lines accurate.

Oh, it wasn't all her fault—he was equally to blame. He couldn't stop looking at her. And what she said in class and out was way above the level of the others. She was brilliant. And serious. And had that crazy forward-leaning grit he admired in women every time. To want, to want, to want. It was life.

For months he'd known she was making herself available to him—the way she leaned forward, teased, called him anything but Professor or Harrison, but often something like friend or sweetheart or honey, the way she caught his eye in class, the blue of her eyes, mesmerizing.

He said over the beers they were having as he touched her hand, "You know where this is going?"

She nodded.

"You know I'm married? Have kids? One of them is practically your age."

She nodded again "Don't worry. You'll get another job. I'll graduate. I won't cause you any grief."

"That easy?"

"I think so," she said.

"I disagree. I'm crazy about you. And obviously, here I am. But...I don't want to hurt you."

"Nobody has to know."

What was it with women wanting him only in the dark? "I think that never quite works."

"I'm so happy you like me. I was pretty low. I didn't think anything was worth it. I was in the depths. And then you came along."

His head spun. He could hardly swallow.

He paid the check with cash on the table.

"That's too big a tip."

"I don't care. Let's go. My place." He was jumping off a cliff, couldn't think about whether he'd live or not.

When they got there, she wandered around maddeningly, touching everything that was his, typewriter, papers, books, frying pan. "So, this is *you*," she said.

He took in her body—not for the first time. She was petite—not that she liked it, he knew. She'd told him she always wanted to be six feet tall. Her hair swung as she picked up a napkin from the floor and searched for a wastebasket. She said, "This place should be more elegant. You're an elegant man."

"It's a temporary rent. Can't be helped. I'm lucky the department found it for me."

"You should have beauty in your life!"

He laughed a little, followed her, and finally caught her. "I do."

The kiss was a little awkward, but they kept going. He breathed in her peppermint and beer breath. Fumbling, they grabbed at each other everywhere; yes, he was crazed. They were together, finally, after months of temptation, and he couldn't slow it down. Oh, she was fascinating. Maddening. He hadn't passed an hour for months without imagining her.

In the bedroom, he took her clothes off impatiently. She groaned, liking that. He knelt before her, worshipful, kissing belly and thighs. He was as hard as he had ever been. He could manage five times tonight, like a boy. When he looked up at her, she looked sad.

"What?"

"Nothing. I… Nothing." She raised him up and they fell on the bed.

Revelations came later. After the third time, she spoke about herself. She disliked her breasts, thought they were too big. His "nonsense" didn't comfort her and so he started to look at them with a measuring eye, even though he didn't really care if her proportions weren't right. She said, "Next time, be rougher. I want you to be rough with me."

"You surely don't mean it?"

"Oh yes."

"I want to love you."

"Then hurt me a little."

Eventually it was three in the morning and he saw her out to her car. He thought about the critique she had given him. He could *pretend* to hurt her—would that do? He started to laugh as he saw himself from the outside, as he imagined rough talk and shoving. No, he couldn't do it, he decided. He was disturbed, unsettled, through the night, through the next day, as he had been from the moment she first came to his office, as he would be in the future when she told him she had survived two suicide attempts. Thus began a five-year period of utter madness during which he would be loved, scorned, cuckolded, used, and whipped this way and that. For all the wrong he had done, he deserved it. He'd found a Maggie-substitute who knew how to punish.

Maggie waited for summers to come with some dread—Harrison was chaotic—and with hope, too, that once again he would add charm to her life. He finished the job in Seattle. Then it was Ohio. She was now used to it—he went away to teach. When he came home on visits, mostly summers, she got to be most herself—an excellent hostess, a cheerful cook, a wise woman who knew what to say. A helpmeet, a reader, a smart, smart woman.

Her mother's advice lived within her. *Let the fishing line out. That's men. He knows where he needs to be in the long run.*

And then he arrived, travel weary for only a day, and the festivities began. Friends! Almost every day—people wanting to see him. Smith and his wife came up from Vassar. Stay overnight, she'd told them on the phone, and they did. Oscar came up with his new wife, Valerie. His former wife Betty did not have a new husband, so she came up alone and they entertained her. Harrison was wonderful at brightening her, saying, "You look very smart in that outfit!" and asking her, "What is your work like?" and listening to all she said, even though Maggie knew he adored Oscar and sympathized with him as well.

Old actor friends came up from the city. Randolph and Sarah once and a woman named Joanie. The former neighbor Sophie who had years before moved to the city even came once with her new guy.

The girls came and went, most of the time with friends.

Harrison painted the back room when Maggie asked him to and he kept after the garden, which this year she had hired Wilson to start.

Maggie read for about seven hours a day when you counted early mornings and late nights. She was sneaking in a chapter of a Stephen King mid-afternoon one day when Harrison came in from the garden.

He watched her until she looked up, and then he said carefully, "I've been thinking... Now, hear me out. You write really well. Why don't you write something on your own? Spend some of your reading time writing instead. Start with a sketch."

"Are you practicing your teaching on me?"

"No. I sort of seem to have that down. It's just... You need something. You read all the time and I—"

"I love it."

He pressed, "You read indiscriminately. *Mademoiselle*, the scandal sheets, Proust, I mean—"

"Look, I'm not one of your students."

"I know but what if you tried to say some of the things inside you—"

"People would be bored. Seriously. Nice of you, but really."

He threw up his hands and went back to the garden, and after a while she heard him singing, "Tell the boys in the backroom—"

She could deploy words, sure, but she didn't have that crazy manic thing that made a person revise the same sentence twenty times. And she was glad not to be that version of nuts.

30

The tractor accident happened one day in the midsummer after he'd been seeing Denise for almost two years. It was very warm, so in the morning when he dressed to go into the field, Harrison put on the purple Guatemalan shorts Maggie had found in a magazine and had made especially for him. He looked comical in the shorts and work boots, sort of Joel McCrea playing something exotic, an innocent colonialist working the land, smiling beatifically at his peasants.

The tractor he'd had forever was an International Harvester, a high-wheel Cub, and he loved it because it was a wonderful machine. It could shovel snow, grade roads, cut hay (for this it had a sickle bar). It also had a rotary motor for lawns, and you could attach a trailer to it to haul firewood. He had bought it mainly to cut field hay, oh, over twenty years ago now, beginning of the time up here. He'd lucked out—found it as a one-thousand-dollar demonstrator at a place that sold farm supplies. He asked Maggie at the time if they could afford it. They decided it would pay for itself because the local farmers charged a lot to mow wild grasses and brush which Harrison and Maggie had plenty of. He realized later that having the tractor made another series of tasks for him to do and took time away from writing. But he didn't blame the machine; he loved it anyway.

The tractor looked like a stripped car, he always thought. It had big rear wheels, five feet high, which he kept filled with antifreeze, heavier than air, for traction. He checked—yep, the tires were full. When he climbed to the saddle seat, he felt like he was riding a horse.

The days he worked on the tractor, away from the house, he let himself be the broken-down person he was. Denise had broken him down. He wanted to cry. Everything she had told him swam in his mind, words and phrases playing over and over. She'd led a murky life. At sixteen she'd had an affair with her paternal uncle, a businessman who was a familiar in her mother's house and who had been perhaps a one-time lover of her mother. She suspected her mother knew of the affair all along. Denise smoked dope while she told Harrison about her various unseemly lovers. There was something about her bizarre calm—or was it cynicism?—that mesmerized and cushioned him, lifted him out of himself as if he'd smoked too. He listened to her tales of ongoing co-caine connections, brushes with violence, and a fast, fast life. He had craved the city. She was the city.

This last year he had to fly to see her from Ohio, where he was teach-ing, or fly her in to see him. It made for crazy excuses and lies, which sickened him and yet he did it, tortured, as if trying to finish a sentence. He had to keep hiding airline ticket stubs for Seattle.

He knew she was with others when she wasn't with him, and yet each visit brought back the puzzle of how to either capture her or end things. She would twine herself around him, enchanting him, only to get up abruptly or to say something outrageously funny.

Her hair was stick straight, jet black, and now almost down to her waist. She said maybe she had East Indian blood from way back some-where, but he wasn't sure what that meant to her if she did.

Back in Seattle she still slept with a pistol under her pillow. The first time he discovered it, he'd been shocked. Now he was used to it and thought, *Better not turn over too abruptly because of the gun.*

She sent him her writing all the way through the Ohio job, usually an envelope a week. He went over it carefully giving her suggestions and it was gratifying to see it got better every time. When he told her things in person, even things she didn't want to hear, she pursed her lips and listened. He'd called her from Ohio just before coming home for the summer. He told her he was desperate with the need to change his life and maybe should give it all up and just go back to Seattle for the sum-mer and be with her. She told him nonsense, go home, he was married.

Yesterday, he took a drive to a pay phone to call her. It wasn't the first time he'd done so. He heard his voice, somehow with a mind of its own, offering to leave Maggie. Denise's voice came at him low and muffled. She told him, "Sweetheart, don't do that. I'm totally fine."

"But we can't go on like this." Had he actually said such trite words?

"We can. It's all right."

"What am I to you?" He'd laughed at himself. Here he was, playing Madame Bovary. He'd always identified with her, after all. Oh yes, he was the Bovary, the Karenina, the Princess Margaret in the room. Des-perate unappreciated women made perfect sense to him.

Denise answered that he had a reputation to protect, that he was a great man, a great writer, and then she added that line about how she hadn't really wanted to live until he found something worthwhile in her. That was a very seductive line. She knew when to deploy it.

"Go, enjoy your good life," she said. "You have it all."

As if to underscore Denise's words, the sun shone brilliantly on him and Maggie as they sat that morning over cereal and coffee. "It's so good to have you home," Maggie said softly. Out the windows their land looked bright and beautiful. Maggie had her correspondence spread out before her. The perfect life, yes.

Harrison got up from the breakfast table to get to work. He passed the pond on the way to the barn to fetch the tractor. He saw that the pond was a mess again because the farmer who rented their fields used too much fertilizer so there was a buildup of nitrogen which was great for the bit of corn Harrison grew but made the weeds and algae in the pond flourish.

He tromped back to the kitchen. "Mag. I need your help. Can you work in the pond today?"

"Sure."

He pulled a few weeds on his way back to the barn and he saw as he got the tractor out that Maggie was already wobbling her way to the pond, wearing his thigh-high wading boots, which didn't fit. The big boots made her lift each foot carefully with each step.

They worked all morning and then came together.

They had lunch—cheese, crusty bread, tomatoes—and went back to it.

Midafternoon, Harrison had to go over some rocky ground, so he lifted the lever that pulled the chain that lifted the cutting bar. He would say later he heard a snap. Anyway, a link of the chain broke and with a big thunk, the bar fell to the ground. Harrison got off the tractor, preparing to lift the eighty-pound bar. He shut the engine off and put the tractor in gear—there were no brakes on the old machine—he was used to making do. He trotted off to the barn for some wire to tie up the bar. In a way he was proud of how good he was at this life even though it was not his kind of life.

He got the bar tied up.

He was tired, despairing, looking for a way to change the life he'd become good at, and, standing in front of his wonderful tractor that kept serving, old as it was, he reached over and pushed the starter button, not remembering that he had the machine in gear. He'd done this thousands of times with the tractor in neutral, not in gear.

The machine started forward.

Harrison was wearing heavy work boots and otherwise just the little purple diaper. He backed up as fast as he could. There was nothing to hold onto. Maggie didn't see. She kept pulling weeds. The tractor kept coming, but he kept escaping. And then he tripped. And the tractor kept coming.

There was no help for it. The wheels would roll over him. He pulled himself into a fetal position, thinking, *This is it. Goodbye everything.*

Maggie jumped when she heard the scream. It took her a while to figure out what had happened, but her husband was trying to sit up and he was yelling, "Stop the tractor, stop it!" She wanted to run toward him, but every move she made was in slow motion because of the wading boots. Against her better sense she went to the tractor instead of her husband and, running, sort of alongside it, moved the gears, choking the thing until she stalled it. Then she started toward him.

He said, "I think you'd better call for help."

She lurched and tripped in his wading boots back to the house.

He had no mind. He wanted to get up, but he knew it was dangerous. A couple thousand pounds had just run over him. As soon as Maggie opened the door, the new dog, Casey II, somehow as much in love as Casey I had been, ran to Harrison and took the spoon position inside him to keep him warm. Maggie came out of the house, this time in shoes and ran to him.

"How did it happen?"

He shook his head. "Dumb, not thinking. I feel funny. I don't think I should move."

Soon there were four fire trucks and one ambulance zooming onto the property. The volunteers all knew him and came running.

"Hey, buddy." "Hey, fella." "Hey, Mirth."

But Casey wouldn't let the rescuers come near. He snarled and barked and threatened them, as if he alone could be the one to cure his owner. Maggie had to show the dog she liked the firemen and ambulance men. She greeted them, hugged them, and said, "Here, boy, here, come, come to me, good boy."

Finally, the dog went to her.

The men strapped Harrison to a big board and zipped him to the hospital in Hudson. Maggie jumped in without Casey who set up a desperate racket, howling as they drove away. She held Harrison's hand. Up front the men were talking. The tractor, they estimated was a ton and a half or two tons.

What they meant was, How is this guy alive?

Maggie said, "Oh, you. Nine lives."

The women in the ER ooohed and aaahed about the Guatemalan fisherman's breeches. "So sweet!" "So sexy!" they said to distract him. But Maggie could hear them talking among themselves. "Something's gotta be broken. Look at the size of his belly. That's all swelling." She listened with panic as they speculated about what they were going to see on X-ray. "Probably spleen, broken bones, vital organs."

They X-rayed him and wheeled him back. They told him it was a miracle but that they found no broken bones. "All this swelling is… maybe like that antifreeze. Your body puffed you up to take the blow."

He tried to sit up but looked dazed and fell back.

"I can take him home?" Maggie asked.

"No, no, he's still under observation. We have to get this swelling down, make sure things are working."

Nine lives, nine lives, thought Maggie, please.

For a long time, his basic organ functions didn't work, and he told Maggie he thought he would never go home again and then all at once, all that air decided to leave him.

It was loud. A very long blast. Nurses came running from down the hall at the trumpeting that could be heard throughout Dutchess and Columbia counties.

People in the neighborhood brought food and flowers once Harrison was at home, in bed, having been told firmly that he had to stay there—which was fun, but only for a day or two. He was a doer. He lay there and thought out how Denise was an accident—she was the sickle bar fallen across the path of what had been a weird but stable marriage. Maggie brought in soup and painkillers and martinis. He held her hand and loved her as never before.

Thomas brought his reading, science fiction these days, into the bedroom to sit with his father. He read silently and patted his father's foot from time to time. "Rest," he said. "Just rest."

But when Harrison thought about Denise, about her having gotten used to his phone calls even if she didn't want them, and now hearing nothing at all from him, he worried about her. What would she think was the *reason* he had stopped calling?

He got out of bed after three days and limped to the VW. "Going into Pine Plains," he said. "Library."

When she answered the phone, Denise sounded winded. "Sorry I haven't called," he said.

"It's okay."

"I was laid up for a while."

"Oh, too bad. Listen, I'm packing. I'm moving. Just got a grand place in San Francisco."

"Wow. You sound…good. Happy."

"A little frantic. Moving is always that way."

He leaned against the glass of the phone booth, still sore from his ordeal. He understood there must be another man in the picture. "You feel good about this move?"

"Yeah. Scared. Good, though."

"I wish you well, my dear. Send your work, if you want."

"I will, believe me."

She wanted a teacher.

He worked at getting back to routine and wondered if he would get another guest artist position. He watched the mail. It would decide his life. And then one day, the unexpected arrived. He'd been granted a Fulbright.

"Maggie!"

"What?" She came into his study and looked, as she always did, with suspicion at the mail piling up. "What?" she asked again.

"Paris! A vacation for you. A job for me. Not a lot of teaching. Some. Mostly research and writing."

"You could do that here."

"It's a Fulbright! It's France! Wine and cheese and cafes and sauces. Maybe Anna would want to stay with us. She hates school. She could paint again."

"She promised she would buckle down this year. She shouldn't have any more interruptions."

"All right. Okay. But you could come." She didn't answer right away, but this was his chance to make things right. He said, "I know it's hard to leave here, but come on! It's the posting everybody dreams of. Maggie?"

"I'll come when I can. I really will." She hurried outdoors. He thought she was going to work at something to prove how much the place needed her, but later he found that she'd probably circled the house and come in the back door and gone to bed for the afternoon.

"What can I bring you?" he asked.

"Headache. Aspirin. Food."

"What food?"

"Anything."

"You're angry."

"No. Sad. Missing you before you go. You have to do what is right, I know."

He brought two aspirin and a couple pieces of toast to tide her over and declared that he would grill some chops for dinner. He was awfully good in the kitchen these days, having cooked for himself these last years in various cities with whatever pots and pans they gave him. He used a little sage on the chops and tried to come up with a sauce. What might the French do? He tried pork drippings with yogurt and rosemary as a compliment, putting the sauce in a bowl on the side in case she didn't like it.

Maggie came to the kitchen when the food was ready.

A week after the accident, neighbors came by to help move the tractor, which was stalled and stuck on the hill where it had come to a stop. Thomas wouldn't touch it. Sometimes he just looked at it, terror on his face. The guys who came to help were fun—joking the whole time. They'd jump-started the beast and got it to the barn and clapped Harrison's shoulders and left. Harrison looked at his beloved tractor. He knew he would never get on it again.

31

Harrison understood that whatever part of him was French (way back) was responsible for his eyes and his taste buds. Paintings and sauces, paintings and sauces.

One day, he had brewed himself a pot of coffee, strong, and run out to the boulangerie he liked best of the three (three!) on his street for a baguette and an almond croissant. By now, they knew him there. They even knew his name. "Monsieur Mirth!"

He wanted to tell them that he was mostly Irish but part English and the part that was English was really French. He had looked up the area and discovered a Mirth coat of arms which he had had imprinted on the mug he drank from in the mornings (as well as four matching mugs he sent to Maggie and the kids). The Norman influence on the area of Westmorland was what had recently captured his imagination. He was writing a wild experimental story of a family that was both modern and ancient, living in two time periods, and being both French and English. Although probably no one would publish the crazy thing, he was at least having fun.

"Baguette, croissant," said madame behind the counter.

Harrison laid out his francs. He didn't want to frighten the owners, but he did hope to bring his camera and capture them—their faces, their beings. What he'd love to get was what they looked like in the early morning hours before they were open, when they were baking.

He took his breads and went back to his apartment. It was in the Fifteenth, rue du Theater, and if he was going to like the name of a rue, well, this was a likely like. He beamed a bonjour to everyone he passed. How right it was to wish people a good day. Perhaps it would stick.

Eating his croissant (he knew he had to stop but he hated to let down the bakers), he winced and poked at his waistline. He craved some old-fashioned toast and egg today, and he wrote that to Maggie while eating his French breakfast. He wrote her almost daily.

Today he sounded the glories of American bacon. He told her what he had learned about his family name. It was wild that his first name, which had come down as part of the family legacy, was often the last name of the Westmorland people. The commonest surnames were

Atkinson, Robinson, Wilson, Thompson, Hodgeson, Harrison, Jackson, Dixon, Taylor, Richardson.

The "son" suffixes are Norman, you see, and then note how some of them became first names, he wrote.

Somewhere along the line, someone had shortened the last name, for which he was grateful. He wouldn't have wanted to go around being Professor Murthwaite, or Myrthwaite, or Mirthwaite.

In a jokey post card to Denise, he wrote *Mirth WAITS for you to fall in love with him again.*

On Denise's first visit, she'd cursed him for putting carbohydrates before her. She'd pronounced the apartment deplorable. But she was lively, and he'd enjoyed her company.

On her second visit, she'd slept from jetlag for one and a half days. His only pleasure was to climb in and lie beside her. The visit was only three days long. By the time he'd taken her to the fancy dinner on day two, she seemed more awake. She carefully scraped the white sauce from the steak before her, but tasted the sauce with her fork, deciding, "beautifully done."

"So, eat it. Dip bread in it!"

"Too much devil butter for my figure."

"You'd look great with more pounds."

She said, "So your people were once lords of the manor. You should live like that, really. You were meant to be posh."

He didn't argue with her—they only had one more day—but he had the thought, the sentiment really, that he'd had so often with Amanda, that he would have liked much better being the descendant of a hard-working coal miner or cheese maker. That was one of the themes of his crazy novel, so crazy an outpouring that he didn't show it to anyone, not even Maggie.

"You're writing?" he asked.

"Always."

"But you haven't sent."

"In about three months I'll have a revision to send you. Only crazy people write, right?"

That was one of the sentiments he'd heard over the years and seen inscribed on mugs: *Drinkers write.* And *Bad parent? So. you're a writer.* And *Writers are nuts.*

"Why are you always so happy?" she asked him.

Was he? Why did it feel the opposite?

That night she let him make love to her. It was awkward but he couldn't say why. She didn't appear to take much pleasure, though he tried mightily with all the parts of him that had worked in the past.

They lay quietly for a while. He didn't want to let in the thought that this visit was a bit of a disaster. He sang a little love song of his making, "It's me and you and together we're we."

Finally, she asked, "Do you have any rope? Scarves?"

"Scarves. I have my wool scarf. Why?"

"I want you to tie me up. We'll need to tear up a bed sheet or something."

He laughed. "I can't tie you up. I'd feel silly."

"We need to do something *interesting*."

He sat up suddenly. "Well, let's think of something interesting that doesn't hurt you."

"It won't hurt. It's playing. It's playing at roles." He leaned over her and saw she was angry with him.

"All right. I'll do it. If that's seriously what you want." He found one of the bed sheets that came with the place. If they took inventory after he left, he would have to explain he'd needed it to do some S and M. Hopefully they wouldn't miss the worn blue-flowered bottom sheet.

He got a scissors and began to cut strips. "I don't believe I'm doing this."

"You have to try something new." She had gotten up and now sashayed past him to the bathroom. He kept cutting. When she passed him coming back to the bedroom, she ruffled his hair, for which he felt grateful. Nobody touched him here in Paris, he realized. Maggie had come once at the beginning for three days, Emma passed through with a friend for one and a half days. That was it.

The bed had a headboard with short posts, but he managed to make the tie hold there. The end on her wrists was bulky because he didn't want to tie the pieces of sheet too tight so he wrapped twice.

"Tighter," she commanded, stretching up to look. "What ugly sheets."

At the foot of the bed, he had to reach under for the frame to tie her in place. He wasn't at all sure he could ravish her with her hardly moving, staring up at him with a fake expression of fear in her deadly blue pathologically opaque criminal eyes. Had Josephine Tey been right, after all, that certain startling blue eyes meant a person was simply dangerous?

"Torture me for a while," she instructed. "Make me beg."

He started to laugh. "Sorry," he said, trying to get with the game. "Really, sorry." Okay, okay, he would do it, but he was reminded of what a lousy actor he was in Maggie's troupe. He tried, "Look at me! Don't move!"

"Call me names."

"Damned...bitch. What are you good for?"

No, he couldn't do name calling. He repeated the "what are you good for?" He took a break after a while and got himself a good slug of bourbon. Then he went back to it and did his best.

After she took a taxi to the airport, he sat, forlorn, at his table-desk, hoping to get back to his manuscript that was right now his only form of play. He could play on paper, not so well in bed.

Sipping from his family herald mug, he admitted it wasn't the trip he'd hoped for. She hadn't run into his arms. She hadn't said she'd come to her senses and now despised her newest lover (whoever she had back in San Fran). She hadn't repeated her old sentiment, "I was nothing until I met you. I wanted to kill myself and then you saw something in me." And he never got to say, "I never tried to kill myself—except if we count my carelessness with the tractor—but I wasn't truly alive until you told me my virtues as a writer and a teacher."

Had she been lying at the start, when he first met her? He examined those early moments every which way and decided not. She had admired him. She had lost faith in him, then. Perhaps she'd come to agree with the publishers that quiet was passé, and transgressive was the new necessity.

It was not going to work out with Denise. He'd known it, always known it, and he hadn't really wanted it to, either. He wanted to solve her, solve *something*.

He dragged his typewriter toward him. In about a hundred more pages he'd have a draft of his crazy experimental time-defying novel. Typing furiously, he remembered something he learned once, that you could renew, refresh yourself, by working on a whole different project in the afternoon when you thought you had nothing left. He would do that on non-teaching days—his class was only on Monday and Wednesday afternoons—he would pull out the other Mirth-related manuscript, an ordinary realistic novel based on his parents and about his childhood. It made him sad to revisit his boyhood. How afraid of his mother he'd been. How he could never get enough of his father. And the way he'd tiptoed around his grandparents, whom he loved, but tried not to bother. They were old. Tired. He wrote his little self and that little self…became a character he could look at, became a romantic boy who worked at joy.

It didn't matter that he wasn't getting published. Only that he do. And do. And do it honestly, one good line a day. With patience. With love of the words. And with love of the truth.

32

It was a glorious summer day—everything about Maggie's life was perfect, the plans for Provincetown made, her husband finally home from France, the garden bursting with vegetables, the grounds glorious, all the pine trees grown to good size, birds of all feather swooping in, the house in order, no appliances broken. But her insides quivered. Harrison wore a silence that she feared. Was he going to ask her again to move to some far-off place? She couldn't. She didn't have it in her. She had made her life right for herself *here* and he kept wanting to be somewhere else.

She watched him out of the corner of her eye. Yes, he was in a constant frowning mood. A slamming door she could handle. Carefully closed doors, a bad sign.

Anna was visiting but down the road at a neighbor's house and Thomas was apprenticing unofficially at the local vet's office. Emma was summering with friends on a Maine beach. The quiet was unnerving instead of peaceful. No happy bumping around sounds, no voices. No muttered "aarrggh," or "damn."

She carried two cups of coffee to the table on the porch and she sat in one of the chairs. Finally, her husband came out and sat in the other.

She had to say something. Her voice sounded whispery to her when she said, "Quiet without the kids."

"Um."

"I can see you're somewhere else."

"What is this to you? Us?" He looked choked, unable to speak. Finally, he said, "We're not happy, we're not right together."

Did people have to be happy? Couldn't they just be? "I guess that's true."

"I think we ought to divorce."

"All right." She said it before she could think what she was saying because she had only wanted to keep being agreeable. But she had always known when the moment came, she would not make a fuss. She would not be a baby. Almost everybody they knew was divorced, and she had rehearsed the moment so many times, it seemed it had already happened.

She had never been a screamer or a fighter; she lived for peace. Her insides were trembling, but she took up the coffee cup without spilling it. "I'll contact our attorney." There. She'd faced it more boldly than he. His face was still swollen with emotion. "Where will you go? The city?" she asked, after a moment.

"Eventually. But I have a job next year in Pittsburgh. I just heard yesterday. I'll need the salary."

"Pittsburgh? Will you be…all right there?"

"The hinterlands? I hope so."

"There are plenty of trains and busses and planes to the city when you need to get out. You'll be all right."

How civilized they were. She found it necessary to say, before she got up to bring out the pot for refills, "We were great for a time. We have three amazing kids." She didn't say, "They hate that you were hardly here these last years." And he didn't say, "I hate that you wouldn't ever come to be with me."

"Thank you for those things," he said instead. "I agree our kids are wonderful."

"Are you marrying somebody else?" she asked.

"No. I don't know what's in front of me at all. I only know it isn't this. I need to be in a different setting. I need to work."

She'd seen that. A good ten years of watching his joy in other places. How could she not see it as escaping *her*?

His voice finally rose. "Why did you not want anything else? Why did you not want to be out in the world?"

"I need calm."

He knew her. Surely, he knew she needed layers and layers of comfort to quell the natural fears in her. Surely, he understood that.

He held his cup slightly away from him and looked into it as if it held an answer. "When I met you, you had so much ambition."

She wasn't good *enough* at anything. It embarrassed her to try. Did he need to shame her with that? And now she was worn, pudgy, and felt more than a little boring. Husbands got that way too. He would one day but at the moment he was fit, looked at least fifteen years younger than he was. She was the slightly older woman he'd married, and he was still bursting with nervous energy.

There were times when she'd managed a brief visit to him in one or the other places where he went to teach and feared someone would say how nice it was that his mother had come to see him. It hadn't happened, except in her mind.

Now here it was, the worst she had imagined: It was over. She rocked a little, kept drinking her coffee. She would stay right here, hire out all the work. It wasn't a problem; her money was growing nicely.

"Will we need two lawyers?" she asked lightly.

"I'm not fighting anything. We can keep it simple."

She looked at her watch. She began to say something about what was on television that she might want to see but stopped herself.

"I'm going to read for a bit."

She wondered if he would come to their bed.

He didn't. There was a lumpy cot in his writing room. He stayed there.

One half of the time, he asked himself what he was doing. The other half of the time, he went crazy with dreams of flight. Away. On his own. A blank slate.

The night he asked for a divorce, he couldn't breathe right for hours. He thought he would have a heart attack right there. But eventually, as he read, this time Malamud, whom he'd socialized with a few more times in the city, he began to calm. They'd been headed to divorce for twenty years. Nobody suspected it, everybody thought they were doing fine. How would he tell people?

Irreconcilable differences. She was rich. He was poor. She wanted calm, rural. He wanted gritty city. She wanted to live on investments. He wanted to earn every donut. That was enough.

After two hours he put down the Malamud and began typing a childhood memory that might fit into something he was writing. The ragged girl touching his arm in the playground, just that, a kindness.

Fred Lewis had begun sending his wild novel out. Maybe someone would love it, maybe not.

He wanted to hold Maggie and comfort her, but that would arouse hope in her. So, he just kept writing.

He tossed through the night. She'd just said, "All right." Just like that. For which he was both grateful and also furious. As if they could have separated years ago and gone on to their real lives. Why had they kept at it, both so unhappy?

They did nothing for a year, just letting the word divorce become real.

33

A new job, a new start.

Harrison was driving down a hill as steep as any in San Francisco, ramshackle houses on one side, wild growth on the other. He rolled down the window and asked a boy trudging up the hill, "What area is this?"

"Polish *Hill*," the boy said, as if any idiot would know that.

Harrison continued to drive downward to find out where this rural lane in the middle of the city ended and he discovered that not far from the bottom of the hill was the warehouse district, where knowing buyers went for vegetables, coffee, cheeses, meats—a bustling, unpretty place that thrilled him. It was called the Strip District. He parked and began to poke into shops, always buying something and getting into conversations with the clerks. Ground sage in one place, biscotti in another. And then he went to a larger store, laughingly called Pennsylvania Macaroni—only to stop laughing when he found more olive oils and cheeses than he'd seen in France. "Oh, my God," he said to a stranger. "This is fantastic! I could go crazy in here."

The man laughed. "Yeah. We all over-buy."

He ordered a pound each of five different cheeses, not considering how he would eat it all.

Harrison had to freeze some of it, and he gave some to a neighbor in his building, but even so, he ate an awful lot of cheese that week.

He went back to the Strip several times that August, buying olives and vegetables and coffee. He went into the office, too, though classes wouldn't start until the next week. He was more or less prepared for those classes—having done courses now in several cities—but he still got plain old stage fright.

He asked questions, borrowed pens, chatted up the secretaries who brightened every time he came in.

One of the women faculty in the department, who also popped in during the summer, invited him to dinner in a couple of days, just a casual dinner, she said, feeding paper into the copy machine. On the Saturday of the event, he bought wine and flowers, then went back to Macaroni for two cheeses, a nice gift for his hostess.

The university was near a park. On his way back to his apartment in Squirrel Hill, he drove through the park, admiring it.

He would have to see to a new used car. His VW was biting the dust. His apartment on Hobart, which looked much like the seven apartments he had had over the years, was surprisingly inexpensive. One good feature was that it was walkable to two movie theaters, several restaurants, and more than one food market. Tomorrow he would take himself to an afternoon movie. If the car held out for a while, he'd be all right.

Sometimes his breathing was shallow and his heart raced and he wondered if he would just drop dead on the spot.

The hostess, Karen, lived in a beautiful house in Shadyside, one of those classic Victorians with a porch. Though it was surrounded by apartment complexes, it had the charm of a *Saturday Evening Post* America. "People must have built all around this over the years," he said, taking in the surroundings. "This house survived it."

Karen was a tall gangly cheerful woman of roughly his age.

He saw the table was set for four. "Who else is coming?"

"Our chair and his wife."

"Oh, good. Good."

Twenty minutes later, those two arrived. The chair, Barry, was a hearty man with a very young wife, Melanie. Barry brought not one but three bottles of wine. "I'll do the honors," he said.

"Apparently we're going to get soused," Karen said, arranging the four glasses she had put out in front of him.

Melanie said, "I hope not," and shot a look at Barry who opened the first bottle and began pouring.

When Karen went to the kitchen, Barry pointed and asked, "Are you two——?"

"Oh no, I just met her at the copy machine, and she told me a few things about the city. Very nice of her to invite me."

"Very nice."

Harrison had had a card from Denise saying she might visit one day to see his new city. Well, her craziness was better than his loneliness.

"I understand you're divorced," Barry said.

"Divorcing." He rocked uncertainly, drinking the delicious wine. He imagined Maggie, surprised, saying, "Such good wines in Pittsburgh?"

School began with its craziness—meetings, names to remember. "A writer of import," one person said, introducing him to another. "A much-published writer." If that was the truth, it wasn't soothing.

One after another, the rejections came. His wild novel was not getting a welcome out there. *Weird, too weird. Couldn't make sense out of it.*

Kind of liked it but wouldn't be able to market it.

Imagination, for sure—how old is this guy?

Critiques of contemporary society are not selling well, sorry.

I rather liked his earlier works. This is a work of genius, but not right for our house.

Etc.

He put them in a box. Finished. He was done with this one. At least he was a passable teacher.

In his journal he wrote one morning after a date that saddened him for its lack of spark, *I see now I am a loner, always was really and will always be alone.* He laughed at the violins playing and somehow went back to finishing up the family novel, which was a new experience in that it was flowing out of him so fast that he finished it in a couple of weeks. Fast though it was, working on it shook him. After all, he was tapping his childhood, writing about being without his parents, and he ended up thinking a lot about how scared he'd been as a child, scared and scarred, a child shunted from here to there, nobody really able to take responsibility.

He could remember two kids making fun of him for having ancient parents and him having to explain they were his grandparents. Shoving. Gravel. Some blood. Him wandering off to another neighborhood, embarrassed that the scuffle had torn his pants. Finally, when the light was leaving the sky, he found his way homeward, only to see his grandmother limping toward him, her arms out, alarm on her face. How she held him. How she held on. He still remembered.

On a Friday at the end of September he looked at the manuscript for a long time and put the novel into an envelope and sent it off to Old Fred.

The next day he called his daughter Emma because she might be home—it was a Saturday, after all. She was happy, living in Brooklyn, riding into Manhattan, grad teaching at NYU. She answered with a bright hello, but her voice became tight when she knew who it was on the phone. And *she* was the least angry of the kids.

"How are you, honey?"

"Fine."

He could hear someone stirring in the background. Could he really imagine she wouldn't take up the single New York life? "Is this a bad time?"

"Not particularly bad," she answered. A muffled voice behind her said something like "shower."

"I'm just checking in. I want to be sure you're okay."

He could hear in the silence *You care?*

"I always cared," he said in answer to the silence. "I'm very proud of you. I want you to choose a really good guy."

He heard the clunk of a coffee cup. She and someone were having morning coffee together.

"Go home, Pop."

"I have a job, a good job."

"The job will end in a year. Go home. Write there."

"Sweetheart. It isn't like that. Your mother and I will be miserable all over again."

"She's miserable now. You are too."

"I'm sorry. But we talk every few weeks and I think she's better without me. She tells me she's really okay." He went to his window and watched two dogged old ladies with their shopping carts, heading up the street, bodies tilted forward.

"And you believe her?"

"Yes. Yes, I do. I want her to get on with her life."

"What life? Reading, sleeping, drinking, hiring folks to take care of things."

That was the point. That was precisely the point. Maggie needed to find a life. Why could Emma, so smart, not see that?

"Gotta go, Pop."

"Come visit. You'd like it here." The apartment, in a street full of such buildings, was not bad. He hadn't decorated very seriously because he would have to find something else in a year.

"I will. Some weekend. Bus is best, I guess."

"Or fly. Or I'd come get you. Anything."

"I love you, Pop."

His voice was telltale hoarse when he managed, "I love you, Emma." Why not get on with it?

He called Anna. Why the hell did she have to be the whole way off in Wisconsin? Not an easy trip for him or her.

"I was sleeping," she growled. "People sleep, you know."

"I'm sorry. I'll call back."

"Don't. I'm busy. Call Mom. She's the one who needs you."

They were consulting each other, ganging up. If only he could capture them all and have them with him. If only. "Listen, are you okay?"

"What do you mean?"

"Going to classes, eating well, spending time with friends, enjoying life. That's what I mean."

"I do okay. I hate my classes this term. The program is really hard."

"I think maybe it's not right for you then. Anna? Anna?"

"What?"

"Well, why are you not an art major? Or a poetry major? I don't understand why you're not doing what you love. Can we talk about that?"

"No."

"Come on."

"I don't want to be a failure."

That again. Afraid to try. "You wouldn't be." His own so-called success was evanescent. "When you wonder if you have talent, try to remember that you do. Okay?"

"So you say."

"I do. This deserves some talk. Can you come visit?"

"No. Out of the question."

"Why not?"

"I don't have time. Plus, I don't like you these days."

"Anna."

"You told me I should be honest."

"Of course, you should be. Call me then when you have more time."

He thought he heard a mumble. Was it "Right?" or "Okay." The line went dead.

He read. He was thinking the line, "Everybody is a failure, don't you understand? It's just life." He tried making notes for some short fiction. He dialed his son who was in school in Connecticut. There was no answer.

Somehow the weekend passed.

He waited for two months to hear about his novel. The school term and his students were the highlight of his life. When all his papers were graded, he went to movies, seeing anything that was playing.

He ate Thanksgiving dinner out at a restaurant, mass produced, better than the one he'd had at Amanda's parents' house those many years ago, not as good as the ones he'd had over the years at the farm. He had decided he would simply stay in Pittsburgh for Christmas. He wanted to see his kids, but how could he, without confusing things? Maggie would think the divorce was off.

He made himself a chicken on Christmas day and he drank a good deal of wine and watched a lot of television and when he couldn't watch anymore, he went out into the cold and took himself to two movies. Somehow the day passed. The next challenge was New Year's Eve and New Year's Day.

He almost managed to stay in the apartment on New Year's Eve, but at the last minute went out to a local bar. The bartender handed him a hat and a horn. A few people told him he was a great party-guy. The bar mirror showed his hat tipped to the side, cockeyed. He blew the horn a lot even after the ball fell. He kissed anyone who showed willingness and made his way home, glad he'd gotten through it.

Soon, a new term and new students occupied him. That January there was a good deal of snow which made suppers of soup and staying indoors more like a necessity. Yes, yes, he told himself. He was getting used to his life.

He padded down to his mailbox. There was a thin envelope from Old Fred. Three rejections, then, this time of the quiet family novel. And a fourth piece of paper, Fred's letter. Oh, God, was Fred abandoning him? His breathing got raspy as he read the rejections before taking up Fred's letter. He sat on the stairway and angled the letter for more light. "Don't lose hope. They liked it. They just didn't see a place for it. The thing is, I think I have another possibility. Small publisher, but classy. I felt a ripple there. Hang on. Seriously, hold on."

When he could breathe again, he went upstairs.

Old Fred said to hold on. He would try to hold on. Radio! Yes, it was a comfort. He clicked it on. The classical music station played him some Brahms and he just sat and listened, trying to compose it, guessing at each next note. All around him in a bit of a mess were the tapes he'd made of the great symphonies playing on the radio. And jazz, he'd taped that too. He had hundreds of dirty cassettes with scratched handwriting barely identifying them. He decided he must play these great works one after another until he'd heard them all again. On his walls were three of Andrew Rosen's paintings. On the coffee table a bookmark in the Proust—why not intimidate himself with greatness?

He would not be great. But he could be classy enough to appreciate greatness.

On Monday, a week later, Barry called him in. "Your position. You understand it was a one-year replacement for a sabbatical."

"Oh, right, I know I'm off again. Nomad life."

"Well, no, the thing is, our old soul, James, just decided he wants to retire. So, the position will open up. Are you interested?"

"This is—" It was such a surprise that he didn't think he'd heard right. "I was just about to write letters to about twenty schools."

"You're doing a great job. We'd have to advertise the position and put you in the mix, but my guess is the votes would go your way. No, I know they would."

Harrison had been standing. He took a seat. "Like, what a three-year contract?"

"Longer, I'd hope. We're talking about tenure track. You're published; you keep publishing, and it looks good."

"I'm a little bit stunned."

"You seem to like it here. The school, the city?"

He liked it more than he could have guessed. He admired the blue-collar workers, sons and grandsons of immigrants who had worked the mills; now you could find them working the roads, painting houses, doing any sort of contracting work. There were ethnic pockets all over the city, Polish Hill being a case in point. The city had a symphony, ballet, the Chamber Music Society, department stores—and football and baseball teams. Even better, the baseball team was National League. Was it possible? He could stay?

Barry was saying you can get a fine house in Oakland or Squirrel Hill for less than in almost any other city.

"I've seen your place. It's beautiful."

"Tell me in three days if you'll apply?"

Harrison didn't think he needed three days, but he took it.

On a strangely warm February day, he taught his class and went home, heady with the possibility of a permanent job. Of course, it could go wrong. They were bringing other candidates in, they had to do a proper search, but he was ready to tell them his hat was in the ring. He bounded up the stairs; he could hear his phone ringing; he expected Barry's voice, saying "So? Your decision?"

But it was Old Fred. "Got an offer on the new novel."

He spelled out the details. "Not much money upfront but a really good publicity campaign. Lots of press. Arranged readings. That sort of thing. I know we were trying for more of an advance, but—"

"Take it! Take it!"

With the rest of the afternoon to spare, he hopped in his car and began driving. He knew what he wanted to see. He'd continued his exploration of the city all through the fall and knew all the stores and restaurants on the South Side. He knew how to get to the odd dirty side streets and dead ends, one of which held a bar and restaurant in the middle of nowhere called Big Jim's where the portions were good and huge and cheap.

But what he was crazy for was the North Side. There he saw houses like the ones in Manhattan he had always wanted to own, houses butted up against each other, some natural brick, some painted brick, most with jazzy colorful paint on the trim. They were a hundred and fifty years old, some of them.

If the job was his, he wanted to live in one of those houses.

In April, they told him the job was his.

He called Maggie to tell her the news about his novel and his job.

"I wish you well on both," she said.

"Thank you. I knew you would."

"You seem to have some luck coming your way. Are we still…divorcing?"

"Yes," he said. And he felt a pain go through his heart right up to his neck, even though it didn't have to be *luck*, did it, couldn't it be his just desserts?

"I can get things started, if you like," she said.

"That's fine with me. Thank you."

Maggie contacted her lawyer; as far as Harrison was concerned there was to be no contesting of anything. If he could have persuaded Maggie to spend six weeks in Reno, he would have accepted that strange scene once more as a way of uncoupling, but she didn't want to be away from the farm. She called to give him a date. He drove into Newark and bussed into New York, then taxied to the big building on Sixth where Maggie waited for him in the lobby, and together they got into the elevator to go to Kline's office.

Harrison had met the attorney once before but mostly Maggie made her visits to Kline alone to deal with financial issues.

Kline was a nice old guy, in his eighties by now, still working, still in the same office with the patina of expensive old furniture, and—if Harrison was not mistaken, which he was unlikely to be since he remembered such things—the same burgundy leather upholstery, meticulously kept and still doing duty.

The carpets and the almost whisper of the secretary made this a place of peace and quiet. Kline had somehow even muted the sounds of traffic way below.

"Mrs. Everholtz is bringing us water and coffee. Would you like anything else?"

"Sounds perfect," Maggie said. "I'll have a coffee."

"Coffee would be fine," Harrison agreed.

When Kline had them settled, he folded his hands and asked, "Now, what may I do for you?" which confused Harrison since Maggie had said Kline was completely primed about initiating divorce proceedings.

"The divorce," Maggie said.

"And you are both certain?"

"Yes," she said.

"Yes," Harrison said.

Kline tuned to him. "Would you like to have your own attorney, Mr. Mirth? You know you have the right?"

He shook his head.

"Well, an attorney would fight for you. You are entitled to half of your wife's money and property. That's why there are generally two attorneys."

"It's all right," he said. "I'm not asking for anything."

Maggie rolled her eyes. "You should ask for *some*thing. I want to give you something."

Kline leaned forward. "It doesn't have to amount to half. Can you propose an amount?"

Harrison frowned. He did not want to be owned ever again. He felt his chest tighten. But there was something he wanted badly—he wanted one of those houses he dreamed about. If he could get a down payment, he could swing the rest. He calculated. "Sixty thousand?" he asked.

"That's all?" Maggie said.

"Are you sure?" Kline then asked.

"That would just about do it, for a house I want."

Maggie and her lawyer shrugged and looked at each other. Cheap house, their looks seemed to say.

"A very efficient meeting," Kline said. They hardly had time for the coffee.

Maggie forwarded the money right away. And then came the period where the divorce papers sat on desktops in two cities and were not yet signed.

34

A ha," Harrison said at the airport as Denise exited the plane. He welcomed her with open arms, then, when she was close enough, he put an arm around her shoulders, and they walked in the misty rain to his car. She wore a dashing pants outfit in deep blue that emphasized her eyes.

"Still runs," she said of his car. "Coughs a little."

"You look good," he said.

"Oh, thanks."

She watched out the window. "Interesting city. It looks like…something, some place. What?"

He shook his head. "Other Midwestern steel belts? And a little bit San Francisco?" He looked at her stretching up in the passenger seat, looking. "You would like it here."

She was working for the city magazine in the Bay Area, doing her own thing in off hours. He asked her what she was writing in her off time.

"Remember that mean novel about the divorced woman? I put it aside. Now I'm writing about a conflict between sisters." But she appeared to be more interested in studying the highway landscapes and the city.

When they came to his neighborhood, he said, "See the buildings—they remind me of parts of the Village and of Brooklyn. That's what I like."

"Old, old buildings," she said. She touched his thigh. "Boyish."

"Because the buildings are old?" he asked irritably. Then the irksomeness floated off and he was cheerful again. "You see the beauty?"

"Oh yes."

He stopped the car and pointed out his house. "That's mine."

She said, "Good street. Very nice. Trees and lights."

But inside the place, her approval disappeared. They looked at the second floor first because she simply climbed the stairs looking at everything and ended up at the upstairs living room. "Why did you choose this furniture?"

"Well, it was a good deal—I got it at a warehouse sale, an amazing event. And it's neutral so I can decorate around it." The wheat-colored sofa and the mauve armchair looked marvelous to his eye. "I'm filling in as I can with the more glorious pieces of the past." He pointed to the tables he'd found at antique shops. He led her downstairs to look at the corner cupboard that was very like the one he had bought with Maggie. "Look what I found."

She nodded toward that piece, giving it her modified approval, but when he showed her the kitchen, she said, "You should have bought better appliances."

"These are great. They work beautifully."

"But people are going to see the Kenmore tags. People judge those things you know."

That comment was the beginning of a wrangling sort of weekend, with a lot of on and off companionship and no secrets revealed on either side.

He took her to the plane Monday morning.

Several months after that, and before Liz ever met him or saw his new house, Maggie called and said, "I'm driving to Virginia next weekend. Could I stop and see the house you bought?"

"Of course. Yes."

"I realize you could be with someone, but I have a curiosity about the house, and I helped you to it, and I wonder if I could just see it as I pass through."

"Yes, yes, and you can stay overnight if you want. I bought a funny little sofa bed at a warehouse sale."

"I'm game to try it."

"No, I'd take that. You can have the bedroom."

His heart felt heavy that she was coming to his sanctuary, where he felt validated, successful, but how could he say no?

He bought flowers for the table and candles and a beautiful piece of salmon, worried that each nicety would confuse the situation.

She drove up to the place as if she had always known how to get there. He welcomed her with a brief hug, and they sat down to a drink.

"It's like a New York brownstone."

Right. It was. A rowhouse. Vertical. Little light. Pine floors. Mirrors to catch what light there was. His old life but bigger, better.

She opened a pack of cigarettes and lit one for herself, waving the smoke away. He'd quit completely a long time ago.

"You aren't tempted?" she asked.

"Tempted, sure, but no." She'd quit and started up again many times by now. He said, "You should quit for good."

"I should. Not completely sure I want to live."

"Maggie. Don't talk like that."

"All right." She stubbed out her cigarette and stood. "Give me a tour."

They climbed to the second floor and then a set of steep narrow stairs to the third floor. He said, "This is where you'll be sleeping. It's the only bedroom at this point, though I could make another one if I wanted. I lifted the roof here so I could have windows." He indicated a run of windows looking out on a huge tree. "This room makes me feel I'm in a tree house." He laughed. "I got a view, right, but I have to do all kinds of tricks to shave, trying to make the windows act like mirrors. Depends on the weather. Sometimes I can't see a thing, so I use this little girl's mirror—"

It was pink with a princess on the back. "Where did you get it?" Maggie asked.

"I found it on the street."

They descended the dangerously steep stairs and he showed off the large living room on the second floor with a whole wall of shelves for his books.

"The furniture isn't fancy. Or the appliances," he found himself saying apologetically, having Denise's criticisms handy. But he had somehow managed to find enough faded mauves and footstools that the room looked almost exactly like the one at the farmhouse. That and the dining room with its new corner cupboard were homages to their past together.

"Looks fine to me. Looks…very *familiar*. Looks like ours."

His home office was on the second floor. It had files and books all over the place. "What's the current project?" she asked.

"Short stories."

"Ah, great. If you ever want me to proofread—"

"What a kind offer. I'll think about it when I'm ready."

He let her look around the first floor—the dining room and the front parlor and the little room he didn't know what to do with—while he assembled a salad and got out the pan to poach the fish. "Very quick dinner," he said when she came to the kitchen. "Easy. Would you like to open the wine? Or set the table?"

"I'll set the table. I do want a drink before dinner. You have scotch,
I hope."

He dug into a cabinet and came up with a bottle. She went about finding ice cubes and getting herself set up for cocktail hour. He grabbed
a can of peanuts and put some in a bowl. He took a slab of St. Andre
from the fridge and a box of crackers from the cabinet down low.

"Didn't you want to build upper cabinets?"

"I took them out. I wanted windows, light."

"Ah."

There were all those hours after dinner to fill. It made him nervous.
When dinner was finished, they took a long walk around the neighborhood until they exhausted themselves and then came back and had a
late coffee.

Maggie said, "Do you have anyone in your life now?"

He wanted to lie and say yes. But he said, "Not in any important
way."

A month later a very large package arrived by special delivery. It was
a specially made imitation of an antique razor stand, tall as a man, with
a round base at the bottom, a long post, a circular tray at hand height for
a razor and cream, another long post, then the circular mirror at head
height. It was beautiful. The note said, *You don't need walls to have a shaving
mirror. Some old guys figured that out once upon a time. Be well. Enjoy it.*

35

T he first time Harrison met Liz was at a party full of writers. He'd brought a block of St. Andre cheese and a baguette; she'd brought raw kibbee.

They exchanged a few words, nothing important, names and jobs. She was a theater director and a prof who taught plays. He loved the theater and had been attending as much as he could around the city. "We should talk sometime," he said, and she said, "Glad to," but he never followed up.

One day out of the blue, Harrison thought about Liz Albert and the fact that he admired what she did for a living and that she was known for it, so (having rescued her name from the depths of his memory) he called her to ask if she would like to go out to a movie.

She said okay.

He put on his lucky Provincetown sandals and his favorite ancient seersucker jacket with jeans, and he dug out his good spirits, which had been flagging lately.

He stood at her door and knocked. She opened it, wearing a no-nonsense skirt and top of striped white and green. "Ready? You look as if you've been in the sun."

"Right. I have. I drag my reading outdoors when I can."

"I hear this film is pretty good."

She told him she had also read a few reviews.

They bumped along down her cobblestone hill in his VW, a car that was not terribly clean; he apologized for the mess. She said, "Oh, that's all right. It reminds me of my youth; it feels like a teenager's car."

He talked about movies and restaurants, but the theater was just down the hill, so they were soon there, after only a few exchanges.

They watched the movie without touching. Harrison laughed at the cynical lines and there were more than several of them in *White Mischief*. It was a good film, brainy and mean, and he wondered what she thought of all those decadent despairing people indulging in drink and orgies because they had nothing else to do.

She said, "I'm glad we saw that. It was very good."

After the movie, he drove to a restaurant on the South Side, saying,

"I thought maybe the Grill? I hope that's okay with you. Do you prefer something else?"

"The Grill is fine with me. I've actually never been."

"They do a good steak, a good chop. Whatever you like."

He consulted with the waiter about wines, and declared, "Oh, now we have to have a starter. Or two! How about oysters?"

She loved oysters, she told him, loved food of all sorts.

They ordered steaks, both, and once all that was done, he gave a resume of his life, from the press agentry to the early brief marriage to the rural family life and the long marriage, to the teaching at various colleges, the long-delayed divorce—a whole life, digested in a paragraph.

"Children?" she asked, working to catch up.

"Two daughters, one son," he said, and then told her about each, how wonderful they were. Emma was teaching history. Anna was finally sending her poems out and they were being accepted. Thomas was a vet. Emma was married and had an adopted son. Anna had never married. Thomas had married a woman with two teenage daughters; he was serious about bringing them up right.

And to be utterly clear he told her, "Also...I've had a couple of semi-serious relationships here in Pittsburgh. I don't regret any of them. Wonderful women, every one of them. Just not—"

"Not it?" She smiled.

He'd lost his faith in the long term, but he didn't want to tell her that. He was afraid of happiness, trained to replace it with good cheer. He would not have that movie-ending he kept loving—people running toward each other—that romantic thing.

The dozen raw oysters he had ordered to share arrived. "Should I prepare for you?" he asked. He brightened when she said, "Yes, thanks." He squeezed a little lemon, added sauce and a dab of horseradish and handed one over. He watched her eat it. "Do you like them this way?"

"Yes! Fantastic."

"Oh, good. And you?" he asked. "Your life."

"I can't get it down to a paragraph. I can get it to a phrase, though. 'A few bad choices and mostly, mostly work.' Nothing more I want to say at the moment."

"Never mind," he said. "When you're ready. Let's eat. So...lots of work?"

She nodded. "Lots. That seems shabby suddenly, without the dramatic shifts of your life or of most of the lives I know."

"I don't know about shabby. Amazingly steady."

"I'm sort of 'stark raving sane.' That's not original. It's a quote."

After the movie and dinner, back at her house, each of them with a glass of wine, she told him she'd dreamt about him. "Very odd dreams, right after you called. In the one, you were trying to light a fire in my fireplace, and you seemed sort of careless with the torch, rolled newspaper or something, and there was a lot of tinder, but you just swept in and boom, a really big blaze." She stopped herself. "Oh, God, that was embarrassing."

He said, "I'm good at making fires," sticking to the literal with no idea of why. They sat across from each other in her living room. He thought she seemed to want him to leave. When he finally did stand to go, she came to him and slipped an arm around his waist, saying, "Thank you, you're doing really well," and then she kissed him lightly.

The VW disappeared down the street. She finished her wine. She felt like an idiot, having told him she was tinder thin and then giving him *a review on the date.* And man, was she dull, her striped clothes, just saying yes to everything. She laughed at herself and went to bed.

But apparently, he liked getting a good review. He called again, asking, "Movie and dinner?"

The VW got them down the hill and into Oakland and to a showing of *Sullivan's Travels,* a movie that could soften any hard heart. She cried a little, saying it was par for the course—that she cried at TV ads and at beauty of any sort. She cried when people she didn't know said goodbye to each other at the airport or ran toward each other in the arrival lounge, she explained. "Comings and goings, all worth tears."

Then they went to dinner and he touched her hand. He sensed a whoosh of the torch to tinder. He understood her to mean she was fragile, but he couldn't guess why. She seemed sturdy enough, though quiet. He said, "I want to know more about you."

She began to talk. "I was never brave about love," she said. "I wish I had been, but it was easier to do without it, to throw it all into work. I do sort of love work."

"And you didn't want love?"

"Sure. Wanted it. Didn't pursue it."

"But why?"

After a while, she said, "I don't feel good about my body. I never did. And I can't believe I told you that."

"I don't get it. Your body is great."

"My mother pointed out to me—I think I was ten—that I had a condition. An uneven back. It mattered to her. It made her totally crazy, actually. It was the center of her attention to me and actually it became the center of my life."

"I don't understand. You look fine to me."

"I still can't *believe* I'm saying these things. You're getting me drunk or...I don't know. I never talk about this." She shook her head. "Did you drop something in this wine?"

They were only on the appetizers, but they were in a corner of the restaurant with no one else around and he wanted to know things. He put an arm around her and said, "Tell me."

"She called me names. I would have preferred sticks and stones. I never got over it. I know it sounds stupid, but I never did."

"What names?"

"Ugly. Cripple."

He gawped. "That makes no sense."

"My back is crooked."

He shook his head. He was sure it wasn't and was about to move his hand, but she held it tight to her waist.

Dinner arrived. He let the conversation go for the moment. But after they began on their fish entrees, he said, "That's very disturbing. It makes no sense. But the thing I don't get is...well, that she would call you names."

"She couldn't help herself. She wanted perfection."

"I think you look lovely."

"Oh, please thank you, but—"

"You do. She must have known that. She must have thought that."

"No. I don't think she did."

"You like your salmon?"

"Yes."

"Good. Let's enjoy it and then you can tell me more. You can tell me anything."

"Oh, don't make me cry again."

He looked closely. "How did I make you cry?"

"Kindness."

He didn't want to upset her, but he was more than curious about her life. "I'm glad you talked to me," he said. "Should I tell you stories? Entertain you?"

"Yes."

He told her about teaching, funny things students said. He told her about the tractor accident that almost killed him but produced the biggest explosion of abdominal gas in Columbia and Dutchess Counties. After they were finished with dinner, he drove her back to her place and asked if he could come in. "Do you have any more wine?"

"Yes."

They sat together—on the same sofa this time—and he put his arm around her waist. After a while he moved it gently upward. "Are you all right with this?"

"How strange it is to be touched there. I've almost never been touched there."

"How in God's name did you manage that?"

"Moved fast. Kept moving."

"That was horrible of your mother. Horrible."

"Yes. She tried to make me solve it, to make the condition disappear."

"I don't understand. What did she want you to do?"

"Oh, everything from watching Oral Roberts to thinking it away."

He urged her from the sofa to the bedroom. "Let's just lie down for a minute and talk, that's all." It was one in the morning. He caressed her into a lying down position.

She wasn't stupid. She was simply willing.

He said, "Tell me. I'm trying to get the picture."

"She said I was doing it to myself to spite her. She wanted me to stop reading because she said it came from reading too much."

"Oh, my God. Reading. *Reading.*"

"She didn't want me to read. She wanted me to be different, bubbly."

He touched her back. "I can't see anything. Let me look."

She kept her clothes on but turned. He touched her back and kissed it through her dress.

"I never talk about this. You're a wizard. Pretty bad to be almost forty-five and still messed up," she said.

He froze. "There's no age limit. How old do you think I am?"

"I don't know. My age, I guess."

"I'm sixty."

She turned over and looked at him with surprise. "Oh."

"Do you know anything about me?"

"You teach. Writing. I used to be a writer before I became a director."

"Have you read anything of mine?"

"No. I will. I will. I read a lot."

"Huh. So, I'm just a pretty face to you," he said a bit sadly.

That was that. He liked her but he was just an old guy to her now that she knew his true age. He got up and left a bit later.

Harrison spent the next morning writing, but he was distracted. Liz had not read *anything* by him. He was nothing to her, not impressive, even though he was a little bit famous locally. His family novel, so clearly about his famous father and his difficult mother, had been immensely well received and thus there was a lot of press on it. Everywhere he went, people were commenting on it, and thank God, loving it. And he'd finished the collection of short stories he'd been at for a long time and that was coming out soon.

She *had* been touched when he told her he had finally been able to write about his childhood, about how long it took to be able to say his mother was *unusual* and almost always gone and his father was *beautiful and brilliant,* but almost always gone.

And it seemed his own revelations had uncorked her. Right? Not wizardry or wine. She'd talked more freely.

He grabbed a copy of his book and signed it to her, but he was so flustered, he made a mistake. He wrote *To Liz from Funny Face.* No, no, that's not what he'd called himself to her. He tossed the book aside and wrote another one. *To Liz from Pretty Face.* He abandoned his writing early and drove to her house. There was no answer to the doorbell. He left the book in her mailbox. Then he went to the office—there were no classes, it was summertime, but he liked to check in. One day he'd taken croissants to the office staff, another day chocolates. The office staff women were the unsung for whom he felt like singing.

Plus, he loved to match-make between things and people. He saw a croissant. He wanted someone to give it to.

He drove aimlessly until he found himself at the butcher shop he liked where after studying everything in the case, he bought four gorgeous pork chops. He had some good wines at home that would go well with the chops. Next, he went to the Strip and found some arugula and radicchio to mix up with the other lettuces he had.

The sun glinted off the hood of his car, hurting his eyes.

Correspondence was his way of keeping contact with people. He had made friends in every city he'd taught in, so he was grateful to see as he carried his groceries into the house that there were, among the bills, two actual letters.

Ah. One from Emory. This one would be about the fate of the country, all opinions said with heart and ungainly wit. And one from a poet friend in Athens, Ohio, the one who'd called Harrison's style "world embracing," a phrase he especially treasured. He read eagerly, forgetting to put the food away. He had a hundred such friends, people like him who needed to say, and to say precisely, what was stirring them.

The kitchen windows were open, and as he read his letters, several birds kept up a cheerful chatter in his yard. All creatures needed to talk.

This house was the best thing that had ever happened to him. It was his, purchased with a down payment from Maggie, and renovated on a bank loan. He'd have to pay for years, but he didn't care, he was fit, he now had a salary; it was his, and it looked like the homes he had visited, brownstone or other, in New York, when the writers or painters had four floors of nineteenth-century features to put in conversation with contemporary fixings. It was the house he'd imagined Maggie and the kids in years ago when he longed so badly for that life. It was his to pad around in, barefoot, windows open. The back yard was expansive for a city yard, oh, not quite eighteen by twenty. He no longer had Guatemalan breeches but in more ordinary shorts he went out every other day to weed and to admire what he called the back forty. Forty square yards, his, property owned, but not property that took all day to attend to, an urban yard, an image from his dreams realized.

He supposed he should make a chop and freeze three. No, he loved a great chop (veal, lamb, pork), so maybe make two and freeze two?

He picked up the phone and dialed. Liz was home now; she answered on the second ring.

"Harrison? Thanks for the book. I would have bought it. I was planning to."

"Oh, you're welcome. Listen, if you don't have dinner and you like pork, come on over for a couple of chops I'm putting on."

"Tonight?"

"Yes. I'm messing around in the kitchen right now." She didn't appear to be saying no. He gave her the address. Fantastic day! Two letters and company for dinner. He got out his largest cast-iron skillet to sauté four chops. With one of his pirated tapes in the deck, he listened to

Billy Eckstein. It was June, the sun was shining, he'd started a new novel today—so he mixed himself a martini and opened a bottle of red. She could eat, Liz could. She didn't mince around about food. He rummaged in the cabinets and found polenta, good. And now he searched for something else, what might it be… Ah, yes, a few stalks of asparagus would do it. He put out his two best cheeses, a bowl of olives, and some crackers.

She arrived at his door, saying, "Beautiful street, and the houses look wonderful. They look like New York."

"You've never been over here?"

"No."

"Well, let me show you." He trotted through the downstairs, two sitting rooms, one developed, one not, dining room, kitchen, identifying each giddily because they were clearly what they were. "If you'd like to go upstairs while I cook, you can see the rest. Or I'll show you later. Do you want a martini or other mixed drink? I have wine opened."

"Wine then."

"Do you like pork?"

"I love pork. It's my favorite. On report card day, my father would give me a dollar for every A and my mother would ask me what I wanted for a reward dinner. I always asked for pork chops."

"Well, you're getting rewarded today. For something."

"Not sure if I deserve it. I've been struggling with *All's Well That Ends Well*. I'm directing it in the fall."

"Oh. Shakespeare, right? I don't know that one." He poured a glass of wine so expansively he had to mop up the counter with a towel.

"I won't tour the house until I've made a dent in this. I don't want to spill," she said, lifting the full glass. "This house is really gorgeous. It's…"

"What?"

"I don't know. Never mind. It's a bit overwhelming, art everywhere."

"Have some cheese."

"Sure."

"I like the way you eat."

"*Valiant trencherman* as Shakespeare would say. A family trait. Everybody in my family loves to eat. Sisters, brother, mother. My mother was a good cook. She did like to feed us. What we asked for, she made."

"Your mother was…complicated, I guess. She rewarded you with food for good grades, but she was awful in other ways."

"Very complicated. Cooked fabulous meals, baked bread every other day, sat over patterns and made our clothes. She scrubbed and painted and beat the rugs. Attended every award ceremony I was ever in. Those were the things she did right. I give her full credit for those."

"To balance the wrong."

"She just…she just got furious when she thought things reflected badly on her. It took me a long time to figure it out."

He wanted to touch her, but she was way across the kitchen and he didn't want to say anything stupid that would reduce the moment.

"This cheese is phenomenal."

"St. Andre. It's sort of my signature by now." Seeing the dent in her wine, he said, "Go ahead, look around anywhere."

She started down the hallway, calling back, "I'm forty pages into your novel. It's spectacular writing."

The little happiness in him ballooned up to a larger happiness. He listened to her walking upstairs, content that she would see parts of him, things the house showed, decisions, choices.

He measured out a cup of polenta and found a can of chicken broth to give it zing.

He listened to the steps above, rapid, then tentative, then rapid.

Only forty-four, not yet forty-five. It won't last, he counseled himself. Be happy for tonight.

What Liz saw upstairs on the second floor and the third floor could be capsulized by one thing in his home office, the way one thing stands for the whole, synecdochally, microcosmically. She saw a copy of his book open on his desk and lifted it tenderly, thinking how eager she was to get back to reading it. She'd felt the pain of the child without the author's ever asking for sympathy. He got at the child by ignoring the child, by describing what the parents were driving at. And it reverberated too. It made her feel the despair of her own mother, who'd done wrong trying to do right.

Liz lifted the book intending to tell Harrison just exactly where she was in it when she noticed on the flyleaf that it had been inscribed to her, then obviously abandoned. This one was signed, "Funny Face," and the one she found in her mailbox was signed "Pretty Face." She understood. He'd been nervous, hasty.

Slapdash, reckless, generous. Nervous. Delicate. Bountiful. His house showed these things. There was something for the eye everywhere.

Sculpture, painting, photographs. She couldn't take it all in. She put the book down as gently as she'd lifted it and made her way down the stairs.

"Hungry?"

"Yes. Your house is…amazing."

"It's what I always wanted. And now I have it."

"That would be a wonderful feeling."

He leaned forward and kissed her. He took her hand and led her to the dining table where he had candles burning and cloth napkins on placemats, a little skewed, a bit hastily put down. As she straightened them, he was saying, "Sit. The pork takes almost no time if you do it right. Unless you like it well done."

"I don't like anything well done."

"Fantastic!"

"Let me help."

"Not today."

He brought polenta to the table, asparagus, a salad. "Now just the pork to come."

Minutes later, he forked two chops onto her plate, each an inch and a half high. "If you can't finish you can take it home."

"How many women have you seduced this way?"

"In this house? Four. I'm a pretty fair cook." He grinned happily.

He was sixty. Run, run, run, she told herself, but she was already in love.

She wanted to run, he sensed that, even as he guided her up the stairs. He'd done a pretty good job of getting her to talk over dinner—more about her mother, and then a bit about her father. She told him her father was a man who had owned three bars, drank without enjoying it, was quiet and lovable, affectionate and loving, and he was the person who made her feel she was okay, better than okay, but he died young.

"You adored him."

"Yes."

"I'm sorry he's gone."

Harrison felt bizarrely that he knew the man, could picture Liz's family in their small town with their lives racing by.

They made it to the second floor and she hadn't bolted. "You like the house?" he asked foolishly. She'd already said.

"Oh, my God, *like* is hardly the word. Well, you must get compliments all the time."

He put a hand on her waist to distract her from the steepness of the climb to the third floor.

He was guessing she probably wouldn't want to be tied up. That was definitely a relief. He just wasn't any good at it.

"I'm nervous," she said when they reached the top.

"Me too."

"This room is awfully hot."

"It was an attic." He gestured to the slanted ceilings. "I built out, put in all the windows."

"I see that."

She was wearing a sundress, easy to get off, but he helped her with it. "Ah," he said. "There we are."

"Here we are."

His shorts came off in a hurry, his shirt over his head and onto the floor. Again, the joy of feeling this kind of lust, what was there to compare?

She got into the bed, trying to pull the sheet up over her.

As gently as he could, he took her hand with the sheet and slowly helped her to reveal herself.

Later, they lay there spooned, a big box fan blowing on them. He could feel the sweat drying.

She said, "I've got to go."

"Home?"

"It's too hot for me up here."

"I never mind it."

"I do. Can't sleep."

"Okay." They didn't move. "Are you bothered by my age—the age difference?"

"Yes."

"You think I'm an old guy."

"Yes. I just didn't know. I thought you were my age."

"I don't plan to die, ever. Does that help?"

"You seem like someone for whom that would be true."

He laughed because he liked that answer, also her previous one that she had thought him her age until in a burst of honesty he put the truth on the table, second date.

"You have a lot of spirit. You 'eat the air, promise crammed.'"

"What is that? I know that."

"*Hamlet*. That's how he describes himself. Of course, he's more or less nuts at that point."

"I'm going to type that up and put it on my wall, right in front of my typewriter. I like it."

"Shakespeare did have a way with words. I love words."

"Do you?"

"Yes. Yes, I do. Always did. Apparently when I was little more than a year old, I slapped my highchair and pronounced a meal *delicious*. I have to go. I'm melting."

"I'll buy more fans."

He couldn't see her face when she turned aside to dress. "I'll walk you down." He slipped on his shorts, but not the shirt or shoes. She got dressed, saying, "Don't poke your feet on anything."

He looked at his feet. "I'm made of tough stuff. Genetic. My father. My grandparents. They all lived to a very old age."

At the door he said, "Want to come to dinner tomorrow? I could do a simple pasta."

"I…happen to have no plans."

"Glad to hear it. Come at six."

He watched her drive off.

And like a miracle, the next day, as if he were building up points in the universe, came the postcard from Denise. *I will come to visit again. How about a weekend in July? Can you by chance pay for the ticket?*

Of *sterner stuff*. She might have said his feet were made of sterner stuff, a better phrase than tough stuff, she thought as she drove home. She loved words too much. They sang in her head all day. She'd wanted to be a writer since she was a child. Tomorrow, pasta, and then what? This was madness. He was too old for her.

She arrived with two bottles of wine and some chocolates.

"Oh, wonderful," he told her. "Thank you so much."

She was dressed this time in a shorter sundress, a sandal with a small heel—sweet.

Before dinner, over wine, Harrison read the summary she'd written for him of the play she was directing while he also stirred his tomato and butter sauce (easy and good). He had put some linguini and a salad aside, ready to go, and on the table were some cheeses and olives and bread to start.

He'd poached some pears.

The kitchen was steamy. He saw Liz dab at her forehead. After a while she took his novel from her bag and began reading. The bookmark was near the end.

The play she was directing was one of the several Elizabethan plays, she'd explained, that had a 'bed trick.' A male character went to bed in the dark thinking he was with one woman but learned later that in the dark he had actually slept with another. *Measure for Measure* had a bed trick. *The Changeling* did too.

"Crazy, this bed trick idea," he said, delighted to be learning something he'd missed in college.

"I know. One of the conventions. If you get literal, you'd have to say, 'Well it couldn't have been a full moon.'"

Harrison laughed to think of the gimmicks dramatists came up with. "One thing about Shakespeare. He makes a person courageous about trying plot. What a bunch of reversals and turns. Who would dare to write this today?"

"I know."

"It makes me want to go right to my typewriter and do something bold."

"I really understand that. I used to think I was going to be a writer. Lately I've been messing around with it again."

Oh, shit.

But, of course, it made sense now. That was why she was at the party of writers where he first met her.

Shit, shit, not another writer in his life, please. He said, betraying irritation, "You and lots of other people. Lots."

Eventually they ate his excellent pasta. As they ate, he forgave her for being another person who wanted to write. Talk was flowing nicely; instead, he asked her, "Would you go to DC with me on Friday to see the Matisse show? Come back Saturday?"

"Well, okay."

"Would you like to go to a ballgame next week? To distract you from *All's Well*?"

And she said yes.

She was so wonderfully *available*.

"You like baseball?"

"I *love* baseball," she said. "Always. Since I was a little kid. I was in love with Ted Williams."

He hastened to say, "I'm booked one weekend at the end of July, but we can have a couple of fun times before that."

Her eyes, he thought, registered a question but she didn't ask it.

He had assured her he loved Arabic foods and she owed him a dinner, but she wasn't a fancy cook. She'd rather have taken him out, treated him, but no, he said he hoped for dinner at her place. When she let him in, she said nervously, "It's just peasant stuff." She had olives, cheese, hummus to start. A large salad for after. For the main dish, she'd stuffed whole zucchinis with rice and lamb and cooked them in tomato sauce. There was bread to dip in the sauce.

He said, "To think you've been hiding this from me! Peasant food is the best, always the best."

"Very kind of you."

When he finished his second large zucchini, he dropped out of his chair and knelt before her. "This was fantastic."

"You like that kneeling thing," she teased. "How did you not become an actor?"

"That's…a long story. I filled in for a little while when my wife had a company. I wasn't any good. I'll tell you about it sometime." He got up and said, "You remember, I'm booked, weekend end of the July."

"I remember."

She watched him as he formulated a lie.

"I have to go visit my mother. I should…stay overnight and the next night, back Sunday. Back, well actually, late Sunday."

36

Denise was wearing jeans and a sweatshirt and carrying only a small bag when she got off the plane. She was quieter than usual when they drove to his place, so that he could hardly see her well, looking to the side as he had to. He kept his eyes on the road. "I was surprised that you wanted to come."

"Our yearly visits," she said. "Filled with angst. Something out of Graham Greene. Except you're divorced now. And I'm not married."

He wasn't sure he could understand her tone. He said, "I made reservations for dinner at a place out in the country. Been hearing about it for a long time but never went. I already know I'm going to want the duck."

"You think about food a lot."

He did. Was it a flaw?

When they got to his place, they sat out back. He'd put out a few slices of ham, some bread, and a gorgeous fruit salad. At first, he thought she was wearing an odd shade of eye makeup, but then he realized the yellowing was a faded bruise. "Did your current lover do that to you?"

"Which one?"

"Whoever you're seeing."

"There are two."

"Not counting me. Three?"

"If we're counting." She spooned herself some fruit salad. "Looks good. Thank you."

"You haven't tried to hurt yourself, have you?"

"No, not that. I'm all right now."

Because of him, she would be all right? Because of this visit?

"Who are the two?" Why did he want to know? To measure himself. But he also worried about her. And he had some ability, so she'd said, to save her from her worst impulses.

"One is Bruno—we go way back. He's a jazz musician. Drums. There. I've told you. We can't seem to be done with each other. The other is a guy named Peter; he owns a wine store. He always wants to feed me, too, just like you."

"Which one hit you?"

"Bruno. Let's not talk about all that."

"I don't understand your life. You have ability and talent. Why do you mess with men who aren't good enough for you?"

For a while she didn't answer. She ate fruit salad and smiled at him. At one point, chewing on a piece of cantaloupe, she said, "I think that's where my talent comes from."

In being around meanness? In adopting meanness? He worried the part about her talent was true.

"I'll always love you. I'll try to be better to you," she said.

"In what way?"

"More attentive. I'll come visit more often. Right now, I think I need an hour to shower, get a ten-minute nap, and then we can do whatever you want. I won't make you tie me up."

"I wasn't good at it."

"I would have to agree."

She was worn out. Sagging. And she looked a little odd with her long black braid down her back. He'd hoped she'd say something about his new book and the one almost out, but she was not thinking about that.

After the shower and the nap, he heard her stirring. He went to the bedroom, and she extended her arms to him. He undressed and went to her.

"It's awfully hot."

"I have all the fans on. I bought new fans."

"Good."

They began to make love in an almost dutiful way. He stopped when he became aware of the fullness of her breasts. "Is this… Is this what I think?"

She nodded.

"Whose?"

"I'm not sure. It doesn't matter."

Not his at any rate. It had been too long. "What are you going to do?"

"I don't know."

He said, "Let's just rest." And she didn't disagree.

After a while, they went to dinner. She was livelier, joking, imitating people. She ended the evening saying, "God, what a good book you wrote. I wish I could do one like that."

"It ripped my guts out, doing it. Sixty-year preparation. I thought it was possibly bad, but people say it's good."

"It is."

They slept in the same bed, but he didn't approach her again sexually, aware as he was of her new pregnancy. She entertained him with stories of people she imitated. She was a wicked mimic. All the while he felt dizzy, living in an alternate narrative from his regular life, hyper-aware, the whole cocaine experience of her again.

As they were getting ready for him to take her to the airport, he said, "What are you going to do?"

"I don't know. I got careless. I know it's my fault and I take responsibility. People say I'll learn to love the kid if I, you know, don't do anything."

"It happens that way a lot of the time I hear."

"Six hundred would help. If you have it."

He went to his study and wrote out a check. He wasn't sure what it was for. He wondered if she asked him to marry her and raise her kid what he would say.

He invited Liz for dinner on Tuesday night—he'd given himself only one day to recover from Denise, brushed up the house a bit, laundered sheets. Breaded pork chops this time, because she'd said she hadn't had them that way for a very long time, the way her mother had made them as a reward for her good report cards. She seemed strange and tentative and exotic when she entered in a long-printed dress, eyes averted, then head turned to the side when he tried to kiss her. No, she wasn't herself. More distant.

"How was your weekend? Your mother?" she asked

"Oh. Critical, as always." He felt a need to keep talking so he blurted, "Look, what do you think of this house?" even though she'd already told him several times it was wonderful.

She looked at him oddly.

He said, "The bowls, the wall hangings, the paintings? The things I collect."

"They're beautiful," she shrugged. "The look? It's you."

"But you don't ordinarily *notice* things," he said with an edge. "You don't stop and look at them."

In the past month he had cut flowers from the garden and put them on the side of the bed she took, but she never saw them. He had cut other flowers—his best gerbers—and put them in the center of the table when they dined the other week and she never noticed. She had faults. Big faults, he reminded himself.

"I don't. You're right. I admit it. I'm often fretting, talking to myself. I see I'm failing some test here. I'm always living in my head, working things out. You on the other hand need to have a lot of visual stimuli, a lot going on." Now *her* voice had an edge.

He took a giant sip of martini. "Want a martini?"

"No, just a sip. I guess you had a good weekend. Your mother likes visual stimuli, I take it."

She had to come close for the sip of his drink, and he murmured in her ear, "Don't, don't be hasty."

"How old is your 'mother'?" she asked, leveling her gaze. "Twenty? Thirty? I'm guessing here. Don't turn away. I'm not dumb. You don't have to lie."

He sank to a chair in the dining room. "Just past thirty."

"That sounds…not so good. Look. This is more complicated than I knew. For the record you could have done it without lying." She took up her bag.

"We can talk over dinner. The chops are all ready to go. Stay to eat at least. I got them for you."

She hesitated. She really, really loved food. He had that card to play at least. He hurried to add, "She was just…old business. Something I had to understand. Please. Please stay. I won't touch you. Talk to me. Just talk."

"Let me see her picture."

"Why?"

"You called her your mother. I'm curious."

"Crap." He was almost laughing with the ridiculousness of it. "I did, didn't I? All right, after dinner." He made the chops, nice gritty bread-crumbs on the outside, a dab of butter with the oil. He asked her to toss the salad and make it like the one she'd served him. His homemade fries splattered grease all over the stove, caught him on the arm, one drop to his left eye. But they were crisp, the way he liked them.

He had another martini while he cooked and slugged a good half bottle or more of his best red at dinner.

"These chops are great," she admitted.

"Good."

What photo would he show? The question interrupted his other thoughts so that they barely spoke much during dinner except to praise the food. He stood uncertainly.

"Several photos," she said.

Aw, fuck it. He went up the stairs to his study and grabbed a folder of pictures of Denise—photos people had taken of them together, photos of her that he had taken—some posed, some candid. If Denise was going to end it for him, that was fate, let it be. Liz would leave—they would say polite hellos at some party, he would eventually date someone else, Denise would show up a year from now with new curiosities about him, maybe with a child, probably not. That was his life.

He tossed the folder down beside Liz's plate, which was licked clean as they say, and he took the plate to the kitchen.

"Oh God," he heard. "Your 'mother' is a tough cookie."

He scraped the dishes clean. He felt drunk with confusions. They were now talking about his actual mother? No.

She said, "If these were resume photos and I were casting a Shakespeare, I'd plug her in for Goneril, Regan."

He thought for a moment about that. He couldn't say, "Ha! What can you tell from a photograph," because he was known for believing you could tell everything from a good photograph.

She said, "Thanks for the chops. I should get going."

He heard her walking toward the front door. He hurried to catch up, touched her shoulder, which she shrugged away, and yet he managed to turn her. She was crying.

"I can't compete. Honestly. Sorry. I mean I *won't*."

"You can. Believe me. You do." He backed up a step. "It's my age."

She nodded. "We're both having a big problem with that."

He let her leave, stood there watching her drive away and he thought, I will always, always be alone. So be it.

It had in many ways been his mother they were talking about. Years later, he understood that.

37

The amazing thing was that Liz made her way back to him and the twenty-something years in the middle of their story were without much drama. There was the beginning—wonderful, sweet. The end—when he felt the end coming, terrible. And as Harrison would say to students, "Get your beginnings and your endings sharp if nothing else." In between was the long middle, and since the middle was largely a time of contentment, it needs only a brief summary.

There was success:

Books kept pouring out of him. His voice was unleashed. He won honors. The mailbox held letters from friends almost every day.

The food was almost always good.

Liz added the work of writing to her other work and began to get published.

Harrison bought Liz dresses, sweaters, coats, scarves, gloves. He got them right almost every time.

She bought him shirts, sweaters, coats, scarves, gloves and she got them right too.

They made some ten trips to Europe. He wrote letters and postcards to his children on an almost weekly basis, and if one of them visited for two days, his joy hit the ceiling. If they came with spouses and kids, he went totally crazy with happiness.

Liz fell in love with his children. Their voices, faces, and quickness were a part of him and she loved to look at them.

He stopped hearing from Denise. Someone told him she worked in real estate these days and had a daughter.

His mother died. He'd driven to see her often (not a lie, his actual mother, Gertrude) sometimes more than once a month, traveling on a non-class day the whole way to Philadelphia and back, ridiculous and dangerous when you counted in fatigue.

"Devoted," the aides said. He wasn't. But he couldn't stop visiting. Perhaps he wanted her to say, "You are a miracle. I never took care of you and you turned out well. You've done well, my son."

Of course, she never did say that. She was herself till the end.

On one afternoon getting toward the end, after he'd been gardening, Harrison came in the back door proffering flowers, but as Liz accepted the flowers, she saw he was unaware that he had blood streaming down both his shins.

"What happened?"

He didn't know what she meant. He was grinning.

She grabbed paper towels, both wet and dry to catch the blood. It wasn't the first time he had not registered pain. How lucky in a way—she felt everything, absolutely everything, emotions, sensations, the pea under the mattress.

"Ah, let it be."

"Hang on. You need Band-Aids."

"I don't need bandages." He tried to move, but she grabbed his leg to stop him. "What?"

"Um, the floors, the rugs, your shoes!"

"I'm *not* still bleeding."

"Actually, you are. Take off your shoes." She kept swabbing.

"You sound like my mother."

"God, please no. Don't assign me that. Just stand still."

By the time she brought the Band-Aids, he asked, "What are you going to do with my shoes?"

"Wipe them."

He reminded her that they were one of a kind, handmade in Provincetown.

"Carefully then. I'll wipe them carefully. Almost no water."

Of the things in his life that were old and therefore, to him, precious, there were many. Luggage, handmade, too, with the dirt of a lifetime; Dopp kit, ditto, he'd had it since boyhood; his sandals, made by an artist; certain pots, certain shirts that had been mended a half dozen times, the house they lived in with its steep stairs and drafty windows. He loved what held memory, what used to be. Given that, Liz asked a couple of times if he missed Maggie, but he just said how sad it was that it hadn't worked, a wonderful person but he was the wrong person in the wrong place for a long time.

Bandages on, Liz began wiping the shoes—carefully while he stretched over to the sink and put the bouquet meant for her in a vase.

It frightened her that his nerve endings did not register pain. She thought of all the horrible things that might happen to him. On the other hand, she couldn't help taking comfort from his strong, unbeatable body. His grandparents and his mother had lived far into their nineties and his father to the upper eighties. So, there was a good chance, given her shorter-lived family, they could die together as they often joked they wanted to do, *sort of together*, not a suicide pact, more like a lucky terrorist attack, them in the wrong place, wrong time, but together, the only victims. Sweet last words to each other, his usual extravagant "You gave me my life. I adore you." Her "I loved you from day one, couldn't help myself."

He simply had to live as long as she did.

He wants to. He's started another novel. Well, research, notes. A photographer. Nineteenth century. He's been reading and reading but he doesn't have all he needs yet.

His protagonist is a photographer, a crusty middle-aged coot who goes from town to town doing what people need, preserving youth or even middle age or old age as an aid to memory. And one time he takes a photo of a young Native American woman. Her innocent face captivates him. He sees hopefulness there and a lack of guile and a lack of anger. Inevitably, he falls in love.

He woos her. He asks if she can cook him some buffalo meat. He lugs the big box of a camera to her and takes another picture. He wins her. And then he needs to move on to make a living, twenty-eight more towns by his reckoning and then he will round out his trip and return, he tells her. But when he returns, she is no longer there. He asks everyone he meets but nobody knows where she is. It's as if she's never been. He travels again, always looking for her. Many years go by. He does not forget her at all, in fact lives a life of longing and of mourning for what almost was. Twenty years later he photographs a young woman. She is lovely and he thinks the picture turned out really well. In fact, he keeps a copy and often looks at it. He travels again and slowly realizes who the young woman reminds him of. Does he have a daughter? Could it be? It takes him a long time to make it back to where he saw her. She is no longer there.

"I think it's going to be good," Liz tells him when he gives her the outline. "Write it."

He's in his study at the typewriter, eyes moist.

"I need to come up with the energy to take it on."

"Maybe he could find her. One of the hers," she says.

"I don't think so. It's a better story if he never does. What's for dinner?"

"I don't have any buffalo steaks," Liz says. "But I did make stuffed green peppers. For some reason, where I come from, people like them with mashed potatoes. Should I make some?"

"Thank you."

Oh, he misses cooking. And serving. He doesn't have the patience these days, or the energy, that crucial thing, energy. In the old days, when he first began to see Liz, he would bring trays with cheese, ripe figs, wine, to the edge of the bathtub for her. He loved amazing her. If they went for a long drive, he would pack a picnic of cheeses, chicken, olives, ripe tomatoes, crusty bread, and wine and he would find a spot on the side of a road to spread a blanket. He would host dinner parties with course after course, pears in molasses, five fancy cheeses "to close the stomach."

Now he works hard to find a little of the old energy that defined him.

He's frantic to say what he sees before it disappears. Birds at the feeder? A wagging stem with a single rose reaching for sunlight. A new cheese at the market. A theater production. An invitation to a garden party. Wonderful. All those things that he believes are worth getting down.

38

I think we should spend next winter and summer in Europe," he announced at dinner one day, spearing a piece of broccoli. They had sabbaticals coming up. He had that defiant look that showed he knew she would say no.

She stopped eating, felt the tightening of her esophagus. "Eight months? No way. First of all, there's affording it."

"We can afford it. I'll pay. France," he said. "France."

"We don't want the house left alone all those months."

"We could get someone to watch it."

"Other people get renters, but—"

"I know. I don't want that either."

"But I don't work well in France."

"I do."

"That's one of us that will do well there!" She scowled. "Seriously, I really don't work well there. It's because of not being good at the language." (She was fueled by English words and she thought this time she would win the argument because he loved the fact that she loved work.)

"You would this time. You would learn to."

"How can you predict that?"

"I can't. I can hope." Then he pulled the big one: "I have to go while I can. Someday I won't be able to do a trip like that!"

Do what! Make change in euros? Walk up and down the metro steps? He had legs like steel cables. "I think you're being very dramatic," she said tightly, "just to get your way."

She was wrong. He, it turns out, was right. Some day he would not be able to do it and that day was soon. He could hardly—though she didn't guess—do it now. His face was so eager, she felt herself caving.

"And I would spend my time how?" she asked. "If I can't write?"

"Read. Eat croissants. Sit in a sliver of sunshine."

"I'll go mad."

The next night he presented pictures of apartments in Paris. They were hard to see because he had printed them in black and white from his computer.

Cold, dark, damp, wintery Paris. Unfortunately, she loved it, too, and he knew that. Though every joint ached in the dank air, there were rewards like croissants and baguette sandwiches, even to the ridiculous hot dog drilled down into the foamy inside of the crusty bread.

Harrison was on a mission. He dealt out more photos like playing cards. "I was thinking this place in Nice for the winter months. Near the old city. Near the place we like with the oysters and brown bread. Walkable too. A good walk gets us to the ocean. We could reduce the whole trip to five months. You could work like the devil in January here. Then we go. February, March, April in the south, May, June in Paris when the flowers are up. He left the photos on the table and took a turn at cleaning up the kitchen. "Just remember. This may be the last time I'm able to do such a trip."

It was a very attractive plan.

And so they went.

The winter months flew.

Three months in Nice could be summarized as: Brown bread and oysters, brown bread and oysters, harrowing European traffic in their rental car, and work, work, work. Liz worked in spite of her frustration with hearing another language everywhere she went. She bit down and concentrated and wrote.

Harrison wrote in a more leisurely manner and went out marketing most days. He dragged her out into the sunshine and to museums. And food. "Wasn't it worth it?" he asked when the third month came to an end. "Now to Paris in springtime."

And as they drove to the airport days later, he said sadly, "Time to give up the car. Ah, well."

He'd been terrible at driving in Nice. She didn't answer. He needed all his concentration on the road.

He turned into the rental lot.

He parked and dropped his hands.

She looked at him and saw his hands were shaking and understood he was secretly glad to be getting rid of the rental car. He hadn't been quick enough for the drivers in Nice, who all knew how to slip into a lane with a quarter inch to spare.

They sat for a moment, breathing the last of their time in Nice.

Once inside the hut of an office, he signed a sheaf of papers at the counter and they looked at their last palm tree of the trip, struggled with luggage, and took two trams. Finally, at their gate, with time to spare, he went off to explore at the airport. She understood he needed to buy her something. She'd nixed bottles of perfume or luggage. One of her sins, he said, was not wanting things. Because he wanted to buy things for her, and she was taking that away from him.

What *were* her other sins? Wishing him young again. Wishing to return the calendar to an earlier year. Wishing him faster at walking.

He bought her a candy bar and a *pain chocolate*. "Keep up your strength," he said.

And then they were in Paris with a whole new set of routines that made him happy: Saying bonjour to the very French neighbors in the apartment above them, frequenting the café at the corner that charged a leg if not an arm as well for an omelet. Going out to buy a newspaper.

Another of their routines—and Harrison loved it—was a walk several times a week to Notre Dame and beyond to a café he liked. It was a mile, two miles, and the perfect reward for a day of wrestling with a manuscript that might or might not see the light of day. Short stories. He had two that chimed together, but he needed to come up with about ten more that fit thematically. Could he? And if he could, where would he send them?

One late afternoon, Harrison watched Liz, lurching ahead, checking out windows here, street signs there, and hopping back to him. Why? They should be walking *together*, right, *strolling*, seeing things—she wasn't a dog breaking a leash. It made him angry. "Why are you racing?" he demanded.

"Why are you dawdling?" she countered.

He did his best to keep up, but he couldn't match her pace. He watched her legs move and then his own. How could she get so far ahead? He couldn't figure it out.

He slowed down. He couldn't help it. She'd called what he did "slogging along." Slogging? He would never slog. Amble. Saunter. Stroll. Good words that spoke of enjoyment, yes.

He insisted on a break and by the time they went into the great cathedral he was breathless with irritation at her *need to be moving*. A light Gregorian chant lifted him and after a while, he was calm again.

She was off lighting candles and then back, smiling, to sit beside him.

"Did you wish something good?" he asked.

"Pray."

He nodded. "Did you?"

"For us, of course. Twenty-five more good years."

Not possible unless he were on a mountain in India eating only rice and not too good at counting. Yes, he wanted twenty-five more years too and couldn't think about it or he would cry.

Lately, he remembered his father moving slowly, feet glued to the pavement. His old pa would stop and try to lift them, crying, "Damn, cah, damn." But no matter how he tried, he couldn't lift them, even with swearing.

There was a slight mist in the air when they left the cathedral and even though it was May, it was only fifty degrees or so, not particularly spring-like yet—or bright in the City of Light. Still, there he was, ambling, strolling, his wife on his arm, drawn by the small glowing lights in cafes, people talking to each other in every restaurant—talk for the French being medicinal—joy filled his heart.

"You're very silent lately," she said.

He didn't really want to answer, so he squeezed her arm closer and urged her toward a restaurant window. "Slow down for a minute," he said. "Let's look in here."

"This place looks pretty ordinary."

"It is. Nothing wrong with the basics." He read the posted menu intently. "See? The basics. Rabbit, beef, chicken. And watch the way the staff moves—see, you can tell they're the owners by the way they run—trying to make it, trying to make good."

"You want to eat here?" she asked, puzzled.

He wondered when she would realize he was faking it, drumming up interest in order to rest. Having caught his breath, he said, "No. You're right. It is ordinary. Let's go."

Slowly it crept over them that Harrison was getting old and that maybe this was his last trip.

One day he was out for a long time with Liz getting very worried, and when he got back finally, huffing with fatigue, he handed over a pair of earrings.

"Oh, what prompted this?"

"For the memory," he said.

Memory.

Before they went to the airport for the trip home, Harrison went out to buy almond croissants from the bakery they liked so much so they could have that little treat on the plane to remember their almost daily indulgence.

Then he looked forward and got excited. "Going home!" he said. "Baseball. The yard. All that."

Twenty-four good years so far, and only the last several with hints of the end.

39

Amanda was in the habit of checking the obits every day, so it was with a jolt that she saw Sam was now gone. She had run into him on the street three years ago—he had left *Time* for *The Times* and God, he looked awful. He had aged a lot, not that she hadn't, not that everyone *didn't* unless they were Romeo and Juliet, cashing out early. Still, it had been a shock, running into him, partly because she could tell he saw himself through her eyes for those seconds on the street.

It felt strange that she had once been in love with him.

After a long illness, the obit said.

His liver, she was pretty sure. He'd had that yellow orange glaze even three years ago. As she read, taking in the details to make his passing real, she saw he had still been married to Louise. It was a strange business, trying to guess what would last, what wouldn't. Ha. One child they had together, now an adult daughter, married.

Her own relationship had lasted. She and her guy bought Christmas gifts for each other, vacationed once a year, and otherwise got together three times a week unless there was something extraordinary going on. Her long-term affair with him may have been the shot that killed her poor mother fifteen years ago. "It's okay to be a couple without marriage, times have changed," she tried to explain, but her mother wasn't having it.

She often looked for Harrison's name among the obits. She'd run into his name in the course of her work at the magazine, when books came in, press releases, even when she went to the Strand to buy reviewer copies of new works. Thank God, she hadn't ruined him. He was a success after all. He'd done what he wanted to do all along, written and published one book after another, to wonderful notices. He even got a brief review in the *New Yorker* for his last one. He was a name now, a known figure on the scene.

She bought each of his books *new* as they came out (knowing as she did that publication produced almost no money for most authors), and always felt a little sad that her purchase contributed only two dollars or so to his royalties.

But he was still alive, apparently, and had made it past Sam in the survival race.

She folded her paper and got up from her chair in the Algonquin lobby. She only worked part time these days because she was "up there" as they said. But it was time to check in to the office.

When she considered Harrison's love of Manhattan, when she considered all the stories of people bumping into each other in that megalopolis, it amazed her that she had never seen him again.

Maggie was thinking about having a drink at the Algonquin when her business was finished at what would probably be three or four o'clock. She was making her yearly visit to the city to see Isaac Kline. Never having dispensed with formality, she'd put on her good gray suit for the meeting. No hat, no gloves, she'd come that far at least. All around her on the street were people in jeans and sweats.

Kline greeted her with a kiss on both cheeks, brought her a sparkling glass of water and offered "drink—or coffee or tea."

She thought for a moment and chose drink.

What arrived was a scotch with water on the side. The man had a wonderful memory. He shuffled now, but in spite of what his legs were doing, he forced his posture upright. After he served her, he sat, hands folded, and waited.

"I've moved some money around," she said, handing over a folded sheet from her handbag. "The will stays the same, except I want to give a hundred to my friend Alice—she's fallen on some hard times. And I want to bequeath two hundred to my ex. The rest is as it was, to be divided equally among the girls and Thomas."

"Last time we talked, you thought your youngest daughter might want the house."

"I don't think that's logical anymore. Her life is pretty settled in Michigan. Somebody told me it might in time be worth two million but that since it's so much work to keep up, I should sell now. I can't. I don't want to. Ah, you never know if I'll stick to that. Anyway, if it should still be mine when I die, the dividing should continue to be equal. You figure it out."

"Very good. I understand. You can trust me to make it absolutely equal. I'll send the new phrasing to you." He leaned forward, asked, "Now, this new bequest to your ex—"

"Harrison."

"Harrison. Yes. You've been in contact lately?" His voice rose with curiosity.

"The usual couple of letters a year. He came to visit a month or so ago." She paused. Suddenly she wasn't sure if he had visited or if she had dreamed it because all she could remember was the figure of him standing at the front door.

Kline watched her for a while. "On this visit, did he ask for money? Of course, he's entitled to it, but he always refused it before."

"Oh no. It's to be a surprise. A last gift. A thank you."

"I see. To help in his retirement, perhaps?"

"I believe I heard he still works, but what sort of salary does a teacher make? I'd like to leave him a little something if I go before he does."

"Very generous of you. Just, my dear, for my sake, don't go too soon. Right?"

"Well, I'm older than he is. I was all along," she said, laughing, as if just realizing this, "his older woman. Not by a decade, but still."

She wished she hadn't laughed. Kline did not have much of a sense of humor.

"He is continuing to live in Pittsburgh?"

"Last I heard, yes."

Kline's gentle smile remained. "I'll do what you want, of course. You think of everyone. The sister-in-law, the niece still on the list?"

"Oh yes."

When she left his office, Maggie walked around a bit, wanting to stroll toward her drink at the Algonquin, but there was so much shoving as younger and fitter people hurried past her, that she gave up walking there and hailed a cab, fully intending to say, "Algonquin," and somehow hearing herself say, "Penn Station" instead.

Had she dreamt the visit? She saw that Kline questioned it. It was very brief if it happened, wasn't it, just him at the door, and they wished each other well, just that.

40

He sits at breakfast, marmalade today on a buttered English muffin. He had a dream, a bad dream, with truth in it. A terrible feeling tugs at Liz until she cannot work. The ship. His quiet. How he *is* these days, halting.

Liz is the do-er. Does there have to be a do-er in couples? She watches him move slowly from the kitchen to the living room. She remembers a colleague of his asking, when the man saw Harrison walking slowly, "Is he okay? Is it Parkinson's?"

But why, then, did his doctor not say so if he's got Parkinson's?

He turns and sees Liz watching him. "Why can't I move faster?" he asks, frustrated.

"We're going to find out."

Many phone calls later, they find themselves facing a very young doctor who orders tests and, once he's studied them, says, "Call it a disease if you want, give it a name, but it's really old age. Let's try some meds. They may help."

Old age. They try to laugh about it. Harrison does his best with the pills, he takes them with a sort of snarl, but they make him so sleepy he has to load in caffeine to get to his classes. He tosses the pills in the garbage. "Better to be awake," he tells Liz.

The same doctor says they *could* try something that sounds kind of crazy, but…hey, isn't medicine always coming up with something? "It's sort of a new procedure. Basically, we treat the pressure on the brain. We go in and we drain the fluid around the brain."

"My brain!" Harrison exclaims. "I thought my legs were the problem."

The doctor winks. "It all comes from the brain."

"Surgery on my brain?"

The doctor laughs. "Well, yes. We go in and free it." He taps his own head and adds lightly, "There have been some miracles."

Harrison is silent for a minute. "Are you saying my feet would move? I would be the old me?"

"Could be. If it works."

On the way to the car, he needs every banister there is and when there isn't one, he uses Liz's shoulder. He says, "I want to be right for you."

"You are," she says. And then she says the thing that will require forgiveness for the rest of her life. "Let's do it."

Harrison tells Oscar and his children in phone calls, "We're going to get me fixed." He sounds his usual upbeat self, which is encouraging. Attitude is half the battle.

But the night before the surgery and also the day of, he is so angry about having to wash with the red stuff three times, he yells at Liz, "They're cutting my head, not my body."

"Let me just get your shoulders—"

"Enough," he tells Liz, batting her away from him. "Let's just do it." But he knows he has to let her help. He can't walk. He can't pee. He just stands in the bathroom for a while letting her dry him. It takes ten minutes to get his pants on. He can't reach for his socks. "Never mind." He slips on shoes without socks, saying, "It can't be that cold out."

No breakfast, no water, nothing. The little pleasures of this life. She *knows* how he's thinking, what he wants.

He limps into his home office before leaving the house. In the center of the desk, he has put the checkbooks and the unpaid bills so that Liz can find them, in case. The rest, the mess all around him, the student papers, the files, the dusty books, she will have to deal with if he doesn't make it.

He closes his office door. Click. Something has closed.

Her car. She must drive. She does everything now, all the cooking, all the marketing, the buttons on the remote control, everything. How that happened, he can't remember.

As she's getting him to her car, he mutters, "My head."

"I know. You have the most beautiful head."

"I'm an old man. I get it."

"Still beautiful."

And after this, he does not want to speak—not while being wheeled into the hospital, not at the desks they stop at, not back in the waiting area. He stays mute, not giving himself.

"We can walk away," Liz says. "If you feel funny, we can cancel. Just say the word."

He hears it, and she thinks he wants to say, *Run with me, yes, let's run out of here*, but he simply shakes his head.

He does want to run. Phrases keep going through his mind, phrases he loves as a writer, and which he said once but has been revising in his mind, though when he said it before, Liz got upset. *I think this is the end, the start of the last chapter.* And *This story is about to end.*

Many nights in the last months he had the dream of the big black ship. At the beginning he thought of it simply as a curious dream, just something to mull over. But then he came to hate the sight of the ship, the memory of it when he woke, the whole idea of it, coming slowly toward him.

In the hospital waiting area, he hears his name being called, but pretends he doesn't.

"You can change your mind," she urges him, but how can he now?

He shakes his head slightly. Sometimes there is just simply movement forward.

Liz waves the courier over to them. "I love you," she says while the courier jerks the wheelchair and whisks him away.

The next part is better—voices, people taking over. "Mr. Mirth. Just a little something to relax you. You'll feel good."

And then the boy-doctor, face looming over his, asks, "Mr. Mirth. What are we going to do?"

"Hurt my head."

The doctor laughs. "A little. For a little while. Why?"

"Make my legs work."

"Very good. Think of something nice."

A few quick photo images appear behind his closed eyes—of him as a boy, eating a cookie his grandmother baked, fighting on the school ground, a series of balls—baseball, dodge ball, basketball, and all the photos start making wild spiral circles, until they disappear.

It goes wrong. Liz knows it before she hears it. She can feel it. Down the hall is the surgeon, tapping something into a tablet. She runs after him. "Tell me."

"Oh yes, I was going to find you. It...went well."

"It did? It took so long."

"Well, we had a little brain bleed, had to work with that for a while. But we're good now."

Her heart tells her a brain bleed is a big black ship.

She hurries to Recovery to find her wounded soldier who said yes to war. His eyes open. He looks at her as if he's never seen her before and doesn't care to know her. Blank, wandering eyes, not even the eye movements of a newborn.

She plays with alternate histories—that she'd never found the young doctor, that she never said yes.

Days later, he is sitting up.

There is a food tray before him. Broth. Jell-O. He closes his eyes, not wanting any of it.

"Sweetheart."

He opens his eyes to a squint and looks for a long time. *Liz.*

"I brought you the newspaper. There you go. I know you miss it." She hands him the *Times.* "I think you need to eat."

He shakes his head.

"You're going to have a physical therapist so you can get moving, get your legs going."

He shakes his head.

"Let me see those gorgeous blue eyes."

He squeezes his eyes closed, points to the bed.

Two days later people keep shaking him, wanting to wake him. All the while he only wants his grandmother to come sit at his bedside and the doctor who makes house calls to put the cold stethoscope on his chest. Buttered toast, tea. The radio. He tries to think what happened. Some kids beat him up in a parking lot, hit his head with a bat. Yes. He sort of remembers. But where is his grandmother? He opens his eyes, finds he is sitting up in bed and there is a newspaper on his lap. He lifts it.

"There. I knew you wanted the paper." Liz. Yes, Liz.

He pretends to read it but sees only black lines going this way and that, just marks, although he has a distinct memory of once being able to figure out those marks.

41

Six weeks now he's been at the skilled nursing home, therapies every day, and he's still not moving well and has no mirth, and whenever Liz gets there, which she does several times a day, he asks where she has been. The answer is home, fretting, cooking to bring special foods to him, making an office/bedroom out of his home office, but she only says, "Mostly here."

His children have visited—four days, three days, two—what they could manage. Liz made meals or they went out or they got takeout and she could feel his life in them, could see his stamp in their faces. Lots of "Love you, Pop" "How are things?" and "What's happening?"

Did their visits scare him? Liz wonders. Does he ask himself why they have hopped on planes, bam, bam bam, all of them suddenly available when getting a visit used to be near impossible? And this time they don't argue, they don't ache aloud for their mother, but look searchingly at him even when he tries to wave their attention to the television or the window. And he's changed too; he doesn't stretch toward them but only smiles and lets them be.

Liz visits three times a day, fevered with the wish to change what is. The nurses and aides have told her he's a bad boy, fighting with them, getting out of bed on his own, falling, and once, so angry at still being imprisoned that he somehow managed to lie under the bed, arms over his chest, like a corpse. He wants to be himself, she understands, he wants to be free to choose his own movement.

There was a horrible scene a week ago when she went along to physical therapy to cheer him on.

"This is not working," he yelled at her.

"What isn't?" she asked.

"This, this, all this."

The therapists told her, "Take a break. We're going to give him a break too."

She couldn't push the thought away any longer. He's dying; this is a person dying. She cried all day, working at the new bedroom, trying to get herself in shape to go back. When she got there, late, his eyes were closed, but he was awake.

She managed to climb in beside him. "Honey. Are you okay?"

"Um."

"Why don't you open your eyes for a bit?"

After a long pause in which she assumes he is not going to answer, he says, "I don't want you to see me." This is not Harrison thinking as a child, the kid who climbed under the bed, the kid who thinks, if you cover your face, you are invisible. This is Harrison as an adult, saying, "I don't want to see you seeing me." Her face, the face she presents to him, must be terrible with grief.

He heard Liz. Thank God for Liz. She told them in firm tones that he is in constant pain. She told them, "Do something. Help him." And now they are taking him somewhere, rough, on a gurney, rough hands, everything bumpy, terrible pain. "Where is the pain?" they keep asking. He tries to gesture at his whole belly, but they always say, "Not your head?"

Yes, that, too, but he points to his belly again.

"Where specifically?"

His arm is weak, but he gestures, *Everywhere from the sternum on down.*

"We're going to the hospital," they tell him. "Get you some hydration. You'll feel lots better. You won't feel this pain you think you're having."

"Where is my wife?" Four words. He managed four.

"She'll meet you at the hospital. She's taking her car."

She will tell them. Liz always tells them what he needs.

"Ah!" he screams when the needle goes in. "No."

"It's fluid. You badly need fluids."

On the phone, one of Liz's friends tells her, "Oh, doctors always want to hydrate. That's a shame. I saw this with my mother."

"Why is that a bad thing?"

Her friend said reluctantly, slowly, "When old people are dehydrated, they're often at peace. They're trying to go."

The new doctor they send him at the hospital is a skinny old lady. Liz can tell immediately that her husband hates this doctor, this Linda Ann Something, who does not look like a Linda Ann, and who keeps shaking his arm to rouse him, asking, "Do you know who you *are*? Do you know *where* you are?"

"A writer," he answers. "Hell."

The doctor laughs but then starts to hammer him in a loud voice.

"Well, all right, okay, you have some mind left. Now listen up. You're going to need to have surgery. Sur-ger-y." He opens his eyes, looks past her to Liz whose face she hopes betrays nothing.

"Yes! Mr. Mirth, listen!" the doctor continues in the loud voice of a person speaking to a bad child or a deaf old man, both of which happen to be almost true. "You have *cancer*. You need surgery. We're going to have to keep you here."

He looks at her without reaction. It's just a word. Delete. Delete. The old white out. The backspace. Start again. Say something else.

There was more wrong. And they didn't know.

Liz grabs the doctor in the hall. "He can't bear another surgery. Not until he's strong. This last one destroyed him."

"We found cancer."

"I know. What would surgery…entail?"

"Take out what we can. Chemo, lots of chemo."

"He's so weak. He's lost forty pounds. Could he possibly survive it?" The last surgery battered his mind. He's only now able to hold a conversation. Somehow, she has to find the strength to say no.

The doctor wags her head and sweeps away down the hallway.

They hydrate him until his cheeks glow, and he is rosy. "Now you must drink water," Liz says. "Even when you don't want to. Good news. They're sending you back to the other place. Where we're used to everything. No surgery just yet. We'll get you stronger first."

But Liz is very worried to see he can't figure out where he is when they wheel him into his room at the nursing home. She tries to leap into his mind, to feel his confusion. She watches him understanding, catching up. After a long time, she's pretty sure the window, the sink, the bed look familiar.

"Would you like something to help you sleep?" the nurse asks.

"Yes. And ice cream."

"Got it. You get both."

Liz hurries home and sleeps for a few hours and then goes back to see him.

"Wow, look at you!" says his favorite aide the next morning. "What a little hydration will do! Rosy cheeks. Mr. Handsome."

He smiles. A compliment!

"You want television?"

"Yes!"

"And your voice. Strong sounding."

"Thank you."

"Well, it's good to have you back. Your wife is beaming. Look at her. I know you're happy about that. You are just fantastic today, Mr. Mirth. So nice to have you like this."

Liz says, "Oh, you look good!"

"I *am* good!"

"I know."

"I had the most wonderful dream last night. We were walking hand in hand in the Strip. Shopping maybe? And we were so happy."

"Oh!" All those words! He's found words. Eyes open, too!

Liz is crying again; she can't help it. "Sorry," she says. "That's such a great dream. What were we buying?"

"I don't know. Something good, but mostly we were just walking. And loving each other."

The aide is still there, attending to supplies. She says, "Why, Mr. Mirth, I didn't know you were so romantic. Are you romantic?"

Liz says, "He is the *most* romantic, the most."

"Well, isn't that wonderful."

He reaches out a hand to Liz and squeezes. She finds a way to fit herself onto a sliver of mattress space to lie beside him, her arm around him.

"Thank you," she says.

"Thank *you*!"

He eats his dinner that night and when Liz sees he has done so, she runs to the snack bar for a burger. She swallows most of it in three minutes, chewing as she hurries back to him.

She finds him working the television remote—a miracle since he usually can't figure out any remote. He appears to be fascinated by a dumb sitcom with canned laughter. "Why are you watching that?" she asks, climbing back onto the sliver of mattress.

He shrugs. "It's a narrative!"

Is his wit and wisdom returning? She does not want to leave the Harrison he is today. Still, after a few more sitcoms, she knows she needs to sleep. She stands at the doorway, assuring him she will be back. "Early tomorrow."

His arms go out in his signature wide-armed gesture. "I love you with all my being!" he says in a full steady voice.

She had him again, for a day.

She finds him the next morning, frowning at untouched food, no chair beside him. She fetches one. His face is very still.

"We should talk," he says, carefully parceling out the words. "I think…the last chapter of this story is being written now."

It is the last chapter. The cancer is everywhere. Surgery will do no good. For weeks she has wanted to have this conversation. Will he tell her how to live without him? Will he tell her how he feels, what to do? She begins to cry. "I'm sorry," she says. "Yes, I want to talk. Don't stop talking because I'm crying."

But then, Lauretta, the favorite aide, the one who cheers him on every day, hurries across the room. "Mr. Mirth. What did you just say to your wife? You've made her cry."

Liz waits as the aide deals with water, pills, bed position, blankets, and all the while she works to stop crying so they can have that important conversation. But after the aide leaves, he closes his eyes and shushes Liz. He never tries again.

He worked on that line, that sentence he wanted to say, she knows that much. He was writing it six months ago. Not something fancy, like, "I'm dying, Egypt," or something simple, like "I'm dying." He wanted to be a novel, something in print that would last for a while.

Home. They keep saying he will go home. He closes his eyes again. Images and sensations fly by, so delicate he can't catch them long enough to enjoy them. The smell of his grandmother's cookies. The farm, the tractor, the New York apartment, the Pittsburgh apartment, one apartment after another. The word, *home*, but he is not sure anymore what it means.

"We're taking you home," Liz says.

Once more the words go the way of images and he can't say them.

A date is set.

A date is changed.

A date is set again. They have to weigh him before they can release him. They put him in a metal scale and lift him up, up, up high as if he's a baby to determine, yes, forty pounds gone.

Finally, he's in the wheelchair being released.

People he doesn't know push and lift and curse and stretch to get him into a car that will take him a mile and a quarter to their house. Liz is in the back seat leaning over, holding onto his shoulder.

"See?" she says. "Your city? The things you love." After a while she says, "Our house."

He must be lifted again; the people he doesn't know lift him, grunting. They can't. Two more are needed, strangers who were just walking down the street and wanted to help. He closes his eyes so as not to see them.

"Your desk, your chair, your computer, everything is here," Liz says nervously. "And your airplanes are still hanging from the ceiling. But it's all painted, clean. And now we have a bed in here, too. I hope you don't hate it."

He shakes his head slightly.

She kisses him.

"Stay," he says.

42

She brings him soup and feeds him, ice pops to cool his throat. The hospice people have explained that this phase could go on for years or weeks or days, nobody knows, the body being mysterious.

She lives, as he does, in a dream world. Nothing seems real or right or solid. They are together in that. She feels his feelings. He loves everything and doesn't want to look because he doesn't want to leave.

"You're distraught," says one of the hospice workers. "You should rest."

"I want him to be glad he's home."

"Look at him. Very peaceful. Go. Sleep."

"He was always so joyful."

"That's wonderful."

Okay, not always, but *mostly*.

How beautiful he looks—they have bathed him, shampooed him, shaved him. She touches the dent in his fine skull. He moans.

He never tries to get out of bed here at home. That was Liz's biggest fear, but he stays put.

The next day she tells the hospice worker she can handle the night shift on her own because he sleeps so well now. "Shift the pillows in about six hours," the worker instructs, so that his body moves a little. The woman shows her how. "Do you think you can do it?"

"Yes."

She sleeps until two in the living room, ten feet away from him, wakes without an alarm, goes to him and leans over him. "All right? Can you hear me? I'm just shifting you a little. That's it. That's right." He's hard to move, but she does it. They have him on oxygen. They said, "It's not completely necessary, but why not give him some help."

She returns to the downstairs sofa and sleeps for two more hours. These are the two hours before she wakes and finds him gone, the cannulas tossed over his shoulder in a gesture of freedom. Or maybe, maybe like a knight tossing a bone to the dogs.

During those two hours, she has the most marvelous dream. He is walking, walking like a young man, in love with the world, and then he runs.

ACKNOWLEDGMENTS

There were teachers in my life who said the right thing at the right time and in doing so gave me permission to write stories. They may be gone from this world, but they are alive in my mind. Marian Varner, Monty Culver, Buddy Nordan, Bert States, Chuck Kinder—I will never forget you.

Thanks to my earliest readers Vivian Preston, Janet Taylor, Joyce Dodd, Eileen Arthurs, and Merrilee Salmon who gave me attention when this project was in its infancy. You moved me forward. Thanks to the readers who read this manuscript in its final form and who provided commentary—Jane Bernstein, Stewart O'Nan, Jane McCafferty, Paul Kameen, Margot Livesey, Hilma Wolitzer, and Meredith Mileti.

I am fortunate in my neighbors who keep me in the world and laughing. Jill, John, Marty, Gary, Nancy, Mark, Patt, Bruce, Jodi, Terri, Rich, Eileen, and Tawny—thank you for comradeship and high spirits.

Joanne Dunmyre at Carnegie Library was a wonderful resource.

My colleagues and staff at the University of Pittsburgh Theatre Arts Department, all of them, but particularly Gianni Downs, Annmarie Duggan, Michelle Granshaw, Ken Bolden, and Ashley Martin, keep me talking about and examining the intersections of fiction and drama. And my students, past and present, too many to name, are a gift. You inspire me and challenge me constantly. It is a privilege to watch you think.

The Pittsburgh writing community (Littsburgh) is a vital and supportive group. I'm glad to be among so many talented and generous people who have made their home here.

Jaynie Royal, Pam Van Dyk, and the whole Regal House operation is a pleasure to work with. They stress collegiality as well as excellence. I am very lucky to have worked with them.